MW00778739

East of the Great Valley

The Story of Merab McCreary

By

Sylvia Ross

This novel is a work of fiction. While the descriptions of geographic regions and cultural attitudes are historically accurate, all characters and elements of plot are imaginary and not intended to portray any actual persons or events.

Dedicated
to
Christopher Matthew Ross
Theodore Noel Ross
Nathan Patrick Ross
Andrew Baird Ross
with
love and pride

~~~>>>O<<<~~~

EAST OF THE GREAT VALLEY, The Story of
Merab McCreary

Copyright 2012 Sylvia Ross
ISBN- 978- 0615700533, Bentley Avenue Books

Cover and end page: George H. Goddard Map, State of California, 1860, used with permission from: Barry Ruderman; Barry Lawrence Ruderman Antique Maps Inc., 1463 Girard Avenue, La Jolla, CA 92037 (USA), BLR@RareMaps.com or RareMaps.com, 858-551-8500; Back Cover image: Lydia Tonantzin Ochoa, image used with permission from Eduardo and Contessa Ochoa, from photo by Andrew Ross 2012; author's photo by Nathan Ross 2010

All text, layout, and cover design is copyright 2012 by Sylvia Ross and registered with the Library of Congress. No part of this publication may be reproduced, stored in a retrieval system or transmitted, in any form or by any means, electronic, photocopy, or other method without the consent of the author or her heirs.

Requests for usage permission or other inquiries should be addressed to: Sylvia Ross, P.O. Box 44040, Lemon Cove, CA 93244-0040; thistles@ocsnet.net   559-594-4743

Other Books by the Author:

ACTS OF KINDNESS, ACTS OF CONTRITION

ACORNS AND ABALONE

BLUE JAY GIRL

LION SINGER

Anthology Inclusions:

THE DIRT IS RED HERE, 2002 Margaret Dubin, ed.

SPRING SALMON, HURRY TO ME, 2008 Margaret Dubin & Kim Hogeland, eds.

SEAWEED, SALMON, AND MANZANITA CIDER, 2008 Margaret Dubin & Sara-Larus Tolley, eds.

THE ILLUMINATED LANDSCAPE, A Sierra e Nevada Anthology, 2010 Gary Noy & Rick Heide, eds.

LEAVES FROM THE VALLEY OAK, 2011 Mary Benton & Gloria Getman, eds.

SIERRA WONDERS, 2013 Karen Kimball, ed. for the Arts Alliance of Three Rivers

Table of Contents:

Part Five ~ The Significance of a Song

Finally, brethren, whatsoeuer things are true, whatsoeuer things are honest, whatsoeuer things are iust, whatsoeuer things are pure, whatsoeuer things are louely, whatsoeuer things are of good report: if there bee any vertue, and if there bee any praise, thinke on these things:

1611 King James Bible

Philippians 4: 8-9

EAST OF THE GREAT VALLEY
February 1856

Prologue:

The child was so young she didn't have language to describe her fear. She cried, and her mother pushed her down in the bushes and covered her mouth. She curved around her mother's belly. Her mother's heart was beating fast.

When it was dark they crawled out and began to walk. She was carried for most of the night. Her mother stopped now and then to put her down and stare up at the sky. They walked until they could go no farther. Then they slept hidden in a wide clump of manzanita and covered with leaves. She wanted her father and her auntie. She wanted her own soft bed in a place that smelled like her family and had a warm fire.

After they rested, they walked again, found water, and slept and walked again. They walked until they heard the noise of children. Her mother watched from the trees, but she couldn't see what her mother saw. She wanted to go home and cried out. Her mother pinched her nostrils shut. She took a deep breath. They stayed crouched where they were until the noise of children went away. When it was quiet, they climbed over logs and down a hill. Her mother took her into a dim place with big animals. The animals smelled and made noise, but her mother wasn't afraid of them, so she wasn't either. Her mother found water in a basket that was hard and smooth. She put some seeds in the young child's mouth. The seeds were sweet but wouldn't soften.

She awoke when it was black in the place of animals. Her mother lifted her and put her in a big hole with hard, curving sides. Her mother pinched her nostrils again, whispering, "ye-na-na". She wanted out of the hole. The child knew that her mother was nearby but wouldn't come and lift her. She wasn't frightened, but she wasn't happy either. She curled up and fell asleep.

<<<<<<<<O>>>>>>>>

Part One: A Dream of Wolves
~~<<<O>>>~~

Chapter One
~ Nancy McCreary ~

At dawn, Nancy McCreary woke from a dream of wolves. As she dressed, she reflected that in the dream she'd stood powerless as snarling wolves raced through the timber behind the barn, leaping through the fences into the ranch's pastures and biting at the legs and bellies of the ranch stock. Pole fences allowed the agile wolves egress through the spaces between the rails. The milk cow and sheep were trapped. The screaming animals ran in circles looking for exit.

Then, in the way of dreams, the images shifted. The stock multiplied, and there were more sheep and cows inside the barn now, frightened and jamming up against each other, bellowing and calling. Black and grey wolves with great teeth were scratching and snarling at the double doors of the barn, pawing and nosing through any spaces between the planks and in knotholes in the barn's walls.

The dream shifted again. The pack multiplied. Packs of wolves, as thick as the pine trees on the mountain behind the corrals, were lunging at the barn's walls. As she watched, she was locked inside the bondage of her dreams, useless as a wax-headed doll or armless marble Venus. The person she was in the dream, so unable to act, frightened her as much as the wolves did. They would smash through the barn's walls, and she could do nothing to protect the poor animals.

The dream unsettled her for the day ahead. Sandy and Mud's barking had awakened her from sleep twice during the night. She hadn't loaded the rifle or gone downstairs though she and the boys were alone. Frederick was hauling goods out of Stockton and wouldn't be home for another week. She'd listened, and then curled back to her pillow. The dogs' barking hadn't sounded alarmed. There was no reason for worry.

She would have heard if anything larger than a raccoon had come near the ranch house, and the McCreary stock was secured in the barn each evening. The horses and mules were the only animals left out in open corral. Bears seldom came around during winter, and equine hooves would keep even a mountain lion at bay. No sensible wild beast would risk a mule's kick. Likely, it was only a fox or badger that aroused the dogs' curiosity, or one of Mr. Lander's big pups who came up the creek during the dark hours and began a conversation that the McCreary dogs wanted to continue.

She didn't know where the dream came from. She'd never seen a live wolf. But she'd seen a carcass once after wolves had savaged it. That was in the sand hills of Nebraska on the trail. The men set guards afterward while traveling through that country.

Light was breaking over the mountains on the other side of the valley. She finished dressing and went downstairs, pinning up her skirt to keep the frosty grass at the verge of the path from dampening it as she brushed by. Before going out, she lit lanterns in both the kitchen and the alcove and built the fire up in the stove. She put on her work cape and went out to her early tasks.

Her days were busy but predictable and starting a new one calmed her. There was enough light for her to find her way now. The day would be cold but sunny. There was no smell of rain, just clean mountain air. All was quiet in the yard. The dogs came to walk with her to the necessary shed as they did most mornings. They were racing ahead, coming back to circle around her and race ahead again. She had to raise her voice at the little tan dog to keep him from bumping into her. The pail had a tight lid, but she didn't want it spilling as she walked. The dogs' barking had woken her more than once during the night. She wasn't disposed to enjoy their antics.

After Nancy used the necessary, she dumped the commode basin and the night pail. She carried the empty containers across the back garden path to the pump house on the opposite side of the yard. The outside pump was running well in spite of the cold. There was just a thin crust of ice on the drip pail below it. She washed the basin and bucket carefully and set them on the frosty winter grass to drain.

Going inside the pump house, Nancy took soap and cleaned her hands well, rubbing lard from the can on the shelf into her fingers afterward against cracks made by the cold. Frederick had erected a sturdy shed around the pump and kept a lantern there to warm it on the coldest nights. It wasn't cold enough here in the valley to freeze the ground beneath a well-housed pump. The lamp and the pads that he had wrapped around the fittings kept the water flowing, and she was grateful that he'd whitewashed the inside of both the necessary and the pump-house. It was a thoughtful thing for him to do. No hissing possum or coiled snake would startle either her or the boys.

Before she went back to the house, she refilled the lantern's oil. Tonight would be cold again. A chill, damp wind was whining down from the pines, and the last of the oak leaves were blowing across into the garden. She'd need to rake when the wind stopped. Nancy hollered at Sandy and Mud to be still. They were too much annoyance this morning, wagging their tails and circling around her as she walked back to the house with the clean containers.

She put the basin and bucket away, and hanging her cape in the coat and boot alcove, she could feel the stove's warmth come radiating through the open doorway. Nancy glanced up at the shotgun strapped in its holder at the side of the back door, and she moved toward it. She was bothered by her memory of the dogs' nighttime barking and the vividness of her dream in the dark of early morning. She reached up and pulled down a box sitting on the lintel beam. From it she dropped some balls and cartridge tubes into her apron pockets.

However, within a half-hour, the boys were up and making noise. Wiley was clumping down the back stairs. His younger brothers were stomping about and hollering at each other as they dressed in the two bedrooms directly above the kitchen. All was well, at least upstairs. She looked out of the window. All was well in the yard; the dogs had calmed and were lying on the veranda. But the vision of wolves wouldn't leave her. Nancy determined to tend the stock animals in the barn this morning. She'd make sure it was safe before sending her boys out to their chores.

Wiley reached for his coat, pulled his cap down and called to her from the alcove. "The dogs were barking last night."

"Might be that some coyotes came into the yard. Our chickens are too smart for coyotes."

"I didn't hear coyotes, Ma. I think it was wolves. I had

a dream about wolves last night."

"A dream? No, son. It was more likely a bear than a wolf. Maybe even a mountain lion. Papa says there aren't any wolves in California."

The boy nodded, but looked unconvinced.

"There might be some, Ma. Mr. Dickey says there aren't, but his Indian says there are."

He hadn't been sassy and so she didn't chide him. The boy smiled at her as he slipped out the door to tend to his business. Looking through the window again, she saw him take a stick to punch through the thin ice on the dogs' water bucket at the side of the veranda steps. Then he went on down the path to the small building most people called an outhouse, but the parson's wife taught her to call, "the necessary." It was a more refined term, and she had grown up trying her best not to sound common, but to use a gentlewoman's voice and learn to use a fancy gentlewoman's words the way the parson's wife did.

Nancy glanced at the garden. Across the fence that kept stock out of the vegetables, but allowed her bug-hungry poultry in, a line of little cabbages and leeks was showing through the frost. Next to them were beets and carrots.

This was a strange land. Many things in her garden were planted after spring thaw in the usual way, but many vegetables took better when planted in fall and harvested in spring. Much that Indiana had taught her needed to be re-learned here. She went about her work, setting out what was needed for breakfast, but her mind was thinking of the strangeness of California and how different it was from Indiana.

Soon her oldest boy was back inside, putting his coat back on its peg and coming into the kitchen to warm his hands at the stove. "If it was a bear or mountain lion, Ma, it surely didn't hurt Mud and Sandy none."

"Well, it surely wasn't wolves," she answered. "Go wash up before you come into my kitchen."

He gave her a sheepish grin and disappeared into the commode closet to wash. Five doors opened into the alcove. One led in from the stairway hall, one opened into the kitchen, another to the long back veranda and the wall opposite the kitchen had two doors, one to the cellar. The other led to the wash-up closet. A smaller pump and sink had been installed there. The alcove had places for hats, boots, coats, and tools, plus space for a drying rack to hang clothes inside during wet weather.

Wiley came back into the kitchen and she sent him down to get a bowl of dried peaches. She'd put them to soak and make a peach pie that afternoon.

"Papa's going to take me on a haul with him, now I'm ten."

"What about school?"

"Only a short haul."

The ranch-wife reached for a crock on the shelf to the right of the sink. She thought it was remarkable that her oldest son had shared her dream. Ten years old, Wiley was his father's son in looks, size, tenacity, and love of hard work; he was hers in the odd kinds of things that came into his mind. But he was more practical than she and prey to none of her strange apprehensions. A real wolf would have sent him racing for the rifle in the alcove, but no mere dream, even a dream of furied, vicious wolves, would unsettle him.

>>>O<<<

Chapter Two
~ Crane Valley ~

Nancy pumped water into the kettle, put it on the stovetop,
laid out two scoops of oats in a bowl, and glanced
across the planked counter to affirm that the salt can
was at hand, sugar in its jar on the table. She went to
the pantry cupboard and brought a bowl of hard-
boiled eggs to add to breakfast, then sent her son back
to the cellar to ladle Letty's good cream from the
cooling can into the table pitcher.

The house was only three years old. It was larger than
the parson's home back east had been, and though it
wasn't papered or painted as the parsonage had been,
it was the finest place within fifty miles. It had been
built with planed lumber toted over the summer of '52
from the mill in Mariposa. Steuben, the man who built
it, had great plans for this house. It wasn't mere rude
logs as most of the mountain homesteads were,
though there weren't many homesteads yet.

The McCreary ranch was a half-mile up from the
Landers place on Crane Valley. There were other
ranches scattered along the creek and the larger
Waukeen River, but not many. Mr. Dickey's store,
built where the Creek met the Waukeen, served them
all.

Dickey also served as Crane Valley post-master. Crane
Valley was ten miles from Fresno Flats. The Flats had
a hotel, livery and bigger general store, a schoolhouse
though no permanent teacher yet. Nancy was satisfied
with Crane Valley, although it wasn't a real town like
the Flats. She was happy for neighbors, and the

nearness of Mr. Dickey's store. She'd expected some loneliness and hardships in the far west, but never thought she'd have such a fine home. Rather, she imagined that for a time they would have to house themselves in a tent or a two-room, dirt-floor cabin.

Frederick had chosen this high wooded valley of California, and the house was a marvel in this western region. Its windows had been brought from San Francisco. They came floating down the Waukeen to the town of Merced and from there were brought by mule wagons to the ranch. Mr. Steuben told Frederick he had himself brought the windows from the landing in three haulings, and nary a one had been broken. He named the ranch *Die Weiden,* for the two big creek-side willows down where the drive turned into the road.

That a property be given a name seemed a vanity to Nancy. But it suited the ranch well. The property was fine too. Seven level aces near the creek were planted in cider apples, and more trees were on order, good New England rootstock that would come around the horn to San Francisco, then Stockton, then here. The rest of the useable ranch was in sloping pasture. Behind the barn and corrals, the land grew steep and was timbered in pine. The trees might remain uncleared. Frederick didn't earn their family's living from the land.

He could have brought them to a town down on the flat land, near Stockton or Sacramento. But he preferred the mountains to the winter bogs and summer heat of the Great Valley of California. When he had first come scouting to set up the business that he had in Indiana, he knew California would profit him. It was a place that had a need for mules and haulers, and there was little competition.

A year later, his business established, Frederick

moved the family by wagon, first to St. Joseph, Missouri then by wagon train across the plains and up and over Sonora Pass to this beautiful place, forested in woods of straight trunked trees that held green all year round.

The Sierra was so different from Indiana's forests where most trees stood naked all winter that it seemed there was no winter at all. Though many people had come here to pluck gold from the streams and rivers, the McCrearys had come to provide service in a freight company that the new state with its growing population demanded. In just two years, McCreary Hauling's wagons were moving throughout the Sierra. Crane Valley had turned up little or no gold. That pleased Frederick. He was leery of settling his family too near mining town riff-raff. He wanted his boys growing up knowing that hard work would bring them prosperity, not stones and colored sand easily plucked from a streambed.

Mr. Steuben's plan had been to rent rooms in the house and produce cider and cheeses for the mining camps. When his industrious wife died, and when only a skimpy return of gold in the region's streams closed many camps, he soured on California. With Frederick's money, Mr. Steuben went back to Pennsylvania. He left a ranch to rival any farm Nancy had seen in Indiana. He also left Letty, the Holland cow whose heifers would sell for a good price, twelve chickens, a ram and two ewes, and a houseful of heavy, dark German furniture for their use.

Frederick needed only set fences, corrals and a long shed for his wagons and mules, and insure that the roads between Crane Valley and Mariposa through Fresno Flats were wide and passable, not only for stages but also tandem wagons, mules and oxen.

He brought a crew of disillusioned French miners from Stockton to make the additions to the property, for there were no men in Crane Valley or the Flats who didn't have employment already. Nancy set to ordering the house and laying down the rules of their new ranch life for the boys.

The stove in Nancy's kitchen was brand new. Frederick hauled it from Sacramento with two others, one for a general store in Merced, and one for the postmaster's home in Mariposa. Mr. Steuben had never put one into the house. She hadn't enjoyed cooking over an open fire on the long months traveling west. She hadn't complained, but her husband gifted her kitchen with the new, shiny black stove. The stove's box banked nicely, its char waiting to spark to life when wanted.

"It was cold out there, Ma," Wiley said, as he put the cream pitcher down on the counter.

She took the kettle and poured hot water over the bowl of dry fruit. "I know. And it may get colder. Although it doesn't feel like rain or smell like snow."

Nancy McCready was proud of her firstborn and chided herself that she'd felt a slight disappointment at his birth. She'd wanted that first child to be a girl who would give her some help when the others came along. Wiley was as good as any girl could be, and his brother Tom looked to be the same. They'd be honest, hard-working men someday, like their father. Wiley was ten years old now, his brother Tom eight, Richard almost seven, and Mason coming up on five.

The baby she lost near the Little Blue River in Nebraska, during the long, tedious wagon train west, came into her mind as she looked at her son. That

child might have been a girl. Forced out of her by
sudden pain and the gush of a bloody clot, it was so
small it washed away with the stains of her petticoat.
It hadn't stayed long enough for her to know what it
was. That might-have-been child was only significant
to her. Frederick didn't think she ought grieve over
something that never was, but she did. She would
have liked a daughter. She had neither mother nor
sister to share her confidences.

She briefly thought she might have held on to the
child, but for the roughness of the journey. But then,
she knew she might have lost it with her life back
home, lugging water from the well to the washtub or
chasing one of the ewes back into the pen. Women
slipped babies. Especially when they were old.

She wished she could have married earlier. Maybe
these fine sons were all she'd live to bear. She was
three years past forty now. She'd been a bride at
thirty-two and thankful that at last a man had liked
her well enough to pay court. She knew herself to be
an uneducated woman past her prime. She thanked
God in her prayers every day that Frederick had
found worth in her and given her his name. Nancy
was happy they'd left Indiana.

In Richmond, she'd been the parson's wife's hired girl.
She was a good hired girl, and when she grew to a full
woman, she became the parson's wife's housekeeper.
She knew her Bible from the Reverend Simmons'
readings, and she knew the meanings of its passages
from his Sunday sermons. But marriage hadn't
elevated her position. Shopkeepers back in Indiana
might greet her as "Mrs. McCreary," but they thought
of her as just Nancy, an orphan child Reverend
Simmons took out of the poorhouse, now a good
woman, but one who couldn't read or write.

Marriage and knowing her Bible verses didn't open the front doors to fine houses. No matter how successful Frederick was in business, she wasn't invited to tea.

Still, the McCrearys had the chance of becoming new people here in this new place. Frederick was valuable to the people in these mountains. He hauled needed items from warehouses in Stockton into the Sierra. He was seen as the provider, more valuable than a parson, schoolmaster or even doctor. Nancy was respected here because her husband was so respected. She was guilty of a vanity, and she knew that vanity robbed virtue. Mrs. Simmons had often righteously quipped, "One is never so low that there is no one below to pity, or never so high that there is no one above to envy. Nancy had taken Mrs. Simmon's lessons to heart. Yet she would rather her place be on the high side.

As soon as she saw the West's rugged beauty, its peaks and quick-running streams she recognized its promise. She lived higher here than Richmond's citizens could dream. And the height was in more than just a matter of California's mountain geography.

There were no shops with glazed windows here, and her sons went to school only twice a month and if they were confounded by their lessons, they had to find a literate neighbor or go to Mr. Dickey for help. For herself, she cared little for the enticement of shops, but she did share hopes with Crane Valley's community that they'd soon have a full time schoolmaster. Wiley and Tom could already understand their father's ledger book and read words she'd never be able to decipher. Richard and Mason were right behind them, learning fast. Her boys would rise higher than their parents, and that thought gave her pride. In California, nothing could hold them back.

Mud scratched at the back door and that brought her out of her reminiscence and back to the present. The men said that there were no wolves in this part of the world. She didn't believe them, in spite of what she'd told her son. The ragged limping Indian who was setting posts down at Mr. Dickey's store told the boys that there were greys roaming in the tall pines between northern mining camps and this valley. The Indian seemed old, though probably no older than Frederick and still well shy of sixty. His English was poor, but she and the boys understood him. The man pointed to the northeastern hills and unhitched a wolf tail he'd strung on some kind of thready twine around his waist.

Her boys petted it and traded it among themselves. It seemed that old man was trying to tell them that the wolf tail held some kind of magic. Frederick, loading the wagon, took notice. He turned, strode over and grabbed the tail out of Tom's hands, and tossed it rudely back at the old man.

If the wolves were gone, the Indians were practically gone. Mr. Dickey told her that the miners in the valley had near wiped them out and burnt their villages before her family arrived. It was sport to shoot at the Indians if they walked on the roads. Her husband knew this, and it bothered her to realize that what had been done gave him no bad feelings. Mrs. Barrow who lived miles up the creek told her they used Mono Indians to dig wells and ditches and to lay fence. They'll work for a little food," she'd said. "Ranchers hire them so as not to have to pay in money."

But Frederick wouldn't.

Mr. Dickey told her there were some Indian women and a few children left. "They live in little dens up in the mountains like the bears. If we aren't killing them outright, we seem to bring them our sicknesses. Alcohol is a poison for them."

She thought of the Reverend Simmons' sermons. "I think that is pitiful, Mr. Dickey," she said. "But alcohol is poisonous to white people too, I think."

"As I do, Mrs. McCreary."

Mr. Dickey took a fancy to the Indians and told he primitives which ranches along Crane Valley and the Waukeen River would give them work and not run them off. He gave them old tools and discarded clothes he came by. Nancy appreciated that. Reverend Simmons had oft quoted Leviticus 23:22 that admonished gleanings be left for the poor. Homeless, sick Indians were certainly poor. She liked Mr. Dickey's actions.

After Frederick's mother died, worn out from the long trek, Nancy thought long on how clothes could be similar to gleanings. She bundled up all her mother-in-law's shawls and dresses that had skirts too worn for her to take apart to turn into shirts for the boys. She took the bundle to Mr. Dickey for the Indians. When Frederick finished loading feed grain sacks, he walked in the store for tobacco and saw what she was doing. He didn't interfere, but out in the wagon on their way back to The Willows, he grew upset enough to chastise her in front of the children. "We're meant to help the godly poor, not give encouragement to idolatrous heathens. I'd rather you burn my mother's clothing than let it touch an Indian's filthy skin," he barked at her. "You could've found some needy Christian woman to dispose of it."

The community of Crane Valley had few women, she thought, Christian or otherwise. Only maybe six or seven other ranch wives lived within seven miles.

None of the women were rich, but all would have taken insult from an offer of his mother's old clothing. She ground her teeth at Frederick's meanness, but she bowed her head and swallowed down what she wanted to say to him. The Bible also bound a wife to honor and obey her husband.

Chapter Three
~ A Gun at the Ready ~

It was her dream that brought Indians and the memory of the boys holding the wolf tail to her mind. She stirred cinnamon into the peaches, and allowed herself some resentment against Frederick. She hadn't thought touching a wolf tail would hurt the boys any. It wouldn't turn them savage or put tattoos all over them. She remembered too, how in the quiet of the night when he was sweet with her, Frederick patiently explained how he wouldn't allow his sons to hear of any pagan nonsense about spirits in wolf tails. Indians were like the pagan tribes in Israel's desert lands. It was God's punishment for idolatry and wicked ways that they had been turned out of His favor. She'd married a good and a righteous man and so she accepted his words. It wasn't right that she should argue against her husband even in her mind.

Wiley was in his usual good cheer, and as he came up to stand beside her, he was humming a hymn from last month's tent meeting. "How long until breakfast is ready? I've got work to do."

"You'll stay in the house and prepare breakfast this morning, son. I'll do the early barn chores myself." She'd decided before she was out of bed that she didn't want him to go out to the barn until she had surveyed it well herself. Even imaginary wolves, the kind only real in dreams, had upset her.

"Ma! I'm supposed to go to the barn. Pa says."

"You'll watch your brothers and set breakfast. If I'm

not back here when the oats are tender, serve your brothers and yourself. You do know what to do."

Nancy slipped from the kitchen to the alcove and took the old cape she'd kept there down from its hook. She looked back through the kitchen doorway, her eyes questioning her son and demanding that he answer her.

"I know what to do. But Ma..." The boy wheedled. He wanted man's work and let his face beg her more than his words could. "Pa told me to take care of the barn and check the mules first thing. I'm supposed to do that, not you."

"You can let Letty and the sheep out to pasture, muck the barn and check the mules after I've come back inside."

"But I'm supposed to do it. My father said I was."

"Well, my husband said I was in charge of this ranch, its animals, and its people. That includes you, son-o-mine."

She'd go herself. The dogs had set her mind to fretting, and she'd not send a ten-year-old out of sight of the house after a dream of wolves, no matter how much he pestered her, or how few wolves there might be in California. She'd go, and she'd take the gun. The mules were enough for Wiley this morning. He'd check that mice weren't in the wagon shed's feed barrels and that the water was clean in the trough. He'd examine each mule's hair and hooves as carefully as his father did, while they ate the grain he'd bucket out to them. Nancy looked down at her son.

"Pa thinks you have a better eye than I do for those McCreary mules' welfare." Chastened by her earlier remark, but pleased with the compliment she'd given him, the boy went right to the cupboards above the oak board counter. He took down five bowls and set them on the table.

"See that your brothers sit and eat properly if I'm not back."

"Yes, Ma."

Looking to the left through the small window by the back door, as she put the cape over her shoulders, she could see that the mules in the south pasture were all right. She scanned across the kitchen garden and up the slope of the hill.

Nancy could see the front of the barn, but not the pasture behind it or the one to its north. The dark pines that covered the hill made a wall, and where some had been left in the yard for summer shade, they blocked her view. She'd not send a child out where there might be trouble.

There were planks on the garden paths near the house, but to go to the barn she'd have to tromp up a muddy track. Deep frost was in the field and the ruts were filled with thin and already melting ice. Little snow fell here, only a few times a winter. She hadn't laced her shoes when she got up this morning. Now she slipped her feet out of them and into a pair of Frederick's worn-out boots that she kept in the anteroom by the back door.

Tom and Richard were coming down the stairs jostling each other. Richard pushed past Tom to be the first one with his coat and cap on going out the door. Mason, still young enough to be clumsy, was dawdling. Instead of heading for his coat and the outside as his brothers had, her youngest boy was moving toward the small curtained closet across the alcove, opposite the kitchen. Wiley saw him through the kitchen doorway and razzed him about using the commode and night bucket.

"The closet is for women and babies," he said trying his best to sound like his father. "Men and boys take their business outside."

Pouting, but heeding his brother, little Mason pulled his coat and cap on and went out trailing his brothers down the path.

Nancy shouldered the rifle and rod and went through the door. One set of steps from the veranda led from the kitchen to the garden and the sheds behind it. Nancy didn't follow the boys down the steps but turned right and went to the end of the veranda. Down its side steps, a long track that they called "the drive" led to the barn. She was still uneasy.

She doubted wolves had come after the stock, but though Wiley was already a good shot, he was a boy. She didn't want him seeing mountain lion scat or other vile beast's trace and go off shooting into the trees on boyish impulse. Frederick had freely wasted ammunition as they came west, making sure she was a good shot before they settled in this wilderness. She wasn't a wasteful woman and didn't want her son wasting it for no reason. And if there was reason, better that she faced danger, not her child.

Nancy heard the low stock door banging the side of the barn before she could see it. The dogs, Sandy and Mud, ran ahead of her around the side of the barn and stood on point before the open doorway. She knew she'd latched that door closed after milking yesterday. It wasn't left open.

She recounted their afternoon work. Mason and Richard had put away any tools; Wiley forked fresh bedding in with Letty. Tom had checked the water buckets for the cow's stall and the two sheep pens. Nancy clearly remembered putting down the milk pails and latching the stock door as the boys went out. She'd picked up the pails, as Tom raced on ahead, wanting to be first around to the front to close the tall doors on the face of the barn. By the time she got to the front of the barn, the boys had set the drop bar in place; she'd seen that the barn was secured. Closing the barn for the night wasn't something that she'd forget. It worried her that the small side door yawed open this morning.

Sandy growled. The dogs didn't go rushing ahead of her through the side door. They stood like hunting hounds on point, waiting. It wasn't like them to hold back. She checked the readiness of the gun in her left hand, feeling beneath her coat with her right hand for the balls and cartridge tubes in the apron pocket. They were where she'd put them. She was as ready as the gun and ram to protect the stock from whatever might be there. Stepping softly forward, she watched the wary dogs. They moved closer for the comfort of her nearness, just as the solid weapon in her hand and the weighty balls and cartridge tubes in her pocket comforted her.

She wedged a large stone against the door to stop it from banging against the barn. She couldn't see into its interior's darkness. She thought about going around to the front and opening the big barn doors to let light in before she stepped inside.

Mud, the bigger dog, whined and bumped up against her. His tail was down. Then she smelled what the dogs' keen noses already knew. An odd sharp smell was mingled with the hay and sweetish grass-eater's manure odors that were always present. The smell was something she knew but couldn't place. She had dreamed of wolves. However this wasn't any wild animal smell, and it was familiar to her. It wasn't the smell of cow piss, hanging or freshly butchered meat, but it was near in sharpness. It held blood's rusty smell and something else too.

Sandy shoved between her and the barn's wall on the other side of Mud. He was making a continual low growling noise, conveying his suspicions. Mud's tail was down and still. Whatever was wrong, it wasn't wolves, bears or mountain lions; the dogs weren't bristling. Standing erect and tensed beside her, they were telling her something wasn't right. She relaxed her hold on the weapon, but kept it ready. She looked around and listened. It seemed a normal day. A mule brayed from the other side of the garden. Birds were calling to each other. Squirrels in the pines were chucking back and forth to each other. A ground squirrel ran under the pile where Frederick had been clearing brush his last visit home.

She leaned forward squinting into the darkness and cocked her head to better isolate the sounds coming from the dim cavern of the barn. The sheep were shoving each other against the planks of their pens and scraping hooves on the floor, each wanting to be first out of their pens and out of the barn. Above her, hens fresh from their boxes were up on the edge of the loft squabbling. Letty's loud bawl told her it was time for her to be milked and let out to pasture grass.

And then, beneath the animals' ruckus, and almost beneath her hearing, Nancy McCready heard a different sound, one that pierced into her. It was a weak but persistent human sound, a newly born baby's thin le-le-le cry, and she quickly recognized the pungent odor coming from the barn for what it was: the peculiar fragrance of blood combined with birthing fluid.

She turned and ran. Her underskirt snagged on a rough splinter at the base of the door's frame. She heard the muslin rip but didn't stop running. The dogs were excited by now by her own quick movement. Rounding the corner of the barn, she reached out to wedge the rifle and its ram across the top of the rain barrel where Sandy and Mud couldn't bump against it.

Next she grappled with lifting the long bracing beam that kept the barn doors from opening, succeeded, and cleared its iron hooks to heave it out of the way. She pushed one door open, then the other. The great wooden building filled with winter light. She signaled the dogs to stay, and they obediently did. Nancy stepped into the barn.

Chapter Four

~ In the Barn ~

The early sunlight penetrated the wide front barn opening, but Nancy's vision was blocked the clutter of the family carriage, the small wagon, hay bales, animal pens and larger ranch implements. Shapes and shadows cut confused her and she stood for a moment listening. She was trying to get a feeling of where in the barn's big space the baby's sound came from. While she was at the side stock door, she'd assumed that it came from near the three small sheep pens inside the barn. Now she wasn't sure.

Another baby cry sounded out. It sounded a hollow, reverberating cry, not a clear baby's sound. And it was stronger and older, not the sound of a newborn. The cry was brief. It became a huh-huh sound, and then faded as though the baby who made it had cried long already, and knew that no one was going to answer. If there were two different cries, there were two different babies. Her mind raced through the possibilities. In less than an instant of time she considered that an itinerant family, strayed from their purpose or lost, may have taken shelter in the barn, but she had to discard that idea. The barn was a long uphill lane from the road. From the road, they would have had to pass the house. Surely she would have woken. Her window was just above the drive. She woke to any odd sound near the house.

Nancy turned toward the sheep pens. She knew that one the grain barrels beyond the sheep pens was near empty. Confinement within that barrel would explain the hollow sound in that brief older baby's cry.

As she moved toward the barrels through an aisle in ranch contraptions and smithy tools, she looked down and saw a thin stream of liquid had stained the floor and seemed still damp. She looked to its origin and saw what looked like a bundle of rags on the barn floor between some bales of hay and the pen closest to her. She wished for more light and fewer shadows.

The smell that had alarmed both the dogs and her grew stronger as she moved deeper into the barn. She frowned, and her nose wrinkled back from the stench. The floor was wet, darkened by slime and blood. It was draining down the grade of the floor, and it came from under what looked to be a dead animal. There was a mound of fur half-hidden in the shadows between the pens and stacked bales of hay. She stepped carefully toward it, her shoes unable to avoid the dampness of the bloody trail in the small space. She stepped closer, ignoring the wet floor, and saw a strangely woven cover of braided rabbit skin, then discerned the top of a head covered in black hair and a woman's thin, small, dark forearm and hand were protruding from the bundle. The hand was stiff and cold to her touch. She uncovered the head to see the woman's face. It was still and dead.

Death didn't shock Nancy. She wasn't a girl. But she shivered at the sight of three heathen lines running vertically from the young mouth down her chin. They'd been tattooed into the woman's skin. The dead woman was an Indian.

The baby in the barrel began wailing again, and she let her eyes go in its direction, glad for a moment's reason to turn away from death. She could see small fingers clenched on the barrel's top edge. She knew the older child was able to stand and was alive and safe. She concentrated her attention on the mound on the floor.

Close enough now, she could see even in the shadow of the hay bales. Two feet covered in shabby wrappings of deerskin jutted out from an edging of woven fabric under the fur. She saw that the soft material was a knob of calico. It was the same faded print as one of her mother-in-law's old dresses. Nancy sensed more than saw a vague movement. She reached down afraid to pull the fur back, but more afraid not to. A tiny, naked living child, still clotted with drying blood and patches of birth paste on its skin, was in the curve of the dead woman's still arm. The calico dress had been pulled opened for feeding, but a dead arm couldn't bring a child to breast.

Nancy drew the fur down further and saw that the baby's still attached cord wound down to a clump of grey afterbirth lying on the floor where the calico had been folded up under the woman's leg. The newborn made a spasm-like shiver as the cold air surrounded it, and Nancy dropped the fur down over it again to preserve what warmth there was.

She couldn't organize her thoughts, but her body seemed to move on its own to do what she needed to do. She straightened up, turned away from the dead woman and baby to run past the sheep pens and Letty's stall. She went back in the barn to the tool rack. It was on the long shelf Frederick had added to the barn near the narrow side door. That's where he kept the kind of tool she needed, the sheep shears. She found them in their place, clean and oiled the way Frederick maintained all that was his. Nancy went back to the dead woman, knelt down, and pulled back the fur again.

The sun was higher now and more light was filtering down into the barn through hay hatch above the big doors. She bent to use her back to block the draft from the doorway to keep the baby protected from chilling more as she worked.

The coiled cord holding the baby to the afterbirth was drying. Blood was no longer passing through it. She forced the woman's stiffened hand away from the baby and used the awkward shears to cut the cord close to the baby's belly. The tiny creature twitched and its head made a slight movement. It was a girl child, and she was probably too small to live. Leaving the shears on the floor beside the body, she unpinned her skirt to let it fall loose around her, and she picked up the now untethered baby. The wee child gave a quiver in her arms.

Nancy moved her to the crook of one arm, and with the hand of the other, she pulled the folds of her skirt up and wrapped them around the baby's tiny body. Murmuring to her, stroking her gently, she awkwardly scrambled to her feet. Holding the baby to the warmth of her own body, she looked down into the grain barrel. The little babe sitting in it was not two years old. It was tan-skinned like the dead woman, surely its mother also. The older child looked up at her quizzically. In the slobber on its chin, bits of oats from the barrel had glazed. It had been eating the animal feed, and was sitting in a smelly mess of its own making.

The child had probably been in the barrel for hours while its mother was in travail. The baby looked up and made some determination. Its dark eyes were gazing at her as though it already knew more than she did. And, in that moment, Nancy felt her heart change its beat. Captivated, she made a determination too. She vowed that she would die to protect this child who was looking at her with such penetrating, knowing, dark eyes.

It looked to be cold and thirsty, but for the time, in the barrel, this one was safe. "I'll be right back, little one," she spoke aloud to the child. "I'll tend to you too. I promise."

Letty was bawling loudly, aware in her slow to respond cow's way of thinking that the person there should have taken her out by now, but the sheep, with their different, more timid reactions, had quieted. The baby in the barrel raised its arms up, wanting her to lift it out of its confinement. The barrel was too deep and Nancy was too short. She couldn't lift the one and still balance the other. She couldn't endure leaving it there in the cold barn. She couldn't abandon it. But she had to move quickly in order to save the newborn.

"I'll promise I'll come back," she whispered. She turned away, cuddling the wee baby in her arms. It had stopped making any sound and was so still, she prayed it hadn't died. Nancy glanced back at the dead woman and marveled that the poor dying mother had sense to put her child in the barrel where no harm would come to it.

Nancy didn't tarry. She turned her thoughts to God in heartfelt petition, and moved away. The deserted child began to cry, but the newborn had the most urgent need. She had to get it to the warm house and into a basin of warm water. It was so cold and frail. Nearly sprinting past the bales of hay and the tool clutter, Nancy moved to carry the newborn to the house and into the warmth of her clean kitchen. She hurried through the wide front barn opening, only vaguely aware of the sheep and cow she had come outside purposed to tend, and no longer with thoughts of wolves.

In the sun, on the drive, where they had been waiting,

Sandy and Mud came to attention. They came too close, trying to sniff at what she was holding. She pulled the newborn as tightly to her body as she could and hollered at the dogs, kneeing Sandy away. Both dogs slunk into place beside her. Halfway down the track, she almost fell on an icy patch and had to restore her balance by clutching the baby tightly in one arm while she grabbed at a stringer on the fence to keep upright.

Moving too fast to do a job right was a child's mistake. She resolutely kept her eyes on the ground and trod slower down the rest of the long slope of the drive to the house.

Chapter Five
~ With the Children's Help ~

As she neared the house she directed the dogs into the garden, then with her free hand she latched the garden gate shut. She had a fear that with the barn opened, once she went into the house, the dogs would go back to the barn and disturb the body of the woman. Sandy yipped protest, but they were often confined to the garden when work was being done. Both dogs settled down. When she opened the door and came into the house, had added more wood to the stove. She was glad to find the house well warmed. Boys and men seemed to like fire as big and bright as they could get it. Ordinarily she would have scolded the boy for being wasteful. She would have put him to the task of chopping more wood for the shed as a punishment for using the new stove as a play toy. But now it suited her need. Heat was what the newly born and barely alive child in her arms most needed.

The boys had clean faces and hands and the younger ones were sitting at the table, waiting for Wiley to finish ladling oatmeal into their bowls. Tom was pouring a glass of milk for Mason. Richard was tracing the grain of the tabletop's maple with his forefinger. Nancy stopped at the doorway to the kitchen looking at them, her cape still on, and her skirt rucked up around something she was holding in the crook of her left arm.

The boys turned toward her, and Tom asked, "What's wrong, Ma?"

She knew she looked frantic and stricken. She took a deep breath and felt herself calming. "Tom, go to the cellar and find the big crate with the new enamelware your father brought us just last month. There's a long oval basin at the bottom of the crate. Unwrap it carefully. I don't want it chipped. Bring it up here."

"I don't know which crate you mean."

"You watched your papa unload it with only Mr. Muller to help him. You should remember. The basin I need matches the enamel pitcher on the countertop beside the pump. It's large but you can carry it."

The boy looked to the sink and nodded. When she saw that he understood she turned to his older brother. "Wiley, put another kettle on to boil."

"Richard, go up to the linen closet at the top of the stairs and bring me all the flannel towels that you find there."

Mason looked up at her as though he awaited a task too, and she gave him one. "Mason, go upstairs with your brother, but you go on into Papa's and my room. In the little closet there you will find a jar of soap. It has roses on its lid."

"Soap, Ma?"

"Yes, the sweet soap I use for my face.

"Carry it down here and go slowly on the stairs. I don't want it broken because you dropped it.

Now scat. All you boys hurry to do what I told you."

The boys, normally quizzical and seldom afraid to speak up, understood the urgency in her words. They scampered to do as they were she'd asked. Wiley, whose orders kept him in the kitchen, started pumping water into an enameled pitcher, and reached with his left hand to pull down the dented secondary kettle from its rack. While the boys did what was asked of them, Nancy set about doing what she needed to do. Opposite the alcove and across the length of the kitchen was a small keeping room. It was always the warmest room in the house, aside from the kitchen itself.

When Nancy's mother-in-law was tired and ill from their long time on the trail to California, Frederick moved the older woman into it so she wouldn't have to climb the stairs to the bedrooms. After her death, the room was aired, and now it stood vacant but for a cot and some quilts, a table and single chair. Frederick had put up shelves with foodstuffs that liked being warm and dry: jars of dried fruits, nuts and molasses. Under the shelves Nancy kept bins of sugar and flour. There was a rack in the keeping room to dry laundry in wet weather.

She crossed the kitchen and pushed the keeping room's door open wider so the room would warm more, and still hugging the infant to her chest, she entered the small room. With one free arm she pulled a soft and tattered cotton lap quilt from its place on the cot's footboard. She managed to carry it back into the kitchen and drape it over the chair where Richard had been sitting. With one hand and her knees she scooted the chair up to the stove.

The quilt was warmed before the boys came back from their errands. Not until all four boys were in the kitchen did she bend down in the stove's heat and pull the folds of her skirt away from the baby. As the boys saw what she had been carrying, they stood frozen and big-eyed. The tiny, naked baby squirmed at the change in air. She stretched her stick-like arms as though reaching to embrace the heat and the fragrance of oatmeal and sugar that filled the kitchen.

"We have to keep this baby alive. Tom, I want you to saddle the pony and go to Landers' Ranch. Tell whomever you find there that I need help here as soon as either Mr. Landers or his son can come. Can you do that?"

The eight-year-old stood straighter as he answered. "Ma, the Burnett place is just across the creek. I can get over there faster."

"I don't want you crossing the creek this time of year. Just keep to the road and bring Mr. Landers back with his son or one of his workmen. Tell him I need help. If you don't find anyone there go to Dickey's store."

"I can, Ma," Wiley interrupted. You don't need to send Tom."

"I need you here with me."

"To help you with the baby?"

"Yes, but not *this* baby." She could see he was thinking quickly and absorbing the knowledge that there was another. She turned toward her second son. "Tom, go quickly. If Mr. Landers or Mr. Dickey can't come back with you leave word that I need help and come back here by yourself. "Don't wait on them. I'll need you back to let me know you have given the word and that they will come."

Tom darted into the alcove and put on his coat and cap, proud he was chosen for an important mission rather than his older brother. Nancy called after him, "Be careful, son. Keep Socks at a steady pace. Don't race him."

Richard, who was only six, but practical, shouted to Tom, "If you make Socks race, you'll make him die.

He's too old to go fast."

Mason was perplexed, but pridefully holding his head up high. In his hands he held the soap jar. He had brought it safely down stairs without dropping it.

"Sit in this chair and spread out one of the flannels on your lap, Richard." When he did what she asked, Nancy placed the baby on the flannel and wrapped the tails of the cloth around her. "Hold her tight. Don't let her slip. I'll get a warm bath for her."

"She has lots of hair," Mason shouted. It was a condition of being youngest. He worked to make his voice heard over the voices of his brothers - even when they weren't talking. "It's very black."

"Is she an Indian, Ma?" Richard asked as he curved his arms protectively around the small bundle on his lap.

"She is one of God's children. We might not be able to save her, but we will try our best."

"Every time we try to save a baby bird, it dies," Richard said sadly.

"We will try harder."

Turning to her oldest son, Nancy said, "Wiley, take the blue and white quilt from the keeping room. Go as fast as you can to the barn. The big doors are open. Don't stop for anything, not even the rifle I left there. It will keep, and I'll get it myself later.

"In the barn, in an empty grain barrel, there is another, bigger baby. Wrap the quilt around it and bring it to the house. If you can't reach down far enough, tip the barrel over easy.

"That baby is cold and dirty and frightened. It may try to fight you, but just hold on tight and bring it here. You're strong enough. Go quickly."

Wiley was out the door in an instant. Tom followed right behind him. Seeing the fragile infant curve its arms and legs in toward the warm bulk of Richard's body, and his arms protecting it from falling, Nancy darted into the keeping room and stripped down to her shift. She took down a clean but patched old gown she kept on a hook behind the door and slipped it over her head. She went back into the kitchen and scrubbed her hands and arms and put on a new apron.

The little boys watched as their mother quickly cleared the table of the breakfast bowls and the pitcher and put the enamel basin on its top. She took two cloths from a chest of drawers on the wall across from the sink. With the first cloth, she wiped out the interior of the basin. She poured the first kettle of water into it, and after filling the matching pitcher at the kitchen's pump, she added cold water to bring the basin's scalding water to warm.

Taking the baby from Richard's gentle care, she put it down into the water, using the other cloth to wipe away all the stains of its first hours. Before Wiley returned, the newborn was no longer grey but turning a soft bronzy pink color. The tiny living thing, now clean and back on Richard's lap was moving her mouth and trying to open her eyes.

"I think this baby's hungry, Ma," Mason said.

"We'll soon feed her."

Nancy lifted the heavy basin and directed the little boy open the back door for her. She dumped the dirty water from the veranda's railing and took it back into the alcove where she began filling it with clean water from the kettle and pitcher. Before she was finished, Wiley had the second baby in the house. The baby was filthy and smelly but happy to be with people around her. They stripped the quilt and buckskin gown away and saw that this baby was a girl also. "Clean her, son, top to bottom."

Wiley, practiced from helping with his brothers, soaped the older baby and scrubbed her clean against her protests. Nancy quickly filled pitcher and pot in the kitchen with warm water. Lining them up on the tabletop where he could reach, she instructed Mason to carry rinsing water to Wiley, as he needed it.

Then she set to work fashioning a nurser out of an empty dosing bottle and a wad of soft cloth. She combined milk from the breakfast jug, a bit of the kettle's hot water, half spoon of sugar and pinch of salt. She filled the bottle. Dampening the cloth to draw, she fashioned a small nipple. When she saw drops of the milk mixture could fall from the cloth as she tipped the bottle, she offered it to the tiny baby on Richard's lap. The baby sucked so ravenously Nancy almost allowed herself hope that warmth and food might keep it alive.

Chapter Six

~ Mr. Landers and Ples ~

After Wiley helped her clean and feed the babies, she sent him to his chores with the mules, knowing he'd first turn Letty and the sheep out to pasture. The little boys helped her settle the babies down in the keeping room, giggling because they were dressed in the boys' long outgrown baby and toddler clothing from the cedar chest under the side windows of the front parlor.

The three of them worked to clean the alcove and kitchen and mop the floors. They rinsed the basins and laid them upside down on the veranda to dry. Mason and Richard went out to collect eggs, though there weren't many this time of year. She had much to do. It wasn't her laundry day, but there was so much that had to be washed after the babies had been cleaned. That couldn't be put off. She carried her apron, the gown she'd worn, and all the flannels and cloths that had come in contact with the babies outside and piled them on the planks near the washtub. She started a good fire under the tub to get water boiling, went back to the house and made biscuits to feed the little boys when they came back in.

Through the window she saw Tom dismount and lead Socks to the corral. Then came the rumble of a wagon. Mr. Landers and his son came in their buckboard. Pleasant, the Landers' boy, was older than Wiley by some years, but still a boy. Ples hunted with her sons and played the fiddle at barn dances but only as far away as Fresno Flats.

The boy brushed his corn silk colored hair out of his eyes, nodded to her and said, "Good Morning, Mrs. McCreary." He jumped down and led the horses down the drive toward the post and rail. His lanky father ambled toward the house.

Sadness was coming to the Landers family. Mrs. Landers had the consumption. Maudie Landers was often flushed, and her cheeks seemed to burn a brighter red each time Nancy visited with her. She'd grown thinner too, and her cough was hard and wracked her whole slim body. She had coughed since they had known each other - three years now. The boy, tall but still not quite a man, had her friend Maudie's fair hair and eyes. In the way of country people, they saw each other seldom, for their work kept them busy. But Nancy considered that they were friends. And, she feared Maudie Landers would never live to see Ples marry or give her grandchildren.

Tom and Ples finished taking care of the animals and came to the house. Tom's urgent ride to the Landers' ranch to plead help made her son pale and jittery. He'd not had breakfast this morning at all. But she put out milk and biscuits for him and Ples while Mr. Landers blew the coffee she'd given him cool enough to sip.

"I brought the wagon, Mrs. McCreary, but there aren't any Indians left in Crane Valley to take the woman's body," Mr. Landers said. "Used to be an encampment, a village really, from the Mono tribe way down the Waukeen, near the sandbar, men mostly, looking for ditches to dig. But they've all disappeared. No one's seen a one of them for days. Even that old man who works for Dickey has run off. He ain't Mono. Speaks some different language and wears different marks. Maybe he's one of the Chancys. I never asked Dickey. I know he don't have no doings with the Monos.

"Dickey thinks he'll come back, but not until the trouble settles down. That might be a while. Don't know if the Monos will ever come back."

Ples Landers spoke up and said, "We'd take the woman's body off your hands, Ma'am. But there ain't a place to take it to."

"No Indians are buried in the cemetery. They're expected to take care of their own." Mr. Landers said.

Seeing her face droop, he added, "We'll bury her for you. You'll only have to tell us where you want her."

She nodded her relief, and said, "The woman left two living babies. I don't know what I must do with them. Surely there is a place, a family, for these babies."

"Tom told us, but we can't help you there. Maudie is down to bed. The winter is hard on her and the cough is back. Mrs. Dickey's gone off to her daughters' in Stockton. Someone down in the big valley might take in a white baby, but not an Indian. No one around here would."

Nancy offered them more coffee and summer jam with their biscuits. She was grateful that Mr. Landers offered to do the burying, for it would be hard for her to manage with just Wiley and Tom to help. She considered the ranch and knew the right place for the woman's grave.

Wiley took Mr. Landers and Ples up to the barn so they could assess the job they needed to do. Tom ran out of the door after them. She was glad that he'd eaten a little. The thinnest of her sons, he'd rather run than eat.

Wiley and the men hadn't been gone long when Mr. Landers sent his son back to fetch her. She wasn't happy at the interference. She didn't want to leave the babies, and she did want to wash the filth from the flannels and quilts she'd used before it set.

But she couldn't refuse to go if Mr. Landers called for her. The man and his son were sacrificing a morning's work to help her. So, she left Richard watching his little brother and the babies, though she was aware that it was too much responsibility for a six-year-old. He wouldn't turn seven until summer, but he was a good boy and seldom made a bad judgment. She had to trust him.

"Don't wake the babies, but watch that they can breathe. Leave the keeping room door open, so the kitchen heat goes in there. You and Mason behave yourselves. I'll be back soon."

She went with Ples, thinking to take two buckets, rags and soap, a clean sheet from the bottom of the cedar chest and her sewing kit. The dead woman may have been a pagan, but she could still be buried respectfully. In the barn, she found that Mr. Landers sent for her, not for her help, but so she would know the reason why the woman died. It wasn't from birthing. The men had raked the area around the woman's corpse and spread fresh hay. They'd left the rabbit skin garment over her and drawn it up to cover her face. When Nancy put down the buckets near the body, the two men turned the stiffened Indian woman onto her side, and the braided fur cloak fell back.

The revelation shocked Nancy. There was a ragged hole in the back of the calico dress. Blood had dried brown and black on the cloth. It was just above the right side of the Indian woman's waist.

"Her face marks are like the Chancy women's. See those stripes on her chin? Looks like she might have been from that tribe. A gun made that hole, Mrs. McCreary. It mighten not to have killed her, but I

42

think it did. You can see the festered wound. I imagine the ball is still in her. She's naught but a girl." Mr. Landers and his son gently set the body back in its original position.

"There was a ruckus over on Coarsegold Creek by the big mining camps two days ago, ma'am," Ples volunteered. "It was a terrible thing. The men were in liquor and raided the Chancys living up 'bout three mile above the camp. They claimed the Indians had been stealing out of their tents. Pa and I were down to Fresno Flats buying grain yesterday and heard their cruel bragging." Turning to his father, he said, "Pa, you think this woman got away from there?"

"She *didn't* get away, son," the older man said sadly.

He turned to Nancy and looked down at the buckets, flannels, and sheet beside her. "Mrs. McCreary, are you going to wash her?"

"She wouldn't be the first person I prepared for burial, Mr. Landers." Nancy answered. The thought of a passage from Scripture where Jesus had once washed his disciples' feet ran through her mind.

"Then I'll leave you to it," he said. "We'll come back for her when we're done digging. Any special place you want us to bury her?"

"Up in the pines, beyond the corral fence a good ways, there is a little meadow. It is flat there. The boys can show you. The ground won't be so rocky."

"Then we'll get on with the diggin'."

The men started to leave the barn, but she called them back. "I need a knife. Would one of you loan one to me? It's for her clothes. I have my scissors, but might need to cut the rawhide bindings. I'll not bury her in these dirty things. I have a clean sheet to wrap her."

Mr. Landers gave her a narrow smile and nodded at the things she brought into the barn from the house. From that she saw again that he was a kindly man.

"Ples?" Mr. Landers gave his son an expectant look, and the young man took the skinning knife from his belt and handed it to Nancy.

"It's sharp, Mrs. McCreary. It'll cut easy."

"And I'll not forget to give it back."

"I know you won't, ma'am," the young man answered. "Sorry you were dealt this burden when your husband was far."

"And, I thank you for your and your father's help."

"It won't take long, but we'll dig deep enough for the animals not to get at her. Then we'll carry her up the hill." Mr. Landers added. "We'll take care of it, Mrs. McCreary. You needn't come. No need for Christian prayers at this one's grave. But we'll bury her right, as we'd do for a white person."

Wiley and Tom gathered shovels and a pick from the barn's long tool rack for the men to use, but Mr. Landers declined to use them. He had his own tools in his wagon. Wiley had been leaning on the pick, looking solemn until the men began to walk to the clearing in the timber. Her oldest son tarried, while second son ran to lead the way.

"Do you need me to help you with her, Ma?" Wiley asked.

"No, son, I do need you to go back to the house and watch after your brothers and the babies. Richard has been on his own about long enough. Tell him and Mason I'll be in the house soon's I can. Keep the house warm and don't worry if the babies cry. Crying's a good sign. Keep wood on the stove and under the wash pot outside to keep it heating."

Wiley lingered until she put her arms around him. "I need your help now, son. Keep Richard and Mason in the house until we are done with this."

When the boy left her, she went outside to the barn's pump and drew water. The Indian woman wouldn't mind that she'd be washed in winter-cold water. Alone then in the barn, she started to use her scissors to cut the woman's clothing away. She thought of the two women who had worn the rose calico dress. She determined to cut some of the worn fabric to keep as a memory of Frederick's mother and the Indian woman.

On that impulse, she cut two squares of the calico from the side of the dress that was free of blood stains, and put them aside up on a high hay bale. She moved the braided rabbit fur away from the body easily, but found she had to soak and pick the dress from the areas around the wound on the Indian woman's back and on her birthing parts. She's just a girl, Nancy thought. Her body is as hairless as a child's. How had she walked this far from Coarsegold Creek, sore wounded and burdened with a baby, and so close to her time of delivery?

Nancy set about washing the body clean. The water was just less than freezing, and it made her hands feel raw in the air of the dank barn. When she was done, she took the long pronged rake and dragged the mess of the dirty, stained calico dress and the braided rabbit skin cloak out of the door of the barn. The damp pile would dry in the sun, and later she would burn it all.

Before she took fresh hay and scattered it on the floor to soak up the residue of wash water, she retrieved the scissors from her sewing kit and cut a length of the Indian woman's hair and put it with the pieces of calico. She unfolded the clean sheet she'd brought from the house and spread it on the hay, then rolled the woman's body onto it. She tucked the ends of the sheet up and rolled the woman again, and then again, swaddling her as tightly as a babe.

With Ples Lander's knife she cut neat lengths from one of the coils of cotton cordage Frederick kept on the wall above the pens. They'd used it to tether calves and lambs, and when Mason walked early during their days on the trail, they used it to keep him from falling out of their wagon. Raising the swaddled body's shoulders and then legs, she was able to bind the cord around the Indian woman in three places. Poor thing weighed next to nothing.

Just as she finished, Tom and the Landers men came back to the barn, finished with the digging. Mr. Landers nodded to her, as if to say he approved that the body was bound and would be easy to carry to the gravesite. "I'll not go up the hill with you," she said. "I have many other things to do this morning."

"As do I, Mrs. McCreary. If you'll forgive us, my son and I will be getting on home as soon as we are done here."

"Tell Maudie I will add her to my prayers today."

The men lifted the body together, but Mr. Landers' boy took her over his shoulder. It didn't take two men to carry such a small woman. Nancy watched as they started up the hill. She did have much to do this day. She couldn't tarry longer, and she trusted Mr. Landers and his son to manage a proper burial, even though it was the burial of a pagan Indian.

Chapter Seven
~ Merab and Mikel ~

A week had gone by. Frederick, his long wagon, its trailer, and six of their mules were due home on Friday, just two days away. Nancy was anxious for his return, wanting her husband back home and thinking of how she would greet him with a fine meal and the ranch in order.

She was also apprehensive. She didn't know how he would respond to the discovery of two Indian children in his house. Mr. Landers had carried the news of the Indian babies at the ranch, but no woman for twenty miles around wanted them or offered help. He told her that for miles the Sierra seemed empty of any natives. Any left after the miners' violence had disappeared. She pulled the quilt up over her shoulder. The babies were sleeping, tucked in. The kitchen stove in the next room kept them warm. Her sons were asleep upstairs. It was quiet but for the intermittent popping of logs in the stove.

She'd adjusted to the work of two more children; the animals were healthy, the house in order, and the older boys had kept their sessions with the schoolmaster down at Mr. Dickey's store during the three weeks their father had been gone. All was in readiness for Frederick's return. She wanted him to judge that the boys were learning, as they should. He could do that better than she.

Reverend Taylor only came to Crane Valley's children twice a month. He lived and preached in Fresno Flats but worked an itinerant route throughout the region. Families with children paid him a fee and Mr. Dickey lent a storeroom to use as a classroom. Frederick himself could read, write and cipher. If he were home, he helped the boys with their schoolwork. If he were away, Wiley helped Tom. And if Wiley himself hit a snag in his studies, he could ride down to the store where Mr. Dickey could help him. The Reverend said that Wiley had a mind for calculus. Neither she nor Frederick knew exactly what calculus was, but they recognized it as praise for their son.

From their ranch to the store, it was three full miles. The Scruggs girls came from more than four miles in the opposite direction. They picked up the Summerfield's boy and his sister in their wagon on the way. The Barrows' older boy only came to school once a month. He spent the night at Mr. Dickey's and went home the next morning taking the family's supplies and the mail. Both the Barrows were learned people. Their boy only needed teaching from the Reverend for the classics and fancy mathematics. Ruyle Barrows was going off to boarding school in Stockton next year. He'd be fifteen.

Richard was almost ready for school. He was near in age to the Summerfield's girl. Wiley and Tom didn't want him going with them. They were afraid Nancy would make them travel in the small wagon once Richard joined them. The two older boys had ridden tandem on Socks every other Monday the whole past year, and liked their time away from the ranch. Hitching the wagon would be more work for them, and a wagon limited after-school exploring. They'd have to keep to the road. They knew better than to leave mules and wagon tied to a tree while they played.

Socks was fond of wandering in the brush and went along with what they wanted to do, though any self-respecting pony would have wanted the barn. Nancy could smell creek weeds on them, over top of the tobacco, cider and licorice smell of Dickey's store when they came home, but she allowed them the time, as long as they were in well before sundown. She smiled to herself in the dark-ness. She might have liked a free hour twice a month herself, but there was no one to allow it.

Since she had found them, she'd spent her nights with the babies. The little one was too frail to leave alone. With the boy's help, she'd wrestled the baby furniture first down from the attic, then down from the second floor. Nancy needed to stay close to the wee ones, and she could keep the kitchen stove burning if it grew colder in the night.

The boys insisted the babies were their sisters and needed names. She supposed that they were the boys' sisters in God's eyes, but she scoffed at any Wiley and Tom suggested from the fancies in their schoolbooks. They offered names like Isabella and Fortuna, Wilhelmine and Jasmine. Richard championed Hansel and Gretel, and refused to consider that Hansel was a boy's name. Mason offered no suggestion. Perhaps he felt moved aside. Nancy would give him extra attention and it would help. He'd been the baby longer than his brothers had been and had grown more accustomed to her attention.

She chose the babies' names from the Bible: Merab, therefore, was the name she gave the older baby. Mikel, she called the newborn. They were names of the daughters of King Saul. The parson's wife would have been proud of her choice. But, in truth, those were the only names of sisters from the Old Testament's stories that Nancy could remember. She felt sleep coming, and she was content. It would be a week tomorrow, and the pitiful early-born baby was still alive.

As small as she was, Mikel greedily swallowed the milk mixture every few hours as any full term baby might nurse. Merab was a pretty, dimpled child and seemed to have forgotten she'd once lived another life. She tottered around after Mason, as wee ones did with any child they saw as close in age. Only occasionally did she stand still and look around with a puzzled expression as though remembering. Even then she didn't cry.

Nancy McCreary awakened with a sharp and certain knowledge that something was wrong, and realized that the wee baby hadn't cried during the night. The dim morning light was just beginning to filter into the room and she got up and went in her bare feet across the rough planks to the cradle. There wasn't enough light yet to really see the baby, but she bent down and touched the infant's face. It was cold. Mikel had lived just six days.

Still in her gown, she wrapped the baby's body carefully and took it into the large front room and placed it up on the high cabinet. She didn't want Merab to climb from the crib and find her sister lifeless, not that the small girl could understand. It would be too sad for Nancy to have to witness such a scene. After she dressed, she went upstairs to her boys' rooms and woke them, telling them what happened in the night, reminding them that it was God's will.

Breakfast and chores finished, Nancy shrouded the tiny body in soft gauze and a small blanket, and she and her sons took Mikel up the hill to the clearing in the woods. Merab wanted to walk. She clung to Richard's hand as they climbed. Merab was dressed warmly and wearing Mason's old scuffed baby shoes.

Tom and Wiley dug the grave in dirt softened by the child's mother's burial. It seemed fitting that they be together. Richard wanted to hold the swaddled baby one last time, and she let him. Mason stood beside him, patting the baby's wrappings tenderly every so often as the older boys dug. Merab watched the boys but ignored the bundle.

Wiley and Tom took turns with the shovel, digging into the grave's dirt. It was still soft enough that either of them could have made a pit three feet deep alone, but they worked together. At three feet deep, Nancy stopped their progress. It was enough.

"Not deeper, Mama?" Tom asked.

"No, we'll cover the grave well with stones." She took the baby's body from Richard and knelt down to give it to Wiley who was still down in the shallow pit. He hand-dug a deeper hollow for it and placed it carefully. Done, he crawled up out of the grave, crying in a way he hadn't done since he was too young to go to school. Nancy stood up, took a shovel and scattered dirt over the flannel and gauze covered body. Wiley and Tom took turns filling the hole with dirt. They took their time. No one was in a hurry.

"I knew she would die, Mama," Richard said softly. "Just like a baby bird."

Nancy pulled the little boys to her. She began to cry against her will.

When the grave was filled in, the family gathered stones as big as each could carry and brought them back to cover the mound. Miming what the family was doing, Merab brought pebbles to help. With the six of them working, it didn't take long.

Tom said, "We need to make a cross."

"She wasn't a Christian, son," Nancy answered.

"That don't matter, Mama. Wiley'n me will make one this afternoon when we got time. Jesus will find her and give her an immortal soul."

"*Have* time, not *got* time," his older brother corrected Tom's lofty thought to find fault with his grammar. Wiley wiped the grave dirt from his hands on his overalls and reached into his back pocket. He took out an old, foxed, leather-covered book of psalms his grandmother had given him before she died. Its miniature browning script was still legible on the yellowed pages. Nancy and the other boys spread out to circle around the grave.

Wiley found the place he wanted in the book, and read the selections his father had chosen for the boys' grandmother's burial. He read as clearly as Frederick had. They stood for a few minutes, quietly, Mason clinging to Nancy's hand.

"She was never a papoose, was she, Mama?" Richard asked, demanding his mother's affirmation. "She was a normal baby."

Tom answered for Nancy. "She was our baby. Papooses live on cradleboards."

"Tom's right," Wiley said, Mikel never had a chance to be an Indian. She never belonged to anyone but us." He composed himself and looked sternly at his brothers. "But we aren't supposed to talk. We should sing hymns. That's what we're supposed to do after the reading."

Nancy began singing, *"Father, Whate'er of Earthly Bliss..."* The boys joined in, the five voices ringing through the morning. Merab toddled farther from the family as they sang. Her black hair was shining in the winter sun. She wandered to the fringe of woods around the clearing. The light seemed to follow her penetrating into the woods in bright patches and odd shafts of brilliance.

The baby found earth-mucked acorns to pocket and pinecones to toss, and twigs to pick up and put down. She sang too, trilling out merrily in sounds from a language the family had never before heard, though in their solemnity, they paid little attention other than to watch that she didn't toddle too far.

 And in this way, Merab's sister, the tiny Mikel was laid to rest with their young mother.

Chapter Eight
~ "She is Merab McCreary" ~

Word came, and Mr. Dickey had passed it along to The Willows. Frederick would be home the next afternoon. Eager to see their Papa, the three older boys rushed their chores and went to the south pasture to sit on the fence where they could watch the road and wait for him. They had a long wait. It was mid-afternoon before the mule team pulling the linked wagons was in sight. As the boys ran toward him, Frederick halted the wagon against the wishes of the mules. The beasts had been gone a long time and could smell their home corral. In scarcely a minute, Richard was up on the seat beside his father and Wiley and Tom had mounted the lead mules, sitting proud as one of the Royal Lancers going into battle.

Soon a clomping of hooves and the rumble of heavy wheels could be felt as the team came up the drive. Mason ran out the back door and rushed to see his father, leaving Merab standing in the kitchen looking puzzled. Nancy quickly covered the vegetables she was paring with a soft cloth. Happy to know her husband was safely home, and as anxious to see him as his sons were, she lifted Merab up on her hip and went outside. Three weeks had seemed long, and she had much to tell him.

Frederick was agile for a tall and heavy man. He swung his body down from the wagon seat and turned to help Richard climb down. Mason was jumping up and down, crying "Papa!" hoping for notice. And Frederick did notice. He picked the small boy up and twirled him around three times before putting him down.

"Hold on," he told his smaller sons as he reached into one of the great pockets of his winter coat and drew up a handful of paper-covered candies. "There is a treat for the both of you boys too," Frederick called to Wiley and Tom, still up on the lead mules. "Drive on to the shed. This team knows where its home is. I'll walk behind you."

The boys nudged the mules, and the wagons rolled up the drive, past the barn and toward the long mule shed. Without looking in Nancy's direction, Frederick trudged behind his sons. She called out to him, but he gave her not a single nod. She called again, but though she knew he heard her, he didn't glance back. The little boys each took one of their father's hands and went to tend the stock with him. Nancy and Merab, left alone, went back to the kitchen.

It took an hour for Frederick, Wiley and Tom to get the mules brushed down, watered and fed, and the wagons separated and backed in under the shed roof. This homecoming was different, in that McCreary shrugged off his sons' chatter until they too fell quiet, miming their father's taciturn silence. But happy just to have him home, Wiley and Tom held to their custom, sweeping out the beds of the wagons, scraping down the heavy wheels, oiling and wiping all the bolts and fittings and inspecting for cracks or weakness in the wooden staves.

Richard and Mason also held to their custom, making more work for their brothers by trying to help. Before long, they younger pair grew bored watching their father and older brothers work at tasks they weren't old enough to do. They went to the house to see what their mother was doing.

When all was in order with wagons and stock,

Frederick said, "It's enough, boys." He and the older boys stopped at the pump house to wash their hands and faces and walk down to the house. The smells of food billowed out as their father opened the back door. Tom nudged Wiley and sniffed the air. Tom smiled and started to say something but their father's harsh voice bellowed out. Directed to their mother and not to them, it startled them and stifled any words they might have said to each other.

Frederick was filling the doorway, shouting into the house. At first the boys behind him on the veranda couldn't understand what their father was saying, for the blast and intensity of his speech was different from any sound they had ever heard come from him. Then the noise separated into words that they knew were meant for their mother.

"I know what you've done, woman! But blast you! Do *you* know what you've done? By Jesus' breath and blood, I'll not have a wife who betrays me. Get that filthy thing out of my house."

Richard, Mason and Merab were standing with Nancy between the kitchen and the alcove. They shrank back, using the folds of her skirt and apron as a shield.

"Blast you woman. Blast you to Hell. You get rid of it. I won't have a poxy savage on my property. Get it out." He went forward through the alcove to loom above his wife. Sucking in air, and letting it out slowly, he said in mock politeness, "I'll have a glass of buttermilk brought up to me and then bring water up for my bath." He pointed down at Merab, and his tone turned sharp. "But the first thing you will do is get rid of that red nigger."

Stunned, not knowing what to say or do, the four boys and their mother did nothing. But then Mason glowered up at his father. The youngest boy seemed to sort things out. He stepped forward in front of his mother. Puffing his chest up with indignation, he said, "Our baby isn't a nigger, Papa. She's ours. We're teaching her to talk."

Frederick pushed the little boy aside with more roughness than he had ever before shown one of his children. He stared down at the Indian child grasping Nancy's hand. "Get it out of my sight!" The wave of sound that came from him seemed it could shake the windows out of their frames.

Defiantly and with clenched fists, Mason punched at his father's thighs and piped, "Papa, she's *ours*. We found her in the barn. Her name is Merab McCreary."

Richard, two years older and much wiser, reached forward and pulled Mason back into the kitchen and behind their mother. The older boys, sweaty and tired from their work, stood on the veranda watching through the open doorway, confused and afraid.

Nancy spoke. "Frederick, let me tell you what happened. I haven't told you yet what happened."

"It's no child of mine. Get it out of my house."

"Please. Let me tell you what happened."

"I can see what you've done, I don't need to hear it told." Venomous spittle slid into the corners of his mouth. "Out. Out. Out!" He threw his hand out toward the door and closer to Nancy and the younger children, stiffening his posture in an attempt to keep control of himself and of his anger.

Tom drew back, but Wiley moved bravely into the alcove and pulled at his father's sleeve until Frederick looked down at him. "Papa," Wiley pleaded, "She's just a little girl. We're the only ones who can take care of her. Mr. Dickey says all her family is gone."

With courage then, to support his brother, Tom came through the doorway to stand firm with Wiley. "Please, Papa. Her mother died here. Ples and Mr. Landers helped us bury her. No one else wants her."

Not wanting her husband's rage directing itself to the boys for speaking up to him, Nancy intervened. "She's an easy child, Frederick. She's been no trouble."

"I want no savage poison in my family," he said in answer. But his shoulders loosened and he took a deep breath. He looked at Wiley and Tom, then back at Nancy. It appeared that his anger was dissipating.

Frederick noted how straight the little girl stood. The child's eyes were open and they appeared to pass an adult's judgment on what was happening. He spoke again, with deep antagonism. It seems my wife and sons have been poisoned already," he said as he took off his hat and hung it on one of the hooks along the wall. Scowling at the coarse leather gloves still on his hands, with a quick movement, he stripped them off and threw them hard at Nancy's face. She flinched and twisted away. The gloves hit her ear and her hair, bounced against the doorframe, and dropped to the floor. Richard scooped them up and Nancy took the gloves from her son, thanking him. She calmly placed them on the shelf next to the doorway.

"Look around you, woman," Frederick said. "Do you see the children who belong here? My children." For a quick moment, a fleeting tenderness showed in his eyes, but only for a moment. He looked longer at his wife and his eyes squinted in hateful assessment of what she had done.

"Yesterday morn, when I dropped supplies at Coarsegold Creek for the miners, they told me they had run out the thieving Chancy Indian scum. With Ezra Hopkin's help on the braking and ropes, we got down the hill to the Flats with wagons and cargo intact. I sent him on home and took supper at Boulange's place.

"It is a hellish grade between Coarsegold Creek and the Flats, and I was tired. There at the table, I overheard three homesteaders laughing about some fool woman who had taken red nigger children into her home. They were laughing!" He pounded the flat of his hand on the wall.

"Are you listening to me, woman?" he shouted. He closed his fist and raised it close to her face. I didn't know that the figure of their fun was my own wife. They knew it all the while. I imagine that it made the jest all the better, laughing behind my back. Mocking me! Woman, I'll not allow you to shame me by what you do in my house."

 Merab, understanding only the anger, not the words, clung to Nancy's apron. Mason and Richard started to cry. Nancy looked at Wiley. Her son understood her. He took Mason and Merab's hands and led them out of the house onto the veranda. Tom did the same with Richard. Nancy reached down to the lower coat rack and took up three small coats. As she walked past her husband, she did not give him her usual deferential nod. She held her back straight. He was still ranting. Under his bombast, Nancy's light voice was like a tinkling bell swallowed in thunder. "Boys! Wait," she called out.

Her sons heard her. The children stopped. Merab was looking up at them, her eyes going from one boy to another. She stepped out on the veranda. "It's getting colder." She said, thrusting the coats toward them.

Frederick stomped through the doorway behind her. "Mrs. McCreary, By the God Jehovah and the Devil himself, get back in here."

Nancy didn't look at him. Trying to keep her voice steady, she said, "Wiley, You are in charge."

"Yes Mama." His voice was husky.

She went inside past Frederick and into the kitchen. She pumped two buckets of water and filled the teakettle and set all to heat on the stove. Frederick watched through the doorway to the alcove as she methodically went about her work. She didn't look up, and soon she heard him climbing the stairs. He had sometimes been loud in correcting the boys, but he had never before spoken so harshly to her. Never before had he thrown anything at her. She placed some dried pears and raisin cookies on the tray with the buttermilk, and slipped a napkin over her left arm. In her days in service the work was done, no matter what conflicts ranged in a household. She knew it was important to concentrate on the tasks at hand.

Nancy looked around the room. The table was clean and clear, the vegetables pared and soaking, the rolls covered and rising on the shelf near the stovepipe. Butter was in the box on the veranda where the butter would stay firm and cool.

Her husband would sleep after his bath. While he slept, she'd go out to the barn and milk Letty. After that, it would be time to put the chickens in the skillet, and the rolls would be ready for the oven.

Chapter Nine
~ The Distraction of Chickens ~

It was still afternoon, but the low sun had arced westerly and, with its movement, winter's chill was back. The older boys were still wearing their outdoor clothing. With Wiley's help, Tom sorted the coats their mother had given them. Wiley helped Merab into the woolen hand-me-down she'd learned was hers. Mason was not yet agile enough to get his coat on, so Tom helped him. Richard proudly worked and was able to get both his arms into the sleeves and only needed help with the buttons.

"We'll take them to play in the barn, Tom." Wiley said. "We can lower the pulley and I know where the matches are. We'll light the lanterns."

"It's too early. Mama hasn't even done the milking yet. She wouldn't want us to waste oil."

"She said I was in charge."

Wiley squatted down and cuddled the baby, then stood and took her hand. "Come on, MeMe. Let's go find the chickens."

Solemn and perplexed, the little girl looked up at the boys.

"Chickens," Tom said as he peered at the little girl, making a silly face to make her smile.

She was young enough that her memory was short. The harshness she had witnessed was completely banished and she smiled as she recognized the word the boy said. "Chi'n. Chi'n," the small girl gurgled. As her face brightened, the boy's apprehensions diminished. Tom darted ahead on the drive.

"MeMe, watch me! I'm a hen." He squatted down and began clucking while he bobbed his head back and forth.

The baby giggled, and Tom, with encouragement, expanded his repertoire. "I'm a duck!" He bent forward and walking with his feet turned out and his head arched back he started quacking. Mason was laughing too. Richard started to mimic Tom's duck walk, which prompted Tom to stick his elbows out straight from his shoulders, jut his head forward and hiss.

"What am I now?" Tom asked as the children followed him up the drive.

"You're a goose! You're a goose!" Mason hollered.

"A goop," Merab imitated. "A goop."

"Goo-ssss. Sssss. Goo-sssss, MeMe," Richard corrected.

"SSSSsss. A goop."

Any wisps of tension left in the younger children receded. Wiley grinned his approval, and Tom led on to the barn. Swaying slightly left to right, his feet plodding like the wide hooves of the mules before their father's wagons, he let out a bray. Richard caught on and pulling his elbows back, he rotated his shoulders forward and back. His forearms and fists, perpendicular to his torso, became wagon wheels going around and around. Mason imitated Richard. Merab tried, but all she could do was wave her fists in the air as the children walked in procession the rest of the way to the sheep and chickens, and the other comforts of the barn.

Bathing did calm Frederick. He had earlier cleverly installed an iron pipe drain in the room upstairs that he called his closet. The drain led from the tub through the outside wall and down the side of the house to a dry well. His wife didn't have to carry the dirty bathwater down bucket by the bucket. He took pride in improvements.

There was still the problem of getting hot water upstairs to the bath without hand-carrying buckets. He rested on the bed and thought how he could plumb a sink and pump to the tub. The cistern was high enough on the hill that there would be a strong gravity flow. There was no reason to plumb only to the first floor of the house. There was the big problem of heating the water. He would have to put one of the fancy water stoves into the closet and pipe the smoke out through the attic or the outside wall. That would only be the first problem. There would be the problem of hauling wood up the stairs to the stove. He had once seen a dumbwaiter in a hotel in Sacramento. It was a marvelous contraption. He pondered ways to add one of those gadgets. Until soothed by the bath and the warmth of the house, he fell asleep.

Her husband slept longer than Nancy expected. She'd had time to bail the bath, do the milking, check on the children, and organize the kitchen before she heard him moving on the floor above her. His footsteps, their pace and weight descending the stairs, told her neither the bath nor the rest had restored him to the husband she had known. She understood the gravity of her situation. The trouble in their home had not ended.

"Where are my boys?" Frederick called tersely from the front room.

Wiping her hands on a kitchen towel, she stepped into the dining room in order to answer him without raising her voice. "They're outdoors. Supper will be ready soon, and I'll call them in to wash and eat."

Frederick leaned forward in his chair so he could see her by looking around the dividing doorway between the rooms. "I won't have that blasted filthy savage in my house. By Jesus' name, I won't. You understand me?"

Nancy raised her eyes to meet his. "I understand you." She turned back to the kitchen, blinking away tears. The baby wasn't filthy. Nancy cleaned her tiny fingernails just as she cleaned Mason's and Frederick's. She made sure that there was no dirt on the child. Merab was bright as the gold in the Sierra. She had already learned to squat on the commode and call to be cleaned, just as their sons had when they first began to walk and talk. She was an Indian. She wasn't filthy.

Good smells filled the kitchen as she worked: spices, lard, sugar and yeast. Nancy had much work to do, and she trusted her older sons to keep the younger children safe and calm while she did it. She roasted potatoes, and prepared tiny new beets and radishes from the gatherings she'd made that morning in the winter garden. She mixed them with summer-dried dill and a splash of cider that had turned vinegar.

When the potatoes were done, she removed them from the oven and put the raised yeast rolls in it. The timing was good. The chicken, killed, plucked and dressed that morning, was in the skillet and ready to go from pan to platter. She worked steadily and surely. The work of a well-run household continued no matter what else might happen, feast, famine or flood.

When all was ready, Nancy set the dining room table and placed covered serving dishes and a pitcher of milk on it. She looked at the table, satisfied. A small picnic basket, not used since the balmy days of fall, was in the kitchen and also held food and a jar of milk.

Nancy took off her apron and hung it on the hook in the keeping room. From a cupboard, she gathered up three soft, well-washed quilts. She went back through the kitchen and deftly took up the basket without unsettling the burden she already carried. She went into the alcove, put the bundle and the basket down long enough to drape her cloak over her shoulders, and stepped outside to head down the path to the pump house.

She looked around the whitewashed planked shed. It was scarcely seven feet square, but it would serve. She put the basket down near the pump and trough, and spread her bundle of blankets on the floor. Then she lit the lantern hanging from its ceiling. It was cold in the pump-house, but it would do. She didn't want to spend the night in the barn. Too much had happened there, and her memories of the Indian woman's dying weren't displaced readily. Her sons, understood life and death flowing through a barn's days as natural, far better than she who had never tended animals as a child and blamed a place for what happened in it. She spread the blankets to make a rough bed.

It had taken only a few minutes to prepare the room, but it was nearly dark when she got to the barn. The boys had already closed the big doors so she entered through the side.

"After you did the milking, Ma, you didn't come back. So I thought we should stay here," Wiley said.

"You did well, son." She smiled lovingly at Wiley as

she reached out and put her arm around Tom. "Thank you, boys. Both of you."

"I told Wiley and Tom it was time to go to the house after they penned the sheep," Richard complained.

Nancy cupped his chin in her hands and kissed his forehead. "Wiley's in charge when I'm not with you. You know that, Dickey-bird. Wiley and Tom were doing the right thing." Richard frowned but made no more complaints. Nancy picked up Mason and kissed both his cheeks lest he felt neglected by her attention to his brothers. Then she spoke to her sons. "Your father wants to see you boys. Supper is ready and on the table. Go to the house. Tell him the chores are done, the animals put to bed."

"Is he still angry?" Wiley asked.

"He is angry with me, not with you. Go to the house, and behave yourselves."

Tom spoke up. "Mama, aren't you coming?"

"I can't take Merab into the house, so she will stay with me in the pump house."

There was a chorus of protest. "Mama...."

"Go, boys. Be good to your father. He's had a hard journey."

Tom and Wiley said nothing, but their faces gave her argument, and she felt she should give them further instruction.

"It will be wise that you not mention Merab. Talk of how well you did your tasks. Tell your papa how much you have learned in school the past weeks. Recite for him. He will be very proud of you."

She picked up the baby, and pointed toward the barn's side door. "Go on now. You boys have done enough." She balanced the baby to lean and kiss each on boy on his forehead, and admonished, "Go and eat your supper."

Wiley bent forward. "Climb on my back, Mason. I'll carry you. You walk too slow."

"He can't help it. He's little," Richard defended.

Nancy, with Merab, followed the boys out of the barn into the night. Outdoors, she paused. "Every-thing will be all right boys. When your father leaves the table, Wiley and Tom, put any food left into the larder, and..."

"...the scraps go in the chickens' pot." Richard piped up completing her sentence.

Nancy and Merab turned away and took the path to the pump house. The lantern soon warmed away the chill. Nancy washed Merab's hands and face and tried to make a feast of the contents of the basket, but Nancy's stomach was knotted, and she was fighting tears. She ate, but the food was hard to swallow.

One of the mouser cats meowed at the door. Nancy let it in and poured a bit of the milk into the trough. The tabby jumped up and lapped up the milk delighting Merab. The two of them went out to relieve themselves, then came back in and bundled down for the night. God gave her this child and she'd care for her well.

The cat curled at Nancy's feet. She didn't mind. Better a tabby than a mouse.

>>>O<<<

Chapter Ten
~ Taking a Great Risk ~

Sleep came to the woman and child. Once, Nancy woke to hear a great horned owl catch some small prey. She recognized the squeal and other sounds, the scratching of a branch against the pump house wall and the skittering of a mouse coming in the night, as natural. She went back to sleep, the baby beside her. Sometime in the night, the door to the pump house crashed open. The noise woke her and caused the baby to squirm, the tabby to flee. Nancy rose up from the blankets to see what had happened.

Frederick was standing in the room's doorway. The lantern he held made his eyes glisten and their sockets look hollow. "You are my wife, and you will come back to the house."

"Not without Merab," she answered.

"I'll have no savages in my home, or on my property! Leave your nigger here until morning, and then I'll take it to Boulange's. Those Frenchies can always find where the Indians are hiding. They'll find a place for it."

His solution did not please her. She kept her voice free of emotion and calmly said, "Merab is my child, Frederick, and I will keep her."

"Then you're no wife of mine."

"Then I am no wife of yours. In the morning, I'll take this child and go to Mr. Dickey's. I know he will find us transport to the Flats and down into the Valley. There's work for skilled housemaids in the cities."

"You'd leave me?"

"If you give me no choice."

"You'd leave your sons?"

"Will you let me take them with me?"

"No, by God! If you go, it's by yourself."

Nancy knew how grave a risk she was taking, but took the gamble. "Then that's what I'll do," she said as she looked unflinchingly at her husband.

Frederick swore vile oaths at her. Words she had never heard before except coming from alleyways or among the drovers on the trail to California came from his mouth.

Yet, he guarded his rage by quieting and keeping distance between them for what seemed to her very long minutes. His intensity tempered at last, he moved closer to glare down at his wife, a woman he'd stood to marry before an ordained preacher twelve years before and who had never before crossed him. "Suit yourself, woman," he said to her. Turning away, he left the pump house door gaping open to the winter night.

Nancy got up and closed it, and then she lay down next to the dear substitute God had sent her, a baby to replace the child she lost two years earlier on that long, trying journey across the plains.

Long before daybreak, Frederick came again into the shed. He filled it with his size and presence.

She gave him no greeting, but when he looked down at her, his wife's face, reflecting the glare of the lantern he held up, showed the firmness of her resolve. They stared at each other, neither ready to turn away, for that would indicate concession.

"Come back to the house," Frederick said. When she didn't respond, he spoke again, hoarsely and too loudly for the small room.

"Come to the house. You can keep your pet."

"In the house? I'll keep Merab in the house? No other place?"

He stared down at two of them, before he spoke. "The house, yes. You may allow her in the keeping room, the alcove and the kitchen – the back rooms. Not in any other part of my home. Not in the rooms to me and my sons' use."

"You'll not be unkind to her?"

"I'll have nothing to do with the red creature."

"But you'll not be unkind?"

"I promise I will never touch her. No more than I touch your jewelry or little things your friends have given you. The savage is yours, not mine. But you must keep her where I will never have to look at her. Come to the house now."

"And you promise not to bring harm to her?"

"So long as you do your part and show respect for my sons and for me."

He raised his head, and took a deep breath, looking at Nancy as they came to a final agreement. He was still full of hostility, his anger near to the surface. The compromise was gravely difficult for him. "You can keep your pet. Mark this well, though," he said in a flat-spoken and determined command, "that damned Indian will never call you mother. You aren't her mother. You're my sons' mother and my wife. Don't forget yourself in your infatuation. Make a servant of her." He tilted his head and smiled at her, but it was a cruel smile and added, "*You* should know well how that's done."

"But you won't harm her?"

"Don't make me say what I've already said. The red creature is yours. I won't interfere. Come."

He made no move toward her, but neither did he leave the shed. He waited. The baby's slanty dark eyes were watching him. Like a cottontail in a field turned stone at the threat of danger, the wee girl's still manner showed neither a movement nor made a sound. Yet there was something very unlike a rabbit in the expression on her face.

Merab wasn't a red creature. Nancy knew that her face and little body were near as light in color as Frederick's were by nature. From his work outdoors, his face had turned darker and redder than hers. Her skin was no darker than Richard's freckles. Nancy had an impulse to point this out to her husband. But, as she scrambled up, pulled on her shoes, and reached for her cloak, the wisdom of discretion won over the foolishness of quick retort.

She leaned down. Leaving the quilts in disarray on the floor, she lifted the baby. She could feel the child's warmth and the child could feel hers. The air would be chilly outside, so with her free hand she pulled her cloak around Merab until only little spikes of her black hair showed out from the wrap.

Frederick stepped back, and Nancy tucked the baby's head to be away from his big body as she carried the child he didn't want, and she wouldn't give up, out of the room.

A great full moon was lighting the way ahead of her to the ranch house. Her husband followed Nancy. He was holding up his unneeded lantern. Its grinding squeak just above her shoulder, and his looming closeness, were pressing her to walk faster.

Frederick was so near behind her that if he were a cattle dog, he'd be nipping at her ankles. She didn't want to walk fast. She didn't want to stumble with a babe in her arms.

Nancy McCreary wanted to walk slowly under that bright moon. She wanted to shout hosannas and to sing all the hymns she knew that were filled with pride and triumph in godliness. She wanted to hold the baby up high in the face of heaven's glow and teach her to count the stars.

Part Two: Settling the Score

~~<<<O>>>~~

Chapter Eleven

~ The Arrival of Ada Cotter ~

The McCreary family had come to California and Crane Valley three years after a trader named James Savage touted the discovery of a natural addition to the Seven Wonders of the World in the mountains of California. The addition was a glacial remnant carved from towering granite. Distinguished by its series of magnificent waterfalls, the valley was of outstanding beauty. Other American explorers and adventurers, including the United States Army, squabbled over having been the first to make this discovery. All of them discounted that a tribe of Indians had lived in the beautiful valley for a thousand years.

The quantity of gold in eastern Mariposa County declined, along with part of its territory, when Fresno County was formed from part of Mariposa County's area in 1856. To the settlers in the Sierra, it was as though the county's name change influenced the region's geology. As the gold disappeared, the brawling and often contentious encampments along the area's streams dwindled. But few of the property owners left the region. Traffic through the mountains continued. Whether discovery of the spectacle of a certain beautiful mountain valley in the Sierra was to Savage's credit, or belonged to another, it resulted in international publicity for the mountains of California.

Aesthetes were coming from all over the world, their

paintbrushes and daguerreotype boxes replacing the miners' picks and pans. The whole world had learned of the grandeur of California's mountains, and that great wonder was very near Crane Valley. Hunters came in expectation of meat they didn't have to raise, and trappers looking for furs. Scientists came on the hunt, looking for new species.

The market for beef, mutton, eggs and vegetables had diminished with decline in gold encampments, but the settler communities were self-sustaining. Lumbering operations brought in new industry. There was still profit to be made in mining other minerals. Men with capital were investing in the Sierra. The small settlement in Crane Valley was prospering. McCreary Hauling was also prospering. Frederick owned a warehouse near the Stockton wharves to hold freight awaiting distribution and had mule corrals and wagon barns with managers hired in a number of mountain and foothill communities.

His duties overseeing the health of mules, weights of wagonloads, reliability of drivers, and difficulty of mountain passages allowed him few visits home. He counted on Nancy's reliability and good sense in running the ranch, managing its business and hired help, and raising their sons.

A great expansion of the hauling business had come about through a round trip-contract for McCreary to guarantee bi-monthly delivery of mining supplies into Angels Camp's mines, and then return well-guarded ore down to Stockton. His freight routes between Stockton, Jimtown, Mariposa, and Fresno Flats were already profitable. Secure in his California ventures profitability by 1860, Frederick began entertaining ideas of moving his family farther north in the state.

That was where the bulk of his enterprise had ultimately centered.

Frederick McCreary could buy a ranch in Tuolumne or El Dorado County, and build a house that had paneled and papered walls for Nancy, and a room of his own for each of the boys, and more. It wasn't time to share this plan with the family, but he was making regular deposits in a Stockton bank to that end.

Early that year, the town of Fresno Flats invited an ordained minister to serve as full time pastor. His arrival usurped the largest community in the Reverend Taylor migrating sinecure as both traveling preacher and schoolteacher. The displaced reverend removed from the Flats to Crane Valley hoping to find a congregation. He found that the community welcomed him with gratitude that he offered a full-time school for its children. The Reverend was a moral man, and if he had some traits of personality that were annoying, they could be overlooked.

Under the leadership of Mr. Dickey and Mr. Barrows, the ranch owners voted unanimously to build a schoolhouse for the Reverend Taylor before they built the church he desired. Mr. Dickey succinctly and somewhat ironically stated, to the agreement of the practical men assembled, "A schoolhouse can serve as school, meeting hall, dance hall, and also as a place of worship. But a chapel can only be used for God."

The ranchers' wives, hearing this decision, all concurred. Frederick McCreary, absent at the time of decision, was notified by a letter from Mr. Barrows. In his reply, Frederick sent back a note of encouragement, and promised financial support.

By September of 1860, when the new school opened, Wiley McCreary was in seventh grade. Tom was in fifth grade, Richard in third grade, and Mason in first grade. The following year, Wiley would be the first graduate of Crane Valley School.

Nancy wanted her firstborn son to continue his education as the Barrows' boy had done, but Frederick wouldn't hold with the idea and scolded her for getting above herself. "By the time he graduates eighth grade he'll be coming up on fifteen. He's as tall as I am now," her husband stated. "I'll apprentice him myself in the Angel's Camp office. He'll learn double entry bookkeeping and how to run the office. The boy doesn't need to speak Greek and Latin; he needs an understanding of the freight business."

"But Reverend Taylor says Wiley has a fine mind."

"And do you want your son educated to become another Reverend Taylor?" Frederick let sarcasm make his point. The reverend knew his Bible and was a good teacher. But he was a pompous, vain, and silly man.

With great regret, Nancy McCreary conceded that her husband had won the argument. She had held to the idea that she, a woman who could not even read, might be mother to a scholar. The idea had given Nancy a sense of glory that was hard for her to abandon.

Later that year, to sooth and surprise his wife, Frederick hired an older woman to come to the ranch as housekeeper and cook. The woman, Mrs. Cotter, was Irish, cheery, and efficient. Frederick often stayed at the Stockton Inn during his business trips. She worked there, managing the dining room. He knew, from his observation, that she was a steady and honest worker.

To his questions about any family considerations that might interfere with her removing to Crane Valley, the woman answered, "I buried two fine husbands, sir. I give fair work fer me keep, like many another does."

"How is it you've no family to help you?"

"When the hunger came t' home in Ireland, me first husband found passage fer the two o' us. Then me second husband wanted t' leave Boston and come t' the west but died in the travel. Me men are gone, sir, and I've no children that lived."

When she found that there was a hired girl already coming to the ranch to help with the laundry and heavy work, Mrs. Cotter agreed. Mr. McCreary offered better pay than she was earning, and lighter work. But no sooner than they had arrived at the ranch, than the woman caused trouble for him. She'd seemed agreeable to Nancy and the work, but Ada Cotter refused to share a room with Nancy's Indian.

"I'd sleep beside a white child, sir. But yer can't expect a righteous Christian woman like meself to share a room with a squaw. Not even yer midget-size squaw. I'd as soon go to me grave as stoop so low."

The woman took up her traveling bag and nodded to Frederick that he should pick up her small case. She marched back out to the drive and climbed back into the carriage. He was forced to take her back to the Flats and pay for her board until a place could be made for her on the ranch. The sewing room was too small for a cot, and the attic wouldn't do. He had to hire two carpenters to build a room adjacent to the bunkhouse for the crotchety woman.

"It'd suit me if that blasted little devil of yours would move out of the house," he groused as the new room was completed. "It's not proper that the good woman I hired for you should have to cross the yard back and forth each day, while a bastard Indian brat lives inside," he shouted at his wife as the new room was added.

With a quick retort, Nancy silenced him. "You granted me that the keeping room would be Merab's. It's no matter to me that you hire twenty housekeepers."

Perceiving the issue settled in her favor, Nancy showed her appreciation in warm affection. However, Frederick sulked during the rest of his visit. The disagreement had proven how insidiously the child had rooted herself in his home. His gifts were less important to his wife than a barn bastard's pleasure.

One afternoon on a visit home in the late spring, he went into the kitchen to find Nancy looking on, while Ada let the child gleefully roll buns and shape them into crescents. Ada and Merab were laughing together, the woman's wrinkled old white face down close to the child's dimpled brown one; Nancy was smiling at their easy compatibility. Frederick's antipathy for the child overcame his good sense. He pulled his wife out of the kitchen and propelled her up the stairs. Insuring privacy, he closed the door before he spun around to face his wife.

"I don't pay Ada's wages and give her a home to have her play up to a black-haired bit of evil." He gripped Nancy's arm and swung her toward him. "I hired her to make your work easier, not to encourage that slippery little maggot downstairs to think she's white. I'll take the woman back where I found her."

Nancy turned her head to look away, but he twisted her chin back. Her own weakness shamed her. Frederick was in the wrong, she wasn't. She felt outraged anger. Its intensity seared her tears dry and strengthened her. She faced him squarely, chin high, until he took his hands from her shoulders.

"You fool of a woman," he said disgustedly. "All I do for you, you throw away."

When she again able to speak with no stammer, she did. "Merab comes with me when I visit Maudie, so she will learn to care for the sick. She goes to Dickey's with me and learns to shop wisely. She sprinkles and rolls the clothes for me when I iron. She helps Ada in the kitchen." Her voice was softly defiant. "She *is* learning to be a servant as you, long ago, demanded."

With no words to say, he remained silent. But without a release through language or action, his anger grew. Nancy was but a serving woman when he married her. He'd bought her a comfortable life, a prized California ranch, and servants of her own. Yet, she would taunt and throw ancient words back at him. His wife favored a dingy child from a race he despised as an equal to the children he'd given her.

Nancy went to the door of the bedroom and opened it. Miming what he had done a few moments before, she turned to look back at him. She tilted her head slightly in the same way he had done. Her plain face confronting him was haughty and defiant, her voice sweetly acid.

"You told me to train her to servitude as I was taught, and that's what I'm doing. I teach her exactly as Mrs. Simmons taught me when I was a girl.

The next morning Frederick checked with Frank and the hired men and gave them instructions for the stock he'd soon send to summer at the ranch. The boys had already gone to school, but Nancy came out on the veranda to wave him off. Her manner was cool with him, as his was with her.

"I'll be in Angel's Camp. I'm adding oxen to the livestock corrals to pull the ore. They are slow, as you well remember from the Trail, but will carry half again as much weight as the mules and take less water and feed. "I've had to have new corrals built and ordered wagons to army design. There is much for me still left to do on this contract. After that, I'll be in Stockton and home again in six or seven weeks," he told her.

He gave her a scowling, half-hearted wave as he left, but she, her eyes soft and face smiling, blew him a kiss. It confounded him that he bested the woman in size, strength, good sense, and education, and he couldn't best her in argument. She did it with clever words that left him unable to answer. As he rode northward, it entered his mind that he would have been a happier man if he'd picked a mute for a wife.

>>>O<<<

Chapter Twelve
~ Singing Hymns ~

Mr. McCreary came across the yard to knock on the door of Ada's room and demand that she refrain from giving Merab any particular attentions. She was not to show any special favor to the Indian. In so doing, he unknowingly made the housekeeper party to a collusion of protection that surrounded MeMe. The woman felt it was not her employer's business to tell her whom to favor, and she'd grown to like the girl's manner and to ignore her heritage.

As time went on, in a conspiracy of understanding by all in the household except Frederick, Merab was never mentioned to him. The child grew in an easy understanding that there were two different rhythms to her life. They were to her as natural as the moon's changes each month out the window of her room.

The family was quiet and constrained when Mr. McCreary was home; it was rowdy and jovial when he was gone. Knowing nothing else, Merab assumed it was the way all families lived. If she couldn't go in some parts of the house, well, it had always been that way. The boys weren't usually allowed in the front part of the house either, but to do their schoolwork. Nancy was seldom in the front of the house either. Ada only went in to polish the furniture. She liked that the room she had always known to be hers was near the kitchen. She always knew what was happening.

After Frederick left once again, Nancy, as she often did, took Merab in the wagon to Dickey's store for weekly purchases. Nancy had been pleased to see that after his long absence, the old Indian man was back and again helping Mr. Dickey.

She was relieved to know that the Indian man hadn't been murdered in the terrible violence in '56. She felt a useless guilt over what her own kind had done to his. If the Indians had thieved, it didn't warrant execution. Nothing excused murdering all for the crime of some.

The Indian's greetings to the wee girl, given in his own language, made Merab giggle. As Nancy put the many items she selected on the store's counter, it seemed fitting to her that the child should like the Indian man, and she nodded to him in a friendly manner.

"This fellow is called Ootie, Mrs. McCreary. He's a good fellow," Mr. Dickey remarked with a gentle grin. "You never need fear him."

Merab didn't seem at all frightened of the old man, and it didn't occur to Nancy to fear him either. "I remember Ootie well, Mr. Dickey. I'm glad you have your helper back with you again."

She couldn't help but remember the day Ootie told her sons about wolves in the California mountains. It hadn't been creatures born with fur that had caused his disappearance; it had been wolves of her very kind, vicious men armed with gun and knife. And though her mind conceded a discomfort with the Indian Ootie's fearsome tattoos, she found him courteous and gentle. After that day, she greeted him in a friendly manner, as she would anyone to whom she had been introduced.

Short weeks after the Indian man's return, Nancy and Merab's bi-monthly visits to the store became less frequent. Maudie Landers, ill with bouts of consumption as long as Nancy had known her, had taken to her bed. Ada and Frank would go to Dickey's for any supplies Nancy needed. Any extra time she had, apart from overseeing the ranch, was given to nursing duties and care for her friend Maudie Landers.

The women had grown to be friends over the years though as busy ranch women their contact had seldom been more frequent than once a month. The Landers family had no housekeeper, and though the Braun's oldest daughter came in twice a week, she was young and uncomfortable with giving Maudie all the care she needed now that she was very ill. Merab loved the visits. She'd look at picture books in the Landers' house and listen to the women talk.

"Aaron and his brothers had the wanderlust, Nancy. His brother Samuel read of the gold strike here and wanted wealth. They had good farms, but couldn't resist the lure of the west. The older boys, Pleasant's cousins, went with them. They traveled by horse to Missouri and joined a wagon train, traveling west as you and your family did."

"Maudie, were you and Mr. Landers after gold?" It surprised her to think of her sedate neighbors with their slow and gentle voices as fortune hunters coming to the Sierra.

Maudie smiled. "Oh, no! Aaron never had an interest in chancy ventures. We moved because doctors said that the air in the west would be better for me. I was sick already, Nancy. Aaron did put some of our money as investment in his brother's venture, but he likes farming. He thought that gold seekers would need fresh milk and cheese, and he was right."

Nancy's eyes welled, and she looked away for a moment as her friend continued the story of her family's move west though obvious fatigue made her voice weak.

"We waited in Philadelphia, until Aaron and his brothers were well settled here. Then we ventured. Pleasant was only nine when we came to California, Nancy." Maudie needed to pause frequently to have breath to go on. "Pleasant and I, with the other Landers' wives and young children, came by ship around the horn.

"Pleasant loved the voyage. I think he might have stowed away to work as a cabin boy, but that he didn't want to leave me. He was just a boy when we came to California. He's nearly twenty now." She fixed her eyes on the window as though the sky outside held images of her memories in its blue.

"Oh, the ship was awful. I'd rather have had the dust of the road than that endless rocking and the terrible storms. One of my sisters-in-law lost half again her weight on that horrid boat. But Ples was not sick or scared even one day. Grandfather's fiddle was already in California, gone by wagon, but my dear hardy boy played the pennywhistle to entertain us even during rough seas, and he played nurse for all of us."

Nancy had never been on water other than standing on a ferry across a river. The swirling currents on rivers frightened her enough. She imagined she was Maudie on the ship. The thought of someone traveling through the storms of two oceans in clash gave her a thrilling kind of fear. But, she pondered that in some ways it would have been easier to come by the sea, for all its violence.

"Now, the trail wasn't so pleasant, Maudie. Cholera struck when we were camped on the Little Blue in Nebraska, and a family whose wagon was near ours lost a young mother and two little daughters. The grandmother was left to keep the babe alive and tend the grieving husband and older children."

Nancy thought of her husband and his frequent generosities to others on the long trip west. "That family had no stock but oxen with them. Frederick gave them one of our ewes for its milk." It seemed time for sharing a confidence. "I lost a babe early, on that trail," Nancy said and was gratified that Maudie's expression showed she understood how a sorrow can last.

"I've only carried but one child that lived. He is healthy. Praise the Lord," Maudie responded, sharing wounds well scarred over but still deeply felt.

"Yes. We both have reason for prayers of thanks."

They were alone in the Landers' house. Clean western air was coming in the window and blowing a fresh pine fragrance toward the sick woman. Nancy would startle no one. She let her strong voice carry *"Praise God from whom all blessings flow..."* and Maudie, though pathetically short of breath, tried to sing along. MeMe knew the words and would have sung too, but for shyness.

Later that evening, when Frank and the hired men came up to the veranda for their supper, Frank made a comment to Nancy. "I was out in the south corral with that new geldin' this afternoon afore Ada rang the bell for the chil'ern t' come in. That little ol' MeMe knows all the hymns I ever did learnt.

"She was singin' 'em to the chickens out by the barn. She knows 'em all, word and tune, and will sing 'em, long's she don't think a body's listenin."

>>>O<<<

Chapter Thirteen
~ The Name Napas ~

By the time school began the next year, Wiley was an eighth grader and as tall as his father. Frederick wanted him to leave school, but Nancy prevailed upon her husband to let the boy finish eighth grade.

The boy himself was anxious to go off and be a man. Ples Landers had been out of school for three years, and in addition to doing ranch work with his father, he played the fiddle for every barn dance around the near Sierra earning his own money. Wiley was driven by a desire to be as independent as his friend, and he made an arrangement with Reverend Taylor. He persuaded the reverend that if he did the work of an entire year by Christmastime and passed his exams, he would earn his diploma at half term. Wiley easily accomplished the task. By the holidays, He brought home a prize for having read all fifty-five of McGuffey's Readers and reciting *The Boat Song* by Sir Walter Scott from memory. He had also taken a penmanship award and earned an eighth grade graduation certificate with honor.

Her son's exuberant joy at being able to leave home and work with his father pained his mother. She was disappointed his school attendance was over and knew he was to leave her. She had no dreams of proud scholarship from her second son. Tom was neither a student nor envious of his brother's achievement. Wiley's academic primacy was unchallenged by his younger brother. Tom liked being the second son, free to walk in his brother's footsteps, to be a clown and play his days away.

Like Wiley, he'd learned to shoot as soon as he could hold a rifle steady and tamp a cartridge. He was the best shot in the family, a skill that filled his older and his younger brothers with envy. It was glory enough for the boy. He didn't envy Wiley's scholarship, or worry about the future.

Frederick came home at Christmas with a sleek young yellow mare for Wiley, and though the other boys each had his own horse, none was the prize that the yellow mare was. And then, on the second day of January, Wiley rode away on the yellow mare with his father to his apprenticeship. He would work and learn to keep a business ledger.

The boy was well over six feet tall. He was as broad shouldered as his father, though he weighed fifty pounds less. They'd be two weeks getting to Angel's Camp; Frederick had many stops to make. Wiley was lost to her now. Wiley, the son who was most like her in his ways of thinking, would never again be hers. Now he belonged only to his father.

That winter was difficult. But Maudie Landers' need for help easing her final days kept Nancy busy, and she had little time to express her grief at losing her eldest son to his father's demands. As the ranch prospered, decisions there also commanded Nancy McCreary's time. She had little time for visiting Mr. Dickey's store. Ada and Frank Sullivan did the errands for her. Little Merab's outings were to the Landers house where she was expected to entertain herself as Nancy cared for Maudie, not to the general store.

Gradually Mr. Dickey's Indian began coming by the ranch every other week or so. He came late in the afternoon and would bring a message or some supplies Nancy had wanted. The supplies were often things that could have waited until Ada or Frank or the boys had time. But it was a kindness Dickey showed The Willows.

The fact that the Indian man brought the supplies was never talked about. Ada, Frank, Lalo and the itinerant hired men had no cause to mention Ootie. It seemed reasonable that Dickey's man would come to the ranch delivering a box or now and again. They knew not to aggravate Frederick when he was home with knowledge he didn't need. If the old man sat in the yard for a few minutes with Mrs. McCreary and Merab, it wasn't a matter of notice. The ranch's mistress usually thought to offer a drink or few moments rest to anyone who stopped by the ranch, no matter how humble.

Nancy, grown to understand Mr. Dickey's subtleties, was well aware that Mr. Dickey was allowing Ootie a chance to see a child who, if not of his band or tribe, was at least of his race. And, so she allowed it.

While she didn't give the old man an active encouragement, she would come out and take a chair on the veranda. For a few minutes after the Indian had given his message, or unloaded what he'd come to deliver, Ootie would sit on a veranda step watching Merab play. He'd talk a bit to Nancy and the child in his corrupted English, and he never stayed long.

Ootie called the child by the name "*Napas.*" That puzzled the child. Nancy explained to Merab that it must be the Indian word for girl, and that satisfied the child who seemed to like the special name that the old man gave her.

It seemed to Merab that people often had different names. Nancy was Mrs. McCreary to Ada, but Mama to the boys. Frank and the hired men called her Missus. Only Mrs. Landers and MeMe called her Nancy. Mrs. Landers had four names. She was Mrs. Landers, Maudie, Maw to Ples, and MeMe called her *Auntie Maudie*. MeMe herself had four different names. Merab, MeMe, *Napas*, and the name Ada called her, *Miss Chif*.

The Indian brought MeMe small gifts, valueless things like stones or feathers. One time he brought a string of animal teeth. Nancy couldn't bring herself to take them away from the child, but she insisted Merab put them away. Ada and Frank might superstitiously fear such things had magic. If Frederick were home, he might become angered if he saw them.

As spring approached, there were times when Nancy wished the Indian's trinkets did have some spirit power. She'd use them to help her poor dying friend, but all she had were prayers. And every day it seemed more likely that God had other plans than this life for Maudie Landers. She didn't know how long Maudie would live, but it couldn't be long now. She and Merab looked for ways to bring a smile to their friend's face.

It had been wet that season and Ootie brought Merab a pair of little buttoned boots, shiny and black. They were new, a rare item that Dickey's store had come by. The summer before the Indian had given her a gingham poke bonnet. This time Nancy considered that it was possible that the man might be stealing from his employer. She made an extra wagon trip without Merab. She wanted to have a talk with Mr. Dickey.

When they spoke, Nancy found that Ootie had earned the boots and bonnet. She was greatly relieved.

Having once witnessed the effects of a massacre of

Indians blamed to theft, she never wanted to be such witness again.

The boots, still too big for the child to wear, were kept out of sight when Frederick was home. They became another part of the conspiracy, for she knew her husband saw her as a careful and frugal woman, and the boots were too fine to be something Nancy herself would have purchased.

On the fourth day of April, when the dogwood was in bud, Maudie Landers died. It was a warm spring, fragrant with new grasses showing under the apple trees and the tips of their branches swelling. Frederick and Wiley were away working, but Nancy put out good clothes for the boys to wear to Maudie's funeral. Reverend Taylor had arranged with Mr. Hopkin's wife, a woman more educated than her husband, to come and hold class during the service he was holding for Maudie, but Nancy declined to send them to school. Her children knew Maudie Landers, neighbor and friend, and would see her buried.

On that day, Merab was dressed in a black wool coat over a mourning dress and she was permitted to wear her new black boots, but was cautioned not to take pride in them. The child tried, but it was hard for her not to look down at the shoes Ootie had given her. Reverend Taylor prayed such long prayers.

Since Frederick was not with them, Nancy was not surprised that all but Aaron and Ples Landers and Mr. Dickey shunned her and the children at the funeral service. Reverend Taylor didn't even find time to speak to her. She had a bitter thought that if Wiley had still been home, the man's teacher-pride in her oldest son's scholarship would have overcome the reverend's distaste for her youngest and adopted child. But Wiley had been gone since Christmas.

None of the women present at the service would look at Nancy or the boys, though they freely gave black looks and snide glances at the child beside her. Merab had given Maudie Landers much cheer, and it annoyed Nancy to endure the snubbing without speaking out. Retorts and sarcastic phrases came to her mind. But it wouldn't help anyone if she caused trouble, and would embarrass Aaron and Ples. She held her head high, and kept her mouth closed. Too, Nancy wanted her own exhibition of gracious manners to set a good example for her children.

As Tom settled in the driver's seat of the McCreary family carriage, she allowed herself to note that the vehicle was nicer than any plain wagons in the community. Perhaps the neighbor women's jealousy prompted the snubbing as much as the presence of a child with tan skin did.

Mrs. Hopkins and Mrs. Barnett had dabbed black trimmed handkerchiefs to their dry eyes at the cemetery, and were solicitous of Mr. Landers and his handsome twenty-year-old son to the point of embarrassing their husbands. But, during all the months that Maudie Landers had needed care, neither woman had come to the sick woman's aid. How "...*like unto whited sepulchers...*" the two women were, Nancy observed, chiding herself for her own unchristian thoughts.

Summer came at last, providing a season's distance from her friend's death. With the summer came warmth and the joy of having three younger sons home from school every day to entertain her and Merab with their tales and teases. The older boys worked with the hired men in the orchard and corrals, the younger boys and Merab helped her with the vegetable garden and in the house.

The news that found its way to Crane Valley was full of President Lincoln and the War of Secession, and Nancy listened to what was being said. But it was distant from her. She felt relief that her sons were too young to be soldiers. At night she prayed for other mothers and their sons who were not so fortunate.

With the season's change, she came to find forgiveness for the women in her community. Those poor women were like Frederick, she told herself. They must not have been taught to share the love of God with all His creatures. They couldn't help their ignorance. It had been her choice to keep the Indian baby and raise her in the light of goodness.

Righteousness had brought its own reward in that the child was a joy to her. Merab had given her happiness from the first day with the McCrearys. The child had even charmed Ada Cotter. The people Nancy had known in the Indiana parsonage would certainly not have disparaged her decision. She was not showing charity to judge these Californians by Indiana's standards of godliness. She released her bitterness into summer's air.

Chapter Fourteen
~ A Murdered Band ~

"Ada, I can count! I can count to a hundred."

"Ah, but do yer know what ye be a'countin'?" The aproned woman held a peeled and cored early apple and was dropping slices from it into a crockery bowl. She was in a jolly mood and let a quizzical eyebrow demand answer from the child.

"I can count anything. Richard made me count all the matches in the blue glass box."

"Oh, weary me! *Ye* didn't go into the dinin' room did ye?"

"No, I only watched from the doorway. Richard brought the blue box in here, and I said my counts at the table." The child's dark eyes were bright.

The old woman suppressed a smile. She had been working at Crane Valley Ranch for over a year and understood its children. "Richard, himself, knew better than bring the box in here for a play toy. Mrs. McCreary loves that glass box. Ye might ha' broken it."

"I was careful."

"Then, Richard might ha' broken it. That disappointed Mrs. McCreary would be. Ye mustn't let those boys pull yer into their shenanigans."

Mason was teaching MeMe numbers, but Richard was testing her. Richard promised her that when she could count to a hundred without mistakes and correctly tell him which was the bigger number or which was the smaller when he gave her two numbers to compare, he'd give her his old school slate and chalk. Then Mason could teach her how to write her numbers not just say them. When she could write her numbers, the boys would teach her how to write her name, *Merab McCreary.*

Nancy said reading and writing weren't as important as numbers and amounts. They should be learned first. But still, she wanted to be able to do what the boys could do. Tom, Richard and Mason went to school and they could read as well as cipher.

The past December, Wiley had finished eighth grade and brought home a prize for having read all fifty-- five McGuffey's Readers and reciting *a very long poem.* Then he went away to work with Mr. McCreary.

MeMe knew Nancy grieved at her oldest child's absence. But MeMe, Mason and Richard were glad Wiley was gone. Once he grew taller than Nancy, He wasn't as nice to them as he had been. He still liked Tom and Ples, but he yelled at the younger children, teased them, and told them to stay out of his things. When Mason complained, Nancy said that was what happened to boys as they turned into men and that in a few years Wiley would surely be nice again, and Tom would become the brother the children complained about. It wasn't a very satisfying answer or a pleasing prospect.

MeMe's two bottom teeth came out, and new ones were coming in. Ada brought a stool from the kitchen into the wash-up closet so the girl could see the white nubs in the high mirror. MeMe knew she was old enough to go to school. The rest of summer she waited for Nancy to mention first grade and Reverend Taylor, but Nancy didn't.

School started and the boys left without her. Ada liked to talk, so while they were laying out tomatoes to dry in the sun, she asked the housekeeper, "Why can't I go to school? I'm big enough."

Ada said, "Now why would ye want to be doing that? Mrs. McCreary and I can teach ye everything ye need to know."

MeMe thought about this that September. She knew girls went to school. The boys talked about them. But she knew Nancy couldn't read, and neither could Ada. They didn't think she needed to know what they didn't know. She'd never learn.

The child was lonely without the boys. One day, she was in the yard alone. Nancy and Ada were boiling big kettles, and didn't want her in the kitchen. To her surprise, she heard Mr. Dickey's wagon. Ootie was coming. He would talk to her.

Ples Landers was with him. The two men brought a package for Nancy. MeMe ran toward them as they got down from the wagon. She was holding one of a litter of kittens - just beginning to come out from under the veranda.

"Ootie, Ples, look!" she called, as the ginger kitten scrambled out of her hands and landed on the ground, only to climb back up using her skirt as a ladder.

"*W-e he- sit*," the Indian said, and grinned at her.

Ples laughed and said, "Ootie says your kitten is a lion."

By then Nancy had come out on the veranda wiping her hands on a towel. Ples was still wearing a black armband for his mother. Maudie was not yet six full months dead. Nancy was glad to see both of the men. She had liked the Indian from the time he'd told her sons about wolves in California, and she felt honest sympathy for the bereaved young man for the loss of his mother.

Ootie greeted Nancy, but swiftly afterward his attention returned to the little girl grappling with the kitten. He cocked his head, and looked at MeMe. Then he pointed to himself, and said, "*En-say.*"

She looked puzzled, so he took a twig and drew a picture of a man in the dirt, pointed at it and said, "*k-oo-te-un.*"

MeMe pointed at him and said, "*k-oo-te-un.* Yes, Ootie." The kitten scrambled away.

But the old man shook his head and frowned. "*Uh-om.* No Ootie, *ka-oo-te-un.*" Beside the figure of the man, he drew a woman, then a very small woman. He pointed to the man and said firmly, "*Ensay.*" and pointed to himself."

MeMe pointed to him. "*En say?*" He broke into a smile and she knew she had it right. She pointed to the smallest figure and asked, "MeMe?"

He nodded while MeMe clapped her hands.

Ples was watching too, and he was studying the old man closely. "Are you MeMe's Papa, Ootie?" he asked.

Ootie frowned, shook his head again, and pointed the twig at the figure in the middle, the woman he had drawn in the dirt. "Thi' papa." he said. His face turned serious. "MeMe ensay." He drew a circle around the smallest figure.

Ples rested his hand on Ootie's back. Nancy drew in her breath, and said, "Oh, Ootie, I'm sorry."

It took MeMe a while to figure it out, but then he understood. She dropped the kitten, squatted down, and drew a circle around the woman figure. "My

Mama? "You're my mama's papa!"

She knew what grandfathers were. She had a grandfather! The boys didn't have a grandfather, but she did. She took both Ootie's hands and jumped up and down dancing her own kind of jig, saying, "You're my *Ensay*, Ootie!"

"Hu!" the old man said. He was embarrassed, but he had tears in his eyes. In his low gruff way he said, "ess."

After Nancy learned that Ootie was Merab's grandfather, she understood much more. Ootie was connected to the Chancy tribe murdered on Coarsegold Creek. His daughter was the woman buried in the meadow.

It was time for her to talk to the child. Nancy McCreary didn't know anything of her own origins, other than that she had been a foundling child. A child should know who she was.

And, so, one evening when they were alone in the sewing room she told Merab the truth of her life. "A long time ago, when you were a baby," Nancy said softly, "some bad men, rude and evil men, killed most of the Indian people around here. It was a terrible thing, but thanks to God, Ootie survived, and so did you."

Merab came and stood in front of her, staring in disbelief. Nancy put aside the britches she was mending and pulled the child down on her lap, although the little girl was getting too big for cuddling in a rocking chair.

"Dear child, long ago, Mr. Dickey saved your grandfather Ootie, and we saved you."

"My Indians were all killed?

"Yes. There may be some members of your family still left way up in the high mountains, but they haven't come back if they are still even alive."

"Even my Mama?"

The child looked at her earnestly, and it was hard for Nancy to go on, for it brought sad memories to her. But the child needed the truth of her own story.

"Yes, my dear girl. She was killed. You were only a baby and can't remember. Before she died, your mother brought you to the ranch where you'd be safe. And ever since that day you have been my dear little girl."

Chapter Fifteen
~ Scarlet Fever Contagion~

It wasn't until afterward that MeMe began to wonder why the miners had killed all her Indian family. She fretted about it, and the question kept coming back to bother her. One Sunday when Richard and Tom were putting up a swing for Mason and her on the big oak tree down at the corner of the mule corral, she decided to ask Tom. Tom was seldom still, and Nancy had to get after him often, but he was the brother who always told MeMe the truth and never told her teases that were only silly things like Richard and Mason did.

She asked him simply, "Why did the miners kill my Indian family?"

Tom dropped the rope and frowned down at her. "Who told you that they did that?"

She stood still and looked scared.

"You can tell me," he said. "You aren't in trouble. I just want to know."

"Nancy."

"Mama told you?" he asked, showing surprise.

"Yes."

Richard pushed forward to blurt out, "Mama says to tell the truth, and now we can finally tell her."

"Who's going to tell her?" asked Mason, obviously not wanting the task.

"I'll tell her," Richard said. "MeMe, lots of people don't like Indians. The miners despised Indians, and they went on a rampage and killed all they could find.

"No one stopped them," Tom said angrily. "It happened to your Indians past the Flats and up over the long grade. But there were people even here in Crane Valley who wanted to kill Indians. Mr. Dickey would have stopped them if he'd been there when it happened. Ples would have stopped them. And Mr. Landers, too."

Richard broke in. "Ples Landers says that people who hurt other people should be locked away for good, but no one ever does it."

"Lots of people don't like Indians." Tom said. "Papa hates Indians. He wouldn't have stopped them."

"Don't say that," Richard snapped.

"Well, it's true."

"Don't say it about Papa." Mason chided.

The boys finished putting the swing up. MeMe could swing high in the air, back and forth. The boys began dropping green acorns down on her, but the acorns didn't hurt and she didn't mind. Going back and forth on the swing let her thoughts come out. One of the acorns plunked on her bonnet. She liked the sound it made.

School days passed leaving her lonely, but the swing helped. Wiley had been gone since December. At Christmas it would be a year. He missed Maudie's funeral, he missed the lupines blooming, and he missed summer. So did Mr. McCreary, but Mr. McCreary had been home four times.

Wiley hadn't come home at all. She realized she missed him, and she wished he'd come home. She wouldn't even mind him teasing her.

MeMe McCreary wiggled her bottom front teeth until first one then the other came out. Ada carried a stool to the alcove closet mirror so MeMe could climb up and see the new bumpy white teeth beginning to come in. Then Ada gave her a shiny penny for each tooth. A pretty lady's head was on each side. The lady had a crown and stars made a circle around her. She looked just like Nancy. Ada said Mrs. McCreary *was* Lady Liberty and winked.

The day before, MeMe had gone down to the store with Nancy to get feed. She didn't get to see Ootie because he was helping Mr. Landers and Ples clear brush up at the cemetery.

After putting the grain bags in the wagon, Mr. Dickey sat her up on the counter and gave her a peppermint. She watched him put the feed money Nancy gave him into a box and write in a book. MeMe tried to pay him her pennies for the peppermint. But he laughed and told her to keep the pennies because she might need them someday. She was wearing her favorite yellow gingham pinafore and a pink bonnet with ribbons. When Mr. Dickey told her she was pretty, Mrs. Barrows and Mrs. Hopkins, who were standing by the yardage shelves, gave her bad looks. Now she understood.

Tom was right. People didn't like Indians. That was why Ada didn't carry a glass of tea out to Ootie when he visited like she did for Mr. Landers, unless Nancy told her to do it twice. It was why Frank never had conversations with Ootie like he did with Lalo and the other hired men. And, that was why she would never go to school with the boys. She wouldn't learn reading. It didn't matter at all that she was old enough to grow big teeth and knew her numbers past a hundred.

Toward the middle of the month MeMe had to stay close to the house because drifters looking for work were coming into the orchard and Nancy and Ada didn't trust the look of them. Nancy asked Frank and their hired men to run off any who came onto the property. She wouldn't let MeMe go down to the swing.

Drifters might be like miners. They might want to kill Indians. MeMe obeyed. She worked in the garden and gathered all the vegetables that were getting rotten and took them down to Frank's pigs, gathered all the eggs each day, and helped Ada in the kitchen as she always had. Nancy said she was old enough to learn embroidery, and she practiced her stitches carefully. Nancy pulled them out if they weren't done right.

"Do I have to do them again?" she asked.

"Yes. Just as I did when I was your age. If you work to learn all your embroidery stitches, and can make a sampler and stitch a quilt, then you'll be able to learn dressmaking."

"How long until I can do that?"

"Oh, it took me about ten years to go from embroidering a border on Mrs. Simmon's dress to making the dress." Nancy laughed.

Then she surprised Merab with a child's silver thimble. She slipped it on second fingertip of the child's right hand. "This will make it easier."

Soon the child could make a lazy-daisy stitch and Nancy let her fill in a pink flower between each of the blue ones Nancy was embroidering on a piece of tan linen. MeMe felt better. She was learning something, although it didn't seem as exciting as what the boys learned at school.

Before long, serious trouble came to the community. It was to acutely affect the family at The Willows. A contagion struck and ran through the children of the school. It began when Louisa, the littlest Scruggs girl, was sent sick to school during the term's second week. Her papa thought she was malingering because she hadn't memorized her spelling list.

A few days after Louisa took sick, other children became ill. Mason was one of them. He came home with a scratchy throat. It became a headache, then a fever burning his cheeks red. From the inflammation in his throat, Nancy and Ada both deduced that he had contracted the canker sickness. Two days later Richard and Tom were also sick, and a day later, MeMe couldn't be persuaded to eat her breakfast.

That afternoon Nancy, who had been running back and forth all day nursing her three sick sons and brewing medicines known to help ease the throat, found the little girl curled up on the boot bench in the alcove, flushed and feverish.

Later that week Doc Braden rode in from the Flats. He diagnosed that scarlet fever had come to Crane Valley. The three McCreary boys, the Wilson and the Braun children had all carried it home to their families. Almost all the children in Crane Valley past weaning were ill. Doc was relieved that the disease was only the canker sickness that most now called it scarlet fever. He'd worried when first called to Crane Valley that he'd find diphtheria and have to ride back home feeling that his calling was as sorry as a gravedigger's.

At the McCreary ranch, Mason was feeling better, but his skin was still red, peeling and itchy. Doc Braden left instructions with Nancy and Ada for an ointment that might ease the children's skin and an elixir to keep the disease at bay in the three children who were still feverish.

Doc said that some gracious angel had waved the small epidemic away from the Robertson and

Creekmore children, for they didn't become sick at all. "At least it isn't diphtheria which can start the same way but is a worse killer," he said by way of reassurance. "Mrs. McCreary, your children are sick and need care, but they are strong and healthy. "Watch the little one, though. It's said that Indians take some sickness extra hard."

Nancy and Ada kept the kettle going day and night. Nancy kept a bad smelling pot of salve to wrap around their necks and cover with flannel, and made a sipping potion of lard, whiskey and herbs from the garden. She put spoons full of the foul tasting liquid in the children's mouths twice daily.

On the sixth day, Nancy woke up with a tight throat. She tried to continue caring for her children, but by the second day she was flushed and feverish. She attempted to come downstairs, but was too dizzy. Soon Nancy was upstairs, so sick she was unable to take care of the children.

Ada, who had much experience with the nursing of illnesses in her lifetime, abandoned her cozy little room and slept in a bed made from two of the soft parlor chairs. Tom, in spite of his thinness, was quickly on the mend. Within a week of taking sick, he and Mason were able to go back to school. MeMe was up and about trying to make herself useful, contrary to Doc's prediction. She spent most of her time curled up in her room, quietly working on a beginner's sampler, or she wandered around the garden, bereft of the company of the people in her life that she most loved.

Nancy was sick upstairs. Two of the boys were back in school and the third was too ill to play, for fever continued in Richard and he was showing little improvement.

Nancy McCreary's fever spiked up and down. Ada knew to give her purgatives, and rub onion on her feet to draw down her temperature. Nothing seemed to help. Finally, on the third day, the fever seemed to break. But Nancy couldn't talk. She'd only turn her eyes away if Ada tried to rouse her. Alarmed, the housekeeper sent MeMe to the mule shed to bring Frank to her. She would rather have called for Lalo, but he was away helping Mr. Hopkins whose sheep had colic.

"Frank, Mrs. McCreary is very ill. Ye must ride to the Flats and get Dr. Braden."

"I'll go. Want I should take the small wagon?"

"No, ye fool. The wagon is too slow. Take a ridin' horse. Saddle up quickly and don't waste time. If the doctor's not t'home, find a pottercary." Ada thrust a small money sack into his hands. "Make a purchase of paregoric and get it back to me as quick as you can travel. But leave word that we need the doctor at Crane Valley Ranch soon's he can get here. Now tell me back what 'tis yer to get."

Frank tried to please. "The doctor and perrygork. I know what that is. But, Ada, ain't there none a that at Dickey's? It'd take but half-hour to git to Dickey's and back. Then I'd go git the doctor."

"Would I be sendin' ye to the Flats if what I needed was at Dickey's? Ye fool, don't argue, get on."

The doctor had been called away for a logging accident miles away northeast, miles above Finegold Camp, but his wife spoke with Frank and she was sympathetic. She had met Mrs. McCreary once some years earlier and liked her. Mrs. Braden sent him across the street to the apothecary for paregoric and gave him a note for a dram of another medicine. Mrs. Braden wrote a list of instructions for its use.

"Can anyone there on your ranch read this?" the doctor's wife asked him sharply.

"Miz McCreary's boys can, missus. They're all good at readin'."

As he rode away, Mrs. Braden wondered what kind of accident had caused that Frank Sullivan to be so lame and palsied. He could scarcely mount his horse. He wasn't yet what she considered old.

Chapter Sixteen
~ Doc Braden's Duty ~

Doc Braden was far up on the north fork of the Fresno River tending an injured miner. It was two days before he received word that he was needed in Crane Valley. Then two more days passed before he could get to the ranch. By that time, it was apparent even to the children that Mrs. McCreary was very ill. Neighbor men both on horseback and in wagons were stopping by the ranch to ask Ada how Nancy was and to tell of how the sickness had affected their own families. They came with jars of different sorts of remedies prepared by their wives. While Nancy wasn't popular with the women, Mr. McCreary, through his strength, reserve, and generous donations to the construction of the schoolhouse, had won their complete affection. Ada thanked the visitors and took their offerings, but she promptly put them on a shelf in the cellar, unopened, suspicious of food that might have been prepared by anyone other than her.

After he'd done all he was able at the ranch, the doctor stopped at Dickey's Store. Its proprietor was sitting in the sun out on the porch of the building. "You've already been to the McCreary ranch?" Dickey asked, standing to greet Doc.

"Just left. I'm on my way to the Jones place up river. His wife is having a difficult time. I need to stop there and see what I can do to hurry that baby down."

Dickey nodded. He knew of Jones' wife's troubles each time she brought out another child. Doc wouldn't make any money there. Jones was both poor and cheap. He'd pay the doctor in pinecones.

"Word around, is that Mrs. McCreary is doing poorly." Dickey led the way into the store and went back behind the counter. "There is cider in the jug. Pour yourself some." He pointed to a jug and tin cup sitting on the top of a barrel. "Now, what is it I can do for you?"

"Nothing for me. I didn't stop in for cider or to make a purchase. Someone needs to go for McCreary. Can you arrange a rider to go and find the man?"

"It is that bad at The Willows?"

"I doubt Mrs. McCreary will live to see her husband's return. But he needs the chance to get home. Do you know where he's hauling? The children told me he and his oldest boy are working up north. They thought out of Stockton."

"He and Wiley are running supplies to the mines from Stockton to Angel's Camp, down through Jamestown and back. Pleasant told me McCreary bought a big piece of property in Angel's Camp for a livery and corrals," Dickey said.

"Then, that's the most likely place to find him. It's my bounden duty to notify him."

The storekeeper frowned. He took a pinch of tobacco and offered the can to the doctor who shook his head. "I'll do what I can, Doc," Dickey promised. "Mrs. McCreary is a fine woman. This pestilence is a damned shame."

Doc reached to shake Mr. Dickey's hand, grateful for the help. Doc's taste for politics and gossip began to show. "You know that there's word around the Flats that 'ol McCreary's a dad-blasted Copperhead?"

Dickey was surprised. "They don't pass that word around in McCreary's hearing, I'd opine." He poured a mug of cider for the doctor against his protest. He knew little of McCreary's political persuasions, in spite of the family having lived near the store for some years now. But Dickey knew how the nation's war climate had brought a split of loyalty to many Californians.

Doc frowned his disgust. "There's a batch of Southern sympathizers down Tulare County. I know they favor the secessionists down in Visalia. Some say the sympathizers fill in the entire state down below Fort Tejon. There's nary one Union man down Visalia way."

"Still, I'd not have thought it of McCreary," Dickey replied. "He pays his men full and fair. He treats them well. Wouldn't think he tolerate slave-keepers."

"Morton, the assayer, not Morton the rancher, saw McCreary coming out of a building that's said to be the headquarters of the dad-blasted Knights of the Golden Circle up near French Camp. If it was McCreary, he's gone swimming in the wrong pond. America just don't need all this dissention and strife! We've got to stamp out that damned rebellion. You know, Dickey, I do like what I hear of a man in San Francisco name of Reed. He's got good ideas."

"Trouble is coming, Doc, and we think the same. However, McCreary's always shown willingness to help anyone needing help. I give him full credit there. We wouldn't have the school without his help. And it's no matter. I'd never take against Mrs. McCreary for her husband's politics. He's lucky to have such a good woman."

The doctor listened nodding his head. "Well, I remember how she gave Mrs. Landers tender care there at the end. I hope she can last until her husband is home."

"I'll ask Braun's young brother-in-law to ride to Angel's Camp. Henry Stegler is quick in mind, though thick in body and sparse in the whiskers. He's good with horses. He'll be able to track McCreary down. 'Sides, I think he'd like a chance to get to know McCreary better. I don't think the boy likes working for that ol' Prussian. Braun considers he's family and won't pay him more'n tobacco money.

"I can write a letter to McCreary telling him to make haste home and why. Henry will get to him faster'n Hall's Stockton mail coach could."

Doc Braden smiled, his mind eased. "I do wonder where

Frederick McCreary found that good housekeeper of theirs. She's a caution. Their man Frank came in and offered to ride for McCreary, but Ada shooed him right back out to the barn.

Raising the pitch of his voice to give Dickey an imitation of the McCreary's housekeeper's brogue, Doc said, *"Why, Doctor, that poor soul of a Frank Sully scarce got to the Flats to fetch ye, and 'tis only ten miles 'tween there and here. If he were t' find McCreary, without ending up in San Francisco Bay, he'd then forget what he was to tell 'im."*

His mission accomplished, Doc Braden saddled up and rode down the Waukeen trail to attend to the Jones woman.

Ples Landers, who was working that day with Stegler breaking colts to harness, volunteered to ride with to Angel's Camp with Stegler. Dickey drew a map for Henry and Ples to McCreary's hauling station in Mariposa. The man there would have maps to direct them the rest of the way. Within an hour the young men were ready to ride, but at the last minute, Mr. Dickey decided he would ride with Henry. He would leave the store in Pleasant Lander's capable hands. Ples had uncommon common sense, and he had been rightly named. It wasn't only his fiddle and country songs made him popular. He liked being kept busy since his ma died, and often helped out.

Dickey had come to the idea that after they found McCreary, he would tarry in the north of the great valley a few days before returning to Crane Valley. He could visit with his wife and daughters. Mrs. Dickey and the girls lived with her brother in Stockton. Mrs. Dickey didn't take to the mountains. Nor did she want their daughters going to a sometime school. They went to a fine seminary in Stockton. She was a good woman, Ella was. But she had high ideas and liked tea parties and soft furniture. They got along somewhat better living apart.

The store could do without him. Mrs. Dickey had long railed at him that he had nothing to dispense but gossip and poor advice. Ples would have Ootie to help him. All the folk for miles around would find a need for something from the store to have a chance to visit a minute with young musician serving as store-clerk. That boy could play a tune on fiddle, flute, or horn, and sing a sweet song if no instrument were at hand. Ples offered a better attraction for the customers of Dickey's goods and supplies than just the storeowner's gossip and poor advice.

Nancy McCreary's life slipped away in the dark of morning three days after Henry Stegler and Mr. Dickey left Crane Valley for Angel's Camp. Ada had been attending her. Nancy gave a little gasp and never made another sound.

It was left to Ada to prepare the body so Nancy's sons and the little girl could see her one last time before the grey color came that accompanied death. Bodies didn't keep, and the Indian summer days were warm. Decisions had to be made. Aaron Landers was there to help. He took thirteen-year-old Tom with him to do what was necessary. They chose a place on Cemetery Hill next to Frederick's mother's grave. Frank and Lalo did the digging; Aaron and Tom rode to the Braun ranch and asked Emil Braun to build a woman's sized coffin and send both his daughters, Greta and Eva, to The Willows to help Ada.

Nancy was put to rest on the day that followed her death. No one asked the Reverend Taylor to leave off teaching school and join the burial party. The ceremonies would wait for Frederick McCreary's arrival. Nancy's sons, the adopted girl, her housekeeper and hired men attended the simple burial. Aaron Landers carried Richard, still feverish with sickness. Frank, Lalo, and the hired men filled in the grave.

Far off, squatting down beside a big oak, Ootie watched the white people. He worried what would become of Napas. His band was gone. He had no family left. His women, Chukchansi women, who could teach his granddaughter the things she needed to know, had been gone for five winters. Mrs. McCreary was gone. This sad day left only Ootie and Ada Cotter to look out for the Indian's twice-orphaned granddaughter.

>>>O<<<

Chapter Seventeen
~ Black Bunting ~

By the time Dickey and Henry Stegler arrived in Stockton and were sent on to Angel's Camp, Nancy had already been two days in the ground. Horse and rider again proved the most reliable way to get a message across counties in the Sierra. Telegraph was in between Stockton and the gold country, but a lightning strike had downed the lines and sparked a fire through the still, dry country.

A grey and black sense of foreboding had been surrounding Frederick for days. The sumac trees were fall colorful, but he felt it winter already. He feared something had happened to one of his teams out on the road, or infection might down the corralled stock at one of his stations. Or, that Jim Birch's California Stage had outbid him on a Twain Harte contract. Frederick was so nervous and impatient that he called the farrier out a month early to circuit the corrals, and fretted over each page of the assets and debits records, as though he distrusted everyone who worked for him in the livery and office.

Wiley, Mr. Harrington the bookkeeper, and the clerk voiced the wish that their boss would go back to McCreary Hauling's warehouses and bank account in Stockton and leave them to their work in peace at the Angel's Camp office.

On the day the Crane Valley men arrived, Frederick glanced out the livery office window at the sound of horses. He recognized Dickey and Braun's young relative dismounting at the rail outside. Frederick's gut bunched up, and he felt he could vomit. He had to force himself to the door to greet the men. His concerns had been misplaced. They should have been for his family.

It took Wiley longer to comprehend that Mr. Dickey and Henry Stegler's appearance wasn't a serendipitous coincidence. The boy had yet to learn that surprise and tragedy often held each other's hand. Dickey only brought word of the grievous sickness in Crane Valley for it was all the man knew to relate, but Frederick sensed that death was waiting for him there. That had caused his dire feelings of foreboding. He wanted to go to Nancy immediately, ready instantly to leave the business that had concerned him so. His wife's face would not leave his thoughts. He told Harrington to manage the business in his absence, and sent Miller, the yardman, to arrange for his favorite riding mount and a second horse to be made ready.

Against his son's protests, he instructed that Wiley stay in Angel's Camp and keep to his work. The two men aforementioned were to share with the boy any business discussions and decisions that were needed before his return. Wiley was to initial any contracts made, any receipts drawn before Harrington's signature as agent of the business.

Frederick left for Crane Valley before two hours had passed. "It's better that you stay with your work. There is nothing you could do in any case," he told the boy. There wasn't anything that his son could add but nuisance to him. Inexperienced in hard, fast riding, Wiley would slow him down. Dickey and Stegler said the canker sickness had struck the whole community hard. Why put another son in the face of contagion? He had made the right decision.

As Frederick rode away, he saw in the angled reflections of the shop windows that Wiley stood in the dust of the street behind him, tears streaming down his young face. Mr. Harrington was standing beside the boy, trying to give him some comfort while Henry Stegler, still holding the letter of employment Frederick had given him, was watching soberly from the office doorway.

McCreary saw the scene reflected clearly. He looked straight ahead and shrugged off guilt he might have felt toward Wiley.

Every mile onward toward Crane Valley worsened Frederick McCreary's dread. Every night camped along the way, he prayed, "Dear God that I've only lost one!" In moments of sincerity, he knew himself to be a greedy man, but he was afraid to be so greedy in his prayers that God's wrath would wreak down punishment on him and send the Angel of Death to take his wife and his children. He slept on the ground only short hours, changing from one horse to the other, tarrying briefly to give them water and graze, taking little rest or food himself.

At last, Frederick rode up the ranch drive certain that death's shadows had already come to drab the joy of his home and tinge his family. He rode through the orchard and saw black bunting stretched from the rail of the veranda; black draperies already showing dust in their folds hung from the lantern post; the curtains in the house were drawn. Though it was Saturday and not a school day, he heard no shouts of greeting from his sons.

Frank met him out on the track and took the horses, saying, "The boys all live, sir. I'll be tending to these animals fer ye." Frederick motioned to the man that he needed say no more. The man's words, never mentioning Nancy, already told him his wife was dead.

Frank gave a bow and led the horses away. The Angel of Death had come to The Willows, but God had stayed his hand. Only one was dead. As he went up the steps, the dust on the folds of the bunting told him they had been hanging along the rail for days. His wife was in the ground before he reached home. He would have no last word, no last kiss, no final look of tenderness from her face. His life, the good life he had anticipated, had unexpectedly changed.

In the parlor, the daguerreotype of Nancy, wearing the dress with the French lace collar, her favorite of all the gowns he'd ever bought for her, was on the mantle. He'd had the photograph made when they were first married. The picture's frame was surrounded with bouquets of dry grasses and the prickly wildflowers that lasted until

September, the other pictures and ornaments in the room had been removed or were covered. Richard lay on the horsehair sofa, a blanket over him. The boy smiled faintly at his father. Frederick knelt by the sofa and took the boy in his arms registering that the boy was wan and feverish, but grateful that at least the child still lived.

Mason and Tom came down the stairs. Both boys were pale but had put on their good clothes, out of respect for their mother. He reached out to embrace them. He had never seen their eyes so dull, their movements so apathetic. Aaron Landers, who had been sitting in the tall chair reading to the ailing Richard, rose to shake Frederick's hand. "I'll leave you 'til you're ready to talk to me. Take good time with your boys. I'll go visit with Ada a while. I'm in no hurry."

As soon as the parlor door closed on their neighbor, Tom came alive to query, "Where's Wiley? Why isn't he with you?"

"He had to keep to his work, son."

"But why, Papa?" Mason asked, his voice quivering, his tone accusing. "Mama's dead. We need Wiley."

"Why, sir?" Tom asked again. His tone better controlled. He knew it was not wise to push his father. Wiley might try, but he should not.

Frederick looked at his sons' beseeching faces and couldn't give them reasons for having left Wiley behind. He wasn't sure of his reason. Nor would he tell them that Wiley begged to be allowed to ride with him, and he'd refused. Frederick hadn't wanted the boy to give him any bother. That was the truth. And more, the boy still needed hardening before he'd be the son Frederick wanted. Perhaps it was simply because he trusted Wiley's good sense even more than Harrington's in the running of the office. All could be true. He chose to say nothing. His sons were left to think what they chose.

After a suitable time, Ada came into the parlor. "Mr. Landers is sittin' out on the back veranda, sir. He'll tell ye what's been done concerning Mrs. McCreary's remains. The man or his boy 'as come every day to sit with the children. "The two have been through just the same kind of sadness this year. They are a grand help and good neighbors to ye, sir."

Frederick gave a nod that she call Aaron back to the room. Ada folded the thin blanket covering Richard and placed it over the arm of the sofa. Taking Nancy's shawl from the rocking chair, she draped it around Richard's shoulders, though the last day of September was warm and there was no chill in the house. She drew the child to his feet and pointed the boys toward the kitchen.

"I'll see that these scamps don't bother ye, none sir."

After the boys were grouped in the kitchen, she went to the window to inform Mr. Landers he was free to go to the parlor whenever he wanted. Then Ada beckoned the boys to the table and said, "Sit yerselves down. 'Tis early for supper, but now your father is t' home again, people will be soon be dropping in to bring their consolations. I won't be wanting ye fine urchins to scarfle up the fancy food I put out for them."

The boys didn't smile, but they didn't argue either. Somber-faced, they took their places. Tom was the first to notice that Merab wasn't in the kitchen.

"Where's MeMe?" he asked accusingly.

Ada was tolerant of his intent. "The girl's not locked up, Tommy. She's nappin' in her room. 'Tis a grief for her too, that yer mother's been called to Heaven." Ada poured milk into the boys' glasses, letting her free hand skim each boy's shoulders affectionately as she passed behind him. MeMe's young, she is. 'Tis all that much confusin' to 'er."

"MeMe knows what dead is, Ada," Richard said flatly. "She was with us when Ples's mother died." It was the strongest his voice had been since he took the fever. "She shouldn't be asleep at this time of day, Ada. She isn't sick."

"I'm going to go and get her." Mason slid off his chair, went to the keeping room and knocked on its door. MeMe didn't answer, so he opened the door, went in, and pulled her up from her cot. "Don't be a lie-a-bed," Mason scolded. "Mama didn't like that."

MeMe looked at him squinty, and her lower lip drooped. But she followed him into the kitchen. Tom jumped up to set another place at the table for her.

With Aaron to accompany him, and a fresh horse to ride, McCreary left the house to ride out to see the spot his son had chosen for Nancy's grave in the small Crane Valley Cemetery. While he was gone, Ada played her part. She let the boys know what would be expected of them at and after their mother's service, and told the children stories of the grand wakes that had been held when she was a child in County Cork.

The children were enthralled with the woman's talk, so she told them of the ghosts who lingered around her village, ghosts of poor men who had been hanged by the English for stealing potatoes, and waited their revenge, and ghosts of doomed women who took their own lives when their fishermen husbands and lovers didn't come home from the sea. And, as frightening apparitions they were cursed to roam the land forever for their grievous sin. For all the morbidity of the housekeeper's stories, the children slept better that night.

Chapter Eighteen
~ Thoughts at A Gravesite~

Frederick's eyes, *tired of looking down at his wife's* mound, glanced around. He couldn't keep his mind from wandering. Reverend Taylor was blessing Nancy's grave in an unnecessarily long service. Few of the crosses and stones were for men. Frederick only knew of two: Mrs. Hopkins' brother who'd come out in 1851 hoping to strike it rich - only to die in a mining camp brawl, and Lanny Hopkins, Ezra and Asa's cousin, who'd been thrown from his horse.

There were children. Babies aplenty. One little girl was drowned in the Waukeen while her mother was sweeping out the family's tent and her father was butchering a hog. One lad broke his arm, and it mortified. His idiot father wouldn't let Braden take it, and the boy died.

Five women had been buried here since Frederick brought his family to Crane Valley. He corrected himself. Not five women, six. Nancy's mound was the last. His mother's had been the second, Aaron's wife, gone to consumption, had been the fifth. The first, third, and fourth died birthing. That was the great killer of women. He'd known many men who had outlived three wives. He sympathized. It was hard losing his mother, but harder losing Nancy. He'd not marry another wife.

As he'd prospered at the hauling trade, and matured, he found he wanted children who would live after him; but as to anything else, he'd never felt he needed the bother of a woman like some men do. But she had grown dear to him. The past night had been filled with anguish, and he'd slept little. Nancy had been a good and loving wife, never shrill, never scolding.

By sunrise that morning, the grieving night was over. His tears were shed. Reverend Taylor droned on and on sounding like a politician running for office. A small dust devil whirled across the cemetery behind the man, twisted away and spent itself. In Angel's Camp, he'd refused Wiley's return to his mother and brother's bedsides, and this morning Frederick refused Ada's attendance at the cemetery service. "You have duties here at the house. Many will be stopping at the ranch afterward. I'll need a proper feast prepared. You'll have Braun girls to help."

Ada's disappointment was showing in her face, but she' stood straight and said, "Yes, sir. I'll do as ye ask and do all ye order. "Now, if I may suggest sir," she softened her look, "although I'll not attend the service, the boys might well want MeMe with them. Mrs. McCreary called her their little sister. They're that fond of 'er, they are."

"Children's whims give me little concern," he'd answered. "She'll *not* be there. I expect you make her work in the kitchen." He was disgusted with the audacity of her petition.

Ada continued to speak curtly and honestly to him. "It may help them if Merab be there. She'd pull their minds from Wiley what's missing to angle them to her young one's need of comforting, If ye understand me way of thinking, sir."

"I understand that you're the housekeeper and I'm the boys' father who pays your wages. The Indian is not to be in sight when guests are here. You should be able to manage that. Keep her working in the kitchen or lock her up," he'd said. "Air the house, and set it right as my wife would have had it. There's still a smell of sickness about the place."

At the Crane Valley Cemetery, Frederick smirked to himself. Reverend Taylor would thank him for keeping the woman and girl away. The man's attitudes didn't call for a papist or a pagan to be sitting in Christian assembly. He'd always given a questioning eye when Nancy insisted she bring the child to Sunday prayer meeting even when the two of them sat at a bench at the back of the tent.

Looking about the cemetery grounds, Frederick felt he too had shown good sense that morning – and fairness. He didn't allow Frank or any of the ranch hands attendance at the service either. It was better that none of the help be at the cemetery, than some be but others not.

As he'd watched, he'd seen Aaron and Ples Landers' bending of their heads toward each other. He knew that they expected the Indian devil to be there with his family. Nancy had softened the Landers to the savage as well as she had his children. However the neighbor men gave him no questions or remarks when he and the children arrived. With none of his other ranch workers there, he knew he couldn't rightly be faulted for disallowing Ada and the Indian child's attendance. He'd excluded all that were on his dole but not of his blood. It was his right.

Dickey wasn't back yet, but McCreary was sure no others from the community but the storekeeper would fault him for leaving a dingy girl and a papist-saint-worshiping housekeeper behind.

He'd excused Richard from the service, but the boy insisted on being there. He was proud of the boy for pushing himself to do what was correct and proper. Of all his sons, this was the one who most pleased him; and though he loved them all equally and saw himself in certain ways in each, Richard was the most practical-minded and therefore in a certain way, the most admirable.

Blasted Tom had disappointed him. He'd begged off, pleading to be excused. "I saw her buried, Papa!" The boy mumbled with a disrespectful barb, "I was here when she died."

"You are as tall as a man, behave like one," his father responded.

Mason had thrown a weeping fit, crying that he wanted to stay home with MeMe and Ada. Mason would soon be nine-years-old and old enough to learn his responsibilities.

As the reverend called the assembly to silent prayer, an idea came to Frederick that his wife's death had released him from promises he might have made to her. It would solve his problems best to put the girl his wife had chosen against his wish, and his sons doted so on, into a Hessen bag and drown her in the river. The thought titillated him. He saw her as the little cat that she was, with her squinty eyes and black fur. Drowning was fitting for her.

He couldn't recall ever having spoken a word to little animal in the near five years she had been his wife's pet. He was moving his family away from Crane Valley, and she wasn't part of his family. The red nigger would not continue to be a dolly for his sons. He had a houseful of boys as weak-headed as their mother had been.

Perhaps it was the Almighty's design that a child's illness would take his wife down. In a moment of great revelation, he saw that Nancy's death was God's way of showing Frederick what He wanted him to do, showing him a direction to take, a direction to reclaim the boys to the strength they ought to have.

The Reverend prayed again, eulogizing Nancy. God knew Nancy was a good woman. Putting her name in Taylor's mouth wouldn't give her a higher place in Heaven. Hymns began.

Music was more soothing to Frederick than words. He liked to sing, and lifted his voice with the others in words and melodies so familiar they didn't interfere with the ideas he was contemplating. He'd already formed a plan to take a short freight-trip tomorrow and had told his sons. He wanted them to go back to school and mind their manners until his return. It would be soon.

He had a plan involving Aaron Landers. However, it wouldn't do if he acted too quickly. Impropriety might offend his neighbor and that might gut the plan's success. Aaron was odd about some things. Settling business on the night of Frederick's wife's funeral wouldn't suit the man. But he'd lay the idea tonight in his neighbor's mind, and finish his plan's completion in two weeks when he was back in Crane Valley. Yes, this was surely the Almighty's plan for the McCreary family. So many things were coming together.

Getting away from The Willows tomorrow would be good. The boys would have time to settle down. They'd be themselves again by the time he returned. Harrington had promised to send a wagon to pick up a small load for a woman in Bailey and transport it to Stockton whenever there was an opportunity. It wasn't an important job, just a common run between Mariposa and Stockton, transporting the effects of an old man who had died and were wanted by the man's daughter. Frederick would do it himself and serve as the driver.

The run would refresh him and turn his mind from this sorry business he'd just endured and give him a new face for the future. Bootjack, midway in that run, brought the solution to another of his problems to his mind. There were rumors that a man named Jared Cobey traded in Indians out of a tavern there. Nancy's vile Indian, who had spirited her way into house to set his wife against him and net his boys attention away to womanishness, might bring him a fifty dollar gold piece.

He would sell her. There was a good market for Indians who were young and docile, particularly females. There was a market in scalps too. He'd heard that in the north state, counties were paying for Indian heads. Money he'd gain by selling her would do to pay him back for all the trouble she'd caused him. Ada told him the red nigger was a quiet child, but she learned as quick as little black ants can find a kitchen. The simile she'd used brought a smile to his face. Not like black ants, like red ants, he thought, the red sting worse than the black.

He heard a cough, and realized that the singing was over. He felt the first relief in nearly two weeks. His time of mourning had come to an end, for he counted his grief beginning when he first felt the strange anxiousness in Angel's Camp.

When his business with the child was finished, he'd take the boys to San Francisco. He'd show them a time and then they'd make a new home in Calaveras County.

As he and his sons led the neighbors back to The Willows, Frederick firmed up his plans. It was a grand scheme. Dickey prattled that Aaron Landers had struck it rich without Aaron ever having had to pick up a gold pan. Landers' investment with his brothers in a mining company had paid off.

Aaron had money in the bank, and the McCreary ranch was a far better property than the Landers' place, better pastures, more timber than rock on the mountainside. The orchards were planted now, and in production. Fifty acres stood in timber against future building. The opportunity should not be ignored, and he had picked his buyer for the ranch. With luck, the McCrearys would leave Crane Valley before the rains started.

Late that afternoon, at the house, Frederick set a rumor going, the first step of his plan, by confiding to Reverend Taylor, "If I find the right buyer, I'll sell The Willows." McCreary could almost watch the rumor pass from ear to ear. He'd chosen the right vector. The Reverend Taylor was dependable as an Indiana quilting bee at passing news. Sure enough, after about a half hour, Landers' son came up to Frederick on the veranda, bringing him a glass of cider.

"Excuse me, Mr. McCreary, but are you thinking of selling the ranch?"

"I might be." Frederick sipped the sweet drink and allowed a little levity to break through at the end of a difficult day. "Just how much money you offering me, son?"

"Oh, none, sir. I was just curious." The young man took him seriously, missing the sarcasm. "I don't intend to be a rancher, Mr. McCreary," Ples said. His face grew bright with the enthusiasms of youth and with words he was bursting to tell someone. "I'll be leaving soon. We are far from the conflict here in California, but to save the Union America needs every man to stand up for the cause. I want to go east and enlist."

"Ah, lad, I doubt your father would allow it."

The young man grinned and gave a sly look. "Papa has nicer things on his mind than me, sir."

Frederick recoiled at the reference. The handsome young man was fine fiddler and good rifle shot, but that gave him little excuse for disrespect. Though Maudie had been in her grave less than five months, it was common knowledge that Aaron was courting a young widow in Fresno Flats. The boy showed bad manners by making a joke at his father's expense.

"My father doesn't know. He believes in the Union, but is against my taking part. I'm old enough to decide for myself, Mr. McCreary."

Chapter Nineteen
~Fortune's Turns~

The conversation with Ples Landers didn't last long.
Shortly after Ples left him on the front veranda, Aaron
Landers came out to join him. "Our wives rest
together, Frederick. It's just eight years since you came
here to Crane Valley, near ten for me. Mrs. McCreary
was a good woman. Those boys of yours are going to
be fine, God-fearing women."

"Yes. Wiley is doing well in the office. And, I'll start
Tom in the business soon too as he graduates come
June."

There was a pause. Frederick waited, pleasantly
anticipating that an inquiry on his property was about
to come. Landers surprised him by moving to a
different subject. "The cemetery has a nice elevation,
Frederick. I'd thought to bury Mrs. McCreary in that
little meadow high in the trees behind your barn, but
Tom said you'd rather have his mother in the
cemetery, so that's where we buried her. Four or five
years ago, my boy and I helped Mrs. McCreary bury
the Indian woman there. It is a peaceful place, a good
place to put someone to rest."

Aaron Landers' words, that he'd have lain Nancy
down in the forest next to a foul Indian, made
Frederick's stomach turn. Landers must be made
maudlin by drink to bring up the one folly Nancy had
committed. Blast Aaron, he thought. Blast him! He
turned his head away from the man's stupidity. But
Landers had more to say, and Frederick was forced to
endure the man's sentimental prattle longer.

"Mrs. McCreary took Maudie up there early last spring," Aaron went on. "They made a picnic and Maudie came home with a basketful of wildflowers. I think Mrs. McCreary knew Maudie was near the end and wanted to give 'er a last look at spring's arrival. We set my Maudie down soft on pillows in the big barrow. Tom and Ples pushed it clear up that steep trail behind the barn with the little boys helping. I scarce had to give a push less there came up a rock.

"Nancy and little Merab carried the hamper along. Your wife surely loved that meadow. You can see across the whole Waukeen Valley from there. I do think it was my Maudie's last fine day."

Frederick rankled, but he worked to keep his words bland and even. "Tom made the right choice, Aaron. Nancy best deserved to lie beside my mother."

"I credit your wife for all her help toward Maudie's end. You won't think so now, but you're lucky Mrs. McCreary went quickly. A lingering sickness can tear at a man. But Mrs. McCreary and the little girl rode over daily to help tend to her needs at the end. It lightened Maudie's day to see the little one. It eased my days too."

Frederick had enough of this wound-picking conversation. He found easy opportunity to turn it. "Praise God. Richard is better today than yesterday. He will rally from the contagion's effects."

Landers responded to the lead. "I envy you your boys, Frederick. I have only the one." Then, he cleared his throat and his Aaron Landers voiced the words Frederick had been waiting for. "My boy tells me you might be thinking of selling The Willows."

"Yes, but not for less than it's worth. There is a good harvest this year. Steuben was wise to wise to start the orchard with prize rootstock. I'm guaranteed a good price from O'Neal's again. My sheep produce long fleece, and the pastures are all in and secure."

Frederick knew Landers coveted his cows as much as his ranch and added the final inducement. "You know that I've been having our Letty bred to Braun's big red, and she's dropped good heifers three times in a row. I was thinking of importing a Holland bull. But, I'd sell the farmyard stock with the ranch and only hold back the hauling stock."

Landers nodded his head, and said, "I'd like to have a serious talk about The Willows, soon's you're ready."

"I have to leave on business in the morning, Aaron. But I'll be back before mid-month." It wasn't yet time for a handshake on the deal, but The Willows was all but sold. The men stood alongside each other looking out over the orchard as the sun sent its final reddish glow across the trees and they finished their drinks.

When there was no more to say, they went back inside. Landers strode directly to the refreshment table where the men were talking of the war. Frederick stopped to thank each of the community's women for showing their respect for Nancy by attending her services. Duty done, he went to the kitchen to check with Ada on the provisions, and found she was managing well. Frank, in clean and mended clothes, and the Braun girls, buxom and tidy, were keeping the pitchers and plates filled.

Braun, Summerfield, Cutler, the Hopkins brothers and Landers, Frederick's nearest neighbors were gathered around the refreshment table, talking of the war. Landers was tipping his glass more than he ought. Frederick joined them and soon heard what he wanted. Landers had money for the deal.

"Why," Landers was bragging. "That hundert dollars I gave my brother seven years ago has come back many times over. He needed financing for a mine up out of Jimtown and promised to share his riches. Howard, Samuel, and brother-in-law Marshall Smith were in it too, but I staked Howard his part. By God, he's kept his word. I'll send Ples to join the Stockton Blues, costumed in style. He can play any horn that they give 'im by day and fiddle dances by night."

"Ya, Der Schtockton Blues ist da finest band in de vest!" Braun shouted. "Hilda unt I saw dem march ven ve comen down der river."

Frederick, too, had seen the Blues on parade in Stockton. Their uniforms were stylish indeed. But from what the young man had said to him, Ples wanted to march with a gun, not with a fiddle in his hand or a cornet in his mouth.

"You're backward, Landers." John Butler called out from where he leaned against a China cabinet. "I heard the Blues disbanded. Couldn't decide if they were for the North or the South."

"No sir! You're backward, Butler," Ezra Hopkins corrected. Ezra proceeded to claim to have seen a Stockton newspaper only two weeks old.

"The Blues *Militia* only changed their *military* name to brag on an allegiance to the Union. The band didn't change its name by one letter. 'Twas too well known. I doubt Washington D. C. or New York City has as good. I know Sacramento doesn't."

Landers, his speech beginning to slur, said, "Making music, that's where my boy belongs. Not dying under any flag's army."

"Now, I know you're loyal to the Union, Aaron. You're a Pennsylvania man. But are you tellin' us Ples ain't good enough to soldier for the United States of America? Fingers that play a fiddle can't figure out how to pull a trigger?" Willy Scruggs needled.

"Ples is better than good enough to soldier. He's one of the finest shots in this valley, as you well know, Willy. Any man's army would be proud to have him," Frederick asserted, knowing no one could disagree.

Willy Scruggs made easy to wave the flag, Frederick reflected. The blasted man with his houseful of women had no sons to worry over. His eyes caught the motion as Tom, a thin rail of a boy, gaunt as the nation's president and nearly as tall, came to stand beside Ples behind the cluster of men.

Landers stared across the table at Willy and made answer. "What I'm saying is I'm a Union man down to the bone. I've pledged gold to the cause until the last Reb is killed. But, I'll be damned if I'll give 'em the only son I've got." He wobbled as he refilled his glass.

Cutler finally added his opinion. "None of us need worry about our sons facing the Rebels. California's militia won't be goin' east. There are still Indians an' pockets of Mesicun hotheads who want our state going back to old days an' old ways."

"We got so many damn Injuns yet to rid we don't have time or ammunition to waste on rebellious white men," Barnett said, to the agreement and applause of most of the men but Dickey and Landers. Dickey frowned and Landers wasn't paying attention until he heard the clapping.

Ezra Hopkins was quick to interject new information. "John, the Governor in Massachusetts approved Captain Reed's proposal to welcome Californians to fight with Massachusetts. There is a ship readying to sail for Boston. In a few months our proud California Battalion will be goin' around the horn. We're invited to fight with the state of Massachusetts." Ada came in from the kitchen and bustled about, replenishing drinks. She set a fresh pot of coffee on the dining room sideboard. The discussion recessed until she was gone then resumed where it had been interrupted.

"If your boy wants to go to war, he'll go, Landers," Barrows said.

"He'll go! You can't hold a brave boy back, Aaron, for all that he's your only child," added Hopkins.

"No, I purely don't approve of him going for a soldier." Landers raised his hand for emphasis and stumbled forward. His eyes began to run water. Cutler kindly led him away from the table and took him out to the veranda. Landers was popular with the men, and if he turned to drink this one night it was understandable.

Fortune was turning things Frederick's favor. He knew what price he'd ask for The Willows. And, he knew that Aaron would meet it. Landers, when he sobered, would want the farm stock. Frederick would part with the cows, sheep and plow horses for additional price, though he'd not sell any of the freight stock. He'd throw the chickens and geese into the deal.

He'd arrange to have the mules, oxen, carriage, and riding horses driven north. The boys' ponies and pups too. The thought came to him that it was also time to rid himself of the other animal on the ranch.

>>>O<<<

Chapter Twenty
~ Settling the Score~

When the long was over, and the sounds of hooves, creaking wheels, and goodbyes had given way to the sounds of crickets and night birds, Frederick went back into the house. He'd noticed that Ada had given the boys spirited cider on the sly. He didn't begrudge her actions. They were exhausted from illness, from losing their mother, and from holding good behavior during a trying time. Her action would help them rest well, and if they slept late, it suited his plans.

He thought about his absent son. Frederick sent word to Wiley, but the message wouldn't have reached Angel's Camp. The boy wouldn't yet know his mother was dead.

Downstairs, with Frank's help, Ada had quickly cleared the rooms of glasses and platters. He could hear his housekeeper's voice scolding Frank as he came down the staircase. In the dining room, Frederick took a bottle of good Kentucky bourbon he'd long stored in a low cupboard, safe from his own hospitality and Landers' thirst. He went into the kitchen and placed it on the table, inviting both Ada and Frank sit down. He rinsed three glasses and took them back to the table where he poured drinks for them.

Ada demurred. He thought it an affectation, and he urged, "Just to honor Mrs. McCreary." Ada smiled her assent. The three of them raised their glasses in toast. And, after a moment given to Nancy's memory, Frederick made his announcement. "I want to tell you it is my intent to sell this ranch."

He paused to let the realization of what he'd said meet their comprehension.

"I think Mr. Landers will buy it. He might want to keep the men and both of you on, and he would be a good employer." He turned to Frank. "But, Frank, wherever my sons and I go, I will always have small stock to care for. You are a good man. I'd like it if you stayed with me. I owe you that."

"You owe me nothin', Mr. McCreary. I was the fool who caused my injury. McCreary Hauling had naught to do with it."

"Then stay with me because I value you." Frederick turned to look at the housekeeper. "I'd appreciate it if you, Ada, would want to stay with my sons and me too." Ada nodded, but didn't answer him. The glasses of good Kentucky corn bourbon sipped down to empty, Frank limped out of the kitchen to the bunkhouse.

Quietly in the stillness of the kitchen, after Frank was gone, Frederick's jovial expression changed. Abruptly he laid out his immediate plans for the housekeeper. "Ada, you and my sons know I must leave on business tomorrow. I'll be home soon." He paused to pour a little more bourbon in the housekeeper's glass.

"I'll be taking the Indian away tomorrow. *She* won't be coming back. Fill a sack with her things. Do it tonight while she sleeps. I'll want her dressed and ready to leave well before daybreak. You will need to be here in the house before dawn to have her ready to leave."

Ada looked down at her hands, then slowly raised her head. Resolutely, understanding his meaning, and knowing that the child would not be back, she said, "I work for ye, sir. I'm bound to do as ye ask."

Frederick stood up to look around the kitchen. Out the window it had long been dark. He looked at his pocket watch. It was past ten o'clock. Ada still sat at the table, frowning, and looking very dour and uncertain.

"Ada," Frederick said. "I'll be increasing your pay, but you needn't tell Frank and rouse his envy." He came and again sat across from her. "I'm wifeless now. Mrs. McCreary is gone from me." His pathetic tone might color his words and elicit the woman's sympathy.

"More responsibility for my boys will fall to you. I'd like you to stay with us. I won't beg. However, I will promise you that if you choose to stay with us, you will have a home for as long as you live."

He watched the woman's response to his words. At first her face didn't change. Then she worked things out for herself and looked straight at him. Ada forced a bright edge to her voice. "The girl will be ready, sir."

"I trust you to take good care of Richard. Keep him quiet and send for Doc Braden if you judge necessary." Frederick stood again and bowed to her. "I thank you for stitching mourning bands for our sleeves. I know you must have stayed up far into the last night and must be tired. The boys may wear them to school at least a month or two in honor of their mother. If they ask about the girl, tell them I've taken her to a new home."

"But what do I say to *her*?"

"You say nothing to her."

"She is but a child. She may be frightened when I wake her so early."

"I expect that you'll be able to manage."

Later Frederick walked down to the bunkhouse and shared a pipe with Frank. "I'll need you up in a few hours. I'll come wake you. No need call Lalo or the men. "When I do, I want you to hitch the two young mules to the small hauling wagon. Set the ramp and roll those three empty barrels into it."

"You goin' hauling? Need me to go along?"

"I've a contract down in Bailey. Small stuff, but I need to deliver it to French Camp. I can handle it by myself." Frederick had seen the old man dote on the savage. Ada would have enough trouble with the boys in the morning when they awoke to find the red nigger gone. She didn't need aggravation from the old man too. He would handle that now. "I'm taking the Indian girl. You needn't say anything. If anyone asks, say you heard I'd found a home for her."

But Frank surprised him. The old man looked up sideways at him. The night's faint illumination bounced a glimmer off one of his remaining teeth as he grinned. "Takin' her off, huh? Well, you're the boss 'round here. You're the one what decides what goes and what stays."

When Ada woke her in the dark of early morning, MeMe was startled, but didn't resist. She remembered that sometimes the household awoke when it was like nighttime and the sun hadn't started. Sometimes the boys needed breakfast before they went birding, or someplace with their school friends. Ada dressed MeMe and brought her out to the drive in the chill before dawn. Only then, did the child balk. By the lantern light, she saw the mules and the wagon. Looking around she saw no one there but Mr. McCreary.

MeMe twisted away from the woman and ran back

into the dark house. Ada dropped the sack she carried to the ground and went running after the child. Frederick took the opportunity to pick up the sack and look through it. He found it full of sturdy well-made clothes and fine knit stockings. Nancy ruffled the blasted girl up like some banker's daughter, he thought. From the bottom of the sack, he pulled up a pair of shiny little black boots, laces tied together. Well, a dog is a dog no matter how fancy its collar or how fine its shoes. He tossed the sack into the wagon, satisfied that as well as a market for the girl, he'd find a market for ruffled frocks and fine stockings.

By the time the housekeeper reached the keeping room, the girl was sitting on the floor by her cot, protectively clutching the buckskin packet where the child kept all her silly little treasures to her chest. The woman took the girl's elbow, pulled her upright, and said, "Do as yer told and all will go well with ye." She gave the child a hug and said, "Come along. You can take that with you."

Gripping the reluctant child by the wrist, she dragged MeMe out of the room. She pulled the girl through the kitchen, the alcove, and across the veranda. MeMe stumbled, but Ada yanked her arm until she was moving again. Down the steps and across the path, she led the child, never letting go until they were back on the drive and standing before Mr. McCreary.

"She's ready fer ye now, and done with her foolishness, sir."

Frederick pulled MeMe's arms apart and took the packet away from her to examine the prize the girl had run back to get. It was just crude buckskin, with a lash stitching at the bottom, tied around the center with a piece of rawhide. He opened it to check its contents against the chance that the child had thieved from his house. The buckskin held a small scraps of worn flowery fabric, a small bonnet, odds and ends of no value, but a ribbon gathered drawstring bag of finely embroidered linen was tucked down inside.

He pulled it up and opened it. In the dim light, the cloth bag seemed to contain bird feathers, a loop of what looked like dark hair, more scraps and a chamois bag. Curiously, he pushed his finger down into the chamois and felt two small coins, some pebbles, worthless baubles only a child would keep.

He had a mind to keep the ribboned linen bag himself as a memory of his wife. But as he held it up close to the lantern light, he saw initials embroidered onto it: M.M. 1860. His wife had made it for the creature. He thrust it back inside the buckskin and, angrily, tossed the packet back at the girl.

The girl held the buckskin in her arms as though afraid he'd take it away again. He didn't want her to start a ruckus and wake the boys. Ada had said that the Indian wasn't one to make trouble, but he'd take no chance. "You can keep it," he said, "If you keep quiet.

Part Three: A Choice of Shoes

~~<<<O>>>~~

Chapter Twenty-one
~ The Pond ~

It was a time of day *Frederick McCreary liked best, still* dark of the morning, the raw beginning of dawn when light was just a greenish edge to the deep indigo-black sky at the eastern mountains. He didn't want anger to disrupt the morning's solitary drive. He felt leaving the ranch that morning was leaving the old for the new. He had looked forward to feeling like he did when he was young and he was all there was of McCreary Hauling.

"Go back to the house," he told Ada.

He lifted the child and the pillowslip of her belongings into the wagon. He moved packing quilts to jam between her and the barrels he was carting to Bailey, lest they roll over on her and tarnish her value before they arrived in Bootjack and he found Cobey, the trader. "Stay there. Don't get up. Don't move. Don't talk."

He shoved the girl's head hard against the board behind the driver's seat, and tossed a heavy hessen bag over her so she was well hidden. It wouldn't please him to pass anyone on the road that might question him. The Indian had come to sour the milk of his family and make its taste bitter to the tongue. He was settling that score at last. That thought helped his mute anger into peaceful satisfaction. He turned the mules out of the drive and onto the road.

Hot and airless under the rough cloth, MeMe thought she might smother. The airlessness made her fall asleep. Only when she woke coughing, did she think to poke a hole making an air tunnel through the heavy folds between her nose and mouth and the outside air. The wagon lurched over some ruts, then found a trough for its wheels and settled into a constant, rumbling roll forward.

Mr. McCreary stopped the wagon twice that day and let her down from the wagon so she could relieve herself. He gave her water when he gave the mules water. The second time he stopped, he gave her some bread and a pear. She thought she would run home the first time he stopped, but she didn't know which way to run.

That afternoon the air had a smell that was different from Crane Valley. Not like apple trees, and not like the weeds around Mr. Dickey's store. It wasn't like the pines up behind the barn either. She wanted to see where she was. Mr. McCreary told her to stay down, and keep the hessen cloth over her.

She fell asleep again to the sound of the mules' hooves and the wagon's creaks. Later, she awoke to hear Mr. McCreary singing. He sang all the hymns she knew; He sang song that Ples played on his fiddle and she and the boys sang, *Billy Boy* and the song about a fly with a blue tail that she liked best. She worried where they were going. She had never been farther away from the ranch than Fresno Flats for a tent meeting with Nancy and the boys. If Mr. McCreary were singing songs the boys liked, maybe they were on their way back home.

The big barrels rattled. She was afraid that they would break loose and crush her. She and Mr. McCreary had been in the wagon all day, turning first one way and then the other way. She peeked out, and through the wagon's slats, she saw different looking country. She knew she'd never be able to find her way back home, and put her head down. The barrels kept rattling. She hoped their bindings wouldn't come loose and the barrels squash her. She moved her head until the heavy folds of hessen cloth and quilted pads blocked the rattling noise some. She fell asleep again.

Frederick was pleased with his progress. The two teams of mules kept a good pace and were familiar with the road. By mid-morning he knew they were making good time. He was picking up an empty chest, its slab lid, and some personal furnishings for the woman he would barrel for her. The proximity of Bailey Flats to Crane Valley made it easy for him to handle the haul alone and have it done. He'd planned, should anyone ask, to say that the girl was more cargo being delivered. If anyone pursued the question, he would comment casually that she was going to some missionaries.

The story he concocted for Aaron's son was a good one. Missionaries of all kinds were ever passing through the plains of the great valley on their way between Los Angeles and Sacramento begging money for their enterprises. The Presbyterians were as apt as the Catholics to take in a savage for conversion. He hoped to be rid of her in Bootjack.

The woman whose property he would transport lived in Campo de Las Franceses, just this side of Stockton. He'd be rid of all of the ranch's baggage and have a good meal with the Frenchies before a return to business with Aaron Landers, and his sons.

As the wagon rolled on, steadily lowering in elevation, scattered oaks marked the landscape. The

142

jack pine was gone. Frederick was looking forward to getting down onto the foothills where the driving was easier.

MeMe woke when the wagon wheels hit a bumpy track. Each time the wagon thudded down hard it hurt her. She got a splinter in one of her hands when she tried to move to a better position. It was dark under the cover, but she didn't need light to pull a splinter out. She sucked the place on her hand. When she was little, Wiley and Tom had taught her that dogs and cats licked their sores and it healed them, so she should do that too if she were outdoors and had no other way to wash a wound. Her mouth was dry and her hand tasted like dirt and salt.

Her low belly hurt from trying not to wet herself or move her bowels. She held back, and pretty soon she went back to sleep. She woke up a long time later and was afraid to get out from under the cloth. She'd wet herself. Later Mr. McCreary stopped so she could pee. He looked mean and scowled at her, but he gave her something to drink and some bread.

The next day was the same. Mr. McCreary would stop the wagon, get down and come back, then say, "Get out of the wagon. Go relieve yourself and get back here." He only gave her food and water when he took care of the mules.

It seemed to be around noon when they stopped just beyond a plank bridge. He told her to get out of the again. She climbed down faster this time and ran down to the water. Nancy had taught her that running wasn't ladylike, but she was so thirsty. She dipped her face and hands in the wallows of the nearly dry creek below the bridge and cupped up water to drink in big gulps, dripping it on her apron.

Mr. McCreary unhitched the mules and took them down to the water. Her clothes were rumpled and dirty from the grit of the wagon. He tossed a piece of bread at her. "Climb back inside." he said, scowling. She did as he told her. He didn't cover her this time. He just got back up on the seat and started them moving again. She ate every crumb of the bread. She wondered what her brothers were doing. Was Richard better? Were they in school? She worried where Mr. McCreary was taking her.

In the late afternoon, when the sun was low in the sky, he stopped the wagon again, and sent her to take care of her needs. There was no creek, though she was thirsty. After she climbed back up he tossed the hessen cloth over her again. "Cover yourself up," he said. "I don't want an inch of you showing, not a finger or a toe. I'll stop soon, and there will be people around. Don't let them see or hear you. I'll bring some food out to you later."

That night, MeMe could hear crickets and also voices and the sound of people walking around the wagon. She heard Mr. McCreary tending the mules. It got quiet for a long time, and then he came back and lifted her out of the wagon and walked her to some bushes in the dark. There were buildings on the other side of the wagon. She could see lights in the windows and hear people laughing and talking.

"Do your business there," he whispered. He took her back to the wagon and gave her a canteen of water, some jerky, crackers and two small, hard apples. "If you let anyone see or hear you, I'll beat the life out of you." He was whispering to her. She knew that he would do what he said.

Ada had *let* him take her. Ada stuffed her clothes in the pillowslip and led her out to Mr. McCreary. She sensed that Ada had betrayed her without knowing the word that described it. By now her brothers knew she was gone. Maybe they were looking for her. She hoped that they'd come and find her.

The next morning, when Mr. McCreary stopped the wagon, he didn't unhitch the mules or give them water. He tied the reins to a fence post and made her climb out. Then he took her by the hand and led her down a gully to a green water pond. Cattails grew half the way around it. There was a three-sided shed near the pond. It had a bench, and a hitching rail. "Take off your shoes," he ordered. She did, and stood in her stocking feet. He picked up her shoes and put them on the bench. She watched, wondering what he was going to do.

He took a small package from his jacket pocket and put it on the bench by her shoes. Then came toward her, picked her up, and threw her in the water. "Wash yourself. You stink," he said.

He turned and walked up to the small three-sided shed on the pond's bank, stopping to look back and say, "Take your clothes off and rub the dirt out of them. Dunk your head and clean your hair until it shines. I'll be back to get you later.

"There's food in the bundle I left for you. Your clothes will dry if you lay them over the rail." He turned and left her

blubbering in the pond trying to find a footing on the slippery bottom. When she cleared the water from her nose and mouth, she looked at the water around her. How could she get clean in dirty water? It wasn't even clean like the pond at home or the Waukeen. She dunked her head. A fish skimmed through the pond near her. Fish were shiny and clean. Maybe the water was clean and only looked green and scummy.

The dust rinsed out of her hair, and she felt better. She took off her stockings and washed each one, tucking them under water into the pocket of her frock, and then slipped down her split-crotch drawers and took them off. She rubbed them the way Ada and Nancy rubbed the small clothes on laundry day. Soon she'd rubbed away the stains. She hung the drawers on the rail and went back into the pond. It felt good to make her clothes clean. She loosened her petticoat's drawstring and worked it down her legs although its wet folds wanted to twist and grab around them. She rubbed it as clean as she could. She kept her frock and pinafore on and patted it as clean as she could. She knew she wasn't supposed to be naked, especially here, outside with fish and dragonflies.

When she thought she was clean enough, she climbed out of the water. She dried quicker than her hair or clothes. She put her under things and stockings back on as soon as they stopped dripping.

The sun moved down lower and the air felt cool. She was scared, but she stayed there on the bench by the three-sided shed. She was afraid that wolves, or coyotes, or dogs would come if it got dark and Mr. McCreary wasn't back. Finally, she heard him. When he got near the shed he shouted, "Don't look so scared of me! I could drown you in that pond and let you sink to the mud on the bottom to rot if I wanted. The pollywogs would eat your bones."

After, he looked slyly at her as though he were waiting for her to cry. Then he said, "Don't worry. I won't." She didn't cry because she thought he wanted her to.

It was fully dark by the time they'd walked back to the wagon. The three barrels now had four small ones more and the cargo filled the wagon's bed. It was packed all the way deep in the wagon, right to the corner where she had ridden for so long right behind Mr. McCreary. She'd left her things there in that part of the wagon.

She was afraid that Mr. McCreary had thrown away the clothing sack to make room for the new things. Then she noticed that the sack was in the far end of the wagon's bed, in a big wooden box that took up one corner. The buckskin packet was in the sack and safe. She was relieved.

Mr. McCreary hollered at her again. "There, right there. Climb in the box. You'll ride in there now." She scrambled up and over the top board, tearing a limp ruffle away from her pinafore on the prickly lumber. She hadn't answered him. She was afraid to say anything.

Nancy wouldn't have liked the way she looked. There was no brush for her hair and without Nancy or Ada's help, she couldn't do up all her back buttons or loop the ties to her pinafore so they'd stay tied. Now her ruffle was torn and hanging down in a big curve. But Nancy was dead, and Ada didn't care enough to talk to her when Mr. McCreary took her away. She curled up in the bottom of the chest and rested her head on the sack. She was glad the chest didn't have a lid and she wasn't covered up the heavy cloth. MeMe could smell her still damp clothes. She didn't think smelling like scum and cattails in the pond made her smell any better than pee had.

>>>O<<<

Chapter Twenty-two
~A Choice of Shoes~

She clutched the buckskin packet to her chest. Everything precious that she owned was in it. Nancy told her that if she took care of the bundle, she'd keep her mother's memory. It held a strand of black hair like hers tied with ribbon, and two pieces of flowered cloth from the dress her mother had worn when she died. If she thought about mothers, she thought about Nancy. The hair and cloth was from her Indian mother. It was hard to keep a memory without knowing how her real mother looked or sounded. She closed her eyes. The sun on her face felt good after having been covered up so long.

She thought about her Ensay Ootie and the little pouch down at the bottom of the buckskin packet. It had four stones in it. He gave her the stones to count her age. Every year when the lupine bloomed she was supposed to add a stone. She would always know how old she was. The lupine was blooming. Ootie took her hand. They invited Nancy to come from the veranda and walk with them. They'd walked down the path until MeMe found a glittery white pebble on the ground. She picked it up, and Ootie said, "*Yit-sil*" He held the pouch open for her while she dropped the pebble in it.

He taught her the names of her own year numbers in a secret language: *ye-et, po-noy, so-pin, hat-pa-nay,* and then he taught her *yit-sil*. She'd said the name of each of her year stones for Nancy after Ootie went back in the wagon to Mr. Dickey's store, and again for the boys when they came home.

She'd remembered each number-name. Nancy hugged her tight and said, "Your Indian Mama would be so proud of you."

This past spring, when the boys were in school and the lupine was blooming, Nancy took her up to the meadow in the pines behind the barn. MeMe added her sixth stone. The next day they took the wagon to Mr. Dickey's store, and when she showed *Ensay* Ootie the new pebble in the pouch, he named it *ka-li-pi-i.* That meant six. It was a long time until the lupine would bloom again. The fall rains hadn't even started. She had to be home in spring when the lupines bloomed so she'd learn the right word for seven.

The wagon stopped under some trees. Mr. McCreary got down and brought buckets of water up from a creek below the roadside for the mules. He told her to get out of the wagon and tend to her business, and she did. He gave her something to eat for breakfast, but afterward he told her to take her clothes off.

That wasn't right. She refused and fought at him. He grabbed her by the hair, pulled her pinafore off and ripped away the buttons on the dress beneath it. She stiffened, crying out, and tried to move away from him, but he blocked attempts with his great big body. Whichever way she went, he stopped her.

His voice boomed at her. "I'm not going to hurt you. Take off your boots and stockings. You need to get cleaned up before we get to town. Take that dingy shift off too."

"Please give me my clothes back."

"Be grateful if I give you a fresh shift from the sack."

She looked down at the gravel, twigs and stones on the dirt beneath her as she undid the laces of her high-top shoes. "I need shoes," she said very softly.

The man took the sack from the wagon and rummaged around in it until he found a white, long sleeved shift and tossed it to her. He ignored her need for shoes. She turned her back, took off her clothes and put the clean shift on. Turning around, she said, "My feet will get dirty."

"You've got those brown shoes and there are black boots in that sack. Make your choice." He climbed up on the edge of the wagon and found the shiny black buckle boots Ootie had given her from Mr. Dickey's store and threw them at her. "Choose. You don't need stockings."

She appraised her high top brown shoes against the shiny black slipper-soft boots from Ootie. The boots were a little too big for her, and gave her a blister on her heel. But they were her choice, and she put them on. "Will you give me my buckskin?"

He laughed at her, but he reached in and pulled the packet out and held it up. "Make me a promise, and I'll give it to you. You can keep this trash if you to tell anyone my name, or your name, or where you came from." He looked down at her. His face was fierce. His eyes frightened her. "Never! You will *never* tell."

"What do I say if someone asks my name?" she whispered.

"Say nothing. Say you came from back in the high hills. Make up some Indian name for yourself."

"I don't know any Indian names."

"Do you want this bundle? You can call yourself Ugh-Ugh for all I care. Now do you want it or not?"

"I'll think a name. Please give it to me!"

"All right, I keep my word. He threw it hard at her. It bounced off her chest, and she had to pick it up from the ground. "You'll keep your promise, Indian, or I'll come find you and beat the blasted life out of you. I'll throw you in water so deep and swift no one will ever find your body."

He jumped down, picked her up and lifted her harshly up into the wagon. He clicked at the mules and they were on the move again. It wasn't far now to Bootjack. Just around a bend or two. She's not ugly, he thought. That might help him sell her off.

Might get forty dollars for her right here if Cobey's around and not have to tote her farther. No. Not so many dollars as forty. She's healthy and doesn't have an ugly tattoo or scar. Her limbs are sound and she speaks English. But she's young for doing worthwhile work, and she's not large in size. He'd heard a young female would call up to one hundred dollars. Prime age was between eleven and eighteen. But this one would need strict training and years to be of use to anyone.

No, on reconsideration, he judged her worth less than he had hoped. The good of it was that he'd be rid of her. He'd not argue with twenty dollars gold or in *Union* paper. His sympathies were with the Confederacy, but he was too practical a man to trust its currency.

>>>O<<<

Chapter Twenty-three
~ Irina and Miss Lucy ~

Cobey offered him far less than he'd hoped. *The little* red nigger was standing near the bar where he'd left her. He didn't know how much she understood. He could tell she knew that they were negotiating over her. No matter what else was happening in the room, her eyes stayed on him and Jared Cobey. She didn't even look away when the tent tavern keeper dropped some glasses and one shattered. Finally they settled on twenty dollars Union paper.

Frederick finished his drink and walked to the tent's flap. He noticed that a robust, fair-haired woman got up from one of the tables as he took the money and walked away from Cobey. She was looking the Indian over carefully and seemed to note that the child understood the transaction. When he'd moved from the bar, the child hadn't followed. She stood there, in her shift and shiny black boots, holding that bundle she treasured so much. He guessed that the Indian was waiting for him to call her. Well, she'd be Cobey's problem now, not his.

Nancy's Indian furtively glanced to him, then back to Cobey, and back to him again, until the bawdy woman took the child's attention by circling around the girl, slowly considering the child.

"Want the little slit-tail, Rinka?" Cobey teasingly jibed. "Someone told me you were in the market for a redskin."

"I give tirty dollarz. I only giving you zo many money because girl is pretty. I want Indian vit no marks on face. But I maybe must to give her you if Indian not working hard. Then you give money back. Yes?"

"Yes, I'll take her back and sell her all over again."
Cobey, an elbow on the bar, leaned forward toward
the woman. "What happened to Mary?" he asked.

"She hev spots on her skin like color dying before she
die. Like ver ugly." Irina made a face, and gave a
dismissive wave to the air. "She like sick. Miss Lucy
turn out of house. Give money and tell to go some ver
else." The saucy woman shrugged her shoulders.
"Nobody lef' to help Ines."

Frederick listened. He was disgusted to think he had
sold the blasted Indian nigger so cheaply. The damned
trader made a fine profit on the Indian. He'd rid
himself of the damned savage at half again what he'd
paid Frederick, having made no expense on his part to
maintain the girl until the sale. Cobey and the woman
made Frederick look the fool. Even today, Nancy's pet
brought him bad luck. The little girl was staring at
him but he glowered at her and put up the flat of his
hand. That motion was enough to stay an ox or mule.
He knew it would surely stay an animal as small as
she was.

He ducked through the tent flap as Cobey called a
man drinking at the bar to come and put his name to
legal papers on the Indian girl giving the trader rights
to her. McCreary's boots left deep prints in the dusty
road as he walked back to the livery to get his wagon.
They'd blow away in an hour. Cobey hadn't even
asked his name. Frederick, feeling free, climbed back
up on his wagon and flicked the backs of the mules. It
was an easy drive down into the valley. He
remembered his plan to have an epicure's grand
supper in French Camp.

Inside the tent, Rinka shook Cobey's hand and said,

"Good. Judge name on paper a'redy. Miss Lucy be happy for legals paper." She glanced down the tent to catch the eye of the man who had given his judicial approval to the sale and blew him a kiss. Then the woman called Rinka paid Cobey in gold coin from a leather bag worn like a holster at her waist. She took the girl by the hand, and they walked together out of the tent.

Down the street, the woman and child walked. They turned at a corner, crossed a street lined with tent stores and makeshift homes, some tents and some shed-like, and they entered a new looking building. Solid and large, it appeared to be part house and part store. It was one of the few actual wooden structures in Bootjack. It was bigger than the ranch house in Crane Valley.

They went inside from the side street through a narrow door that opened into a room filled with bins and crates. From there, the woman led her down a hall as narrow as the door was, past other doors, and into a large closet with stacks of folded garments, blankets and sheets. Pillows covered in ticking were stacked on the highest shelves, near the ceiling.

"Girl, ver are clothes? You haf only but boots an shift?" she questioned MeMe.

When the child didn't answer, the woman's face seemed to pinch in on itself. "You not know English?"

"I know English. I don't have any other clothes."

"Den vat's in pikpik buntle you holt?"

"My things."

"Nod clothes?"

"No."

"Too sad for girl. Girly need clothes. Vat you nem?"

MeMe couldn't speak. If she said Merab McCreary, Mr. McCreary would come back. He'd put her in a hessen bag and drown her in that slimy pond. She had no doubt.   Mr. McCreary kept his promises to the boys, good or bad, and she was certain he would keep this bad one to her. She stood, there, embarrassed and feeling naked, and she was frightened. Mr. McCreary said for her to choose an Indian name. She knew no Indian names, only a few numbers.

And then a bright glimmer came to relieve her panic. Her grandfather had given her an Indian name. A warm feeling came into her in spite of everything. She was saved from Mr. McCreary killing her.

"Nem?" the woman prodded as she looked through stacks of folded clothing.

MeMe said, "I'm Napas."

Irina smiled, relieved that the Indian at least knew who she was. "How old you, Napas?"

"Almost seven."

"Good. I must put nem an' age on paper."

She waved the paper Cobey had given her at MeMe. "Vat do you know to do? If you vant eat, must vork. Vere you vork already?"

MeMe figured out how to give the information without breaking her promise to Mr. McCreary. She wanted to please the woman so she wouldn't be sent back to the man called Cobey. "I know how to embroider flowers. I can help in the kitchen. I know how to feed chickens, put new straw in their nests and gather eggs. "I also know how to scrub things and how to clean up the mess that hired men make when they eat on the veranda."

"See you know talk too. Vell, Napas, is all right. Same

vat you vill do here. I show you ver you sleep."

"Not here?"

"Not in clothes room of house. Here I fin' clothes for you." She gathered a bundle together. The woman led her through another door and through a large, empty room with drains in its stone floor and big tubs set up on legs. It had a long table under a south window and long open cupboards with folds of fabrics and spools of threads in different colors. The girl wanted to stay and examine them. It was a cool and quiet room. A brown skinned woman was working there but she didn't turn around as they walked by.

"Come. Is path to privy behind you room. You find it by nose." The woman who had paid for her took her outdoors. Behind the house was a grassy yard. They came to a small lean-to against a stable. Its door hung from just one hinge. The woman had to lift it open and closed.

"This you room. If door too heavy, Ines help. Or you go in and oud by window," the woman who bought her said merrily and pointed to the single window.

MeMe, who was now called Napas, didn't know who Ines was. A shutter hung from a pair of hinges from the top of the window frame. The woman went over to a pile of odds and ends of lumber and found a small crate. She brought it over and put it below the window. "See, like zo. Climb up. Go in easy."

Inside the room, the floor was made of dirt and flat stones. There were two box-like low bins on the floor. One was spread neatly. The other box was filled with straw and a sheet and blanket were neatly folded on it. Beside each bed there was a small chest. There was a table with a pitcher and basin on top, a rack with some rags and a towel. The planks of the walls around the beds had nails in to them.

Clothes were hanging from the nails by the bed that had been made up. This dark room wasn't at all like Ada's pretty, cozy little room at the ranch. There were holes in the walls. Nancy wouldn't like it.

"Ines sleep there." The woman pointed to the made up bed. "You sleep on other side room. I bring pillow. You to vash face and hands, and careful to clean body ever day. Use soap. Share soap vit Ines. Vater outside. Dirty clothes go to laundry. You need get up early, vork hard. You must vork no talking. Ines is deaf vooman and is Mexican vooman. You like. Is brown like you."

If she were brown like Napas, Ines must be the woman from the room with the table. MeMe knew what deaf was. One of the hired men at The Willows was deaf. He only understood if you looked right at him when you talked. She knew Lalo who worked at the ranch was Mexican, but he wasn't very brown. His skin looked like Mr. Dickey's not like Ootie's.

"I boss of you and Ines and maids. I live in house. If you need, my room is by kitchen. I share vit Cook. She not like, but is big room. I like."

"What's your name if I need to find you?"

"You don' know?" The woman laughed. She said something in a strange sounding language. Then she puffed up and said, "I am Irina Dimitrichna Ivanova, and I Miss Lucy right han' vooman.

"Everbody know me. Friend like Cobey and Horace call me Rinka. But it is not pretty name. *Irina* is pretty name." She stretched up to loom self-importantly over MeMe. "Only Miss Lucy is more boss from me. I boss everbody but not Miss Lucy girls. I boss maids, Horace, Ruben, Ines. I boss Cook."

MeMe found the privy. A horse was carved on one

privy door, and a tulip on the other. She figured out
that the horse was for the men, and used the privy
with the flower. It had a row of seats so others could
use it while she was, and there was no latch on the
door. She washed up at the pump in the yard. A stone
path led back to the big house between the grass and a
tall fence.

Soon, Irina brought her a pillow and clothing: two
pretty skirts, two plain, long sleeved shifts, three
aprons, five sets of small clothes, six pair of stockings
and handkerchiefs.

The woman explained that the two buttons on each
shift, just at her collarbones, were where the aprons
would attach when she was working during the day.
That didn't seem sensible because buttons could come
off and be lost. The aprons in Crane Valley had a loop
that went over her head. They didn't need buttons.
MeMe didn't quite approve of this place. At home,
Nancy and Ada had always done sensible things. But
Irina was nicer to her than Mr. McCreary had been. It
wasn't home, but she'd rather be here than in the
wagon.

"I find you a nightdrez too. Don't to sleeping in
daytime shift. Everbody in Miss Lucy house must
keep clothes nice," Irina said. "Sewing vooman
daughter die last year. Clothes ver daughter clothes."

"Did her daughter die from a fever?"

"No, girl die by horse in road. Mother too sad. Go
away, mebe to San Franzeesco. Now Ines sewing
vooman for Miss Lucy. You vill help Ines sewing. She
teach you."

A puzzled expression came to Irina's face. "Vere you
Indian girl learn speak English? You sound same
American girl."

"I just knew."

"Important to don't talk good around Miss Lucy. She think you show-offs and beat you. Keep mouth shut. Make Miss Lucy like you."

The little girl kept her mouth shut, but it didn't make Miss Lucy like her any better. "Your Indian gives me the dang willies!" Miss Lucy yelled. "I don't like the way the little brown dog looks at me. And what kind of Indian speaks English, Irina? Tell me that. Cook says she sounds like a priggish little schoolteacher. You tell me where some Indian brat learned to talk like that?

"Maybe back in Kansas in some mission school, but not out here. You wanted to buy a kid, so you deal with her, but keep her dark-skinned face out of my sight. She's yours. We have that settled. Now go back to work. But come to my room, my pretty Russkie, after the men have gone. I'm feeling lonely."

For the next few weeks, Irina gave MeMe work to do in the kitchen and washroom. She had Ines show the child how to clean the privies with a bucket and brush. MeMe didn't like doing it, but she didn't want to be sent back to Mr. Cobey. He smelled as bad as the privies did.

She was afraid of Ines at first, because the woman had a white scar running down across her forehead to a knot of an ear. But Ines seemed willing to help her. The woman seemed to understand about Miss Lucy. She found reasons to keep Napas busy mending clothes and away from working in any room Miss Lucy might wander into.

A week later, Irina told MeMe that she was to go out into the town helping Ines every day but Sunday. The two of them would cart the dirty laundry to the Chinaman's laundry and bring it back. The maids would distribute throughout the house. Other than that, her work was to help Ines keep all the clothing and linens of the household in good repair and do some light housework. A lot of women, but only two men, worked for Miss Lucy. Ruben drove Miss Lucy's carriage and tended the yard around the house. He wore a gun in a holster. Mr. McCreary did too, but Mr. Dickey and Mr. Landers didn't.

Horace played the piano in the big parlor. Both men's skin was very dark. They didn't look Indian like Ootie and her or Mexican like Lalo. They had a room up above the building next door to Miss Lucy's. Irina told her the men's room had its own stove and was very nice because they were part of Miss Lucy's business.

Horace's piano in the south parlor was the best thing Napas had ever seen. He polished it himself. One morning she almost touched one of its keys, hoping she could catch its music with her fingertip. Horace appeared in the doorway from the middle parlor. He shouted, "Napas, I'll cut off your hands if you touch my piano."

She didn't think he meant it because he was a tease, but she never went near it again.

From her room most nights she could hear its music. It reminded her of Ples Landers' fiddle. Horace played tunes Ples played at picnics with the McCrearys. She was sad on those nights. She didn't cry. She could have. Ines would never have heard her. She could have sobbed and wept and squalled if she'd wanted, but she didn't.

>>>O<<<

Chapter Twenty-four
~ Selling the Willows ~

Frederick had been gone more than two weeks before he returned to the ranch. Ada met him with a scowl, and she was primed to voice her complaint. "It wasn't right that ye left it to me to deal with those boys about the girl. They were persistent with their questions. Sir, I tell ye, it wasn't right."

"You made an agreement with me to stay and be part of my family. I pay you well to carry some of my responsibilities, Ada Cotter," he said. "If they ask you anything, tell them I found a home for her in a church school for Indians." A moment too late, he added, "For that's what I did."

Her suspicions then aroused, she asserted, "I don't like to be lying to them, sir, as I'm with those boys every day," she protested.

"You aren't lying. You are taking my word. Are you saying you question my word?"

Knowing now how close she was to the boundaries of his tolerance, she humbly replied, "No, sir." And, that made an end of it.

If Frederick had been disappointed with Ada's welcome, he found his sons sulky to the point of rudeness. Tom wouldn't speak to him, or meet his eyes. The boy answered questions only in yes and no, refusing even to use the courtesy of *Papa* or respect of *sir*. With odd formality of speech, the boy asked, "Where is our sister, Father?"

Frederick answered, "She is adopted out."

Richard was up and about, but when he met Frederick's eyes, his boy's eyes grew slitty. The man recognized his own stubbornness in the child. Mason would answer his father, though he didn't talk much. Frederick didn't worry. Mason was young enough to forget unpleasant things quickly.

The boys' father convinced himself that his sons would all recover, and that the reason for their silence was grief over their mother's death, not through any true concern for the Indian girl's disappearance.

Mr. Dickey had at last returned from his long visit to Stockton. When Frederick visited the store, from the man's terse talk and lack of questioning, McCreary assumed that Ada had passed the word along that the Indian girl was gone from The Willows. He expected Dickey's tension. The man had always been soft on savages.

Frederick rode by the Landers' ranch after letting Dickey know he was back in Crane Valley. Aaron seemed to accept Frederick's story about the missionaries. Aaron had shown partiality to the child in little ways that Frederick had noted but were too slight for him to have voiced any objection. Landers was shrewd enough that he wouldn't say anything to squelch the sale of The Willows. The man wanted the property. It was a fine ranch, one that others with money would find bid-worthy if it went to an open market. The men agreed to meet at the bank in Fresno Flats the following day, sign the papers before a notary and arrange payment, closing the sale of Frederick's property.

Then, Aaron called his son into the room and told him of their agreement. Ples nodded, he reached to shake Frederick's outstretched hand, but Ples seemed reluctant, hesitated, and withdrew his hand.

"Something wrong, son?" Aaron asked. "Don't you want me to buy The Willows? I do love that property, and its land butts up to ours. You love it too, I know you do!"

"It's not that, Paw. I know it is a good idea. But I want Mr. McCreary to tell us honest what happened to Merab."

Ples wasn't equal to Frederick McCreary in height, but he stood as straight as he could and kept his eyes on the taller man. "Mr. McCreary, Mrs. Cotter told Tom and me that Merab was adopted out. You told Tom that she's with some preachers building an Indian mission in the south of the state. Where is she? What's the truth of it?"

Frederick felt his rage to fill his belly and come to his throat. He swallowed down and tried to quell it. Not that it mattered what happened to any of the savages. He needn't justify himself to Aaron Landers' barely grown son. "This isn't your matter, son."

"I think it is," Ples insisted. "My paw and I buried her mother for your wife. Your sons and me, Mr. McCreary, we've watched her grow. I think MeMe *is* my matter."

If Frederick had killed the girl outright in front of a street full of witnesses, the law wouldn't have done a blasted thing - but consider him clearing trash. No young whip of a neighbor boy ought question him. Not that he cared a penny whistle's toot what this ignorant fool of a fiddle player might think or say. But Frederick did care that the business move along unimpeded. He wanted badly to get the fuss of moving his family and stock finished and them settled closer to the center of his business operation before the rains started.

He knew appeasement was necessary to completion of his desire. It's the details that do convince, Frederick thought, and he'd already created details to puff out his lie.

He looked Ples Landers in the eye, and said, "Yes, Pleasant, dear boy, you can be assured it's true." Frederick affected a most sincere and honest demeanor. "I shook the hands of two reverends and met their fine wives. Presbyterians, they were. The girl will be well cared for at the mission in Southern California. You can take my word on that.

"They were good people. Fine people. The child will be happier with her own kind, and she will receive a Christian education. It's time our state provided American education for Indians to free them from the mumbo-jumbo the Spanish brought in with the padres. She'll be well off in the southern part of our state with her own kind of people."

Aaron looked at Ples. "Son, you know we can trust our neighbor. Mr. McCreary has always been reliable, honest and good neighbor. He's been a friend to the whole valley here for nigh on to eight year. You must trust in what he has to say."

Everything the man said rang false. Ples couldn't extend his hand to the man. The young man turned, and with a slight bow to his father, left the room.

Frederick did a good job of making light of the young man's rudeness, consoling Aaron for the impetuousness of Ples' behavior. They soon came to agreement on an equitable price for The Willows. The papers would be signed at a notary's office in Fresno Flats the following morning. By noon, Aaron's money was in Frederick's case and would go in his safe.

The next morning, before Frederick left the Flats, he'd stopped at the stage depot and sent a post to Harrington in Angel's Camp orders to assign two oxen wagons and drivers to Crane Valley. They would be used to port the family furniture to one of his warehouses in Stockton.

He'd keep the sturdy walnut furniture that Steuben left, and the stove and move them with the family's personal effects in wagons with his hired men to help. There would be room for Ada's and Frank's belongings as well. He'd ask if Lalo wanted the job as a driver and to stay in Angel's Camp to work. He was sure Lalo would accept. Old Frank Sullivan could drive a single wagon the distance to Angel's Camp, but not a tandem set or a team of mules. Lalo would quickly learn. He was clever and strong, the best of the ranch's hired men.

All Frederick had left to do now was to inform his sons of the move. They should be glad to leave Crane Valley. After all it was the place where their mother and grandmother lay buried, a woeful place now, a good place to leave. Early that morning before he rode out to the Flats, Frederick ordered Ada to prepare a grand meal for supper that evening. She'd told him she had haunches of venison Tom had brought home that week and she'd make a salad of new little carrots and currants Nancy had kept in the pantry.

Frederick gave the younger two boys the job of catching and dressing out two ducks to fill out the feast. They'd have venison and roast duck. Ada could send for a Barrow's girl. The Braun girls were off to Merced for some festivity or other.

Aaron had gone courting his lady friend and wasn't riding back with him that afternoon, and as he rode toward Crane Valley Frederick pondered the story he'd told Ples Landers. He rankled at the boy's accusations. He was sorry he hadn't discouraged his boys close association with him.

He had fibbed some to defer to his Lander's vanity when he'd honored Ples Landers by calling him the finest shot in the valley. Now, the deed transferred, he was sorry he had said it. His own skinny Tom, always on the run here and there, was the best. He wasn't old enough yet to pass the entry limit for a grown man's contest to prove it, but no man or boy could beat him, and Tom's rifle eye was finer than Ples' ever was. Tom would find the hunting as good in Angel's Camp as in the hills around Crane Valley.

Trouble began when Frederick came home to smell burned meat as he entered the alcove. The kitchen was smoky. "Before you have anything to say," Ada began, "I'll not have that Barrows girl here to help again. I set her to watch the oven and she fell asleep. The meat is charred, sir, but I can save enough to make you and the boys a fine supper still. I paid her but half of what I would have given her and sent her home."

This kitchen squabble was nothing to him compared to the troubling and annoying reaction he received from his boys when he announced the sale of the ranch and the impending move to Angel's Camp. Mason and Richard began to cry. Tom just stared at him, then got up and stomped outside.

Frederick stayed calmly at his place at the head of the table. "It is going to be good for you boys," he told his younger sons. "You'll see, and Tom will come around. You're just surprised. I promise that we'll find a house better than this one, or I'll have one built. There is a school there, and you'll be with Wiley again."

When he saw Mason look up at the mention of his oldest brother, Frederick took that as a signal that he had happened on the right inducement. His sons would cooperate with his desires without argument or unpleasantness. It was time to reunite the family. Surely they understood that. "We need to be together. Your mother would be pleased to look down on us from heaven and know we McCrearys weren't separated.

"You boys know I have business to attend and can't be always with you to act your true father. But I will not leave you boys here on your own."

Mason reached for Richard's hand. The table blocked his father's view of an act so babyish. Richard squeezed Mason's hand, and spoke for both of them. "Can't you run the company from here, Papa?" the older boy asked.

"No, Richard. I was already planning to move the family north when word came of the contagion at Crane Valley."

"But Mama liked it here. She wouldn't have left."

"Your mother liked it in Indiana too. But she left it."

Mason sat at the table but he didn't want to finish his supper. He'd been thinking as their father spoke of the wonders that the move would bring and how the family's life would improve. Mason was thinking of his mother, and when he spoke, the boy voiced a fantasy.

"Mama is an angel now," the boy had said. "She'll like an Angel's Camp and she'll be able to watch over all of us easier there."

Mason's dream suited Frederick well and gave him pleasure. It wasn't something he would have conceived of through his own way of thinking, but it fit his needs perfectly, although he could hear a little too much of Reverend Taylor in the picture his youngest son drew.

Frederick went to bed pleased with himself. It had been a difficult evening, but the younger boys would be reconciled. He'd promised them that their ponies and dogs would be able to come along. Mud was gone but Sandy still chased after them, and they'd added two new pups. The younger boys seemed reassured to know that Ada, Frank and Lalo were coming along. He only had to reconcile Tom. He would handle the problem of that son in the morning.

But when morning came, Tom didn't come to breakfast. Frederick discovered that the boy had taken his Bible, the seventh grade issue of McGuffey's reader, his rifle, the fine racing pony Frederick had given him for his birthday sometime in the night, and he had run away.

Soon, Aaron Landers rode up the drive of the ranch he now owned. "Have you seen my son?" he shouted from the saddle.

Frederick, who was sitting out on the veranda, stood up. "No, I haven't seen him," he barked back to Aaron. He was angered, knowing that both their sons were gone. And suspicious of what the two lads were up to, he asked, "Did Ples take his fiddle and horse?"

"Yes. They're gone. He said nothing to me. Nothing! Not a word or note. Why would he leave?"

Frederick walked out to the drive so Aaron wouldn't have to shout and neither would he.

"My Tom's gone with him."

"Tom?" Landers seemed to ponder for a moment or

two, then said, "Yes, Tom might go, but why'd Ples leave *me*? There ain't no reason for Ples to go away. He loved The Willows. I been going to sign our old place over to him soon's he comes of age. We'd work the two ranches together." Landers dropped the reins and slid down from his horse.

The two men walked back toward the house. Tears were running down Landers' cheeks. He needed his handkerchief to wipe his nose and Frederick's hand at his elbow to steady him up the veranda steps. "He didn't want me marrying again. He thinks I should be true to his mother. Oh, Frederick, Maudie was sick for so long, and I *am* not an old man yet." Aaron shook his head. "She wouldn't hold it against me. Our son didn't even say good-bye. He left no note." Aaron wiped his eyes again.

Frederick looked away. He'd liked Landers in spite of the man's self-pitying weaknesses, drunk or sober. But this morning he wanted the man gone. Aaron's face was still running tears. Frederick wanted to go tend the mules, but waited, pretending to patience he didn't feel. He called out to Ada to bring coffee for their neighbor.

When Landers recovered himself, he said, "Frederick, Tom was powerful angry 'bout you selling me the ranch and the disappearance of that little MeMe. Your Tom might have had some reason to run off. That's true. But I've taken nothing from Ples."

No matter the circumstances, Aaron had been tactless. Frederick understood only too clearly and too well the reasons why Tom had run away. He hadn't liked a neighbor spelling it out for him.

>>>O<<<

Chapter Twenty-five
~ Troubled Days ~

Frederick left word with Reverend Taylor, Mr. Dickey, and the constable in charge of the district that his son, Thomas Jefferson McCreary, had left home and was underage. However, Frederick McCreary had no intentions of running after his son. Aaron Landers, with the good counsel of the men of the community, had come to feel that the boys had gone to San Francisco where Ples would try to finagle himself into the California Battalion that was forming. He knew how much his son wanted take arms against the insurgents who were trying to split the United States apart. Ples was only weeks away from twenty-one, and so Aaron reconciled himself to allowing his son to choose his own way, though it tortured his heart.

No, Aaron wouldn't go chasing after a grown son either. And, besides, Aaron was preoccupied with settling into his ownership of The Willows and finding a buyer for his ranch. He was also concentrating on pursuing ownership of the slim, comely young widow in Fresno Flats. He was young yet. He knew she was closer to agreeing to marry him now that he could move her into the nicest house in the entire county.

Frederick agreed that it was probable that San Francisco was the boys' goal. Although Tom was a tall boy, Frederick didn't believe that any recruitment officer would assess him as old enough to enlist. The boy inherited his height from Frederick, but his voice hadn't turned yet. The renegade Tom was smart enough to be able to find his way to any of McCreary

Hauling's stations when he got hungry enough. The station managers would see him home. Either that, or once winter set in and the boy found himself hungry with only a horse and a blanket, Tom would find his way to Angels' Camp on his own. He knew the fool boy would be full of apologies for causing annoyance to his father and adding to his brothers' grief.

Within six weeks, the McCreary family and most of the ranch hands had departed Crane Valley. The only traces left were some of the farm stock that with the deed belonged to Landers, two marked graves with the surname McCreary in the Crane Valley Cemetery, and another, rougher, mound marked with two crudely made crosses in a meadow high on the hill above the barn.

Ada, Frank and Lalo, with Richard and Mason, arrived in Angel's Camp a week before Frederick, who had stayed in Stockton to arrange storage for the family furniture, and also to bank Landers' money. Mr. Harrington, his orders having come by post and telegram, had found boarding house where Ada and the boys could live temporarily. He would settle Frank, Lalo and all the McCreary four-legged stock into livery quarters and corrals, and assign the men work once they arrived.

In Angel's Camp, Wiley watched the wagons approach, but he was so dulled by his own sorrow, he could scarcely greet his brothers. Denied his mother's last honors, he saw himself abandoned as worthless by his father and evicted from his position in the McCreary family.

But the sight of Mason jumping and waving from the first wagon gave him joy. "Where's Tom?" he called to his youngest brother as the wagons pulled into the freight yard. Richard and Mason were shouting whoops in greeting, but Wiley couldn't see his brother nearest in age.

He looked toward the family's carriage, pulling up behind the wagons. Seeing Ada there, he turned back to shout, "Where's MeMe?"

Mason leapt down from the wagon and ran to embrace Wiley. The smaller boy broke into weeping.

Richard, always slower and more cautious, climbed down from the wagon, but once down, ran to them. "Wiley, Tom ran away!" Richard exclaimed. "We don't know where he is. Papa wouldn't go after him. He and Ples ran away together. I tried to send you a letter, but Ada and Papa wouldn't let me take it to Dickey's. They said we'd be here before the letter would arrive."

Mason nodded, then blubbered, "Papa took MeMe away. He says she went to live with missionaries."

"I don't believe him, Wiley," Richard said. "I want to believe him but he took her away without telling us." He leaned against the wagon. "Laura Barrows," he said with his eyebrows tight and his chin held high, "Laura told me there weren't any missionaries in Crane Valley, or even in Fresno Flats. She knows. Her uncle is a preacher and told her. So, how would missionaries adopt MeMe? How would Papa have known where to take her?"

"MeMe *did* go to their mission. He wouldn't tell a lie."

Mason looked questioningly at Wiley and Richard wanting them to reassure him that what he thought was so, that the boy's father hadn't lied to them. But Wiley was moving toward fifteen now. Richard was eleven. Their father himself had taught them never to rely on a man's words but to look into his previous actions before giving him trust.

Mason had been only four, but Wiley and Tom were old enough to remember the day their father's hatred for MeMe had been loud and vociferous. And though that hatred had been tamped down during the intervening years, the older boys knew Frederick had never come to a liking for the child they called their sister. Neither Wiley nor Richard could give Mason the words of reassurance he needed, or erase the skepticism showing on their own faces. The three boys stood by the wagons, not knowing what to say or do.

By this time, Ada had climbed down from the carriage with Harrington's help. She came to join them, brushing off the dust of the road from her skirt. She took off her shawl to shake it out before she spoke. "Wiley, boy, aren't yer goin' to greet me a'tall-a'tall, though I've come this whole long way t' see yer."

Richard gave a frown to Ada's playful chiding of his brother. He felt a needling awareness that the housekeeper was involved in MeMe's dis-appearance.

"What has happened to my family, Ada?" Wiley asked her. "Where have they gone? Are we all broken apart?"

"Now, Wiley-boy, you'll see God has his plan. It will all fix itself in time, as all things do." She was so cheery that even Mason gave her an incredulous glower.

There was activity all around. The company men came out to unhitch the weary stock and lead them to water and familiar corrals. Ada scurried away like a well-fed rodent to find a bench where she could sit. Harrington, the clerk, and the livery roust-a-bouts were busy organizing the dispersal of all the goods in the wagons. Harrington caught a feeling of trouble in the looks of McCreary's sons and sought to calm it.

"Here boys," the man said. "I'm Mr. Harrington. I'll drive Mrs. Cotter and the carriage down the street. You can walk with Wiley and take a nice look at your new town. We're going just three blocks down, to the big brown house with the rooms-to-let sign in front.

"I've done the best I could to make you all comfortable. Mrs. Cotter, you'll be free of cooking duties while you are at Martha's Boarding House. It'll be a vacation for you. Boys, you will like it there too. Martha serves a fine meal. We have a good school for you too here in Angel's Camp. Come along with us, Wiley."

He smiled widely at Wiley. "I've had your clothes moved from the bunkhouse to the boarding house this morning, son. Your father wants you and your brothers to live at Martha's with him until he builds a new home."

With a youthful lack of restraint, his apprentice, young Wiley, using a steady, low voice darkened by anger said, "He's not my father anymore."

Harrington had liked working for Frederick McCreary. The man was fair. He had liked the boy for his steadfast character. Harrington wasn't completely happy with Wiley's response. He'd never heard anger come from the boy before. But he stood with Wiley while his father had left him behind a month earlier. It was not an employee's business to pry into his boss's problems.

With the younger boys enrolled in school and Wiley working, Ada came to feel she was queen of the boarding house. She had little to do but mending, though she went down to help Martha's laundress on washing day. She had never had a period of such leisure in her whole life.

Wiley enjoyed being with his brothers, but he kept to his work, doing what he was expected to do, seething as he scribed numbers into columns. He was anxious for his father's return from Stockton. He planned for that day by stashing a change of clothing and his rifle under his old cot in the bunkhouse.

Frederick, his business finished, didn't arrive until the end of the second week of Ada and the boys' tenure in the boarding house. Wiley scarcely waited for his father to slip from the saddle when he confronted the older man in the street in front of the office.

"You are a liar and a scoundrel, Papa. I'm leaving here. I don't want anything from you but the wages coming to me. I'll take nothing else."

"What is this? Why are you talking to me this way?"

Frederick grabbed the boy's elbow and hurled him into the office. Better that his employees see this than townspeople and strangers passing on the street. As Frederick entered the hauling office he found it empty. He was glad, for he had a contentious boy to deal with. Frederick let go of Wiley's arm and turned to the boy. "Now explain yourself," he demanded.

"I stayed here, Papa, as you ordered while you robbed me of my mother, my brother and my sister. You aren't a father, and I'm no longer your son. I won't stay here."

"You stupid boy. Your mother died of the contagion; I didn't take her from you. "And that red devil *wasn't* your sister. Your damned fool of a mother made you softheaded over her. The Indian was nothing to you. She was worth absolutely nothing but trouble to our family. As to your brother, he's made his own choice. I didn't send him away. I wash my hands of him."

"My mother wasn't a fool." Though his anger was erupting; his voice was unquavering. "Tom is only thirteen, Papa!"

"He's man enough to live with his choices."

Wiley looked at Frederick. His grievance was deeply felt. "You're my father, but you're an evil man. I won't work for you. You're cruel and selfish. I meant what I said. I want my wages. I'm going to find my brother."

McCreary registered the boy's feelings calmly and made no rebuttal. He looked at his son with amused tolerance. All boys had a moment when they crossed their father. And at just about this age. He had his moment once. This was Wiley's.

The patronizing tolerance that the boy saw on his father's face infuriated Wiley. "What did you do to MeMe? Where is she?" The boy grabbed his father by the shoulders as if to shake the heavier man. "Tell me what you did with her! Did you kill her? Did you leave her some place she was sure to die? Where is she, Papa?"

Frederick had had enough. He slammed his hand into the boy's head. As Wiley tried to recover his balance, Frederick shoved him backward with all his massive body's force.

Wiley crashed into the tall double desk, but nearly his father's equal in size, he managed to stay on his feet. An inkwell slid from the desk and crashed to the floor. The acrid smell filled the office.

"You'll do nothing of the kind," Frederick said, dismissing the boy and pointing to the ink spreading on the floor. You'll keep to your work and keep your mouth closed. "Clean that mess up. It's only mid-afternoon and you're to work 'til six. If you've finished your own work, do the clerk's. Harrington tells me he is slow. You, stupid boy, you're naught but an apprentice. I owe you no wages."

Frederick's gelding was standing at the rail waiting for him. He looked out the window and made up his mind that checking the office could be done later. He needed to find refreshment after the long day's ride. "I assume that the family is settled at Martha's," McCreary said arrogantly, as though nothing unpleasant had passed between them. "I'll see you in her dining room this evening. Bring the books for the Jim Town station for the past three years. I'll look it over and tell to you about what I expect of you."

Frederick left the office, mounted and rode down the street. Wiley, dizzy from the blow, saw his father leave, and only then did he slide to the floor. The ink was dripping down through the cracks. It had puddled a stain as large as one of his father's hands. He still felt the shock of the heavy blow. He couldn't recall that his father had ever raised a hand to him before.

"You won't have a chance to tell me anything, Papa," Wiley murmured to himself. The sturdy boy had no idea where MeMe was, or if she was even alive, but he was sure he could find Tom.

He went to the safe and opened it. The boy counted out just what was due him as wages for ten full months clerking work, judging his value modestly and only taking what he knew the lowly paid clerk earned. He felt justified that in Angel's Camp he had done Harrington's work well enough that the man needed only prove it each day and seldom found error. The boy had also done more than half the clerk's daily duties.

Wiley locked the safe carefully and wrote a note of appreciation to Mr. Harrington for the man's kindness and patience teaching him the bookkeeper's trade. He left it on the man's desk, tucked under the ledger.

The boy went out to the company yard and asked a stockman to bring the yellow mare to him, saddled to ride. He climbed up into the rafter attic and picked up the rifle and bedroll he'd put there long before in readiness for this day, a day that he knew was coming from the day when his mother was dying and his father left him behind. He'd go to San Francisco. He knew Ples would be there.

Ples had written Wiley a letter about his plan to join the California Battalion. Wiley was sure Tom would be with him. He'd find his brother. He'd get a job and send Tom back to school to finish eighth grade. Then they'd both get jobs and save enough money to go to Angel's Camp and get their brothers.

He rode west, through the mountains to the foothills. From them he could see across the whole great valley to the mountains on the other side. The winter rains had started.

He had an oiled tarp in his saddlebag. The yellow mare didn't mind the wet. They set out to cross the wide flatness of California's great valley.

Chapter Twenty-six
~ A Minor Forgery ~

November rains pounding down made the rivers rush faster and deeper in the mountains. Here in the valley, the rivers and creeks spread together to make swampy bogs. Wiley had never seen so much water before.

He slept where he found places that were dry enough and he could rest the yellow mare and lie down. He spent little on food, hoarding his money by eating only once a day. Travel to San Francisco cost him more money than he had expected, and the expense was used in ferry fees. The horse would have tried to swim and disliked the ferry, but he calmed her. Often the yellow mare was covered in thick mud up to her belly from fording rainwater ponds and the muck around them.

He and the mare traveled more by guessing where the road lay ahead of them, than by knowing. If there was ever a country that needed bridges built and plank roads laid, it was this one. All the rivers and streams of the Sierra came rushing down and turned the great valley into a lake, most of it shallow but it was still all but impassable. It took Wiley until late November to reach his goal.

He understood better why freight in across the valley was tediously slow and expensive in the flat land during California's winter. His experience was proving what he had learned in the office using pencil and paper, ink and ledger book. He'd skirted the long bay, and come up from the south, finding higher ground again and better roads.

Wiley stopped first in San Jose. The mines McCreary Hauling served bought supplies of the mercury from San Jose. The city was a grand place, far larger than Stockton. He liked the city's look. It was very different from any place he had ever known.

The first people he met looked like Indians but weren't. The dark hair and high cheekbones of most of the people he saw reminded him of his sister more than they reminded him of Lalo Cordero who worked for the family in Crane Valley. Lalo was brown skinned but he had green eyes and brown hair. San Jose and the small communities around him introduced him to Mexican California and he found it intriguing. The courtesies that greeted him used words he didn't know, "Ola", and "Buenos tardes." He remembered Reverend Taylor telling the class that the Waukeen River was properly spelled S-a-n J-o-a-q-u-i-n. The Spanish language used the alphabet differently from the English. Wiley had remembered that oddity, and he had recognized the city's name on his road's signposts as he neared the city, San Jose, it was spelled, though spoken San Hosay.

For the first time he saw California as it might have been as under the Mexican flag, its adobe buildings quaint yet coming from a time not very long past. It was a so different from the towns of the Sierra. He knew, from Reverend Taylor's teaching, that back when Wiley was just four years old, this Mexican city, San Jose, became the new state's first capital. It no longer was, but he liked the chance to feel be here and feel its history.

He stopped, found feed and water for the yellow mare, and the stockman's allowance to sleep in the straw at the livery, and he went out to eat what the

Mexican's ate to see if he'd like their food. He did. Chiles burned his tongue, but that didn't discourage his appetite for the savory foods he was served.

Early the next morning, Wiley rose and saddled up, anxious to get on with his journey. He and the mare followed the road at the edge of the bay northerly until they came to San Francisco. The city was magnificent. It was a marvel!

He'd never seen anything so grand. He knew from school that California's capital had been moved to Sacramento, but he couldn't understand why this miraculous city with its hills overlooking the bay had *not* been chosen. Wiley looked down on the ships in the sparkling water below him and then surveyed the thriving city, and he wondered what Sacramento was like, how it could possibly be a better place than this.

In the heart of the city, he found a boarding house with a roomy stable for the yellow mare. As much as he wanted to find Tom and Ples, he needed rest. So did his horse.

The next day Wiley and the horse went exploring. They ran up and down hills. He'd learned the word peninsula from his geography book in fifth grade, and now he stood in a city at a peninsula's tip, seeing what it was and charmed by all he saw. He viewed ships docked at the wharves, islands in the bay, headlands beyond. He had never seen so many people or heard so many languages. In the Sierra country he knew, people had come from all over the world. There were Chinese, and there were bushy haired men with tattoos - islanders from the Pacific. Frenchmen, Italians and Russians, all were staking a claim on this city.

The proprietress of his boarding house was a Swedish woman who was married to a man as German as the

Braun family. Her tenants were as international as the placer miners that came down into Angel's Camp to the assay office with their findings.

With luck, and because he impulsively picked up a sodden newspaper from the street, he knew how and where he would find the two people, out of the more than fifty-six thousand living in this city, whom he had come to find. An ad was posted on the front page of the San Francisco paper asking for volunteers to ride with the cavalry. Wiley would go to the address, and surely find Ples and Tom. He tore out the bit of paper, wiped it clear of dirt. He blew on it and shook it until it was well dried and put it in his coat pocket, determined to find the Assembly Hall that very same day.

Cavalry Company for the East.

 THE UNDERSIGNED HAS BEEN authorized by the Secretary of War to raise a company of Cavalry for services to the East to make part of the Massachusetts quota.

A poll of the company is at Assembly Hall corner of Post and Kearny Streets, where persons desirous of joining can enroll their names.

No one need apply who is not a good horseman and in good health. Men from the country preferred. The Roll will be kept open a reasonable time before selections are made.

All expenses will be paid as soon as accepted. Further particulars apply to Office, corner Post and Kearny street.

oc28 - 20tf   J. SEWALL REED

He was successful. An enrollment officer at the corner of Post and Kearny Streets was seated behind a long walnut desk. The officer pointed to names on the list. These are the men you're seeking?"

"Yes, sir." Wiley's eyes glistened. "Thomas is my brother. I'm Wiley McCreary, from Crane Valley."

"Your age, son?"

"Twenty-two, sir." The boy, not a liar, easily lied.

"Ah, you and Thomas must be twins. He claims to be that identical age." The officer winked at him.

"We are, sir, but not identical. He is three inches taller, and I am thirty pounds wider."

"I can see that, but any man would recognize that you two are indeed brothers." the army man chuckled.

"Tell me boy, can you shoot a rifle as well as your brother can? The lad and his friend convinced me to come out to the range and watch their prowess. They impressed all the military men on the range."

"I'm not as good as Tom, sir, to be honest. But I can hit a deer moving through brush better than most. And I never hit but what I'm aiming to."

The man grinned up at Wiley, and added Wiley H. McCreary to the candidate roster. "J. Sewall Reed was right to call out to you country boys to enlist."

"I expect so, sir."

"Surgeon wants your brother and Mr. Pleasant Landers in for health examination at two o'clock this afternoon. I suppose you would like me to schedule you at the same time."

"Yes, sir."

"Well, I'll be glad to do it for you. But now, young

man, while I'm sure Mr. Landers is of age, I'd like a letter from the two of you boys from a parent or guardian that will confirm your eligibility. I must file it for the commission before we can accept an enlistment. Your brother is very callow looking, and you, though sturdier, don't look nearly as old as you claim. Can you produce such a document for me?"

"Yes, sir. I shall, and by tomorrow. Is the surgeon's exam held in this same building?"

"Upstairs, and down the hall."

Wiley rode back to the boarding house to immediately beg a pen and writing paper from his landlady. That evening, after much practice, he commenced to write a document allowing Thomas Jefferson McCreary and Wiley Howard McCreary the right to enlistment with the California Battalion. He signed his father's name to it with a flourish, in his best imitation of the signature of Frederick McCreary. In the small parlor, he found two boarders who were only too willing to sign their endorsements to a paper, written in a language that neither could yet read, for the open-faced and honest young American born lad who wanted to be a soldier.

Wiley, Ples and Tom needed provide their own uniforms, but by selling their horses, and working as brick layers for a building being constructed on Market Street not far from their room, they had the money. The day of mustering, they went on the government payroll.

There was no doubt that if Ples hadn't been as accomplished on coronet as fiddle so a Battalion band would seek him, and if Tom hadn't been such a champion rifle shooter, and if Wiley hadn't been

Tom's brother, the three boys would have been turned away.

But they each offered exactly what Captain J. Sewall Reed wanted for the California One Hundred. And if the authenticity of the document from Frederick McCreary permitting his sons' enlistment might possibly have been a forgery, the fact went un-noticed. The paper was promptly sealed away in the Assembly Hall files at Post and Kearney.

The army's advertisement in the newspaper stated, "No one need apply who is not a good horseman and in good health. Men from the country preferred." These young men from the country could find their land bearings from the sun in the day and from the stars at night and never lose their way. In the Captain's experienced eyes, the three were the ideal boys to turn into soldiers for the grand Union Army.

Pleasant Richard Landers and the McCreary brothers sailed out of San Francisco on the 11th of December 1862 on the steamer *Golden Age*, bound for Nicaragua. From there, they cross the isthmus, then go again by ship to New York harbor, then again to Massachusetts. It was rumored that Company A was to be greeted by the mayor of the Boston City. No parents were there to see the three young Crane Valley men off to war; their mothers were dead, and their fathers estranged from them.

However, San Francisco had taken the company and its captain to the city's heart with pride and indulgence. The soldiers had fancy, well-made uniforms and velvet caps. Five companies of Home Guards escorted the outfit to the wharf, accompanied by a twenty-piece band, cheering groups of abolitionists and religious leaders, and many of the City's more

City's more prominent citizens. In among the masses gathered, to witness and wave, was a small group of foreign-looking people. They were new Americans, stood in the throng at the wharf, waving the Golden Age away as it steamed from its dock the valiant California 100 soldiers lined at the rail and waving back were young.

Few men in the ranks were older than twenty-two. The band sounded out *Hail Columbia! Happy Land!* Unashamed tears flowed down the proud cheeks of a Swedish landlady, her husband, and three of her boarders including the men who had aided Wiley's patriotic forgery. With the great and festive crowd gathered at the embarcadero, they tossed confetti and cheered for their own brave, eager boys from the country.

Pleasant Landers had hoped to sail around the horn again, as he had as a child. He remembered the he felt when the ship nearly stood on its tail pointing its nose to the cloudy skies, or when it pointed its nose to the center of the earth as storms, huge waves, lightning split the sky like nothing he had seen in his ten years of life. He'd be able to travel in reverse the shipboard route to San Francisco he had taken with his mother ten years earlier. He'd wanted to show his young friends and new comrades the distant outlines of Chile and Tierra del Fuego as he had seen them, but it was not to be. The *Golden Age* would not go around the horn. An army must be efficient. Crossing Nicaragua at Panama on a cog railway was a much more practical and less costly way to move the California 100 to Boston. They would get to training with the Second Massachusetts, and the war, all the sooner by way of Nicaragua.

>>>O<<<

Chapter Twenty-seven

~ A Letter from Virginia ~

With his two elder sons gone and their names never mentioned in his presence, Frederick McCreary set about making sure that his younger sons were tied very tightly to him and to the future he planned for them. The boys were enrolled in school, with Ada to guide their domestic lives, and Frederick to supervise their free time either personally or by way of his delegation of responsibility to Mr. Harrington. Frederick McCreary, owner of the most successful freight business in the state, indulged any of Mason and Richard's whims if it were possible. They had fine clothing, fine saddles and finer horses.

While the Angel's Camp office of McCreary Hauling was the company's main office, work in Stockton took much of Frederick's time. In addition, he often had to travel to see for himself how his freight stations, wagons, and animals were maintained. He wasn't a man to run his business on the trust of reports sent from distant employees. The Angel's Camp office was open from seven in the morning until six in the evening every day but Sunday. If the boys weren't in school, they were expected to report to the office.

Richard, still pale and easily tired, had not completely recovered from his mother's death. He finished seventh grade in Angel's Camp, and enough time had passed that Frederick and Ada both expected that he would have made full recovery. He still tired and lost color easily and it appeared that the boy would be an invalid for the rest of his life. He turned thirteen.

When summer's recess ended, Frederick determined it

would be better for the boy's health to leave the active life of a schoolboy for a safer and more sedentary role in the company office.

Mason, though, was a sturdy, tall boy who looked older than eleven, and liked working in the livery stable and corrals better than in the office. He was happy to be in school. He was in sixth grade, eleven years of age, and he liked to listen to the schoolmarm's voice. She reminded him of his mother. Ada was good to him, but had a tendency to be shrill. His teacher's voice was gentle music.

Frederick had some trouble with the boy. At the end of the school day, Mason didn't like being cooped up in the office under Mr. Harrington's tutelage as his brother had. He preferred the livery and corrals. The animals reminded him of The Willows, and his barn chores there.

Mason missed his old home and found nothing in the office of McCreary Hauling that was in any way similar to the ranch where he had spent his early days. It might be all right for Richard, but the horses, mules and oxen in the company corrals were the only things that made him feel as free as he had in Crane Valley.

Both boys grieved silently and separately over the loss of their mother, MeMe, and their older brothers. It was as though one of the earthquakes that their state was prone to have had happened to their family. It was cracked and fragmented, strewn hither and thither. All they could do was cling to each other, but neither wanted to bring tears to the other's eyes. Any mention of their life before Angel's Camp was squelched before it was spoken.

Harrington tried his best to interest Mason in the office operations of the business, debits and credits, but Mason stubbornly resisted learning until, finally,

Frederick told the boy that once he well understood the *systems* of the freight company, the man would apprentice him to a noted animal doctor in Stockton, a man who had trained the veterinarian whom Frederick contracted for any problems with the company's stock. That inducement was compelling, the boy saw his future clearly, and paid better attention to Mr. Harrington's office instruction.

Harrington soon grew as fond of Richard and Mason as he had been of Wiley. They seemed to have McCreary's strengths, but none of his abrasive stubbornness. Neither boy was as quick to learn as Wiley had been, but both were willing to work hard to master the business operations from drawing contracts to tallying accounts to payroll to daily records. Mr. Edward Harrington was very satisfied with his office help.

In late January of 1863, more than a year after the departures of first Tom and then Wiley McCreary from the family, the clerk, in the office of McCreary Hauling sorting through the day's delivery, was surprised to find a letter addressed to Mr. Harrington. It was unusual for Harrington's mail to come to the office, for he had a wife, daughters and a home on a side street in town. The mail from his family in Boston normally went by postman to his house.

When the clerk handed the envelope to the bookkeeper, Edward Harrington wondered at its origin. There was no name, only a return address of Readville, Massachusetts. He didn't know whom the letter might be from, though he had family in Boston, not far away from Readville.

Assuming that it was a personal letter, although curious, he didn't open it. He was being paid to work not read letters.

Harrington slipped it into his coat pocket, and went back to work compiling the farrier bills sent in from each of the company's liveries the prior month. Harrington was confounded by the cost of shoeing the hooves of oxen vs. the cost of shoeing the hooves of mules; and determined to persuade Mr. McCreary that it would be better for the company to have its own sets of traveling farriers on salary, than to hire the work done and billed by such as resided in the localities of each of McCreary Hauling's liveries scattered throughout the regions it served.

It wasn't until after supper, when he and his wife were in alone in the parlor, that the bookkeeper remembered the odd envelope from Massachusetts. The envelope produced a thick letter, which when unfolded revealed to be in fact three letters, for two were contained within the folds of the one addressed to him. Edward placed the interior letters on the table beside his chair, and spread the first letter open under the lamp. He then recognized the elegant script, amazed that Wiley McCreary had sent him a letter from so far away, but relieved to know the boy was alive and well.

Carrie Harrington had taken up her knitting and was seated across from him but nearer the fire. Edward called her attention. "My dear, I've received an unusual letter."

"I didn't notice any mail this day but from my cousin Margaret," she remarked, not looking up from the green sweater she was knitting for their married daughter in the east.

"It's from Wiley."

"Wiley McCreary?" she asked in surprise.

"We know no other by that name, my dearest."

"I've missed that boy. I enjoyed the nights you brought him home for a meal better than the livery's cook would prepare. What does he say, Edward? Where has the boy gone?"

"This will surprise you, Carrie. Wiley has gone to Massachusetts to train as a soldier."

"But he's too young. He's but sixteen or seventeen."

"That may be, but he is enlisted."

Mr. Harrington then read Wiley's letter to his wife. He had not read a sentence before Carrie was no longer paying attention to the long needles or the garment in her hands, but watching the expression on Edward's face. He showed worry, but also admiration for the boy who had worked hard and well under his instruction. Carrie remembered the many times that Wiley had come to their house to eat with them when his father was traveling. Her daughters admired the young man, and she appreciated his good manners.

January 7th, 1863

My Dear Friend, Mr. Harrington,

I hope that this letter finds you and your family well, and that you did not suffer greatly from the loss of your assistant. If you found my letter to you, you know the reason that it was necessary for me to leave the office and pursue a life elsewhere. And you know that I'm ever grateful to you for all the tutelage you so generously gave me.

You will find enclosed two letters for my brothers. I beg you to give them to Richard and Mason in the greatest secrecy.

Though our father could do nothing now to remove Tom or me from the battalion, he might forbid our brothers from sharing correspondence with us. With my greatest hopes, I ask that you allow my brother Tom and me to use you as a clandestine post office, that we brothers might continue to communicate with each other.

If this is agreeable to you, please let me know by writing to Wiley H. McCreary, in care of Company A, 2nd Massachusetts Cavalry, United States Army.

We will be removing soon to Virginia, now our training at Camp Meigs is at an end. It is rumored that we will fall under the command of General Phillip Sheridan, but this has yet to be announced. I'm sure that Papa's newspapers will let you know where we may be fighting before any letters from the field will reach you. I remain your most sincere and humble friend, and beg you give my truest regards to Mrs. Harrington

Tell your daughters I have not forgotten them.

Private Wiley H. McCreary

Company A 2nd Massachusetts Cavalry

By the time Edward Harrington had finished reading, both he and his wife had tears in their eyes. Harrington said, "The boy must have forgotten the address of our home to risk a letter to the office."

"You must surely help the boys, Edward."

"I don't think I can, as much as I might wish."

The normally quiet and taciturn woman tucked the handwork down into a basket of yarn near her chair. "Edward, you *must* help them."

"It could mean my job, should McCreary find out," Harrington answered, a deep frown rippling across his forehead, reinforcing the concern spoken in his words.

"I know you like living here in California, and the man pays you well. But my dear husband, a good man must serve his conscience first, even before his duties to his employer." Carrie got up from her chair and went to sit on the rug at her husband's feet. The flames from the fireplace put golden sparkles in her eyes.

"You're very good at your job, husband. And, you are well experienced. There would surely be other jobs if the man should turn you out for your loyalty to his sons. Wherever you go, the girls and I'll go with you without complaint. "I married you for your goodness. Other employers will see in you what I see."

She patted his knee and added saucily, "Why, if no other job should happen, I can take in boarders. You'll be my handyman and keep the pump handles oiled and the trash burned."

With those words of merry encouragement, Mrs. Carrie Harrington of Angel's Camp unknowingly became the earthly successor and maternal agent of a woman she had never met and never would meet, the late Nancy, Mrs. Frederick McCreary, of Crane Valley California.

After Frederick left the office the following day, Mr. Harrington found himself alone with the McCreary brothers. He finally was able to give them the letters Wiley had enclosed for them.

August 20, 1863

Richard and Mason, my beloved brothers,

Tom and Ples Landers are here with me in Virginia. We are fighting for the Union with other Californians and men from many foreign nationalities in addition to the Americans in our Company A. Tom and I share a tent with two Englishmen. You would like them. They are well- trained and good soldiers.

The three of us enlisted in San Francisco and came here by ship, except over Panama when we crossed the mountains by railway. It has been a grand adventure. We trained at Camp Meigs in Massachusetts, and then we were transported here where we will go against Jubal Early and his Rebs.

Tom is the best rifleman of Company A, and you should be very proud to be his brother. Ples shares a tent with others who play music, but we see him often. He is in the Company Band, however it has had little time to assemble and give us concerts. The war keeps all busy.

I miss you both and promise to come for you and MeMe as soon as this war is over.

With my love and great regards,

Your fond brother, Wiley

The second letter was brief and undated:

My dear brothers, I'm sorry I left you. I could no longer tolerate Papa's thoughtless actions. I knew Ples was going off to enlist. I went with him. I promise you that you are not abandoned. When the war is over, Wiley and I are coming back for you.

We have made a vow that if MeMe is still alive, when we are free of our duty, we will find her.

Tom

"Oh, Mason, what has become of MeMe? Maybe the Presbyterians did adopt her as Papa said."

Richard looked skeptical. "Do you believe him?"

"I must believe him. I don't think a father would lie to his sons," Mason answered.

Richard's face remained doubting. "Papa's a Methodist. Why would Papa have given her to the

Presbyterians?"

"Mr. Harrington, how can Tom have gone to be a soldier? He is only fifteen, not two years older than Richard." Mason questioned, his face drawn up in perplexity.

"Wiley looks grown, but Tom doesn't."

"I don't know, son. Perhaps they took him as a drummer boy. They took young lads to fight against the British in our Revolution. My own grandfather served as a boy in Boston. He was at Yorktown, no older than your brother."

"Tom was the best shot in Crane Valley. They wouldn't give him a drum if they knew that."

"Maybe they knew." There was a serious look in Harrington's eyes.

Both the boys looked earnestly at Harrington, and Richard spoke out, "Please, keep the letters secret, Mr. Harrington, and help us write back under your name. I think Papa is a good man, but this isn't something he's to know. He's very angry with our brothers, but they are our brothers."

Mr. Harrington looked at them, and felt he had already made his decision to help them answer. "I don't know Tom, but your brother Wiley was fine and brave. He gave up your father's favor and generosity for his principles. Whether or not I agree,

I admire him for that." He saw the honesty of the McCreary brothers and felt he owed something more to them than to their father. "Wiley grieved when your mother died, and he was left to grieve alone here. It wounded him when your father left him behind."

"Our mother loved us all, but I think she was most proud of Wiley."

Harrington decided that if he were joining a plot with the four young McCrearys, he might as well join it in full. "I'll help you in full, and in secrecy."

But Edward Harrington had a question for them. "Who is MeMe, if I may ask you? Tom mentioned MeMe."

Mason's face lit up. A sweet smile played across Richard's pale face. "She is our sister, sir," the younger boy said.

Chapter Twenty-eight
~ Miss Lucy's Establishment ~

The girl now called Napas had found her place in Miss Lucy's establishment by never being seen. It was an easy task for her, learned by Mr. McCreary's visits home during all the life she could remember. Miss Lucy screamed, but as long as Napas was never in the same room, she was never the cause of the screaming. The second day she was at Miss Lucy's Establishment, she overheard Miss Lucy say that the little Indian girl gave her the shivers. But that kept Napas from having to empty chamber pots or clean in the women's rooms upstairs. Two old white women, Miss Lucy's women's maids, did those jobs. The downstairs workers never went upstairs.

Napas cleaned the parlors in the early morning. She worked in the kitchen. Another daily task was repairing the women's clothing. She liked that, though her fingers and back sometimes hurt. Mending with silent Ines was like working embroidery with Nancy when she was still Merab McCreary. She took pleasure in the tidy weaving of the needle through the bands of thread, and she took pride in the softness of the places where she had moored thread so as not to make a lump of a knot. Ines grinned at her with approval.

Every day but Sunday, she helped Ines cart the mounds of laundry the maids had gathered. Napas and Ines took the soiled clothing and linens to the laundry every morning, except Sundays. They had a different cart to pull on rainy days to keep the clean laundry dry as they hauled it home again. The covered cart was heavy and very hard to pull and even harder to turn.

In the afternoon they took on the burden of pulling the cart back to the Chinaman's laundry where the two picked up the clean laundry from the day before and returned it to Miss Lucy's Establishment.

Once back, they folded and stacked everything neatly sorted in piles of stockings, petticoats, and gowns and other items for the maids to collect. All the women who worked for Miss Lucy had tabs with their marks on their clothes. They took the marked laundry upstairs to be distributed. Ines and Napas shelved the downstairs items. When they delivered or picked up the laundry, Ines counted off every garment, towel and sheet before she put her own mark in the laundry book. She had her own way of writing that didn't look like what the boys had done in their school slates and papers. But Ines always knew if the count was right.

Napas didn't think the Chinaman who ran the laundry spoke English. He never said anything. He just nodded and pointed. The first time she went with Ines to cart the laundry, when she said, "Good morning," he looked disdainfully at her. She didn't think he liked Indians or Mexicans, although his skin was brown like theirs.

As the nights grew colder, Ines brought tattered blankets down from the house's attic and tacked them over the inside walls of the room where the two of them slept. The blankets insulated them from the cold, and a small charcoal brazier warmed the room. Ines showed Napas through signs that the window needed be left open when the brazier was used. Ines was a solemn person, though. She kept to herself.

The maids, Cook, Ines and Napas worked early in the day. They worked quietly, so not to wake Miss Lucy or the women who worked upstairs in the house late into the night and were still asleep. Napas soon learned that she, Ines and Cook had to keep out of sight when the house was open for visitors.

Napas and Ines spent hours mending. Sewing with silent Ines was much like doing embroidery with Nancy when she was still Merab McCreary. Napas took pleasure in neatly weaving the needle through the bands of thread making repairs to garments, and she took pride in the tidy nearly invisible points she made mooring thread without creating an obvious of a knot. Ines, who seldom smiled, would grin an approval. Seeing Ines's rare smile encouraged her.

They worked together every day, but she knew as little of the Mexican woman as when she first met her. The only one at Miss Lucy's who Napas felt she really knew was Irina. But she liked Ines, though the silent woman seemed as forever sad as deaf and never seemed to care whether Napas was there or not.

The Indian girl was puzzled by one odd thing that Inez did. On their way to and from the Chinaman's laundry they passed a large oak tree. Ines would stop, pat its massive trunk, and stand there for a moment or two. After a while, Napas got used to Ines and didn't think about it anymore.

At Christmas, the second year she lived at Miss Lucy's, Cook, Ines and MeMe each received as small bag of candies and fruit from Miss Lucy. Irina brought Ines and Napas two new gowns and six pair of stockings each.

"Break apart old dresses to make new petticoats," Irina said. She made a comedy of trying to explain what she meant to Ines, and finally took the scissors to cut an old dress apart, separating bodice from its skirt. She held the skirt up to Inez's waist, and nodded at the woman. Then showed off her own brightly colored underskirt.

Napas was laughing at the pantomime. "May I have new boots too, Irina?"

"Boots good. No need new."

"But my toes don't fit anymore."

"I vant see feet."

Napas sat on the floor and pulled off her boots. Her toes were red and the nails of her big toes were swollen from pressure.

"I tink you not need new boots. Put back on."

Nothing more was said about new boots for Napas. But, on a morning thirteen days after Christmas, the child woke up to find a box at the foot of her bed. Inside were a pair of almost new brown boots, and they fit her well, allowing just a little growing space.

That morning at servant's breakfast, Irina winked at her. "Today Jesu get present from Vise Men. Good idea give present."

It was the nicest thing that had happened to her in over a year. She wanted to keep the old boots and put them in the box she kept with her buckskin packet. That was where she kept her worn out shiny black shoes from Ootie. But later Irina came and got the boots.

"Mayn't I keep them?" Napas asked.

"Vy? Not to be wearing too small boots. Vy keep? I give to Cobey for some other Indian girl can ver."

Napas had never thought that Cobey might sell other Indian children. She was shocked to consider that she wasn't the only one. She stood staring at Irina and wondering what happened to the others. She had never met another Indian child. Maybe they were all dead like her mother.

"Is good idea?" The Russian woman held up the too-small boots shaking them like a bell.

And Napas managed to say, "Yes, Irina. It's a good idea." But it was very hard for her to give up the boots Ootie had given her.

After that, when she and Ines went to the laundry she peered up and down the streets they crossed hoping to see an Indian child. She thought that maybe all Indians had been killed until one morning she and Ines saw something terrible. A young woman, who looked like an older version of her and wearing a ragged dress, was in the road. A man was jabbing at her with a tree branch and shouting at the woman to go back to the hills where she belonged. The man looked up and saw Ines and Napas.

"This is a white man's town and you stay the hell away from it, you dirty brown bitches," he yelled.

Napas' heart began beating too fast. They pushed the laundry cart faster along, but the man with the branch was coming toward them. From a side street, another man intervened. He tree branch away from the first man saying, "Leave those two alone. They belong to Lucy."

That evening after dinner, before she went out to the room for the night, she went to find Irina. Irina looked up. "Vat's wrong dat need me?"

Timidly Napas asked, "Do you own Ines too?"

"No. She vork here. Not buy Mexican vomans. Only

can buy Indian peoples. Mexican vant pay. Miss Lucy keep Ines money in safe for some day Ines grow old an' not vork." She looked intently at Napas. "Indian not get pay."

"Don't Mexicans get killed?"

Cook was listening and she answered for Irina. "No. Not use-ily don't. But Ines don't like white men an' can't say I blame her. Her poor husband got in trouble, long time ago. Years ago. He opened his mouth to the wrong man. A bunch of them from the Blue Tent Tavern hung him from that big oak tree on the corner down two blocks. Hung him dead. Ines's fine with us women, but you might unnerstand she's kind'a skeered of white men since that happened."

"Is true. Horace tell me," Irina assented. When Irina mentioned Horace's name, Cook gave her an odd look. But then Cook went on talking.

"Mexicans are all right. They used to own this whole land afore we Americans got it away from them. What happened in this piss of a town after that handsome Alejandro was kilt was nobody wanted a deaf woman. Nobody but Miss Lucy gave her a home when her man was dead an' she had no place to go." Cook looked as though she was very proud of Miss Lucy. "Miss Lucy gave Ines a room and work she could do."

"How did you find out her name was Ines if she couldn't talk?"

"Why, girl, Alejandro used to work right here! He drove for Miss Lucy and did odd jobs before Ruben came. Ines' husband was a truly a fine man. And so good looking! He used to sit in this room at this very table and tell me how he come to pursue Ines and persuade her to marry him. They lived down the valley near Tulare Lake on an old Spaniard's ranch.

"Miss Lucy raised all holy Ned with the sheriff. She wanted him to arrest the men who hung Alejandro. But all the witnesses took off and there was no proof. So the fool sheriff said."

"That gang knew better than to ever step foot in Miss Lucy's Establishment again. She'd do 'em in fast. Sheriff would find no witnesses around here either."

Cook was a very large woman. She could lift heavy pots of boiling broth from a burner on the huge wood stove to the sink with no effort at all. She turned her head to look at Napas, raised an eyebrow and shook the wooden spoon in her hand at the girl. "You pay attention to this story, my girl. Alejandro chose his wife because she was tidy and quiet. He had a wit though, and he wasn't so quiet. He got hisself hung from an oak tree and it was all because he talked out to the wrong person. There is a lesson here for you to take note, girl."

Irina was compelled to defend Napas from Cook's implication. "Napas not talking out. My Indian is ver quviet. Never is talk out. Leetle girl is more quviet even to ask quvestion."

"I know, Rinka. I know. I'm just reminding this gal of yours she better *stay* quiet if she knows what's good for her. People like to dump their troubles on somebody else. That brown skin makes her an easy target."

From then on, Napas understood more. She liked Cook better for having told the story.

Chapter Twenty-nine
~ In Angel's Camp ~

Tom had always been better with horse and gun than with paper and pen. Mason and Richard understood. But Tom's reluctance had to do with giving time to sit down and write, and nothing to do with a lack of fluency, more a lack of inclination. He had been Reverend Taylor's student, and Mason and Richard smiled to see how much of the reverend's style Tom had retained from his seven years of schooling in Crane Valley. But it was left to Wiley to give them most of the news that came.

...The California 100 has as many foreign born as it does true Americans. When the gold began to show thin in the Sierra, I think half the miners in our creeks with their odd pronunciations of English must have joined the army.

Tom, Ples and I have bunked down with Russians, Germans, Swedes and Frenchmen, as often as our own kind. They greet each other with such a profusion of words and syllables in their native tongues, that it seems the California Hundred has entered the conflict as a polyglot force worthy of an origin in Babel.

As much as I want to be raised to the rank of sergeant, it doesn't seem likely that I will be. Our sergeants are all Englishmen. I know you boys will find this surprising. However, these English-men are warriors, trained in Afghanistan and the Crimea. I admit that they are fine men and keep us at our drills. When we succeed in driving Mosby's Confederacy up the valley, it will be with the help of seasoned soldiers....

The words from Wiley came in a letter received in April from Gloucester Point, Virginia, where Company A was posted to protect Washington D.C.

It was hard for the brothers in Angel's Camp to refrain from talking of their soldier brothers' adventures, and racing for newspapers with bulletins about the war. But fear of their father's vindictive rage gave them concern for the Harrington family and kept them silent. They behaved as though they were as orphaned of their brothers as they were of their mother. They didn't even speak with Ada, who would have been relieved to know that Wiley and Tom were well.

Neither in their home nor in the office, did words pass between the brothers that could be overheard. Their talk was confined to walks home from the office in the evening, or in visits to the Harrington household. There, they never spoke of their brothers in the presence of the couple's family. Only Edward Harrington would be party to any conversations of Wiley or the war.

Carrie Harrington felt great sympathy for the two boys. She urged Edward to bring the boys home from the office often, and gradually they were eating at the Harrington house two or three times a week if Frederick were away. By the nature of his business, this was often.

Ada didn't complain that they were so often gone. She was busy maintaining the large house Frederick had purchased up a steep hill about a half-mile out of Angel's Camp. She noted that less of her time needed to be spent in the kitchen, and all she asked was that the boys let her know she need not prepare their supper.

The new house had two rooms in a wing off the kitchen for Ada, nicer quarters than she had ever known. She had a staff of day maids to boss around, old Frank and two other yardmen to tote and fetch for her. Frederick seldom took more than breakfast and a small supper at home. Her life was easier in Angel's Camp than it had ever been.

Mr. McCreary released Frank from any duties at the livery, as soon as the McCreary's new home, called *"the mansion"* by envious townspeople. Frank was invited to leave the livery bunkhouse and live in airy quarters above the stable at the grand new manse. He only had responsibility for the family's riding horses, and a half-time groom was hired to help him with them. Many days of the week, when Frederick was traveling, Ada needed only dinner and supper for Frank and herself. The housekeeper understood the attraction of the Harrington household for the boys. It was a busy home with children's noise and a loving mother.

Mr. McCreary hardly noticed that his sons had for all purposes moved out of the mansion, and had no objection to familiarity between his bookkeeper's family and his own. As long as his sons were learning as much of his company's management as he desired, he had no concerns for them.

Of the two young McCrearys left in Angel's Camp, Richard was the better letter writer, careful to return letters to his brothers. To him, fell the job of correspondent. Richard, always practical-minded and thinking ahead, anticipated that under the duress of warfare, his soldier brothers might be billeted separately and unable to share the news of the California branch of the McCreary family he was writing. He wrote letters to Corporal Wiley McCreary and Private Tom McCreary and mailed them in separate envelopes though often they received the same letter, re-copied.

It pleased both Wiley and Tom, far across a continent, to hear their name at mail call, and each have a letter to open and savor. And after Tom was moved to sharpshooter and scouting detail, and Wiley sent to be the aide to the company commander, the brothers saw less of each other. Though they and their friend Ples continued to seek each other out whenever there was a brief furlough or recreation time. Wherever there was music in camp, Ples Landers could be found.

Frederick subscribed to the Sacramento and Stockton newspapers at the beginning of 1864. This had a benefit for Richard and Mason. The newspapers came to the McCreary Hauling office, not the mansion. Frederick ordered the clerk to go through them carefully for any news that might pertain to the freight business. The McCreary sons were able then to read the news and follow the Union victories with quiet triumph. The news from the front was always weeks late, but compensated for the letters that came less frequently as the war waged with more ferocity.

Richard and Mason followed the movements of the cavalry under General Sheridan with care, knowing that is where their brothers and Ples Landers were fighting. The letters became less frequent once Sheridan moved Company A into the Shenandoah Valley. One letter was particularly poignant. On February 22, 1864, on a piece of good paper, Wiley penned:

...Tom and Ples were involved in a skirmish that turned very grave today. I write to tell you what you surely already will know from news telegrams to California - long before my letter will reach you.

Captain J. Sewall Reed has died in battle.

I was elsewhere in the fight, but our friends who were in position near the Captain at Dranesville, told us of his death. Tom's fine shooting that day credited our army. Were it not for our brother, many more of our company would have been sacrificed for victory.

But, brothers, I have not heard Ples' fiddle come sweetly through the tents this night, or been able to obtain word of him. I worry to have heard no word of him and pray God he survived.

We are contributing what money we have in order that the Captain's body will be shipped to his family's home in Dorchester, Massachusetts for burial with military honor, not committed to the ground here in this unfamiliar place. But we wish it were to go back to California. In our own state the captain is indeed a hero of the first order. I again confess my concern for Ples. My fear for him overshadows my grief at losing our good captain...

Another letter followed in the next week. Pleasant Richard Landers had been taken prisoner during the fighting at Dranesville. The men captured in battle were thought to have been marched clear away to Camp Sumpter, in Andersonville, Georgia.

... Keep your prayers said, brothers, that God not forget our friend. Tom has taken his fiddle and I have his mother's Bible for safekeeping. We will hold them cushioned in our bedrolls until we are reunited with our friend again. They, his horse, and rifle were all that Ples brought with him when he and Tom left Crane Valley.

We have heard that Camp Sumpter is a horrible place where three die for every man who lives, but we trust we will one day be able to return these two treasures to our friend...

In an attempt to cheer their brothers during the war, Richard kept writing letters though the spring and summer months though fewer letters came for them from Wiley or Tom.

In July, the California men became part of Sheridan's Army of the Shenandoah and sent to rout Jubal Early and his Rebels. The Union army had orders to put to waste the entire valley if necessary. If Jubal Early's treacherous army could not be destroyed in battle, it could be destroyed by starvation. By this time, it was known even in Angel's Camp, that while the great breadbasket of the western states of Illinois, Ohio and Indiana were sending bread to the Union encampments, cotton plantations in the south produced little that was edible. Grant had ordered nothing left in the Shenandoah that could aid the Rebels. Sheridan's army would execute the order.

From then through August Company A was continually on the move and in constant battle or putting fields and crops to the torch. A very short letter, so short its envelope had no weight, came from Tom.

...Sheridan has us laying waste to this entire valley and I feel like a devil when I set fire to a crop awaiting harvest. War is such horror whether one is on the side of good or evil. Please continue to write us. The letters you send, telling us of your life in Angel's Camp and the good Harrington family, bring us all the pleasure there is in our lives....

In a returning letter from Angel's Camp to Virginia, Richard, attempting humor, scribed:

...Our baby brother, Mason, is a student to challenge Wiley's record. His class is assigned to a schoolmaster now, rather than the schoolmarm of last year.

It takes a man with a strong grip to manage the ruffians that come from the miners' camps. They brawl and curse like their fathers, and the girls are not much better. Mason as likely could be in the Shenandoah with you two as in an Angel's Camp schoolyard.

I feel the weakness that remains from our illness was a blessing to me, in that I may work here in the office at my own pace, learning new things daily. I do not have to face the barbarism of the schoolyard.

But still our young brother learns. He is in eighth grade now and is doing geometry. This week he ignored Papa's work schedule to spend his time determining the square areas of every section of the livery, office and our new house. He is not thirteen yet, but prefers to help the farrier hoof the oxen above learning to keep records from Mr. Harrington. Papa wants him to learn the office after his school day, but our brother's inclination is to choose his own work.

Looking over Richard's shoulder as he penned these words, Mason corrected him. "School isn't barbaric, Richard. It is rather enjoyable. If I tell you of the roughhouse students, it is only to entertain, not to complain. You are penning with too much operatic verve."

"Fancy words don't become you, my little brother. You have never been to an opera, and you find that schoolyard entertaining, Mason, because no one challenges you, not even the eighth graders. The big bulk of you *is* your protection. But if I were there, those ruffians would sense my weakness and I'd be bullied mercilessly."

"But not if I were there beside you," Mason grinned.

>>>O<<<

Chapter Thirty
~ The Shenandoah Valley ~

Wiley wrote in September, that both he and Tom gained a great honor of placement in Sheridan's Reserve Brigade of Cavalry. But their concern for Ples sharpened.

> *...We have been issued excellent new rifles, Spencer Repeating Carbines. They are very much an improvement. But we have had no word of the captured men of our company. Tom and I hear of the piteous condition of prisoners of war and can only pray that Ples remains brave until this is over....*

Wiley's letter brought Mason, Frederick, and the Harringtons worry. Ples' capture put the dangers of war into clearer imagery of the peril Wiley and Tom, and all the other California boys, were facing daily. The newspapers had revealed the horrors of prison camps, and The Harringtons added Ples Landers' name to their daily prayers knowing he faced as much danger as any battle could threaten.

In early November, on a sunny afternoon, Frederick sat in the office making a play of checking through the old records of the company. A letter came for him. Clerk had gone to the post office, and one letter, scuffed in the post, seemed to be personal, not a business letter. The young man placed it on the top of the other mail and returned to his own stool behind the counter where he was tediously hand-copying yesterday's ledger.

Two men, intent on their own work, hadn't looked up. Richard and Mr. Harrington kept to their work, eyes down, across from each other at the bookkeeper's desk impervious to distraction, until a crashing noise brought their heads up from their work. Frederick had raised forward from his chair, knocking his desktop awry. An inkwell, books, and lantern were on the floor and his booming voice, raw and enraged, shouted out. "I'll not have it! By God, I'll not have it."

The men working in the office, startled at the outburst, were fixed in place at their work desks waiting for him to say more. Frederick peered around, his eyes finally stopping to fix on Richard. "The devil has found me. Oh, Jesus God! The devil has found me!"

"Papa!" Richard exclaimed, shocked to stone, wanting to go to his father, but unable to leave his stool or make any other move.

The intensity of his father's violent emotion washed around the room like the waves of a typhoon, drenching him, clerk and Harrington in a wash of cursing anger. And then the cursing and rage subsided. Frederick crumpled, his voice trembling as he wailed, "I've sent pounds in gold to prove my allegiance. Gold trickling out of my California! Gold I've earned and could have spent elsewhere. All it has done is buy my own and best beloved son's death!"

He slumped back down in his chair, and looked around the room, reaching up to whatever god might exist in the ceiling of the room.

"Oh, Wiley, Wiley. How did you come to be there in that cursed place? How did you come to be killed so far from me? I damn the battle. I damn every living thing there to hell. I damn every man who held a gun or manned a cannon to kill you."

The man dropped his arms to his desk and burrowed his head into them, his bombastic eloquence completed, he shamelessly wept. The letter brought by messenger, elbowed aside on the desk, spun down to the floor. Harrington recovered faster than Richard or the clerk. He moved to McCreary to put his hand on the man's back, in a gesture he knew would bring no comfort, but nevertheless needed to be made.

While clerk sat still motionless, Richard ran to pick up the letter and rapidly scan it. Then he went to the door, turning back saying, "I have to go to the school, Papa. I have to go to my brother."

His father neither listened nor cared.

The boy was out the door and running up street after street until he came to stand sweating and breathless at the door of Mason's classroom. He threw it open and stood panting in the doorway trying to catch his breath.

Mason was out of his desk and on his feet in less than a second. No one questioned him. Even the teacher could understand the urgency of Richard's need. Mason reached for his book-bag, came quickly down the aisle of desks and went to his brother. As soon as the schoolroom door closed behind them, Mason begged, "What's wrong? Is it Papa? Has there been an accident? Tell me."

A last momentum carried Richard on his feet to the edge of the schoolyard where he slumped to the ground beneath a tree and sat catching his breath.

When he could again talk, he said, "Papa got a letter from Tom. Wiley's dead."

After the shock, and his breath returned, Mason asked, "What happened? Was Wiley shot?"

"Yes. In battle at Cedar Creek. The letter was dated

October 20. Wiley's dead, and Papa's destroyed. Mr. Harrington is helping him." Richard had breath for no more. He slipped down until he was lying in the dirt of the schoolyard.

Mason appraised his brother's situation at hand, not heeding shock or sentiment. One brother might be dead, but, Richard, the brother on the ground in front of him was shaking and his lips were blue. "Stay here and don't move," the younger boy commanded. "I'll be right back."

Mason raced for Carrie Harrington. She would help him. And help she quickly gave the boys. Carrie was a tall and sturdy woman. She took the wheelbarrow from their shed and between the two of them she and Mason ported Richard back to the Harrington house and eased him onto the sofa. "One of us needs to go for the doctor," she said. She tucked a pillow beneath the boy's head as she talked. "If you aren't too worn yourself, Mason, you should go. Insist that he comes back with you. Tell him it is Frederick McCreary's boy who needs him."

"I'll go."

"Do you know where his office is?"

"Yes."

"Go."

While Mason went for the doctor, Carrie Harrington went to the kitchen and mixed sugar and a sprinkle of salt into a cup of water and took it back to Richard. He turned away, but she'd raised six children of her own and was very insistent that the lad do as she told him. He downed half the glass and let his head drop back.

"I'm all right," Richard said. "I get tired easily, that's all. I had to get Mason. I had to tell him our brother died."

214

"Your brother?"

"Wiley, He's dead in Virginia." His voice came out only in short sentences, but his normal pale color was coming back, the blue around his lips turning pink again, his skin not so moist and deadly white.

"How do you know? No letters from your brothers have come to the house in two months. Edward would have known if there had been a letter." The woman, strong in times of stress, was holding back tears for young Wiley.

"Tom sent a letter directly to Papa. It came to the office. He is destroyed. Our father is destroyed."

Dr. Grainger arrived and took Richard's pulse and measured the depth and frequency of the boy's breathing. He asked questions, and when he learned that the boy had been very ill with scarlet fever a few years earlier, he said nothing but frowned.

Opening his bag he took out his stethoscope and listened to Richard's chest, front and back. When he was finished and folding the instrument to put it back in its bag, Carrie Harrington couldn't help but ask, "Is that a good tool, Doctor? It has but one bell?"

"It is superior to the one you've seen me use when your children were young, madam. This Cammann is the newest and best on the market. I appreciate that you have always been a fond mother. You've also been a tad overly fond of questioning your doctor."

Dr. Grainger put his arm around Carrie with the simple and genuine affection of long time acquaintance. "The boy will be all right for now, but he mustn't exert. His heart is weak; his pulse excited.I advise he stay here for at least a day or two."

They chatted for a few moments about the grown Harrington children, and Carrie bragged that she had grandchildren now, but complained that the older Harrington children had moved far away. Howard had moved to Boston and when Sally went there to visit him, she found a husband there. Small talk quickly completed, Carrie took the doctor's attention to another matter. "Would you go to Mr. McCreary's office, Doctor. I'd like you to tell Mr. McCreary that it was you who insisted that Richard stay with us until he recovers."

"Certainly, I will," the doctor interrupted. "It was already my plan to do so."

"Mr. McCreary needs you for more than that, Doctor Grainger. His son has died in battle. Richard told me the news was harsh for the poor man, and he is in a bad state. I know how I'd be if something happened to one of mine."

The men in the office looked to Dr. Grainger for relief. During the past half-hour, they had been helpless while Frederick had gone from sobbing over his desk to standing, violently tossing furniture across the room and roaming the room and smashing everything within reach. When the doctor entered the building, Frederick had crumpled down against a wall, making himself as small as a big man can, and mumbling over and over, "I've killed my son."

The doctor knelt down beside him to rouse him. But the man continued murmuring senselessly, rocking back and forth. "Do you have brandy here?" Dr. Grainger asked.

"No sir. It's not allowed. Mr. McCreary's a temperate man."

Dr. Grainger stifled a smirk at the irony, for from many shared noontime meals in the tavern, he and other men of business in Angel's Camp knew Frederick McCreary to be a man who seldom declined to take strong drink, though usually a man of intelligence and good company. "Then open my bag and give me the small flask there," he instructed. The men in the office moved to aid Dr. Grainger, make Frederick more comfortable, and restore the office to its usual neat placements.

By evening, Dr. Grainger had gone home. Harrington called for the small carriage and he, with the clerk's help, took Frederick home where Ada and Mason tried to give him what comfort his belligerence would permit. But the man crashed into the study, pulled its drapes closed, and closed the door to them.

"Do ye think Mr. McCreary might harm hisself, Mason?" Ada whispered.

The boy could know no better than she what his father might do. But he answered. "Call Frank in to stay in the house this night, Ada. He can help you or go for the doctor if Papa shows troublesome again. I'll be with Richard at the Harrington house should you need my help. But I'll arrange nurses to watch so you get rest."

>>>O<<<

Part Four: At War's End

~~<<<O>>>~~

Chapter Thirty-one
~ At War's End ~

There were no more letters until after the news reached California and had headlined all of its newspapers that the war was over. Lee had surrendered his sword at Appomattox Court House in April.

Frederick didn't recover from Wiley's death. He sat as a dullard at his desk doing little work during the months after the news reached him that Wiley had been killed in the Battle of Cedar Creek. Richard and Harrington were jointly making the decisions for McCreary Hauling. If they asked Frederick to sign his name to a check or a contract, he did so. But he would have signed anything they asked. He no longer took interest. Harrington could make any office decisions, Henry Stegler could manage the Stockton warehouses, but someone was needed to ride circuit and oversee the freight stations, the work Frederick had heretofore done himself.

By the time the war had ended, Mason had left school and joined Henry and Lalo Cabrera. Working mainly out of the Stockton office, the three were managing the operations of the company, riding to oversee stations and authorize stock purchases and necessary repairs.

When in Angel's Camp, Mason aided Mr. Harrington and fifteen year old Richard McCreary, as they both learned how the business operated. Frederick spent more and more leisure visiting the businesses of his fellow businessmen. They were few, just Bulleton, the lawyer, and Trumble, who had the hardware store. He spent a great deal of time with old men. Trumble's father-in-law was one. Another was Dr. Grainger's father. Those men had retired from business life, and though there was no lodge in Angel's Camp, the men were all were Masons and lodge brothers. They had time to while away afternoons in the Buckhorn Tavern. Frederick found the company of old men soothing.

A new bookkeeper, a trustworthy and competent uncle of Carrie Harrington's who still had many good years of employment ahead of him, was sent a ticket and brought out from Boston by stage. The new man, Harvey Yates, took his place at the bookkeeper's desk and released Edward for work of greater responsibility. Two new desks were purchased and set adjacent to Frederick McCreary's own.

Frederick came to the office a few hours each morning, then ate his noon dinner at the tavern with his cronies, and returned home to the solicitude of the housekeeper. Ada arranged that his days were easy and comfortable. The boys worried that their father had found too much relief in Dr. Grainger's prescribed medication, for a messenger boy brought a new bottle of brandy to the large McCreary mansion daily, and one was kept in a cabinet in the office also.

A letter from Tom, in his tiny script, arrived in early August.

21 July 1865

Dear Father and brothers,

I hope this note finds you well. I have been mustered out from my company here at Camp Meigs here in Massachusetts. I have a little money, as we were given an amount for transport home. However, I must find Ples. I have heard that many of the prisoners are in hospitals near Washington. I have kept his fiddle and his Bible safe throughout the conflict with help from his fellows in the company band and our Captain. I feel that, and pray that, Ples is alive.

I will write you from Washington. I was allowed to keep the fine rifle the army gave me, but my black gelding would have had greater value for me. As it is, I must travel by stage, steamer or railroad, like a city man.

With great regard, your son and brother,

Tom McCreary

After Richard read the letter and shared it with Harrington, he carried it to the house to read it to his father and assure him that Tom at least had survived the war. Frederick snatched the letter out of his hand and tore it apart, shouting drunkenly, "What do I care for some fool of a neighbor boy. Landers' son ought be dead. I wish him dead and damned. Oh, I've killed my Wiley!"

The man's eyes were bloodshot and full of bitterness and rage. He turned his back to Richard and pounded on the wall as though he wanted to punch it through. Then he twisted his massive body around to shout at his son, "You can't bring me news that Wiley is alive, so why do you bring me news of anyone else!"

"I was bringing you news that proved your son Tom survived the war, Papa," Richard said.

His father was no longer listening.

Ada, hearing the outburst and the noise, ran through the hall from the kitchen to stand gaping in the doorway. Richard saw her there. His brother's long awaited letter in was in pieces on the carpet in the front parlor of the fine house his father had built. He came to a judgment on the deterioration in the man, his disheveled condition, and the reek of alcohol, and decided to leave his father to the more than able ministrations of the housekeeper.

Richard picked up the torn letter and said, "He is your job, Ada. Take care of him. If he is too difficult, send word and I will hire nurses to help you." And Richard left his father's house.

Louisa, one of two daughters still young and living at home with Edward and Carrie Harrington, opened the door to Richard's knock. She was shocked at the pallor on his face and the desperation in his manner. She led him into the house and to a soft chair. When he was settled, she went for her mother and Carrie swiftly brought a clean towel to wipe the boy's face. Louisa made a fresh pot of tea and found biscuits to put on a tray.

She was more than willing to sit with Richard, and when he was rested and his color returned, she lifted the flowered teapot and tipped milk into it and poured the steaming brew. He sipped slowly and thoughtfully. "I should like to talk to your mother, you, and your sister too," he said.

Louisa promptly brought Carrie and Lucinda, who had been occupied with meal preparation, into the room.

"Need we sit down? Will this take long, Richard?"

"No, Mrs. Harrington. It will just take a moment for me to ask what I have to ask, but it may take some days for you to find the answer."

"Then don't hesitate to ask your question. You know you and your brother can ask anything of me and mine. We are your friends, dear boy."

"I want to come and live here with you. I would be no trouble. When my brother is here in Angel's Camp, I'd like him to stay here also. Our home is no longer a welcoming place for us.

"Don't feel compelled to take us in. We would be made comfortable at the boarding house. Martha knows us from our stay when we first arrived. But if you would have us, we would stay here with your family."

The gentle smiles on the three women's faces gave him reassurance of their feelings. "Oh, please, Mama." Louisa said. "Lucinda, you wouldn't mind at all, would you?"

Carrie Harrington smiled her response, but said, "I'll need to talk to your father. But the rooms that Howard, Sally, and my dear father used are empty now, only used for sewing materials and storage better kept in the attic. There is certainly space for Richard and Mason."

She looked tenderly at Richard and said, "My dear boy, you and your brother have taken supper at our table more nights than not. I'm very certain Edward will welcome you as my daughters and I do."

Louisa winked at Richard. He, as well as she, knew Edward would agree.

Regretfully, because thoughts of his mother, Crane Valley, and 'what might have been' also stole into his mind, he knew his father in his preoccupation with himself would scarcely notice Richard or Mason's absence from the mansion.

Within the month, it was apparent to all that Frederick no longer came to the office regularly and when he did he made little sense. It also became apparent that legal matters needed to be settled pertaining to

McCreary Hauling and the guardianship of its owner's minor children. Mr. Harrington called Dr. Grainger and the doctor arranged to pay a vagrant to shadow Frederick and report on all he observed, since the McCreary would not allow himself to be examined. The doctor could come to no adequate diagnosis. He believed Mr. McCreary was suffering some catastrophic incapacity brought on by the death of his son, but could not rule out a tumor of the brain or diseases known to cause dementia. He advised that two nurses be hired to alternately assist Mrs. Cotter in the care of Mr. McCreary and to administer laudanum, to be given every three hours if the man seemed anxious. Ada was to keep the house free of any alcoholic beverages. A man was hired to accompany Frederick should he want to leave the house. Frederick responded to treatment, and the laudanum calmed his need for brandy. Ada didn't approve, but did as the doctor asked.

Gradually, Frederick became steadier. But from that time on, he took little interest in either the business or the welfare of his sons. Dr. Grainger and James Buellton, Esq. met on two consecutive afternoons. They were both lodge brothers of Frederick's, and his friends. After careful discussion the men made the necessary joint recommendation before a judge at the Calaveras County Court House.

Their recommendation was that Mr. Edward Harrington be appointed guardian for the minor children of Frederick McCreary and executor of Mr. McCreary's business affairs until such time as Mr. McCreary prove himself to be in sufficient condition to again resume his parental and business duties. A provision was set that at the return to California of Thomas McCreary, these accommodations for the welfare of the family's minor children would be altered. A formal call was made to apprise Frederick of the ruling by the court. The man looked up and said, "Do what you want," and slipped back into a deep and noisy sleep in his chair, Nurse Keller hovering over him.

Many months later, Mr. Harrington received an unusually long letter from Tom to share with Richard and Mason.

25 June, 1866

Mr. Harrington and my dear brothers,

I am now in Washington after an easy trip. I have taken lodgings here and will be boarding here for some time. I've written to you, Mr. Harrington, for I do not know what kind of temper my father is in, if he will even now allow letters to pass between my brothers and me. Wiley trusted you and therefore I also trust you.

My brothers, I have found Ples. He was sent, by grace of God, not to Camp Sumpter, but rather to a prison camp in North Carolina. During an escape attempt, he was badly injured. After release, he was carried on one of the Flag of Truce boats to a Union hospital near Washington. His leg, which had broken in more than one bone, mended poorly. Doctors in an army hospital have tried to re-set it, but as of now he is sorely crippled.

You will understand that our reunion was happy. Ples was overcome with joy at owning his possessions again, but sadly aggrieved at the loss of our brother Wiley. The fiddle was in good condition, for all the war and devastation that surrounded it these past years. With new strings and tuning, it plays as well as ever, and Ples played a concert in his ward of our childhood hymns ~ to Wiley's memory. I have encouraged him to write to his father. If Mr. Landers responds, and will send him money, we will both return to California. I trust our old neighbor will do so, in our mother's remembrance. I remember him as generous in spirit.

As anxious as I am to be reunited with you both, my plan is to accompany Ples to Crane Valley, and then find work. When I have the money, I will come to Angel's Camp. I know you are surprised to receive such a long letter from your brother who has so seldom put pen to paper, but I am happy for the first time in many long months to have found our friend, and have found a job as a guard at a bank in Washington, near to Ples.

I will write again, should our situation change.

Your fond brother, Tom

18 Penwick Alley, 600 New Hampshire Ave, NW

Foggy Bottom, Washington D.C.

Mr. Harrington and Richard had already arranged that adequate funds be sent to Washington to insure that both Tom and Ples Landers could return to California as soon as possible.

Three days after the receipt of Tom's long and triumphant letter, Carrie Harrington held a festive supper to celebrate the fact that Tom had survived the war in good health, and his friend Ples Landers had been found. She invited the clerk, her uncle the new bookkeeper, all the men from the livery, and arranged that both nurses be on duty at the McCreary mansion so that Ada Cotter and Frank Sullivan could attend.

Chapter Thirty-two
~ The Return Delayed ~

It would be three years before Tom and Ples were free from Washington and able to travel back to California. It took time for Aaron Landers and McCreary Hauling to arrange that money be transferred securely to the young men. Booking passage, amid so many thousands of the mustered out also trying to get back to Illinois, Ohio, Indiana and other western states, had proved difficult. Thousands of soldiers had been mustered out. For long months the rail stations and stage depots were jammed.

The two men were anxious to leave Washington. Tom wanted to return to California and search for MeMe. Ples was as concerned for the girl's welfare as her brother. She had often been the subject of their campfire conversations in the Shenandoah. But another loyalty trapped Tom. He had pledged not to leave Washington until Ples impaired and alone in the eastern city. He'd wait until Ples could travel with him.

Railway tickets were hard to come by. The stages provided a harsh and painful ride. Frequent stops during the day, to change out horses and allow passengers respite, were especially difficult for a person without full use of his legs. Traveling by horse would have been just as difficult. Work was progressing on a grand railroad scheme to join the Atlantic and Pacific coast. The Central Pacific and Union Pacific railroads had hired droves of the young men's fellow former soldiers and Chinese laborers to work laying rail across the continent. But Tom had investigated, but found that it might be well into another decade before the grand railroad was complete and an ordinary civilian could ride in style from Washington D.C. to Sacramento.

Ples had been admitted to a soldier's hostel for recuperation where he and other handicapped musician veterans were given occupation by the formation of a Grand Orchestra of the Valiant Union. An ambulance wagon, provided by many donations from wealthy, patriotic Washingtonians, transported the members to rehearsal and performance halls. Tom kept his lodging and his job at the bank, and within a year, he was promoted to sergeant of the guard and given a boost in pay.

Early in 1867, just when the men had decided to purchase tickets of passage by railroad to Dodge, Kansas, and go from there to Southern California by stage on the southern route, through the territories, an ulcer broke out on Ples' leg. It refused to heal, became badly infected, and he returned to the hospital. It was eventually determined that a piece of bone deep in his thigh was trying to surface. The bone fragment needed removal. Still thin and very weak from his long internment in the Confederate prison camp, the surgery was deferred until nurses could encourage him to eat well and he had regained strength.

After the surgery, the young veteran's healing was slow to begin and slow to progress. Tom could not leave Ples during this crisis. He continued to wait in Washington until his friend was able to travel, though his thoughts were with his brothers, and MeMe. He sent a letter to Richard and Mason explaining his decision to continue to wait until Ples could travel with him.

My Dear Brothers,

I much appreciate the letters that you write me, and apologize that I do not return a letter of my own for each one of yours. If our brother Wiley were still here with me, you'd be deluged in paper for his telling of the wonders of the city. Thank you for giving me news of Papa. I wish that I could help you. I think you good, caring sons to visit him and make sure he is not left alone. I have seen much such vile cruelty in this war. I was rash to judge him so harshly.

Ples suffered a setback with infection. The hospital where our friend is now awaiting surgery is far from my lodging. I visit only on Sundays, and it takes much of my pay to ride the stage to the Capitol, then the streetcar, then another stage to reach St. Elizabeth's, the name folks here use for the hospital, though its official name is different. It is a huge facility built to house the insane, but much of it now used for soldiers such as our friend. But it is at the opposite end diagonally across the city from Foggy Bottom. Our friend is of good cheer, and for not being able to stand, he is well.

He has organized his own ward band. You would be touched with tender sentiment to see a once brave soldier, who now has just one arm, beating a drum and keeping time, while another soldier with bandages over his eyes plays a flute, and our Ples sits in his wheeled chair fiddling for all his worth. It is merry there on a Sunday afternoon. I've invited two sisters, who live in my boarding house, to go with me and hear his band. They are jolly girls, hard-working and on their own since the death of their parents and the loss of their brothers in the war.

I do not think the hospital will be too dismal a prospect for them, for the ward's men are cheery, and on the grounds of the hospital are housed many foreign animals from Africa and even India. If the ward sister will allow, we will push Ples' chair about the grounds that he might see the elephant and two magnificent tigers we've read are there. The address, should you wish to write Ples directly, to cheer him further, is ~

Pleasant R. Landers , 2nd Massachusetts,
% St. Elizabeth' Soldiers Hospital, G.H. I.
1100 Alabama, Avenue, SE, Washington D.C.

Your fond brother,

Tom

When Richard, late that evening, read aloud the letter from Tom, even Edward Harrington had to wipe his eyes. "At last I know the character of the only one of the McCreary boys I've never met.

"Tom is as stalwart, true and loyal as the rest of you young men, and has as good a nature," Carrie cried out.

Louisa announced, "I shall begin knitting socks for every man on the ward this night."

"And, sister for every pair you knit, I shall knit a muffler against the winter cold. How many soldiers are in the ward? Did Tom say?" Lucinda asked.

Neither Mason nor Richard could answer her. Lucinda looked primly at them and said, "Then you must promptly write your brother and ask him!"

>>>O<<<

Chapter Thirty-three
~ In A Cage ~

The girl named Napas had no way of knowing what her brothers had suffered. She didn't know that Richard and Mason lived in the town of Angel's Camp, miles north of Bootjack, or that Tom and Wiley were on the far other side of the continent.

No one talked of war at Miss Lucy's. Cook and Irina were interested in the here and now, not what was happening across the continent. Ines didn't talk at all. If Napas had seen a newspaper, she wouldn't have been able to read it. Her life was measured in grief for the family she'd lost, and in tallying her daily tasks completed. But she didn't mind the sameness of her days. Work kept her thoughts from dwelling on Crane Valley.

The year after the war ended in the outside world, in Bootjack, an event occurred to shake Miss Lucy's establishment out of its routine. Irina ran away with Horace. Summer was just over and the nights starting to get cool. Napas felt the loss of the cheerfully insolent Russian woman as she would physical pain. This loss brought back a sharp awareness of her old life and the other losses she had suffered.

Napas' memories seemed sharp only in dreams. But she had not forgotten. There was a clump of lupine dying down in one of the yards near the laundry, for summer was over. Every spring when the lupine had bloomed she put a pebble into the chamois bag her grandfather had given her.

The bag had ten pebbles. In spring she'd watched for

the blue wildflower to bloom again. She tried to remember the names of the first six pebbles. Waking one morning after Irina was gone, she knew the words Ootie had once taught her. They came back in a dream. *Ye-et*-one, *po-noy*-two, *so-pin*-three, *ha-pa-nay*-four, *yit-sil*-five, *ka-pi-li*-six, she made the words into a song to sing to herself. She didn't know seven, eight, nine, ten, or eleven. She'd be eleven the next spring but she didn't know how to say that number in her own true language.

Napas tried to remember the faces of the people she loved when she had been MeMe. She couldn't remember Nancy's face, or her grandfather's, or that of Mrs. Landers who read to her. She knew she'd forget Irina too. She felt she was MeMe only in her dreams. She could remember clearly the expressions on their faces; the way they stood or worked, their voices and smiles. But she saw the actual features of their faces only when she slept. She wondered if she would ever dream of Irina or Horace.

Cook had become irritable after Irina left. The position Irina and Cook took as enemies in the household was satisfying to both of them. Miss Lucy suffered the most from Irina's absence. The woman howled for days and everyone in the front of the house was afraid to make a sound. Ruben was hurt as much over Horace's defection as Cook and Miss Lucy, but hurt was a quieter emotion than suffering. He didn't snarl or howl. Back in the kitchen, Cook made the maids laugh by saying that maybe Miss Lucy was mad enough to send the U.S. Army after Horace to hang him by the neck for stealing her Russian princess. Napas didn't think it very funny because they might do it. Horace had dark skin too.

Napas was young and she recovered. And, with time, she found she missed Horace nearly as much as she did Irina. She missed his music and hoped he'd come back for his piano, until Cook told her that piano didn't belong to Horace. It belonged to Miss Lucy. Until then, Napas had imagined that she herself belonged to Irina. She hoped that when Horace came for the piano, Irina would come for her. Her spirits sank to a brooding memory of the day Irina bought her. It was in a tent, and rough men were laughing at Mr. McCreary as he went out through the tent flap, leaving her there.

All that while, she'd been wrong. She was owned by Miss Lucy, a woman who didn't like her. She didn't know what would happen to her. She thought more and more of the home she had once had. The work she did was dreary now all but for the daily trip to the Chinaman's laundry.

A family lived in a tent that they passed when she and Ines pulled the laundry cart. The family there had children, chickens and a goat. One day she found a rooster's tail feather on the road near that yard. It was brown with black at the tip. She kept it and put it in her buckskin packet. It might only have been a chicken feather, but it reminded her of The Willows. Yet, the girl liked pushing the handcart with Ines in the mornings. The air was fresh, and few people were about to heckle or tease them.

They didn't hurry but enjoyed the walk most mornings. But not long after Irina left, when they had passed the tent family but not yet to the oak tree, Ines looked startled. She seemed to be listening, but Napas knew she couldn't hear. Then the girl felt a rumble through her shoes from the earth and heard the fast clopping sounds of horses. The two of them rushed to get across the street and out of the way of whatever was coming. Twisting the cumbersome cart around, they pulled it into a narrow alleyway between a stable and a tent store and huddled there behind it.

Ines was shaking. When Napas looked toward the woman, she had tears streaming down her face. And Napas realized that they were very near the corner with the oak tree. It seemed only seconds had passed when the vibrations from the ground grew stronger, the noise louder. Soldiers came racing fast, their horses' hooves throwing up dirt and gravel.

Napas, so suddenly frightened, couldn't catch her breath. Miners had killed her mother and she had heard many stories of how soldiers killed Indians from Cook and Irina. Irina said they did worse to Indian women than kill them. Napas didn't know what could be worse than being killed. She feared she and Ines would die that day. But, as fast as the troop came, they were gone. The quiet of the morning returned. Ines used her striped petticoat to wipe her face of tears and dust, and the two dragged the cart out of between the buildings and out into the street to continue on to the Chinaman's laundry.

The Chinaman's face was stern. He shook his finger at Ines and Napas. "Be wery clalfo. A'my go kill Indians in mountain ri' now." He reached behind the counter and pulled out two candies and gave one to Ines and one to Napas. "Be wery wery clalfo."

The man, who had seldom spoken to them before, had a thoughtful look on his face. He wanted to help them. "A'my alus like China pepo. China pepo wok for a'my in keechen an laun'ry an rayroad. 'Cept you not China pepo. A'my not like In dan pepo. You be clalfo. If soldiers come, you hide hea. Not in sleet. Safe hea. Maybe soldiers think you China peopo."

The candy was a treat. Napas thought Inez also understood the Chinaman wanted to protect them.

Still, the girl grew twitchy and watchful when she left Miss Lucy's from that day. She only felt safe on Sundays when she and Ines didn't have to leave their sewing to pull the cart. Even then, she worried what kind of dangers might come the next week. Ines looked like an Indian. Napas knew she was also afraid. They no longer loitered at the oak tree.

Soldiers were frequently in town and often rowdy. If they didn't deliberately kill her, Napas was afraid she and Ines would be trampled accidentally as the seamstress's daughter had been. She pondered how Inez couldn't hear, but the ground told her that the soldiers were coming before Napas heard them. She tried to feel danger through her feet as Ines had done. She found she could feel many things. If Cook dropped a pot in the kitchen, she could feel it vibrate in the floor of the sewing room as well as hear its boom. She began to pay attention to more senses than just eyes and ears.

The house was sadder without Irina and Horace. The women who worked in Miss Lucy's establishment crabbed and complained, and demanded that all their small clothes have lace edgings, so Napas and Irina felt backaches from sitting long in the workroom tatting and crocheting.

A fiddler and different piano player came in to make music in the evening, and music sang out across the yard to the small room where Napas and Ines spent their nights. But the music wasn't like it had been. This fiddle was screechy and raw, the piano harsh. Napas liked the jingley-jangly music, but it wasn't the same as Horace's piano music. She heard notes wrongly hit and seldom did the musicians play tunes that reminded her of Nancy's hymns or Ples's fiddle melodies that made her want to sing.

She had a dream of sweet fiddle music that came and went, repeating itself through the night. She welcomed that dream. Horace's piano music had been more like the music that came in her dream than the music that the fiddler and piano player were making now. She began to remember Ples Landers and think about him as often as she thought of her brothers. She wished if she couldn't be there, they could be here; she wished Ples were the one who was making the music at Miss Lucy's.

Without Irina to run things for her, Miss Lucy, who had never been up and around early in the day, was marching through the house picking at cook and frowning at the maids. Ines and Napas made themselves smaller and quieter, though they both were small and quiet already. But sometimes Miss Lucy came into the workroom where they sewed to shriek at them. Then Napas envied Ines's deafness. One other thing that had changed was odd but it was good. Ever since the day the soldiers had ridden wild through town, the Chinaman bowed to Ines and Napas when he saw them come into the laundry. His solemn face would almost smile, and to Napas it seemed that he felt a friendship with the two of them.

At Christmas that year, the Chinaman came and left pretty red streamers and cones of strange candy for Ines and Napas. Cook joked at his accent and began calling Ines and her "*laun ly we men.*" Cook told her the Chinaman's name. She said maybe Hai Leong was in love with Ines. Napas thought that might be true. He smiled at both of them, but his eyes stayed on Ines longer than on her.

She recognized that he had become a better friend to both of them, in his quiet way, than any she had had since she left Crane Valley. Hai Leong wasn't as entertaining as Irina had been, but he seemed to care about her and Ines. Although he was Chinese, he rather reminded her of the man named Mr. Dickey. They both had counters to stand behind and money to count. Sometimes they were quiet, but neither ever seemed angry with anyone.

Ruben went away the day after Christmas. The women's maids whispered to Cook that Miss Lucy had fired him. Miss Lucy had often been heard raving and ranting, and she blamed Ruben for driving Horace and Irina away. Cook responded with a smirk. It was clear to anyone seeing Cook's face that she felt that it was Miss Lucy herself who had driven the pair away with her demands and complaints. Irina, Horace and now Ruben had disappeared from Napas' daily life. She felt that changes were like barrels in a wagon tumbling toward her. She grew jumpy and woke often in the night.

After Christmas, there was a great party for Miss Lucy's girls. It was a celebration of the New Year, 1866. Ines could sleep, but the wild noise all night kept Napas' eyes open. Then, on the sixth day of the New Year, a change did come. But it seemed a wicked change. It happened on Irina's Russian day of presents. Instead of a getting a new pair of boots or a shawl on that gift day, the man hired to replace Ruben came and took her from the workroom. He made her gather her belongings, put them in the old pillowcase, and he walked her down to the laundry.

Hai Leong gave Miss Lucy's new man a fat envelope. The new man went out the door, closing it without even a glance back at her. Napas, eleven-years-old and sick at heart, understood that once again, she had been sold. Why had Hai Leong, whom she thought was a friend, bought her? She liked him, but she didn't like being sold the way grain or potatoes were sold. She'd miss Ines and Cook. What kind of work would she be expected to do for the laundry? Hai Leong was busy. He left her sitting on the bench and had said nothing to her.

A wagon pulled up at the back door of the laundry that afternoon. The wagon had a cage in its bed, and a single horse was drawing it. A man, who looked a little like the Chinaman but younger and not as tall, got down and came into the room where the Chinaman sat waiting with Napas. The man took her to the wagon. He tossed the pillowslip with the few things she owned casually through the open door of the cage and indicated she should climb into it. The cage smelled like sheep. She put her hand down and crushed a sheep pellet. There was hay in one corner, and she grasped a handful to wipe the cage clean as best she could.

The man locked the cage. He took out a moneybag and gave it to the Hai Leong before he climbed up on the bench to gee the horses on. Hai Leong smiled and said something to her. Thinking she might not have understood, he said it again more slowly.

As well as she could understand, he'd said, "Be lucky girl. Go happy laundly. No more stay in bad whoe house." She didn't know what was bad about a whole house. But he hadn't explained, and he'd left before she could think to ask.

The wind came through the slats of the cage. The driver of the wagon stopped the horses. He gave her a blanket through the slats of the cage. It was dark out and cold. She curled up around the old patched pillowcase that held both her clothes and the buckskin packet and covered herself with the blanket. She had no idea where she was going.

As the wagon bumped along the road in the night, she remembered the day Mr. McCreary took her away from her family and Crane Valley. Napas didn't know why Hai Leong looked so happy to send her off in a cage. She felt very unhappy.

She knew it wouldn't have been good for her at Miss Lucy's now that Irina was gone and everything changing. There were worse people in Bootjack she could have been sold to than the Chinaman and this driver who had given her a blanket. At least the Chinaman and the driver were clean and not rude. Miss Lucy's new man hadn't taken her back to the canvas saloon filled with rough men, the place where Mr. McCreary sold her and Irina bought her.

She wanted to go back to The Willows and her little room next to the kitchen. She wanted Nancy and her brothers. She began to cry. That shamed her. The boys hadn't liked crybabies. She hoped the man driving the wagon couldn't hear her sniffle. She wanted to be back there at the ranch with the boys. She wanted the swing and to see her grandfather. She wished so much that Nancy hadn't died.

Chapter Thirty-four
~ The White Dove ~

Once the man driving the cart found out she was not going to run away, he let her ride up on the wagon seat beside him. "What is your name?" he asked.

"Napas," she answered, and looked away. She hadn't said her real name for so long. She couldn't say her own name or mention Crane Valley. She wanted to say Merab McCreary.

"Is that all?" he asked. "Napas?"

She nodded, but he was looking ahead at the road and didn't see her nod. So she said, "Yes."

They stopped in some towns at places, a laundry once, a camp another time. They always where there were other Chinese people who welcomed the man and gave them both a meal and places to sleep for the night. At each stop, the Chinese people looked oddly at her, and called out to her in Chinese. When the man spoke sharply to them, they didn't bother her again. She and the driver were each served a small bowl of rice and vegetables and given little sticks to use to pull it into their mouths. The food was different from what she had known, but she was hungry and it was good.

When they were back in the cart, she asked the man what the Chinese people were saying to her. The man who drove the cart was handsome, and when he smiled his eyes seemed merry. "They say you are fat for a Chinese girl. They ask what part of China you come from."

"I'm not Chinese. I don't come from any part of China," she said. "I'm not fat either."

He laughed at her and said, "I know."

Then he said, "Why do you talk like white people when you are an Indian?"

"Why do you talk like white people when you are Chinese?"

He laughed so hard he dropped the reins, and it was the first time she felt normal again since she left Miss Lucy's house. His laugher made her bold enough to ask, "Where are you taking me?"

"You are going to White Dove Laundry in Sonora."

"What will I do there?

"You will learn to use a sewing machine and do the mending of laundry clothes that need mending."

"I'll be a seamstress."

"Yes, but that is not all for you. Hai Leong understands many things. He said were a lucky girl and surrounded by good spirits. And, he saw your sewing on clothes that came to the laundry. Good sewing. He thought it was wrong that you stay in a bad place like Miss Lucy's and he wanted his cousin to gain your good luck. Sin Shang agreed."

The man looked over at her, seeming happy to have a lucky girl riding with him. "You will work in one of his laundries and bring luck to the White Dove. You will also have a machine that sews for you. Sin Shang is going to send a man to teach you how to use it."

She thought about that as they traveled. Laundries smelled good and they were warm in the winter. It might not be so bad. "Will the other workers at the laundry be Chinese?" she asked the man that afternoon.

"No. They are white women. Some Chinese men work in the laundry but they are guards and clean and do other work. Feng Goh hires white women from the town to wash the clothes. There are not many Chinese women in America.

They rode quietly for a time, and then the man spoke. "The laundry in Sonora is very busy. You will repair clothes, not wash them. Many, many people ask to have their clothes sewn. Other work goes on there too, but it won't concern you."

"Will I live with the white women?"

"No! That would *not* be lucky. There is a special room for you at White Dove Laundry where no one will bother you. Hai Leong sent a message to Sin Shang if he buys a sewing machine and sends someone to show you how it's used, you will increase Fen Goh's income from the White Dove. That will increase Sin Shang's prosperity also." The man looked over at her and winked. "Hai Leong made Sin Shang agree to keep you safe.

"The women do not live at the White Dove. They are lazy and would teach you bad things. They only come to the laundry to work by day. You will live at the White Dove. Sin Shang wants you to stay lucky. You must not associate with laundry women. They are not lucky."

"I don't belong to Hai Leong? I saw him pay for me."

"No, you belong to Sin Shang. *He* paid for you. You'll work for Feng Goh owns the White Dove, and he will take good care of you."

"How do you speak English so well?"

"You asked me before."

"But you didn't tell me."

"I was the child of a fourth wife. I lived in a mission's school in a city called Hong Kong. There I learned to speak in English and was beaten and not given enough food. It was a bad place for boys. So, when I was old enough, I ran away. I found others who were coming to America. Sin Shang hired me over all the others because I could speak English." He looked at her with merriment and said, "You see I'm lucky too."

"And all you do is drive a cart and pick up Indians?"

"No. I am more important than that. I only came to these mountains because Hai Leong is Sin Shang's cousin. I came as a favor to Sin Shang's honored cousin. Hai Leong was flattered I came to Bootjack on his word." The man made a face of great distaste. "I don't usually have to pick up children and move them from one place to another - or drive a farm cart."

"What do you usually do?"

"I'm a most important man for Sin Shang. I am *the buyer*. I find what Sin Shang's needs and I carry his money. I keep what he buys safe."

Napas thought about the soldiers on horseback and so many rough men passing them on the road. The Buyer was just one man alone. "Can you keep me safe?" she asked as they sat on the bench of the wagon and the horse plodded along the road.

"I have this, and I can use it very quickly and very well," he bragged. He opened his jacket and showed her a gun. It was larger than the small derringer that Ruben had kept in his boot but much smaller than the rifles at The Willows.

"It is a Walker Colt," The Buyer said proudly. "Sin Shang bought it for me to protect what he buys."

Napas thought it had a very odd name for a gun. A colt was a young horse or mule. "Does Sin Shang buy valuable things?"

"Many valuable things. Jewels and silks. Remedies that come from far away. I purchase them for him."

Napas didn't she was considered a valuable thing.

In a few days they arrived in the city of Sonora. It was a real city, and as they turned onto a street from the highway, Napas looked around gawking. There were many stores and people on the street looked busy. Up on a high hill she saw a red church, its steeple catching the sunlight. She wondered if she had come to either San Francisco or Stockton, for they were the cities she had heard Irina and Cook say were beautiful. She asked The Buyer.

"No," the man said. "This is Sonora. San Francisco is a big city. Sonora is not. San Francisco has an ocean on one side and a bay on the other. Do you see boats and ships here?"

"No, but it's big."

It's not big," The Buyer said indignantly. "It is just bigger than Bootjack."

"Do you live in San Francisco?"

"Yes. Sin Shang lives there in a fine building. But Feng Goh's laundry is bigger than that small laundry Hai Leong had in your old tent city. Many Chinese who work in mountains come to the White Dove to play games, sometimes at night. You must not worry. They won't hurt you. Feng Goh will take good care of you."

He was reassuring her, so she nodded her understanding but didn't say anything.

"You, Indian girl, will bring luck to the White Dove, but you must also work hard, very hard. Chinese people work harder than American people do."

"I'm not American," she quipped, and he laughed at her again.

A long time later, Napas realized that she had enjoyed a pleasant conversation for the first time since she left Crane Valley. She liked The Buyer, and she hadn't even asked his name.

Chapter Thirty-five
~ Wearing White Clothes ~

The large laundry was a quieter place than Miss Lucy's had been for the child who once was Merab McCreary. The Buyer had warned her that there would be men and noise at night. She seldom saw the men, although her room had three windows and she could look down on the street. It was always night when they came to the White Dove. She could hear them from the other side of the wall behind her cot. The sounds rumbled through the wall, men's voices sometimes grumbling and sometimes cheering. The Chinese people, who came at night to shout and make the noises that came through the wall of her room, never knew she existed. They were never as noisy as the men who came to Miss Lucy's on Saturday night. She didn't mind the now-and-then shouts that came through the wall. She just wondered what they were doing that gave them reason to shout.

Feng Goh gave Napas a room to herself. It was a long, narrow room above the laundry's front office. The room was full of light from five windows. Three looked down on the street. Two looked across an alley and drive at the rooftops. A wall separated her room from the rest of the second floor. There was no door.

Her room was accessed by a ladder against the wall of a small alcove behind the laundry's counter. The alcove held a cloakroom and Feng Goh's small desk. The ladder led up to her room's entrance in a trap door in the ceiling. A bar on the inside of her new room prevented the door from being opened from below. When she slid the bar, she felt very safe.

She ate at a little table in a room between the office and the big washrooms of the laundry. One of the men brought her a tray of food and tea every morning and evening. They didn't eat in the middle of the day, and Cook wasn't here with the many treats that were in Miss Lucy's kitchen. She grew thinner, but felt all right. If she ate everything that the men brought her, the next day they brought her a larger portion of food. She knew she wouldn't starve. There were rules. She was not to talk to the women who came daily to work in the laundry. She was only to use one side of a small clean privy. It was far from the privy that the laundry women used.

The women had three large rooms in the lower floor for their work. They needed space for vats and buckets, lines and ironing and folding tables. She only needed space for the sewing machine with space and shelves to stack the garments needing repair and a small table and chair. She could see the women working and they could see her. She wondered if they thought she was Chinese.

One or another of the Chinese men was always unobtrusively on guard insuring that the women were working, not talking. They watched that ruffians didn't try to make off with some britches or shirts hanging on the lines to dry in the sun. They watched her too. Instead of being annoyed by the presence the men, they helped her feel safe in the White Dove Laundry.

Only once was Napas allowed to see the secret room upstairs, and then only because her sewing skill was needed. She was sent up the stairs to sew a rip in some draperies. The rip was minor. The window had caught the drape and someone had torn it loose roughly. The room was very beautiful and very long. The floors were polished. The walls and ceiling were white like her clothes. Its windows were draped with white linen. It had a barred enclosure, big enough to fit only three or four people.

Inside the enclosure was a white table holding four white china bowls. Underneath the table was a large tin basin. Papers were on the table in stacks weighed down by stones of the white glassy kind the boys had once found by the creek. They were next to small wooden blocks and some jars. White papers were tacked on the walls of the room, with Chinese marks inked on them. Benches were placed around the room where people could sit. It was the strangest room Napas had ever seen. She recognized that she was especially important to that important room in some way, because she was given clean white clothes and soft white shoes to wear she looked like the room - all decorated in white. When she grew, she was given new clothes to replace the ones she'd outgrown.

She was treated well, but she was isolated. No one talked to her. She listened to the laundry women, but they didn't say very much because they were working so hard. If the laundry women did say a word or two at all, it often rude and they addressed to each other, never her. Even that was rare. It was hot, hard work that they did, wringing garments from the boiling tubs.

She was glad she was a seamstress. When she lived at Miss Lucy's, Miss Lucy was often complaining and Cook was often snarling or shouting about something or other. Especially after Irina left. Perhaps quiet was better. Ines lived without talking.

When she was alone in her room, she told herself all the stories she remembered the boys, Ada and Nancy telling her. She said all the prayers she had learned. She sang all the songs she knew. But in all the time since she'd left Crane Valley, she had never had anyone to talk, really talk, with. It was very lonely being sold to do work.

There were good things at the White Dove. It was warm in the winter in the room above the office. She liked the long room with its windows that overlooked the town. It was the nicest room she had ever had. Nicer than her small room in Crane Valley. From her room in Sonora, she could see across the rooftops and up the hill all the way to the red church. Its bells let her know when it was Sunday and she let it kept time for her. She remembered that Nancy wanted a real church in Crane Valley. She'd drawn a picture for MeMe of what churches in Indiana looked like. The drawing looked like the red church.

Sometimes, on Sunday, when the laundresses didn't work, Feng Goh gave her coins and he or one of his men would walk with her to the Jew's store. It was always busy on Sunday, because most of the other stores were closed. She could buy trinkets and she quickly learned the value of coins by watching what people did. From somewhere she remembered that numbers were better than words. She learned the store's numbers and how to count out the coins Feng Goh had given her.

People jostled her in the store but never spoke to her. She was with either Feng Goh or one of the other White Dove men. That was her protection. As long as she didn't talk, they would think she was Chinese.

The man Feng Goh called "the Jew" always made time to be pleasant even when the store was very crowded and busy. He smiled at her, but he must have thought she didn't speak English because he never said anything to her. He took her coins and wrapped her purchases. She never once said anything to him. Hai

Leong was wise. It was better to have people think she was Chinese. She was as quiet as the Chinese men who worked for Sin Shang when she was in the store. Napas had a memory of the store in Crane Valley, and although she couldn't read the words and labels, she remembered the way transactions took place. She gradually taught herself the values of coins and price marks in the Jew's store. Candies had little value, but yarn and hairbrushes were expensive. She began to make purchases by herself pointing to what she wanted, and counting out the coins Feng Goh had given her.

Only once did she make a mistake. She bought some colored ribbons, and used them to tie back her hair. At the White Dove, Feng Goh frowned and shook his head. He gently pulled them from her hair and went to the Jew's store and brought back white replacements for her.

He explained, "Red, pupo no lucky." Whi' alus lucky! Indan girl mus be alus lucky. Mus wear lucky whi' co'or." He tied back her hair with the white ribbons, then he bowed to her and went back to his own work.

One morning she thought something bad had happened to her. Not many months after she had gone upstairs to mend the tear in the linen, her low stomach ached and something was happening to her. She was scared. Napas tried to do her work, but she was shaking and couldn't hold the needle and thread in her hand steady. When she went to the privy, she found blood on her clothing. She hadn't been injured. Since there was no reason for her bleeding, she thought she was going to die.

One of the laundry women, a heavy woman with an easy smile, noticed that Feng Goh's young seamstress was holding her skirt and petticoat bunched up. She was sitting very still and too upset to work. The woman dried her hands and left her washboard propped against the tub where she was working. She dragged Napas by the hand and led her back to the washerwomen's privy.

"I know you'll understand me, girly. I heard the boss speak English to you when he was fixing that rackety machine of yours. I think you need me to help you."

Napas was too frightened to object. The woman then told the girl how to tear an old flannel skirt or petticoat and make a band from it to go around her waist and use it to secure long pieces of flannel draped between her legs. "The blood will wash out of your skirt and petticoat in cold water if you rub hard."

"Wash the stained flannels and hang to dry in your room. Men don't like to see our bloody rags. Well, girl," she laughed, "I don't like to see them myself."

"You aren't a child anymore. It'll happen to you every month, just like it does t' all women 'til we get old. Keep your worn out petticoats to make your drapery rags. A woman's work doesn't stop because her time has come. Today you should go to your room. Clean yourself and rest. Ol' Feng Goh will understand why you aren't at your work. She shook her head. "It is too bad that you don't have a mother to tell you this. My mother tol' me, and hers tol' her."

In this way, Napas understood at last why Feng Goh had given her the flannel cloths when he gave her a room of her own above the White Dove Laundry. The woman who helped her had orange hair pinned on her head and coarse hairs growing on her chin. Her sleeves were rolled up and her dress unbuttoned so her great breasts showed. Sweat was running down between them. But she had stopped her work to help Napas.

If the girl was lonely at the White Dove, she was also safe. Feng Goh was kind to her and pleased with the work she did by hand or with the sewing machine. She had a nice room with windows. She could look out at trees when they changed color. There were hills with pine trees around the town, and she liked sitting at her high window looking over the rooftops and up the hill to the red church that reminded her of Nancy.

Nothing bad had happened to her at all at the White Dove. No one scolded her. She didn't have to pull a heavy laundry cart in the dust of a road and watch out for horses and carriage wheels. No one gave her mean looks. There weren't so many soldiers in Sonora. She missed Irina, Ines and Cook, but Hai Leong had done a great favor for her by buying her for Sin Shang. Changes sometimes weren't good. She didn't want anything to change.

Chapter Thirty-six
~ For Lack of Luck ~

She heard noises and bells ringing in the night. Napas quickly came awake and ran to the window closest to her bed. People were running in the street and yelling, "Fire! Fire!" She didn't know how close the fire was, but the street was bright with red flickering light, and she could smell smoke. Napas swiftly put her clothes on and went to the side of the room where the shutter opened for her to draw up water.

When she first came to The White Dove, Feng Goh told her that if there were ever a fire or an earthquake, she could use the bucket's stout rope to slide down. He'd said it was important to remember, and she'd remembered.

She looked out the hinged shutter and saw that the alley way was free of flames. Feng Goh and the other men were racing back and forth from the pump carrying buckets around the corner of the building next door. Other men were running down the street doing the same thing, carrying buckets and hauling barrels. She ran to the shelf where she kept her shoes and stockings, put them on and grabbed the old pillowcase where she kept her belongings. She tossed them down through the shutter window, hoping that they wouldn't scatter, she watched the pillowcase land intact, and then she reached out for the rope and slid down as cinders blew about her like glowing orange stars.

She didn't know how long she had been sitting at the edge of a street. It felt like hours. She was blocks beyond the White Dove, keeping out of the men's way. Wagons had come by with kegs of water. Men dragged hoses. They carried buckets. Frightened stock animals were led away. Dogs and cats were running wild. Shrieks and yells reverberated through the night. On the roof of the building nearest her, women and men both were passing buckets of water in relays to pour on the heavy blankets that they had hung over the buildings' upper edges.

The fire ate its way closer. Looking far down an alley, she saw a sign with characters that Feng Goh had told her meant *White Dove.* She watched it ignite. She knew the fire would eat the laundry. She couldn't see Feng Goh or any of the other men in the crowd. She had never heard such awful noise. In the burning buildings glass was cracking; floors were collapsing; a roof caved in on a block nearer her and crashed down into a basement.

The heat was increasing and flames advancing, so she took her sack and ran down a side street to find a place further away from the danger. She found a little cove for herself out of the running people's way. It was in the doorway of a brick building. She could see what she thought was the back of the Jew's store, and farther across rooftops, she could see the tall shape of the laundry's second floor. The air was cooler here. She leaned back against the dark door.

The laundry was the tallest building she could see from where she sat in the shallow doorway. She couldn't see her own room, but she saw flames coming from windows of the upstairs room where she had mended the drapes, the beautiful white room.

She watched The White Dove burn down with the other buildings on its block. The long, quiet, safe room she liked disappeared.

Napas prayed that the fire wouldn't reach the place where she sat watching, but if it did, she'd move farther away again. She didn't speak to anyone. Everyone was frantic, and she didn't want to be a bother. She couldn't help. People not working seemed not to know where to go. The same people went by going one way then the other.

Then, after what seemed many hours, She felt the wind change. She watched from the doorway as the wind blew the flames back over what had already burned. The wind change came too late for Feng Goh's laundry and many other buildings.

By morning the men of the city who had been fighting the fire were walking around stomping out cinders in the rubble. It was smoky and oddly quiet. Napas knew she had slept there in the entry, because when she stretched, her neck was stiff. She coughed. Her eyes burned and there was soot on her white jacket and skirt. When she tried to brush herself off, she smeared the soot. She noticed that her petticoats were dirty and damp where the run-off from the buckets' water had made a river past the step where she was crumpled dozing against a heavy door. The soft white shoes she wore were filthy and soggy.

"Come, come, child. Come with me." A familiar man's voice was speaking to her.

She looked up and saw the man who owned the Jew's store. He wasn't alone. A woman and a girl about her age were with him. They were wearing scarves over their heads and were dressed in black. They were smiling encouragingly at her but didn't say anything.

"You understand me, don't you? My wife does not speak English, and my daughter is shy," the man explained. "We are looking to see if anyone needs to

share our home. We know your home is gone. Thanks
to God, our store was spared. It is where we live. We
will give you food and drink, and a place to wait until
your people come for you."

"Have you seen Feng Goh? Is he all right? What about
the other Chinese men?"

"I don't know. I think everyone from the laundry
escaped. There was time. No Chinese names are
posted as dead."

He looked down at her curiously. "The fire started
down at the blacksmith's shop late in the night. The
wind blew it away from our street, but two blocks of
your street's buildings are gone. They weren't as
lucky. The wind changed too late."

The woman smiled at Napas, and beckoned to her.
The girl looked down at the sack at Napas' feet and
picked it up. She was stiff from sitting so long. The
man from the store put his arm around her and he
helped her walk. The four of them made a small
procession down the street.

Through a charred ruin of an alleyway, Napas
thought she could see the still smoldering ruins of
what had once been the small house where the
Chinese men lived at the back of the White Dove. The
laundry had collapsed into a jumble of charred beams.
But she wasn't sure. Everything was black and
charred. There was nothing she recognized. She
worried about the Feng Goh and the men, and
couldn't know for certain that they had escaped the
fire.

There was a space in the back of the Jew's store that
had been made into a tiny home. Napas saw it had
two small rooms, a room with a bed, a stove and sink,

and another room adjoining. There were three chairs, and the man led her to one and told her to sit.

"Thank you," she said. She was grateful to be out of the street and the dirt and grime of the fire that covered it and the outsides of the buildings of the neighborhood that hadn't burned.

"My wife is Chava. Our daughter is Rivka.

They will make you comfortable."

"I don't know your name."

"You've been in my store so many times and don't know my name. I don't know yours either!"

"I'm called Napas."

"That doesn't sound like a Chinese name."

"I'm not Chinese."

The storekeeper stepped back and peered at her. "You are not? Then, why do you live at the laundry? Don't you have a family?"

"The laundry owns me," Napas shrugged her shoulders.

"Then you are an Indian girl?" He didn't expect her to answer, and she looked at him and knew she didn't need to say anything. From his kindness, she knew it didn't matter to him that she was an Indian although he was a white man.

"Welcome to my home, Napas. My family and I own nothing but what you can see. Our place is humble, but you can stay here until we find where you should be. I am Moshe Benesch."

While they were talking, Rivka filled a basin at the pump and brought it and a clean flannel to Napas so she could wash her face and hands clean of the night's grime.

Napas balanced the basin on her knees, and dipped her hands into the water. Her hands stung from the abrasion of the rope during her escape. She only now noticed. She looked for her sack. Chava saw her glance around the room, understood, and lifted the sack from behind the curtain to the shop to put it at Napas' feet to reassure her that her belongings were safe.

Rivka, who was not much older than she was, poured fresh water from a pitcher brought it to her with some cracker-like bread. Chava went into the adjoining room and brought out clean stockings for her and took her shoes near the stove to dry. Chava seemed to show an apologetic look in her eyes as she handed the dark stockings to Napas because they weren't white. Mr. Benesch sat and talked to the girl softly and told her all he knew of what had happened during the fire.

It had been a long time since she had felt such warm companionship. The Jew's family lived in a space smaller than her room at the White Dove had been, but they filled it with kindness and for now they were sharing it with her. The small quarters where they lived seemed to have more in common with the ranch in Crane Valley than with Miss Lucy's or the White Dove. She realized she was with a family for the first time in nearly seven years.

The sheriff came and demanded she go with him. He took Napas to a big hall where other people who had been burned out camped here and there clinging to what they'd salvaged.

The sheriff walked her down the right hand side of the hall to a place where the men from the laundry were together. Two of the men were sitting on heavy bundles and wearing leather sheathed knives around their necks as well as the ones that they usually wore on their belts. Feng Goh sat with them.

He turned when the sheriff called him. "This is your girl from the laundry, ain't it? She was taken in by ol' Moshe and his family."

Feng Goh had a strange look on his face, mournful and sad. He spoke about her, but not to her. "Napas not lucky girl."

The sheriff grimaced. "Well, she was lucky she didn't die, and you're lucky you still have all that money you people hoard.

"The building may of burnt down but all four of you are still alive. Not so many were as lucky this week as you Chinese were. The blacksmith's body was found this morning. Mrs. Jackson and five of her tenants died in the boarding house behind the smithy. Hope the smoke got 'em before the flame." He put his hands together and said, "Bless the Lord my family don't live in this neighborhood. You better thank whatever god you pray to, Feng Goh. You people were damned lucky."

But in spite of what the sheriff had said, Feng Goh, who had treated her kindly for two years, never spoke or looked at her again.

The people from the White Dove were moved to the home of a Methodist minister and his wife who'd had a mission in Shanghai for ten years and could speak to them in their language. The minister's wife fixed a bed for Napas in a small room away from the men of the laundry. The woman was disappointed and confused when she spoke to the girl in Cantonese and Napas couldn't answer her.

She gave Napas very few tasks to do, but expected the girl to pray with her in the chapel many times a day. She only answered Napas' questions by saying, "Pray, sister, and the Lord will provide." It didn't seem a practical answer.

She would rather have had work to do than stay idle in the little room called the chapel listening to Sister Violet or Reverend John pray aloud for hours on end, but she not given either occupation or choice.

In three weeks, Sin Shang sent a man to get Napas. He came in the same wagon that The Buyer had driven nearly three years before. The cage was still in it. But this man wasn't the pleasant young man she remembered, neither cheerful nor handsome, and certainly not talkative.

This buyer treated her as though she were diseased. He made her sit as far away from him as the wagon allowed, but she was glad he didn't expect her to get in the cage.

"Is Sin Shang selling me?" she asked him.

"You aledy sol. You go up in mountain now."

"To a laundry?"

"To white man. Sin Shang say you no lucky fo' Chinese pepo. I no like you talk."

He said nothing more after that, nor did she. They traveled out of Sonora driving up the hill and past the red church she had always wanted to see. But the driver wouldn't slow so she could admire the building. She twisted on the wagon seat to look back down at the town. She had a sense that she was traveling farther and farther away from Crane Valley.

When they'd turned away from the red church, she felt bleak. Finally, hours later, she asked the man where they were going. He said, "Noth." He wouldn't say anything more.

Sister Violet, the minister's wife had given her adequate clothing and a pair of shoes. The clothes weren't new, but were in good condition. A good thing had happened, and she was grateful. The woman had taken an almost new carpetbag out of a closet and given it to her. It was much nicer than a patched pillowcase for her clothes, and it had room for the buckskin packet.

Chapter Thirty-seven
~ Cobey's Warehouse ~

The new buyer took them far away. They traveled for long days. At night he put her in the cage and chained its door. She'd promised him that she wouldn't run away, but he ignored her.

He'd build a fire, dip water out of a cask and cook rice until it was soft, then he'd add oil and some vegetables he kept in a hessen sack like the ones in Mr. McCreary's wagon under the wagon seat. He'd chopped the vegetables finely and the food was good. The new buyer packed away the food that they didn't eat and they ate it the next morning for breakfast. He was kind to his horse, drove quietly, never sang, and never talked. She stopped asking him anything about where they were, because he wouldn't answer.

Going north, they crossed three rivers on ferries. The ferryman said the last river was called the Stanislaus River. It was much bigger than the Waukeen, and bigger than any she had crossed with Mr. McCreary when she was little. She didn't know the names of those rivers. But it was spring. She had crossed the other rivers in the fall. At that time, after dry summer the water was low under the bridges they crossed. The snow was melting on the Sierra now and winter rains made the rivers and creeks deeper and wider. The water was swift and dirty and it frightened her.

This Chinese buyer didn't seem to be in a hurry. He got up late and stopped traveling early. After he cooked and they ate, he smoked a pipe, and he left her to do as she wished until the stars came out. Then she had to climb into the cage.

They passed many travelers on the road. Most of them were men on horseback, but some were walking. There were people with wagons or carriages, and once they passed a long set of oxen pulling three heavy wagons.

One of the days they traveled, a group of people on horses passed them. A girl about her age smiled at her from the back of a grey dappled horse. No one stopped to talk to a Chinese man and an Indian girl. And eventually, they came to a town. It was closer in size to Bootjack than Sonora. But it had more buildings and fewer tents. She saw few structures as tall as the laundry where she had lived.

She felt a change in the man driving her. He began humming and seemed happier. She thought perhaps this was where they were going and that he'd be happy to be alone again. She wondered what would happen to her.

"What town is this?" she asked, encouraged by his humming.

"Moo fees Cam'. Hea' you go to white man. An I lef. Go home to fa'ly."

"Do you have a family?"

He was smiling for the first time since he had picked her up at the Methodist minister's house. "I haf wi and chilen in San Flansico." He put out his hand and showed her three fingers. "I haf tlee gil." He put out two fingers. "I haf two boy." He didn't talk again.

He turned the wagon off the wide road and onto a narrower one before they came to the center of town. After a while the buyer stopped the wagon. He consulted a paper with the ink drawings in columns that Napas knew had meaning. From then on, he watched the right side of the road until a track led from the road into a cleft between two hills. They turned off onto the track and soon crossed the narrow valley and went into the cleft. The track twisted around a hill into a smaller valley where a barn stood. There were other wagons and teams around the barn, and some men were standing talking.

A man in a big hat came out and led them inside while a boy took the team and wagon around to the side of the barn where there was a trough.

Inside the barn, men were standing around a circle of brown skinned boys. Each boy was tied from the wrists to a long rope that ran across the cavern of the barn from one post to another. Napas was led to a horse stall. In it, two Indian girls were sitting on some hay, leaning against the back wall. They looked up when she was shoved in and the stall gate closed behind her. It was the first time she was had been with any Indians except Ootie.

She tried not to stare at them, but she was very curious. They were girls like her. One of the girls looked back with a puzzled expression. The other seemed dispirited and kept her eyes on the floor. The first girl asked her something. It sounded like "*Si mik mee ko?*"

"I don't know what you asked me," she answered. They had bundles with them, but small bundles. They reminded her of how she must have appeared the dreadful day Irina bought her from the man in Bootjack and Mr. McCreary stood at the opening of the tent and watched.

The first girl turned to the other and said something else in a voice too low for Napas to hear. The sad looking girl nodded, saying, "*ee oo ee te*" and putting her head down. Both the girls looked thin and hungry.

Sin Shang's buyer had given her vegetables at noon, but perhaps their buyers hadn't fed them. There was a bucket with water in the stall. It smelled fresh and clean. She used its dipper to scoop up some water to freshen her hands, dried them on her petticoat. The first girl just watched her. The other one said, "*kiki*," and smiled timidly. It didn't look as though the girls had underclothing, only the old faded dresses. Both were barefooted and their feet looked cracked and dry.

Napas smiled back and said, "I'm an Indian too." But she didn't think they understood her. She didn't know what language the girls spoke. She said the numbers Ootie taught her, but the girls just stared at her.

A different man, with a voice she thought she remembered, came and picked up Napas' sack and carpetbag. He led her to the front of the barn. The buyer was outside, already up on the seat of the wagon, and as she stood there with the man, she watched the wagon roll away from the barn and turn toward the highway. She felt scared, surrounded by the tall space of the big barn, so full of white men. She wanted to run after the wagon and the Chinese man, but she knew he didn't want her and would not stop for her.

The man who sold Indians twisted her arm and pulled her into the sunlight. "See, Billy, no marks. Not one," he said to someone standing behind her. She didn't recognize the man who was talking by his face or grey beard, only his voice. She couldn't remember where she had heard it before.

The man behind her came around to examine her. She tried to turn from his thin face and evil way of looking at her, but he grabbed her chin and pulled her face back.

"I won't take her with devil marks on her, Cobey. You guarantee me there's nary a one on her anywhere. I don't want to find out she's poxy either. No disease! I'll have no disease in my servant girl."

"There are no tattoos on her. I ought to know. I'm the one bought and sold her when she was a little tyke. I know where she's been. "She's a virgin, Henon. The Chinese worshiped her like a little goddess and gave her protection day and night. Nobody got near this girl at all."

Napas didn't know what a virgin was, but she knew that Feng Goh and the other men didn't worship her. No one ever bowed down to her. They gave her sewing to do, gave her clothes and food and safety for her work. It was all right. She didn't want the man with the thin evil face to buy her. His eyebrows bushed out and his grim face looked like it never stopped scowling. His voice was too loud, twice as loud as the man he called Cobey. Then, from his voice, she remembered the day she was sold in the tent tavern, the day she became Napas and not MeMe.

The man let go of her. "I won't take her if she's used and poxy."

"She's but twelve or thirteen, Henon. She's showing red with her moons, but still a child. You can see that she's healthy. $250.00 in hair or $200.00 in gold is my price. Give me the bag if you want her, but don't doubt my word.

"It was blasted hard finding this girl, you old fool. There's not a scab or sore on her. I could sell her for $250.00 today, right here in this room. But you ordered her, and you get the first right to buy her. Take her over there in the corner, strip her down and see for yourself." He made a funny noise, almost a laugh.

"But she'll draw a crowd, and the price goes up $50.00 more because you didn't show me more trust."

"I won't look on woman's nakedness or see the corruption of her lust. I stand before God's ever watchful eye." The man's voice boomed through the room and made all the men in the building stare around in the direction of the barn doorway. Napas sensed Cobey's distaste for his customer. It was no greater than her distaste for both of them.

"You listen to me, Billy. This is what you wanted. Give me $200.00 gold for her, or give me that sack you got as is worth more. Then get out of my barn. This Indian is a prize. She even understands English and can speak it."

Billy reached down and easily picked up the big canvas bag and tossed it to the trader. "Lord stay before me, Satan get thee behind me!"

Cobey looked down at Napas and said, "Go along with Pastor Henon, girl. I hope you please him, but if not, I'll see you again." The seller's rude speech and mean pinched grin made him look as evil as the man who was buying her.

Napas had been sold two times before but never had been as frightened as she was this time. Pastor Henon directed her to climb up into the bed of his wagon.

It was filthy. There was no place she could sit that wasn't stained by what looked like clods of dirt, brittle twigs and big sweeps of black. The caged sheep wagon had been cleaner and smelled better. She picked the cleanest spot she could, and she sat down, putting her sack and the carpetbag on her lap. Her Methodist dress would get dirty, but she could keep her other things clean. She couldn't be going to a good place in this kind of wagon. The sound of its wheels was ominous. The man was harsh with the animal pulling it. Pastor Henon turned the wagon on the main road to the east, so they were going higher into the mountains. She watched the roadside for landmarks.

It had grown late in the day by the time they got where they were going. She found that she'd live in a little lean-to behind a rough barn. The lean-to was dirty and she had to get dry grass to use as a broom to clean the rodent leavings out. Pastor Henon's wife came out with a lantern and brought her two worn blankets and dark dresses. They were long and she'd have to take them up. They looked like they fit Pastor's wife.

"Pastor's my husbin. He believes in plain clothes that won't tempt demons. I won't take your old clothes away, but you wear these here, not what you brung." The woman smiled shyly. "I'm pleased you're here for company. I ain't talked to nobody else in five year.

Pastor goes out to find what we need, but I have to stay with our girl. She's feeble and can't talk. I'm Anna. Come to the kitchen an ring the bell if you need sumthin' else." She didn't offer food though it was late. Perhaps Anna Henon was so thin and wracked looking because she didn't get enough to eat herself.

Chapter Thirty-eight
~ Tom McCreary Returns ~

The McCreary boys learned early on from Reverend Taylor that "...the love of money is the root of all evil." But they knew that the use of money *in good cause* was not evil. They desperately wanted to find MeMe. She had been too much a part of their lives to allow themselves to abandon her. And, so to that end, Mr. Edward Harrington, legal guardian for the minor McCreary boys, and Mr. James Buellton Esq., lawyer for the firm of McCreary Hauling, gave Tom their full financial support to carry out the search.

With money from both McCreary Hauling and Aaron Landers financing their venture, Tom and Ples crossed the nation by a complicated route. They traveled by railroad in regions where rails had been laid down, and by stage where they hadn't. The men chose the southerly route, Washington D.C. to Kansas City, on into Santa Fe, then by stage and rail to California. Once across the state line, their goal was to stop and search through the both the deserts and coastal areas for any trace of the girl.

Tom left Ples waiting in a dreary sand-swept boarding house while he crossed the mountains on horseback into San Diego to search, on the chance that she'd be found there. Ples kept busy practicing his violin and scribbling records of the Indian missions, schools and orphanages Tom visited and kept a good, neat record of their expenses. He sent a wire to the Presbyterian Council in San Francisco and confirmed that the denomination had not as of yet established any Indian missions or schools established in the southern part of the state.

The men searched. They found excellent records in neat script dating back to early days of the padres in the missions, records written in Spanish. But no English speaking Indian girl using the name Merab McCreary, or matching her description, was found.

At the end of their search, the men had spent months working to find trace of MeMe, but without progress. Tom had even searched through burial records, thinking she might have died at one of the places where he looked. The men knew then, that Frederick McCreary's tale was a lie.

Tom's bitterness grew. Ples only felt sadness. He was happy to be back in the west and going home. But he'd hoped that they would find some trace of Merab McCreary, and in all the past months, they hadn't. They bought tickets on the Butterfield Stage Line that ran along the foothills of the great valley. They were going home. Ples planned to travel with Tom as far as Fort Miller. Then Ples would go to Crane Valley and create as good a life as he could given his war injuries, and Tom would go on to Angel's Camp to a reunion with his brothers and what he hoped would be a reconciliation with is father.

It was spring. The brilliant vibrancy of the season was yet to come. The peaks of the Sierra were to their east, the great space of the valley to their west. Tom wished he were on horseback, riding free. But he needed to see his friend returned home to his people first.

Orange poppies and blue lupine had not yet begun their blooms. Rosy owl's clover and red maids were still to cover the hills. But the land welcomed the men home in glory. The purple Sierra was capped with white snow. Its foothills were deep as a grown man's knee in green native grasses; the buckeye already in leaf. Below them the great valley was a bog of water from the rush of rivers carrying melted snow from the Sierra to spread out as an immense lake across the flat valley to their west. High spots formed wide islands of the most vivid green.

Tom could not help but think of all the cattle they had seen along their route across the nation. How cattle would fatten on this rich grass that grew all through the foggy winter months!

Ples had not seen his father in over seven years. He only knew his stepmother but from the letters she had written him. Seven years and a war had passed, and Ples could see how hard it was for Aaron Landers to see him returned lame and twisted in body. He resolved to show his father love and apology for the youthful impulse that brashly took him away.

Mrs. Landers greeted her stepson with warmth and grace. The couple lived in Fresno Flats, and had since they married. Young Mrs. Landers liked living in town with neighbors nearby. They still owned The Willows, its Crane Valley apple orchard even more valuable with maturity. It was to be Ples' own property. The deed already prepared.

Tom helped Ples down from the stage at Fort Miller where his father would meet him. Tom wanted to greet Mr. Landers and to be introduced to Mrs. Landers, whom he also had not yet met.

They had a short, pleasant visit and refreshments while the stage changed horses and drivers at Fort Miller. As anxious as Tom was to go again to the Flats and then on to see his old childhood home in Crane Valley, he was more anxious to see his brothers. He wouldn't loiter here long. It had been too long a time since he has seen his family.

Gradually, during Tom's long absence, Frederick McCreary became aware that his sons no longer lived in his mansion. It didn't trouble him greatly. He knew he could find them in the hauling company office each day. They were where he wanted them. Doing what he wanted. One or the other came to the mansion daily to visit with him, Ada or Frank.

In the years since his eldest son's death on the battlefield in the Shenandoah Valley, Frederick McCreary had recovered some of his capabilities, and behaved tolerably in public though Dr. Grainger monitored him closely. The doctor noted the descriptions given by Ada Cotter and Frank Sullivan on Frederick's deteriorating behaviors during his weekly visits to the mansion.

Frederick seldom rode with Mason to check stations and corrals anymore. He liked to walk to the Buckeye Tavern to take his noon meal, and would often come to the office for an hour or two following. However, he no longer attended to the work of the business.

Richard and Mr. Harrington checked the books and did the accounts. Mason inspected the stations and stock with Lalo Cabrera. Henry Stegler was trusted to do the majority of the banking and supervise freight handling in Stockton. There were banks nearer than Stockton since the war, but a state bank in the city seemed more secure than a small bank in Angel's Camp for the volume of business of the freight company.

The owner of the business came to the office primarily to draw out pocket money and was often jovial. His old energetic personality seemed intact. However, his intellectual functioning had never fully returned.

Richard and Mason, Henry Stegler and Edward Harrington watched out for him, under the careful legal advisement of James Buellton, Esq. In too regular occurrences, the titular head of the company would sink into a depression, stagger home from a tavern where he'd spent an afternoon, and weep, reliving Wiley's death over and over.

"I helped win a war that couldn't be won, and killed my own Wiley, my best son," became his refrain between bouts of tearful weeping.

Ada sent for Doctor Grainger, who prescribed laudanum to help Frederick sleep. It was of little use. Nurses were hired, and a man to manage the still large Mr. McCreary from chair to bed. For weeks Frederick was confined, then he'd seem to improve. But each time it was to a weaker point of recovery. Richard or Mason, one or the other, made a point of calling at the mansion each day.

On an afternoon's visit shortly before Tom was due home, Richard walked into the McCreary mansion to hear his father bellowing, his voice echoing through the high ceilinged rooms. "Ada, you ratty-faced trollop, marry me! If you order me about so and deny me drink, you're as bad as any man's wife!"

Ada called her response from across the hallway in the dining room as loudly as he had shouted to her. "Be silent, ye silly man. I've been married enough, and wouldn't stoop so low as to marry the likes of you."

"Do you hear me, woman? Bring my bottle back, you ugly, dried up creature, and you'll be a rich widow when I die."

Richard grew still, disgusted with his father, but entertained by Ada's rebuttal to Frederick's abuse.

"Aye, I'm not old enough to be yer mam, ye big drunken lug, but I'm old enough to have changed yer nappies. I'd take on the feeble cripple out in the horse stable afore I'd take on ye. His manners are better."

"You blasted woman, you're murdering me! Bring my bottle."

Ada and his father might feel embarrassed knowing they were overheard. Richard reopened the front door and closed it loudly. He stepped heavily on the floor of the mansion's wide entrance hallway.

The housekeeper came rushing from the dining room to pull him from the parlor doorway and whisper, "Richard, boy, yer father's in his cups again and ranting most terrible. Now, ye don't mind what nonsense he says. I'll manage his foolishness."

"I never mind what Papa says, Ada. You know that."

"Indeed I do. Ye are good boys, all. Mr. McCreary is lucky to have yer. But I'm telling ye, I'm weary of the drinkin'. If he gets wild again, I'm calling Doctor to bring the opium for 'im. I'd rather him sleep than bray."

"Laudanum, Ada, not opium," Richard corrected gently.

"Ye calls it as ye like. I calls it as it is," she piped back.

For the grand celebration of Tom's return, Carrie Harrington wanted to include Mr. McCreary and the family's housekeeper to the supper her family was busily preparing, but after Richard considered his father's behavior, he spoke with Edward.

"I think it wise to leave Papa and Ada home on Thursday evening, Edward. Papa is drinking heavily again."

The next day the two McCreary brothers met with Mr. Harrington to talk of personal things away from the clerk and office. They sat in the small park across from the Catholic Church. Richard began. "We appreciate that you and Carrie have invited the whole family for Tom's homecoming celebration, Edward. But Papa isn't in condition to come to a social gathering. We'd rather that he and Ada stay home. We haven't told him that Tom is due home."

"No, Edward. He doesn't know, and we think it best to take him straight away to see Papa," Mason added.

"Then, if all goes well, and Papa holds his temper, Tom can rest and clean up at the mansion. We three will come to your house in the evening. If it doesn't go well, we may take Tom to Martha's and take rooms there for a few days."

"Your father seems to be coming back to himself," said their guardian, remembering that Frederick had blamed Tom for Wiley's death.

"We both saw Papa yesterday. He's not improved enough for other than a rowdy tavern, Edward. I can't trust him in your home. Ada copes well with him, but your family's gentle women would be offended at our father's speech."

"My good womenfolk realize Mr. McCreary has been ill. They are sympathetic to grief."

"It might come to more than that, Edward. He often is angry. We can't subject them to a disturbing scene."

"Papa has never had patience with Tom," Mason said.

"Nor Tom with him. The celebration is for our brother's return. Tom will want to talk of his search for MeMe. He may want to speak of Wiley. He could not do either in Papa's presence."

"Then I understand and will explain to my wife."

That evening, the brothers spoke privately in the study at the Harrington house. "I'm glad Edward agreed. The Harringtons have been good to us. I shouldn't want to offend them," Richard said.

"Perhaps you're thinking of not offending Louisa."

"To be sure. Nor Lucinda either."

"You missed my meaning." Mason gave his brother a wry glance.

"I missed nothing, brother. I confess that I love Louisa and she loves me. She would marry me tomorrow in spite of my faint health, youth, and poor prospects for long life.

"Dr. Grainger has been candid with me about the weakness of my heart and limitations of my future."

"You are old enough and well enough, Richard. Best you do marry young -- if you are going to die young."

"Would it be a fair thing to do to Louisa? That is my great worry. She'd have to face the prospect of widowhood. And if we had a child..."

"If you have a child it will be well cared for. Tom and I would see to that. Louisa will want for nothing. There is only one thing to do. You must ask Edward for her hand. Better she be a widow, than never be wed at all. Waste no more time. We both have learned how precious it is."

"Papa might try to interfere. I'm not of age."

"Papa doesn't matter. He is not our guardian, Edward is."

Tom arrived at the stage depot the next day, dusty, and tired from riding in confinement. He carried a Civil War

issue rifle, a banjo case, and one small suitcase. He didn't smell of drink or tobacco, but a pack of playing cards was jammed into his coat pocket. His brothers met him with joy and laughter and tears that welled but didn't fall. Richard and Mason had been schoolboys when Tom left and now they were both nearly as tall as he was. When Tom looked at Mason, the younger of his two brothers so resembled Wiley, the brother he'd lost on a battlefield, tears came again to his eyes.

Mason didn't notice. "Tell us about Ples. Is he recovered?"

"Yes, we wished you could have persuaded him to come here."

"He'll come, but he needed to visit with his family. Our friend has told me he doesn't mind being a cripple if he can play for the barn dances on Saturday and sing in church on Sunday."

"But his leg. Is it sound?"

"No, and he is in great pain. But he staunchly refuses medicine or strong drink as relief. He says he must become accustomed to the way he will have to live. He walks some with a crutch, and can't mount a horse. And, brothers, I am his hero for I saved that old fiddle of his grandfather's. It is true. It took great deviousness and stealth to find places of safety for it while I was riding off to battle."

"Tell us about the battles!" Mason cried.

"Tell us what's in the case you're carrying," Richard said, pointing to the banjo case's odd shape.

The brothers finished their glad reunion inside the stage office. It was a usual day for early March. The spring rains were pelting down. They waited for a lessening of the storm in the small building. Richard sat on the bench across from the ticket booth, his brothers preferring to stand. Richard and Mason both tried to prepare Tom for the meeting with their father. They explained how much they depended on Ada to handle his temper and bursts of rancor, so at odds with periods of childlike flightiness.

"Ah, Ada," Tom said. "I'll be happy to see her. Will she give me biscuits and milk, do *ye* think?"

The rain stopped. Tom was pleased with the mount Mason had purchased for him. It was a black gelding, and a finer horse than he'd ever ridden, even with the Massachusetts Cavalry.

Chapter Thirty-nine
~ The Threat of Asylum ~

Tom's meeting with his father at the McCreary mansion began calmly. Ada took the boys' damp coats to the kitchen to dry them near the stove. Frederick was in the parlor, sitting with a book in his lap, but though he gave an appearance of reading, he had been in a stupor for the past hour. Laudanum helped by the flask in his breast pocket dulled down Frederick's troubling memories.

Tom's mouth was tight and eyes aged by war, but Frederick recognized him. Tom went to his father. The old man who hadn't been able to rise to greet his son, seemed to flush with warm feeling. They shook hands and Frederick spoke out, not ranting, but in a subdued manner.

"I hope you stay here, son, and don't go off again. There is room for you. Your brothers are always over at the Harrington house these days. I think they even sleep there." It was indicative of Frederick McCreary's decline that he didn't realize that both his younger sons had lived at the Harrington home for years, while Tom was well aware of that fact from their letters.

The old man glanced suspiciously at Mason and Richard. The look on his face told Tom that his father had not changed. He was still a man who looked for slights and became petulant. "Those two have abandoned me, just like you and Wiley did."

Tom stepped back, and surveyed the room. There was little in it that reminded him of The Willows or Crane

Valley. There were only traces remaining of the father he had known, no photograph or drawing of his mother. No relic of her presence.

"How old are you, boy?" Frederick growled.

"I was twenty-one two weeks ago."

"No. Don't lie to me. You were born in January."

"No, Papa. Mason was born in January."

"Liar. You always work at tormenting me. Just like your mother." Frederick picked up his book and threw it at Tom. Tom stepped out of the books arc. It bounced once and came to light on Turkish rug.

"Get out of my house," Frederick shouted. His chair was strong and heavy, suitable for a man of his size. He leaned down, fumbling for his cane in an attempt to throw it at Tom. He almost lost his balance, but the chair held.

Mason and Richard stepped forward but Tom motioned them back. "Give me my turn, brothers," the war-educated man said.

Tom stepped over the book and came nearer Frederick. War and time had changed them both. The pathetic grey hulk in the chair was not the man who had caused the boy Tom to leave home. The old man in the chair was no longer that grand Frederick McCreary, businessman from Stockton and Angel's Camp, Crane Valley rancher and benefactor. Frederick's son Tom was no longer a thirteen-year-old boy, six foot three and spindly. He was a strong and intelligent man who had served in a war with honor. His broad and muscled back bent forward, and he placed strong cavalryman's hands on the arms of his father's chair.

He leaned in close to the old man's face. "Where is she, Papa? What did you do with Merab?"

Frederick drew back as far as he could, cowering into the upholstery. "The Presbyterians! The Presbyterians have her."

"What Presbyterians? Tell me where they are. I've been to Los Angeles! There is no Presbyterian mission in the whole of the southern state, Papa. You're the liar. "I'm done with you Papa, as Wiley was done with you."

Richard put his arm around Tom and tried to lead him away from their father. But Tom shrugged him away and asked again, "Where is she Papa?"

Richard spoke too. "Yes. Where is she? Tell us now. Mason and I as well want to know what happened to her? Did you kill her, Papa?"

Frederick slumped further down in the chair, and in a ragged voice he said. "I didn't kill her. I should have killed her. The hell with you jackals! I sold her to a trader in Bootjack. I got twenty dollars for her. Do you want the money? I'll give you the money."

Mason, who had come quietly back into the room, said softly, but clearly, "We already have your money, Papa."

Frederick looked at the boys in confusion as he tried to puzzle out the difference between what Mason had said and the other thing his son seemed to mean.

Richard took charge of the situation. "Go on, Mason. Take Tom to Martha's Boarding House and register him in. Make sure he's comfortable. I'll watch Papa for a time, and then I'll meet you there."

"No. I must to go to Bootjack." Tom cried out.

"Come along, Tom." Mason said. "Tomorrow *we'll* go to Bootjack, you and I together. Tonight we celebrate your homecoming."

The two brothers left the room, and Richard helped Frederick sit more comfortably in his chair. "Listen to me, Papa. We are in charge now. We have been for a long time. We McCrearys will always take care of you. Nothing will change in your life. But Tom is home now, and he will stay. He's as much of the business as Mason or I am. You must remember that when you come to the office and see him. Do you understand?"

Frederick roused himself to protest. "He's an ingrate. He's a liar. I don't like that boy."

"Then learn to act like you do, or I'll have you locked in the state asylum."

"I'm not a lunatic. You'll not have me locked up." Frederick tried to stand but couldn't manage and sat with a thud back down into his chair. With pompous arrogance he said, "Dr. Grainger won't allow it. He'll tell you I'm sound."

"Grainger will do no such thing. He says you have congestion of the brain, and are suffering from fatal intemperance. He has already suggested that we agree to send you to Alameda to the asylum there."

"I want Wiley. Call Wiley! Wiley will turn you ruffians out."

"Wiley's dead, Papa. If you behave you'll have good care and your freedom here. People on the street know you and will treat you well. Any who work for McCreary Hauling will assist you should you need help, and Mason or I will visit you daily.

"Ada will be here, Dr. Grainger on call. When you feel well, you may lunch at the tavern and come to the office and visit us. But you must accept our Tom, for he is home now."

Ada and Frank came in and helped Frederick upstairs. Richard went to find his brothers.

That evening, after he had bathed and dressed, Tom McCreary turned from thoughts of his father, and worked his charm on the Harrington family. Lucinda's interest in the tall McCreary guest-of-honor caused the dismay of the itinerant Reverend Martin, visiting this week on loan from the church in Sonora. Of all the gold towns he visited on his traveling circuit, Angel's Camp was his favorite. The reverend, with Mr. and Mrs. Buellton, had been invited to the party as last minute substitutes for Mr. McCreary and his household.

After supper, Louisa went to the piano, and Tom brought out his banjo. The family and guests sang all the old familiar songs and hymns. Lucinda dared propriety and gave up any pretense at maidenly reserve. She moved to sit on a footstool at Tom's feet. Her preference was apparent to all present, to the chagrin of the reverend. However, the

Reverend Martin recovered. He had a pleasing tenor, Louisa was a talent at the keyboard, Tom's banjo added a note of cheery jangle, and the evening was very pleasant for all.

Later as Mason and Richard were walking Tom back to the boarding house, Mason, reminiscing over the evening, asked, "Did you and Ples leave sweethearts in Washington?"

"Ah, there were two girls from my boarding house who visited Ples in hospital with me many times. We called on them when Ples was out and testing his recuperation. We took them to tea in a hired carriage on one Sunday afternoon."

"Don't you miss them?"

"No. They were jolly girls, but Ples is too ruined and ashamed of his twisted leg and painful movement. He'd give no girl encouragement, though there was a pretty buxom girl who came and sang for the boys in the hospital. She favored him. But he's a cripple and sees he always will be. He still looks the handsome man, but his poor body is shriveled smaller since the prison camp, and he is painful twisted to one side to ease the bad leg.

"In truth, brothers, I confess I asked the tall girl, Isabella, for her hand. But she wouldn't have me. The girls were Catholics, you see. They wouldn't marry Protestant boys. They were looking for lads of their own faith. Too, Bella was afraid of the west. She thought it full of wild Indians, painted ponies and danger. She mistrusted our land."

"You didn't tell her of MeMe and Ootie? The Indians of the far west?" Richard asked.

"I did. Oh, I did. But she didn't believe me. She'd seen the magazines, you see. I had no pictures to convince her Ootie wasn't wearing a headdress and carrying a tomahawk to fetch her scalp."

"Then, Tommy, if she wouldn't take your word, it is well she wouldn't marry you."

"Don't I just know!" he laughed. "Brothers, when I marry, it will be to a girl who loves our western country."

Tom's banjo case was banging against his leg as he walked. It made a pleasant rhythm.

He began whistling the tunes he and Louisa had played together that evening, remembering how her pretty sister Lucinda smiled up at him from the cushion. "And, boys, I think this very day, I've found the girl."

"Louisa and I are going to marry at Christmas, Tom. We've already talked to her parents." Richard said.

"Then I must get busy. If Lucinda likes me as well as I like her, we'll plan a double wedding."

The decision was rapid, but war had taught Tom all too well how short life can be. That night he slept well. He thought he could like living in Angel's Camp. He'd certainly be happy near his brothers. But he awoke thinking of what poor luck he had searching for MeMe. He would never give up the search. He'd promised Wiley.

Tom had always been Ada's favorite, and she had often championed his cause with his father when he was a boy. She'd grieved when he ran away. The afternoon he arrived at the mansion, so many years later, she made sure she was in a position to eavesdrop on the meeting between Tom and Mr. McCreary. Therefore she heard all of the grand confrontation that had occurred.

She sat in the kitchen with Dr. Grainger and spoke firmly.

"If Frederick McCreary bellows and goes to bully me, or any as works here, I *will* threaten him with the insane asylum in Alameda, Doctor. Ye mark my words. It's one thing for him to rail and rant at me, sir. But the fool man won't control himself with our serving persons who work to help him, and now he's mean and rude with his own sons, and they are good boys. I'll stay here and do me work, but the man's lost me sympathy."

Dr. Grainger had sympathy for anyone caring for the mentally afflicted, and he had greater sympathy for Ada since he had seen Frederick's anger and the way the man focused it so irrationally at anyone nearby. The doctor had often shared a teapot with Ada when he called on Mr. McCreary. She deserved his recognition, and reminded him of his own mam, born in Belfast and not to a lace-curtain family.

On his next visit, Dr. Grainger read McCreary's old housekeeper news from the Stockton paper. Two columns of space on its front page were devoted to the state's plans to build a new lunacy hospital in Stockton.

"*Sacramento* needs the asylum!" His eyes showed merry rage over his teacup. "Our capital is full of lunatics disguised as politicians. However, the legislature doesn't want the blight of the asylum in its city, so the lunatics will be kept elsewhere."

"Tis a shame that Stockton will be known by that place, not as the grand city it is. 'Tis where I met Mr. McCreary, Doctor. He was a good man then, he was. Until his wife was put into the ground. May the saints preserve him." She poured the last ounces of tea into the doctor's cup. "It's still warm enough, but I'll give ye a drop of boilin' from the kettle to top it off."

The doctor knew that her threats of the asylum had been often made to Frederick, but as a warning, not a true indication of what she wanted for him. She had become too much a McCreary herself.

"I'd hate to see the man locked away in a cage, Doctor. As bad as he gets, 'tis better he's here in his home."

"Ada, you are a good soul. Do the sons give you

ample reward for the work you do?"

"Aye, they do. Like their mother, they are. Not in their look so much, but in their ways." She paused to wipe her eyes. "They make sure I want for nothing, and have this grand mansion to live in.

"I'm mistress here and can hire and fire who 'tis I want. There's a good Catholic church here so's I can attend Mass. That feriner priest speaks some langige beyond my ken, but the holy Mass is still in Latin as't always was. The good father there hears me confession though he may not know what 'tis I'm confessin'.

It brings me great peace, saying me rosary in a church does. Ada Cotter sighed and took a sip of her tea as she considered her life in Angel's Camp.

"Yes, Dr. Grainger, There's few women in this world who are fortunate as old Ada Cotter is."

Chapter Forty

~ The Search Continues ~

With knowledge that Merab McCreary might be in Bootjack, Tom and Mason left Angel's Camp traveling south early the next morning, each with two horses to travel fast. The creeks were running high, and they were glad of the ferryboats. Richard wanted MeMe found as much as they, but hard travel was beyond his capabilities, and the thriving office needed attention by at least one brother in addition to Mr. Harrington.

The two brothers arrived late in an evening. Bootjack wasn't a large town. It had been mostly tents when Mason had first ridden through it on one of his inspection trips and was scarcely more. They stepped into the first good-sized tavern they found and ordered a meal of beans, tortillas, butter and beef-steak. After they ate, Tom went up to the bar and plunked money down, ordering a big jug of water with two glasses and two bourbons neat. Tom came back to the table, the barman following with their order.

"I won't drink it," Mason said as soon as the barman left them. "I'll never be like Papa."

"Neither will I," Tom bitterly remarked. The joy of the homecoming had been damaged by his father's destructive words. Frederick's tirade had hurt him badly. "But we'll get more welcome and more information if it looks that we do. There's some who say they won't play game poker with a man who doesn't drink." He drew a deck of cards out of his breast pocket. "I plan to get in a game and act the free-drinking greenhorn. Best way I know to get people talking." He winked at his brother.

"My gun is at hand, big brother. I'll guard you against trouble. Mostly, its only use has been to put down severely injured animals for McCreary Hauling."

"McCreary Hauling's own veterinarian! I do approve of that. For business as well as kindness, I hope you are able to mend more of our stock than you shoot."

"I do. But some accidents are terrible. Mason, do you remember how we loved when Papa told us about the runaway wagons and his adventures having to use hoists to get a team out of a ravine? It isn't exciting now. When I save one animal, I feel victorious. I'm good at this work and would tire of the office."

"We are men for outdoors, Mason. I'll have a ranch someday, cattle on the hills, vineyards and trees around the house, woods for hunting." Tom had been looking at Mason while they talked, but his eyes had continually darted to the tavern door. "The barman clued me to watch for a man wearing an eye patch. He runs the high money games here. Everyone else plays poor man, penny-ante stakes."

Soon four or five men came in together. They split and took two tables near each other. Tom picked up the solitaire game he had set out in the place of his empty dinner plate, and spoke in a low voice, "It's time for me to exercise a skill I learned in the Union Army that Mama wouldn't have liked."

Tom wandered over to the table where the big man with the eye patch sat. Mason moved his chair back against the wall, let his bourbon trickle down its raw planks. The whiskey ran to the sawdust floor showing scarcely a stain. When the barman came by, he ordered another. Time passed, Mason paid for another round to feed the sawdust. He watched as Tom deliberately lost a game five times in a row, leaving money on the table. Tom's defection thereby was amiable. The brothers left the tavern.

"Made a little bundle, and I've found out what we need to know, but it won't help us." He beckoned and Mason walked down to their horses. "Let's take a room and stable the horses. I don't want to sleep by the roadside. It's too wet out."

"Tell me what you found."

"It does us no good. The men had some good to say about the Indian trader. He was named Jake Cobey. He had a place here and carried on trade in a tavern, but he died while running Indians out of Oroville eight months ago. The men remembered him as a man willing to treat the bar whenever he came home from a good business trip. Much of his trade was done up north, above Sacramento. But the men bought from him now and again. "

"He died of sickness? He wasn't murdered?"

"I didn't ask. How he died didn't matter to our business. I found he worked without a partner, just hired riders to guard his commodity by the job. So our trail ends."

"Commodity? That's the word for Indians now?"

"Nope. That's what the card players said that Cobey called them. They had worse names."

"Before we leave in the morning, I'll talk to the stock dealers and mule men here. That's the language I know. If any stock dealers here know anything, they'll tell me."

Mason found out more. Cobey had sold an Indian child to a Russian woman named Irina Dimitrichna who had been popular in town. She'd left town about five years previously. No one knew where she'd gone. But no one remembered seeing the little Indian after she left so they thought she might have taken the girl.

Tom was aghast. "Papa sold her into whoredom? She was just a child!"

"The men said the girl was a little slavey, used for work and to do laundry and stitching, too young and anyway she was too red to be part of the house's trade. The women providing entertainment there were all white women.

"The men remembered the little Indian girl used to pull a great, heavy handcart through the streets helping a deaf Mexican woman. None of them knew her name."

"But can we save her?"

"We must try. The Russian left with a piano player. We might be able to track him easier than her."

"Go back and see if you can get a description of the man."

In ten minutes, Mason was back with a good description. It satisfied Tom because it seemed unusual enough to be possible to trace. "He was tall and lean, had dark skin and bright eyes the color of pond water. He had wooly hair, the stable men said. They didn't know his name. Everyone called him Piano Man."

"We'll find him."

After months of frustrating search and hundreds of dollars in bribery spent first in Southern California, and here in Mariposa and surrounding counties, the only thing that Tom had learned was that a stage master in the town of Merced had once sold two tickets to a man who fit the description of the piano-player. The man traveled with an unforgettable and buxom foreign woman. The stage master found the woman charming enough to remember, but he didn't remember a child traveling with them. However, the ticket seller said the couple was traveling to Grant's Pass, Oregon. He remembered because he had a cousin living in that place.

Tom rode alone to Oregon knowing that it was almost certainly a false lead. Too much time had passed. If MeMe had been with the Russian woman and the piano-player, the man would have remembered selling a ticket for the child.

He returned to Angel's Camp two months later, having found no trace even of the piano-player. More time was lost, but Tom's stubborn concern for MeMe only strengthened -- as was his promise to Wiley that he'd find her.

Ples Landers, from his home in Crane Valley, contacted many of the musicians in Fresno and Mariposa Counties.
Through the mail, he sent queries to traveling musicians he knew asking if any had seen a dark, green-eyed piano player. None who answered his notes had seen a man of that description. After months of failure, he sent a letter letting the brothers know he'd had no luck in the search. But his letter told them of the old neighborhood, the people they had known as children, and of Ootie, Dickey's Indian.

.....Old Ootie still works for Dickey. He's white headed now, but keeps the place clean with broom and duster. I ast him if he'd seen MeMe. The old man near brok down and tol me the last time he seen her was the day my dad and all of us buried your mother.

Dickey says he grieved somthin awful after you left.

There is war against Induns down around here again. Dickey watches out for him. Says that Ootie turned old over-nite when his granddaughter disappeared. He herd from Ada and Frank that she'd gone to some church or other. He didn't take it well. Just withered up. Dickey keeps him as a charity. I went to talk to the old man. He says he wants to help you find his Napas. But I don't know as to what he could do. His mind don't seem all that clear. I'll do whatever I can too. Tell me how I can help.

Pleasant R. Landers

ps. write me at your old address. My father's deeded me The Willows. I've hired young Asa Hopkins and his new wife to work here. Come down whenever you want. You boys can have your old rooms back. We'll polish up the floor in the big parlor and invite the grils in the neighborhood. I'll fiddle, and you boys can spin the grils around the room.

The brothers knew that they could count on Ples to help, but Mason remarked on Ples' weakness. "Reverend Taylor would hide his face in shame over his spelling. Our friend writes much, but not well."

"Don't ridicule Pleasant." Richard said. "He never had more than itinerant schooling. You were lucky. We older children in Crane Valley had school but twice a month. We weren't so lucky in our education."

"Richard's right. Ples may be a poor speller, but then you can't play a fiddle."

"Aw, Tom."

Through his letters to his brothers over the years, Lucinda Harrington had fallen in love with Tom McCreary years before she actually met him. She continued to see him in a heroic light after his return though he was no longer a brave cavalryman. Tom was extraordinarily tall, with the darkest hair and lightest eyes of the McCrearys. She wasn't put off by his need for activity. She was the liveliest of the Harringtons. Lucinda cast Tom as a Knight of the Round Table in his avid search for his lost sister, and loved him all the more because of it. And consequently, within a very short time, Tom and Lucinda became engaged.

The Harrington home's Christmas tree and greenery made the double wedding cheery, though a hoped-for snow didn't fall to turn the town white.

The young reverend who had been on the verge of paying court to Lucinda was the man who married them in the Harrington home in front of the glowing fireplace. It mattered not to the young couple what denomination the reverend was, as long as he was Protestant. In the scattered gold towns, one couldn't be too choosy.

Frederick McCreary was invited, and he came, buoyed up by both Ada and a manservant. He was dressed well, and stayed an hour at the wedding breakfast without becoming loud. Then, he and his servant removed to the tavern and the company of some of his lodge brothers who tolerated him better than his sons did.

Richard and Louisa made a short honeymoon trip to Sonora where they stayed in the newest hotel, far grander than anything in Angel's Camp. They returned within two weeks and took up residence in the Harrington household, to the great pleasure of Edward and Carrie Harrington. They'd happily urged the young couple to make no change but continue to live with them. Edward hired a carpenter to put a door between two bedrooms that Louisa and Richard might have a sitting room in addition to the bedroom.

Tom and Lucinda went to San Francisco to see the

sights. Tom would only take her to the famous Barbary Coast during the day though she begged to visit the scandalous district. But they rode a carriage through Chinatown stopping to buy trinkets and a bracelet of jade for the bride. Lucinda would gladly have stayed in the city longer, but Tom was anxious that they return soon to Angel's Camp.

At home, they rented a dear little cottage only two blocks from the Harrington's home. Tom now had to find a place for himself in the company business, and he continued to hope that he would find MeMe.

Shortly after the couple's homecoming, Mr. Harrington obliged Tom's request, by calling a meeting of the three young McCreary men at the office. He dismissed the clerk and bookkeeper for an afternoon. "Sit at my desk, Tom. It is properly yours, sir." Harrington pointed to the large manager's desk he had occupied since Wiley's death had incapacitated Frederick McCreary.

"No, Edward. I'm not a businessman. I have other plans. I don't want your desk or your job.

"But you are the eldest. I propose that I turn over my guardianship of your brothers to you. Richard won't be of age for nearly two years, but it's just a formality. Your young brothers are both fine men and very capable. They will eventually run the business causing no burden to you."

"I know that sir, and still I propose that you continue as you have been. We trust you."

"That suits me as well," Richard said. "You have done more for us than any natural father would have done, and I, for one, will need your advice long into the future."

"I agree with my brother," Mason said.

"And there you have it," Tom emphatically stated.

"I don't wish to exploit my position here," Edward said. "I should be happy to return to the job of simply keeping the books and proofing the clerk's daily work."

Tom, spoke up. "No. That won't do." He turned to his brothers and made a dramatic sweeping swing of his right arm to indicate Edward. "I propose that Mr. Edward Harrington continue to serve as general manager and declare that we *four* should own this company in equal shares, as partners." He beamed at Richard and Mason, certain that they approved his proposal.

"Edward," he continued, "your good counsel has done well for all of us. If Wiley were here, I know he'd concur. He told me many times of your kindnesses and patience, and of your sound judgment. If my brothers agree, I would like to offer you a quarter share of McCreary Hauling."

"But I've made no investment in the firm. I'm merely an employee."

"You have made the investment of your family, your honor, and your loyalty." Mason said, coming forward to shake Edward's hand.

"You have entrusted your daughters to us. We may certainly trust Papa's business to you," Richard said.

By the end of that day, James Buellton, Esq. had drawn up partnership documents. The four men met at the lawyer's office and each put his signature to the paper and on the copies that would be file both in the law office and the Calaveras County Courthouse.

The next morning there was a meeting of the new partners. I have ideas, Edward," Tom began. "I've talked my brothers, but not yet at length with you. Your opinion is vital to my interest. I will need capital, and have none on my own, only through our company. You see, my time in the east and my travels across the nation and its territories has made it clear to me that change is coming.

"The railroad is not in the Sierra yet, but it will be. There is revolution already in the way cargo is managed. This will affect McCreary Hauling Company. Business will fall away for freight companies like ours. We need to invest in other areas. I'd like to buy land. My brothers may want to invest in businesses, even rail stock, or banking, choosing each to his own interest. If we remain unified in that way we have freedom to invest, yet no one of us takes an inordinate risk. Nor can he risk the whole of the company."

"Our friend Ples Landers' father and his brothers did well with their partnership. We will too," Richard affirmed.

Tom continued. "From what Ples has told me, his father only invested money and has acted the silent partner ever since. I'd rather that we all be active."

He saw Edward's mouth tighten. "Edward. It will be enough that you handle disbursements from the company to our investments in such as way as to protect the company. For myself, I vow never to argue should you refuse an investment you feel takes risk. I'd never want to imperil Lucinda's future, or my brothers' comfort."

'Here, hear," Mason said with a boyish chuckle.

"We can make the central valley of the state as lush with fruit and vegetables as the gardens I've seen in

San Diego or Los Angeles. There can be citrus trees and grapes in the warmer southern valley and stone fruit orchards.

The Sierra has cattle land in abundance here on the valley's eastern fringe," Tom vigorously declared. "If you three concur, I'll buy land and coax it to produce for all of us." His words met a willing audience, and he was encouraged to speak further. "I've talked with Lucinda. We hill people laugh at the flat valley farmers and call them sandlappers. But the sandlappers are succeeding. A farmer's wife has grown orange trees from seed down on the King's River. There is a vineyard producing grapes at Millerton. Johnny Jones in Escalon is a rich man already from producing winter wheat." Enthusiasm added light to the room.

But Richard's caution and down-to-earth sense spoke out. "All well and good, Tom, all well and good. But you move too fast with your investment schemes." And then his eyes twinkled. "First, gentlemen, we must order new signs for the offices and stations and wagons. They shall read *McCreary and Harrington Hauling Company.*"

>>>O<<<

Part Five: The Significance of a Song
~~<<<O>>>~~

Chapter Forty-one
~ Anna Henon's Stories ~

Napas didn't know what month it was, but she knew the season. It was fall. She had been in the woods near the town the driver had called Avery for more than a year. She'd seldom been inside the Henon house. Anna brought her food to her in a pail, and she ate outdoors as she worked. Her hands were rough and her muscles strong from the work; her only joy was thinking going home to Crane Valley and The Willows as she worked.

In the seasons that passed, no one had ever come to visit. Anna and her daughter had never left the property, nor had she. Her job was to take care of the barn, horses, pigs and the five sheep. She had never done that kind of dirty work before, but her brothers had and she'd often watched them. Her reward was seeing the tameness and good health of the animals as she fed and tended them. She enjoyed the beasts' companionship. If she did anything wrong, in the work she was asked to do, Anna corrected her. She never argued. She understood in an instinctive and primitive way that Pastor's rule was never to be questioned.

He was often gone. With every week that he was home, she had grown more frightened of the man. He

298

tormented his family, and someday, when he was home, he was going to torment her too. She knew Mr. McCreary had frightened her once. He threatened to kill her. But Pastor Henon would enjoy doing it.

Napas had begun putting things from her meals that would keep, dry scraps of biscuit, burned rinds of pork skin, and hardened crusts of corn meal mush into a small cloth sack she made and hiding it in loft of the crude barn at the Henon place. It was furtive work. She coaxed the barn cats with food scraps to keep the rats and mice from her storage.

Anna told her horrible stories, and in the past year she had seen enough to believe them. The man was vicious and cruel. He'd threatened if she ever left the yard, he'd kill her. She knew he would. He'd run her down with his whip and his horse. "He gets raged up. He can't help it." Anna told her. "Pastor says I slept with the devil and that's why Trial is like she is. But I ne'er, Napas, I ne'er," she lamented.

"Pastor could see this baby wasn't right as she was borned. He says she ain't from his seed. But, girl, I never slept with no devil nor any man but him. He's allus I ever wed."

Anna's nose had stopped bleeding from where Pastor hit her, but the cut on her forehead was still running. Napas took the cloth and washed in under the pump and gave it back to the woman.

"He weren't called Pastor then. He were young and handsome. He were Billy Henon when we wed in Illinois. An' he had his own farm. My Pa admired that....." The woman's talk drifted away to a happier time. She'd talk to the leaves and grass about the beautiful children she'd borne, if Napas weren't there to listen.

Once the girl asked about Anna's children and what had happened to them, for Anna and Pastor were old enough to have grown children. During a week when Pastor Henon was gone, and in her rambling way, Anna told Napas about them. "My babies went off one at a time," she said. Soon's they was big enough to walk down the road, they ran off. They waited until Billy was gone like he is now, so's he couldn't come after them. An' one by one, my pretty chilrun all disappeared."

Napas had to go quickly and pull Trial back because the child was wandering too close to the creek. But Anna hadn't seemed to notice. The little girl settled down near the place where they were raking hay and began to circle around and around the stacks.

"Oh, I had a pretty girl named Caroline. She weren't like Trial. *You* amind me of my Caroline. Course she weren't no nigger kind of girl. Then I had a boy, then another boy, then a girl." The thin, old woman stared at nothing, smiling at her memory of a different and more pleasant time.

Anna couldn't hold the comforting image very long. Her face drew down. She began talking again, and Napas listened.

"Then, girl, I lost some. Wee, puny things they were. Billy cursed me so bad. He said that I was having baby piglets. He said it were good they couldn't breathe, so's he didn't have to cull them himself. Or if one lived a bit afore she died, he said my milk kilt her. But it wasn't true 'cause then I had anither pretty boy and carried him all the way, like I was aposed to.

Oh, he were fine and fat. He were the prettiest babe you e're did see! I named him Francis Marion, so's he could grow up and be famous.

"Pastor never called him Francis Marion, cause there warn't no Francis in the Bible. He called my pretty boy Elias. He was a good boy. But he sassed Billy when he got big enough. The others had gone away, and there was no one left to stand up for Francis Marion. He sassed Billy to his face.

"An' that's what turned Billy to make hisself a pastor." Anna stood straight, leaning on the rake, smug as though she had just made a discovery. "That sassy day he commenced to beat my pretty boy righteous for the sassing. Billy said he had to beat the demons out of my boy. An' Francis Marion never woke up after them demons was beaten out." Anna choked up and looked away. Napas didn't know what to do or say. The woman recovered in a few moments to return to their work. Anna bent over and began raking fast and hard enough to break the prongs of the rake from its long stem.

Trial was wandering behind them with her tongue hanging out the way she did, but Napas saw that she was staying away from the creek.

"Billy named hisself Pastor e'er after that." Anna was talking as fast as she was whacking down and pulling the rake. "He said he was truer to God than Abraham ere was, and God loved him better than he e're did Abraham. He said it were my fault he kilt Francis Marion 'cuz I didn't teach him proper not to talk up. "Guess it was. But I don't know how you kin teach a boy not to talk up to his pa. Some like to talk up and some don't, like some babies cry and some just lie in the cradle looking about so sweet.

"Francis Marion didn't have no funeral. Billy just took my pretty boy out and buried him in the weeds like those little wee ones what didn't live. He didn't have no funeral at all."

Napas believed every one of Anna's tales and, she came to believe that Trial's father was the devil. She grew determined to persuade Anna and Trial to run away with her. Though, she didn't know how to go about persuading Anna.

As months passed, Napas became as mute as deaf Ines back at Miss Lucy's had been. If she voiced sympathy for Anna, the woman took it as criticism of Pastor. And if she seemed to criticize Pastor, even in the most mild of ways, Anna's voice grew loud in his defense.

The girl worried that listening the woman's stories encouraged the woman to think on her troubles even more. But the woman wanted to talk. Napas didn't know what she could do to help Anna and poor little Trial Henon. Napas had nearly stopped talking. But she didn't stop worrying.

On a horrible day in the winter, Pastor Henon lost a shirt button and made Anna strip naked out in the yard, crawling the paths looking for it, while he hit the woman with a knobbed tree switch. It was the worst thing Napas had ever witnessed. The cold on Anna's bare white skin turned its pallor to blue-grey, and the switch left tiny blood spots tracing along its path on her back and buttocks.

Trial was sobbing, and Napas risked leaving her own work to comfort the little girl. She put her arms around the child and turned her little face away from the scene, patting her, and singing to her. Pastor kept hitting Anna, but was watching Napas. His face and smile grew more hellish each time the switch came down on his wife.

Abruptly, the man tossed the switch away, hitched up his pants, and buttoned his coat all the while watching her. Then, shook himself, and thus composed, he left the yard. Napas ran to help Anna up from the ground and get her clothes back on. "Anna, we'll leave. I'll go with you," she whispered. "We'll take Trial and go to Avery. People will help you."

She remembered the Methodists and how they had helped after the fire in Sonora. "Anna, is there a church in Avery? We could take the old wagon and go all the way to Murphy's Camp. Is there a church there? Do you know?"

"Church people can't help. Them church people is skeered of Pastor." She tilted her head back and smiled. "He brags to me how's he calls God down on his side an' God comes ever time. He says the wrath of God skeers those false prophets in their churches so much they has to call the sheriff on him, but God will prevail. Sheriffs can't win o'er the Almighty."

Anna looked as though she were proud of Pastor, not frightened or horrified. This was something Napas had never seen and couldn't understand, and she found it confusing.

"After Francis Marion died God came down an' anointed Billy the true prophet of the Lord. He'd made the sacrifice of Abraham and Billy was made the new Abraham, the man who kilt his son for God." Anna sat down on the big stump behind the house. Trial came over and climbed on her lap. "My husbin, he's made Pastor by God Almighty."

"My kin didn't honor that," she continued. "They didn't give any honor to God's work in Billy. An' so we came here to the Promised Land.

"The Lord said we should. We walked out of Illinois. Pastor preached wherever we went, an' I did housework and washin'. We walked our way to the golden hills of California, him preaching the word of God everwhere. Soon's we got here I knew I'd have me another baby that I could keep. But I sinned from being too proud of Francis Marion, so God sent me a kind o' baby as wouldn't tempt me to pride.

"You see, Napas? You surely see. Trial is God's baby, not the Devil's."

Napas nodded and smiled at Anna. "She's God's baby truly, Anna," she said honestly. The child was sweet and showed no malice.

Anna looked up and grinned, finally worn out from talking. But that evening, Anna rang the bell that summoned Napas up to the house and gave her some stockings that were scarcely worn, and a knit vest she'd made for herself that had shrunk in washing down to Napas' size.

Pastor Henon had carried a big bag that smelled bad when he bought her from Cobey. The contents of the bag were worth two hundred dollars. She couldn't figure out what was in it or where he made his living. He didn't do any kind of work, but the Henon place, though shabby, had good animals.

Good animals were expensive. Pastor had a fine horse. He had good clothing, and his wagon, though filthy, was sturdy. The family all wore well-made clothes. He took the horses away to have them shod, paying a blacksmith rather than doing it himself. His saddle was good. He brought in bags of sugar and flour, even coffee. Anna wasn't thin for lack of food. The Henons weren't poor people.

Before Pastor left again on one of his trips, Anna wanted him to allow Napas to do more to help her.

One morning when they were in the barn, Anna asked that the milking be done by Napas. The girl was willing, and she liked the gentle animals.

The man turned from saddling his horse his eyebrows twisted up, and he hollered at Anna telling her that Napas' touch would turn the milk and spoil the eggs. He shrieked out again so loud he scared them all. He made Trial cry and almost made the trees shudder with his loudness.

Pastor screamed, "You never done heard of savages what kept cows and chicks, did you, you stupid woman? They can't. The Almighty don't allow for them to live like white people who stand in the glory of His beauteous sight."

The girl grew firmer in her resolve to run away and take Anna and Trial with her. Napas had an old coat of Pastor's hidden in the barn. He'd told her to burn it after he came home in a fine new one after one of his travels. She didn't burn the coat. She threw wet leaves on the fire to make smoke so he'd think she'd burnt it. She hid the coat until he was gone and she could find time to wash it in the creek with laundry soap. If she had to leave while it was still wintery, she'd take it with her, but she didn't want it to smell like him. He often had a foul odor about him when he rode up the track from the woods. She had the buckskin packet, the carpetbag the Methodist minister's wife had given her a year earlier, and a hoard of food. She had other little throw away things too. Things that she'd asked Anna to let her keep, a sliver of soap, a spoon that was chipped and too sharp on the tongue to use, and a knife with a broken blade.

The next time he left, she'd plead with Anna to come with her. She found the old handcart in the back of the barn and checked its bolts to see if they were still tight. They could put Trial in the handcart and go to Avery. They could go to Murphy's Camp. It was very far, but she knew the way. She made plans to save them.

Chapter Forty-two
~ But for the Bending of a Nail ~

Things happened that she hadn't planned. She woke in the middle of one night frightened. She heard noises that weren't just from a fox or raccoon trying to get into her rough little room. Pastor was kicking his way into it. He was ranting at her the way he ranted at Anna but with different words, evil words. "You lust filled whore! Woman, Satan sent you to tempt me, but I won't succumb to your temptations. Hear me, Almighty? I stand here and I resist this demon. I am your true servant, Lord."

She drew the covers around her, shrinking back, afraid he'd do more than rant, afraid he'd beat and torture her. She was afraid to move.

"Woman, you do not tempt me! You think that you can net me for Satan." His voice was so loud she thought Anna could be heard as far away as the house. "Your savage eyes and the very scent of you have come to pull me into Hell's door. But you won't net me. I have the shield of the Lord around me."

There was no hope Anna would come to help her. Anna couldn't help herself. The man's words made no sense to her. She had never willingly gone near him. She never looked at him or talked to him. She thought she was something he reviled, a bush hog or a ground rodent and that made her feel safe. She'd never wanted his notice. He tortured those he noticed.

He was standing in the doorway, illuminated by only the starlight behind him. She could see him moving his arms. She heard him gasp, "Oh God above!" and she smelled something raw, and heard him moan.

She was trapped and praying to a different God than his that he'd move away from the doorway so she could run to the woods. She was quick. She'd run where he couldn't find her. His voice was lower now, cunning and he was forming his words slowly. "I'll whip you bloody, you creature of Satan. You have defiled me. You've brought me low and pulled me down into your pagan hell. You see what you've done? Not the whores of Babylon could do this to me, but you did. The devil is in you that you've made an adulterer out of me."

She heard the clink of his belt buckle hitting the floor as he came toward her. He blotted out what dim moonlight filtered into the room, and he flung the belt out. She ducked her head, but the buckle caught her above her eyebrow and slashed down her cheek. Pastor tossed the belt down and grabbed her up by his big hands. Her face was bleeding. She felt blood drip sticky on her neck and smelled her own blood's rusty odor.

Pulling the covers from her, with one hand the man lifted her up to twist her shift over her hair, yanking her arms free of the garment, tugging until he pulled it from her. His voice was loud again. "I take you as my concubine, like Solomon did Bathsheba. Hear me, God. I am Solomon! This is the woman you have sent me, God. I take her in your name and wash the devil out of her with my seed! I purify her! I am Solomon!"

The pain, and the blood running down her face, had stolen any fight from her. He was banging her head against the wood of the pallet over and over, and she couldn't scream or struggle because of the press of his body on hers. She felt a terrible, searing pain, then a raw scraping began and kept repeating into her body, and she just let herself slip away.

The next morning she woke up to agony. Her mouth was cut, and there was blood scabbing on her face where the buckle cut her. When she tried to move her legs, unbearable pain stabbed up through her to her belly button. She drew in her breath. Breathing hurt her. She was cold and reached out to find her covers. Reaching hurt her more. She couldn't find her covers unless she sat up. She didn't think she could. She was in great pain, and thought she was bleeding from her head, from cuts on her breasts and belly and between her legs. The cold took her and she slept.

When she woke later, it was brighter in the shed. She thought she could hear Trial crying. She tried to sit and to listen, but her body hurt too much. There was scabbed blood on one side of her face and in her hair. Dried blood tightened the skin on her neck and chest. The eye on the side where the buckle cut her didn't want to open, and her tears stung her face. She waited a few minutes, and tried to stand. She saw she was naked and her thighs were bloody too, though it wasn't her woman time. She felt she had been ripped apart, and she stunk. She realized that it wasn't the bloody bed clothing around her, but Pastor's own foul smell on her that made her not want to breathe.

She imagined she could hear Trial crying, but her head hurt and she was dizzy when she moved. She couldn't think anymore.

It was cold, but she was drawn to the creek. She could not stop to think of clothing. She stumbled away from the shed to the dry, crumpled weeds at the water's edge. New little grasses were just breaking through the ground. The water was clear and carrying leaves and bits of winter debris away in its current. She stepped into the cold water and welcomed its numbness creeping up her legs. She walked farther out and sat down on the pebbly bottom of the creek. Her head hurt more for walking, and she couldn't look at the trees beside the creek without them spinning and making her sick.

The frigid water rushed around her. She dunked her head, and kept it turned so that the blood caked side of her face was in the water. She wondered that Anna hadn't come looking for her, for the sun was well up. Today was washday. She should be carrying buckets of water to the tub in the small yard behind the kitchen. She knew Anna wanted her for the washing, but she stayed in the water.

She was shivering when she started back to find clothes. She could hear Trial crying again. She remembered that she'd heard it earlier. Napas followed the sound.

It led her to the privy. The child's hoarse noise was muffled and strange. Napas paused, still dizzy,. She had to hold on to the privy's wall for steadiness. Trial was there, but she wasn't. Napas took a breath of the foul air, and bent down carefully so the privy's walls didn't spin more. The little girl was down below her in the foul muck of the privy.

The privy's bench wasn't hinged. It was just a wide board with a hole in its middle, laid over a frame. She lifted it off, ignoring the sharp pains that ran up between her legs and into her belly as she lifted its weight. She could then look down to see Trial shadowy below her down in the pit. The child was whimpering. Something was dangling from her neck, and the filth of the privy's pit contents covered her legs, arms and clothing.

Naked, but with a rush of anger that took away cold and pain and shame, Napas ran to the barn and grasped a narrow pit ladder. She tugged it back to the privy and worked it through the door and down into the pit. The child was smeared in foul muck even to her fair, thin hair. There was a rope around her neck and it coiled around in the filth below the privy like some whip snake.

On the boards of the bench frame near the ladder was a spike nail. It was bent down. Threads of rope fiber clung to it. Trial reached up to her as she went down the rungs. With her feet in the foul muck, she took the rope from the child's neck. She lifted Trial, bunching up the child's foul gown. The ladder wanted to slide on the slippery footing. She had to lean their weight into its angle to keep it steady. Then they were up the ladder and out into the cold morning air.

She took Trial's filthy nightgown off the child and washed her in the creek, next washed herself, and then washed Trial again. They sat in the water, and she washed their hair and took twigs to clean under their finger and toenails. When they were as clean as icy water and laundry soap allowed, she wrapped the little girl in a blanket. They were both blue, but they were both alive. Her thoughts were as cold as the air. Before she left the Henon place, she was going to kill the devil.

Chapter Forty -Three
~ A Talisman ~

Napas wrapped the child in a cover to warm her, while she dressed and pinned her wet hair back. When she was ready, she honed the knife with the broken blade on a stone, wrapped it in a rag that it not tear through the fabric, and put in her pocket. She carried Trial tucked up in one of her other work dresses, and went to find Anna. She expected that they'd meet Pastor Henon on the path, but they didn't. She pushed the kitchen door open and lugged the child through. Anna was in a rocking chair pulled near the table, bent over and hugging herself. Napas didn't see or hear the man anywhere. The house was quiet.

She could tell Anna's shoulders weren't situated right and weren't set evenly. The woman had been badly beaten and was dazed. When Anna looked up, she recognized her child. Though Trial was still shivering, the child gurgled happily seeing her mother again.

Anna tried to reach to the girl but let out a cry and pulled her arm back. Her mouth was bathed in strings of mucus, tears and blood. Her eyes were almost swollen shut. She was still in her sleeping gown. It was torn and saturated red with blood. There was blood all over the woman, even to her hair. So much that even in the dim shadows of the west facing kitchen, Napas knew Pastor had done to Anna as bad as he'd done to her.

"Is she alive?" Anna asked. "Is my sweet baby alive?" Her voice was softer than a whisper. "Billy said he'd killed this one too. But he didn't."

"Oh, is she a ghost? Napas, is she a ghost? Are you a ghost? I don't mind if you are ghosts. Billy said he kilt you too. He alus kills what he says he's goin' to kill an' he kills some as he don't say."

Napas placed the little girl, still wrapped in her shawl, on the woman's lap. Trial needed her mother, and Anna needed her. "She's not a ghost, Anna. Pastor hanged her in the privy, but the rope fell and then I got her out. She's truly alive. Is he here? Tell me, Anna, is he here?"

The woman began humming, but her voice was making what sounded like moans. There was no music in the noise, only fear and pain. The woman held her child and began rocking. The little girl's color began to pink up as she drew warmth from her mother and the house.

Napas had asked Anna once how old Trial was, and Anna said she was eight or maybe nine years. Anna wasn't quite sure. The child looked to be around four. But whatever her age, she was an infant forever, too young to be bothered by the blood on her mother's face and gown. Blood meant nothing to her but a color. Napas sat down for a minute. Maybe he's still here she thought as her mind opened up again. She didn't know how much time had passed. Her terror came back and made her stealthy and sly. She drew water from the pump into the tin cup the little girl used and found biscuits to put on the table within Trial's reach. Then, with her hand on the broken blade knife, she crept out to the hallway and looked into the parlor.

Pastor wasn't there. She crept toward the back rooms silently, watchfully. Her fingertips were touching the knife. She didn't trust that he'd gone.

Through an open doorway on the east side of the house, she saw a morning-bright room, but it was splattered with blood. The sticky red liquid drenched the bed and pooled on the floor. An axe that was usually left in the stump out by the pump was on the bed, its head smearing the folds of a blanket, its handle lying across one of Pastor's legs. Napas knew the axe. Every Sunday morning, after Pastor's Bible reading, while Napas curried Pastor's horse, Anna used the axe to kill a chicken for the man's Sunday supper.

Pastor lay there on the bed in front of her, his head a mass of bone and blood, the mess of his brain on his pillow. His neck hadn't been cleanly cut with one stroke as a chicken's would be. It had taken many downward strikes of the blade smashing him into the bed to kill him.

As carefully and soundlessly as Napas had come through the hall to the door of the room, she crept back to the kitchen. Anna looked up at her. "Don't you go wake up Pastor, Napas. He'll kill us all o're agin if you wake him. Oh, he'll kill us agin."

"He's dead, Anna. He is dead. He can't kill us."

Anna looked at Napas and shook her head. "No, he won't ne'er die. He kilt us all. I shouldn't have made a baby like I did. Billy that was, an' Pastor that is, didn't like that I made this sweet idjit child. When I saw Pastor dressed an' up before me, though it wasn't yet morning light, he bragged as how he kilt the devil's wanton temptress. I knew it was you he kilt. He kilt you surely. I talked up to him. I said that he kilt everthin' that was mine. He did that. He kilt my fine Francis Marion, an' it was him as drove all our sound chilrun off.

Once started, Anna couldn't stop talking. "He didn't move or say nothin', Napas. He just listened to me sassing him as how you were just a girl an' didn't know what the devil was about yet." She shook her head woefully.

"You were like my Caroline. You hadn't learned no wantonness. You were but a girl. He had no right killin' you. I put the blame on him, I did. I sassed him good. I told him poor Trial was the only one I had left, an' if the devil was in Trial it come from him. Then he stopped listening an' stood up. I watched his rage take over him. He beat me bad, Napas. I think my arm's broken. But I'm not kilt. You said I'm not kilt.

"He told me he was goin' to get rid of that devil's chil' and come back an' beat me again for bearing her. I screamed and screamed but he took her. He alus kilt what he said.

"He were too tired to beat on me when he come back from killing Trial. He said to wait in the kitchen an' he'd beat me later on. I'm waitin'." Anna was rocking faster. Trial looked alarmed by the speed of the chair's movement. Napas tried to calm the woman to slow her.

"He can't beat you. Come with me. We'll take Trial go away. Pastor is dead. He's dead."

Some of what Napas said began to penetrate Anna's mind. "No," she said. "I can't go off with you today, Indian girl. We can't go away. If he's dead, I have to see my Billy buried proper. I'll take my baby in the wagon. We'll go and call the undertaker. I don't want my Billy buried out back like Francis Marion an' all my dead babies. I want my Billy in a green cemetery with a stone an' carved angels, cause he's Abraham the prophet."

315

"Let me take Trial with me. I'll take care of her, Anna. I promise."

Anna leaned forward, still hugging the child, and looked at Napas. "You, Indian girl, you resurrected her, an' I thanks you. But I has to kill you too if you takes her from me."

Napas feared the expressions playing on the crazed woman's face. The woman's mind had never been all the way sensible, but there was a sense to what Anna said. She couldn't take away all the woman had left. "I won't take her away. Just let me take care of her until you get Billy buried."

Anna's face grew wildly hostile. "No! You go outside an' do the washing like you're aposed to. You know it's washin' day. You go now."

"I'm going, Anna. I have to go."

The woman calmed, settled back again, and her frenetic rocking began again. "That's good. You start the fire under the big tub. I'm going to take Trial to her room an' we'll lay ourselves down and take a nap. Then we'll go to town an' get the undertaker," she said swiftly, sounding as merry as if they were going to a picnic.

The woman cried out as she stood with the child clinging to her, but she shrugged away as Napas tried to help her. Anna let Trial down on the floor.

"That's good, Napas. That's real good. But you go begin the wash 'thout me today. I thanks you that you found my Trial." The woman turned away and stumbled down the hallway dragging the sadly abused, but still living child along behind her.

Napas heated water but not over the washtub in the kitchen yard. She heated it in little pit where she often burned trash or offal that could attract vermin. She wrapped rags around her hands. The pail's handle was hot. She carried the heated water to her room.

She took her time and used soap again to wash every trace of her blood and the stench of the privy from her hair. The creek had cleaned her but didn't rid the smell. Her breasts and private parts stung so badly when the soapy water touched them that she cried out. When she looked down she saw that her breasts, belly, and thighs were bruised and had small cuts and bite marks.

She clawed at her skin and scraped with the rag. She dumped the basin outside and poured more hot water into it. The smell of Pastor on her skin was worse to her than the smell of the privy had been. Finally, the lye soap cleansed her, and though she still hurt, she felt better.

Then Napas dressed. From the old carpetbag she took out one of the dresses the minister's wife had given her. The dress's skirt was well above her ankles when she put it on. Her underskirt rimmed the hem for four inches around. She took the old dark frocks Pastor and Anna insisted she wear. The coals of the fire were still glowing, and she fanned the cotton fabric until it caught and sent up red flames. She threw on more kindling and dragged a big log over to the fire. For a long while she watched the fire burn. She felt some rain drops and realized it had clouded over in thick dark clouds. It was time for her to go. She couldn't stop for rain. She climbed up to the barn rafters and gathered everything she had carefully secreted. She was glad she'd kept the man's old coat. It would protect her against the rain until she could find shelter somewhere. She took down a tarp hanging near the tool rack. It was big enough to cover her, but light enough to carry.

With her carpetbag, and a sack of old, dried, scarcely palatable food, she crossed the creek and then the road. She came to the highway. One direction was Avery and one Murphy's Camp. She turned neither way. She crossed the highway and began climbing the hill south from the Henon property. The buckskin packet, bulky but not heavy, was secured inside her shift, held in place by a cord around her chest and back. It held a strand of her mother's hair, some calico, a linen bag she and Nancy had embroidered, and a chamois bag her grandfather had given her to record the progress of her life. Tucked in the bottom of the bag, beneath fourteen small pebbles, were a ring, a thimble, and two liberty pennies.

The packet had been with her since she lived in Crane Valley. She was determined to keep it safe. It was the talisman that would help lead her home to The Willows.

Chapter Forty-four
~ Posted on a Fence ~

On good days, Frederick McCreary took lunch at the tavern. He and his companions lived in the successes of their past lives. They talked of the weather, and politics, and silently damned the times for making them old. They'd gone together to the dedication of the lodge in Murphy's Camp in May two years back and taken two carriages. It was the last time Frederick had left Angel's Camp. His lodge brothers were solicitous of McCreary. He drank too much, but he was one of them. They'd walk him home, or call one of his sons to fetch him, when he was unsteady on his feet.

After lunch, those good days, Frederick would walk to the office for a short visit before returning to the mansion for a portion of Ada's tea and Dr. Grainger's tonic. Then, he'd nap.

He hadn't noticed the change in the sign over the door until Mason and Richard walked him back outside and pointed it out to him. Frederick just said, "Red. I like red. Well done. We needed a new sign painted." He seemed to miss the significance of the addition of Harrington's name. On this day, which wasn't good, as he stormed into the office tossing the door back hard enough to hit the cabinet and crack its glass. Clerk, bookkeeper, Richard and Edward, alarmed by the noise and startled at Frederick's expression, came to their feet.

"Papa, what's wrong?" Richard was standing, and he was the first to speak. Frederick waved a paper at them all, caught his breath and began raving.

"Murderess! I knew she would grow more evil with time. She's killed a man of God. The red nigger is a murderess!"

"Mr. McCreary, calm yourself. What is this all about?" Edward moved to calm the old man.

Clerk assisted as the bookkeeper tried to persuade Frederick away from the open doorway. Richard was locked in place, staring at his father and trying to put sense into what the man had said. He saw the large poster in his father's hand and he forced his legs to move toward Frederick.

"Give it to me, Papa," he said.

"See. I was right!" Frederick waved it toward Richard. "You and your mother were all so soft-headed, but I knew what she was." The man flushed, and fell forward onto the floor face down.

"I'll get Grainger," clerk said and was out the door.

The three men turned Frederick and pulled him further from the door. Using a chair cushion and taking off his coat, Harrington made a pillow for the stricken man's head. Richard took a coat from the back of one of the desk chairs and put it over his father's chest. With Edward and Miller, the bookkeeper, to tend his father, Richard picked up the paper. It had been torn from nails on a post or wall. Dingy road dust filmed it but only lightly. The smell of ink was still sharp. It was a wanted poster.

There was a printed sketch of a young Indian woman on the poster. Looking at it the way his father might have, the woman *was* similar to what MeMe might have grown to look like. But it might have been any other Indian woman. The face was oval, hair dark, eyes almond shaped. The artist might have drawn any exotic young woman at all.

"A guilty conscience, Papa. That's what colors your vision." Richard's voice was soft as he whispered to his father while Edward and Miller went for water and a robe to cover McCreary who seemed to be recovering. Richard's actions with his father remained tender, but his sentiments had hardened. The drawing did look like MeMe. What had his father done to her that he'd think she might be here in Calaveras County in this kind of a situation? Richard suppressed any overt response, but he was overcome with anger at his father's duplicity.

Frederick was taken home to the mansion on a stretcher in a closed wagon, with Dr. Grainger in attendance, and Richard came to a time of reckoning. If his father's certainty hadn't convinced him that the girl on the poster was his sister, when he examined the poster the name of the Calaveras County murderess did. **"THE INDIAN WOMAN NAUPEZ"** the letters proclaimed in large, bold print.

Napas was what Ootie had called MeMe as a child. It was close in sound to Naupez. MeMe was but a young girl, but the *woman* on the poster had to be her. Before he talked to Edward, before he went home to Louisa, or went to find Tom, he locked the poster in his desk drawer and made a decision.

Mason should have arrived in Mariposa today, and his work there would keep him at the McCreary corrals for at least four days. Ples was in Crane Valley, but his father and stepmother were near in Fresno Flats. Wasting no time, Richard went to the telegraph office and there sent three telegrams. Knowing it would reach Ples if sent to him, or his father, he sent:

NEED PLES STOP DICKEY STOP OOTIE IN A CAMP STOP URGENT +
RICHARD

To Mason he sent:

OUR SEARCH MAY END STOP NEED YOU A CAMP + RICHARD

Done, he went to the livery and took a carriage to drive to Tom and Lucinda's home. He was breathless from exertion and couldn't afford sickness now. The carriage allowed him to catch his breath.

"Lucinda, dear, I need to see Tom."

"He's in the study. Go in and rouse him from his thoughts and plans. He banished my attentions for the hour, but he won't mind your visit."

He found Tom at his desk with crop journals before him. His brother didn't mind the interruption. "Richard! Come in and sit! I have wonderful things to tell you.

"Winter wheat will bring a good crop in the lower valley if the spring flooding isn't too deep. It might be necessary to raise plantings, and dig ponds to siphon from during the dry season. The real gold of California is in what it will grow. Down around Tulare Lake there is..."

Richard held up his hand to stop the flow of his brother's words.

"It's not Papa?" Tom worriedly asked.

"No, not Papa. Well, it is Papa. I'll tell you that story soon. First I must tell you that I may have found our sister."

"You? *You've* been successful where Ples, Mason and I have failed? You, who scarce ever leave Angel's Camp?" The look on Tom's face was incredulous.

"Yes. But if it is she, our sister is in a desperate way. I feel it is. She is wanted for murder and being sought in our own county. The murder took place out of Avery. A man was killed."

"That can't be. Richard, she's not yet fifteen!"

"Let me tell you what happened. I'm certain it is she. I'm certain also that she is not a murderess. But posters are going up all about the county with her face and description. Papa brought one to the office less than an hour ago. I saw another in the telegraph office before I came here."

"Telegraph? You've sent for Ples?"

"Ples, yes. And Mr. Dickey and Ootie. And I sent another to our brother. We must plan for them to arrive. If they get the message, they will be here as fast as they can."

"We must find her before anyone else does."

"Exactly so. And we must be careful to tell *no one*. We become criminals as we move contrary to the law."

"The law *will* kill her if it finds her. You know that. But, we will save her this time, Richard. We will not fail."

"Ootie may be of help, if he is able to travel. He's old. And there is one other person who may help, though I don't want her to assume our risk."

"Whom are you thinking of? Ada?"

"We need a woman with us, should we be fortunate enough to find our sister. I want to take Carrie into our confidence. She can help find lodging for Ootie and Mr. Dickey. Ples can stay with us. There is room. Carrie can manage comings and goings. She's about town with her good works. The thing is, we may find MeMe in poor condition. She may need someone like Carrie."

"I already have formed my role as you've been speaking." Tom was too serious to smile. "My job will be to give reason for Dickey and Ples to visit and the five of us travel about. I'll tell Lucinda that they want to venture in a financial scheme I'm planning. We will be working together looking at properties. Lucy will gossip and complain to Louisa that my head is too much in business, but our traveling about will seem reasonable. Ootie will seem Dickey's Indian hire and no one will question his presence.

"If he doesn't speak, we'll dress him up, put a sombrero on him and people will think him a Mexican manservant," Tom quipped. "But I worry about involving Carrie. We may also want to leave Mason out of it.

"But he must be allowed the opportunity to choose. He's young, and this is a dangerous venture, but he is MeMe's brother too as much as we are.

Chapter Forty-five
~ With the Miwok ~

The rain in the mountains south of Avery continued on for four days, and if it weren't for the old black coat, Napas would have been sick from exposure to the damp and cold. But wool insulates even when wet, and the small tarp, folded and worn like a headscarf over her hair and upper body kept her semi-dry.

Her only conscious determination was to avoid white people who might capture and take her back to the man named Cobey to be sold again.

She was in pain and feeling very troubled by what had happened. She crossed three tracks that were wide enough for a wagon, and they were deserted and overgrown. She heard nothing but natural sounds around her, rain, not heavy, but accumulating in the trees and dripping to the ground. The birds were keeping to their nests, and she scarcely heard the scurry of rabbits and squirrel at all. It was hard to keep to a southerly direction. Above the oaks and jack pines, the dark clouds veiled the sun's movement too well.

On the fifth day, the rain stopped. The sun rose banishing the grey and ominous clouds that had chilled and oppressed her. Without thinking of what she was doing, she took her bearings again from the sun. She began following down a creek that was too small to attract miners, scarcely more than a rain run-off.

She walked on, only allowing herself small bites of the

food she had conserved. She had slept as high from the muddy ground as possible, finding fallen logs wide enough for her slim body, or building a nest in the vault of roots in big trees. When she woke she was stiff and cold enough that when she splashed water on her face, it held no sudden shock.

Twice, as she walked, she thought she heard human sounds and smelled coffee. She moved further from the widening creek lest she find miners working the grit there. When it was quiet again, she would near the water. Gradually, with the sun's return, her clothes dried, her body healed, and her mind cleared. She hoped to find an Indian encampment. The only Indian she had ever known had been very good to her. She tried not to think of the things Pastor Henon had done to her, or of the crazed woman and pitiful child she'd left behind. But the clearer her mind became, the more she carried the memory of his viciousness with her.

The Stanislaus River was a great barrier to her progress, but when she reached it she knew she was traveling the way she wanted. She wasted many days wandering up river, wending her way though brush and scrub oak, walking parallel to the miner's trace, but keeping well aware of the danger of being seen by anyone. She would surely be sold again if any white people found her. She moved away from the river when she thought there might any kind of habitation or encampment of white people near. She scrambled back down to the river to drink only when it seemed safe.

Napas couldn't remember exactly why it was important for her to cross the river, but she knew she had to cross it. She had judged that as every creek she forded made the great river wider, traveling east higher into the mountains it would smaller. She was correct in her judgment. The higher into the Sierra she climbed, the fewer streams ran into the river and the narrower and easier to cross the river became. The rain had made the river higher and its water swifter, but each day that passed without rain lowered the river's depth. She watched for boulders and snags that would help her cross.

Early one afternoon, she smelled wood smoke, and though there were no sounds, she went up into the woods again, skirting away from the water. She was very hungry and tired from all she carried with her. Through the trees, she could see men working at the edge of the water.

They had built a rough cave out of the earth near the river, like the root cellar at the Henon place. They had also built some type of low structures that she couldn't identify near an eddy of the river. Below their camp, there were large, flat rocks jutting out. A fallen tree was wedged between them that dammed back the water enough to create a sandy eddy where they worked. She stayed quiet, and watched.

At nightfall, the men made coffee and bacon. The smell tantalized her. That day, all she had eaten was a gathering of the mild tasting, round leafed green plant that she and the boys nibbled in the spring while at play. All her hoarded food was gone. That morning, she had turned the food sack inside out and scraped every bit of the cornbread grains that had lodged along its seam. She'd sucked on the bag itself, savoring the sweetness left in its weave. For two days, all else she had eaten was the green plant but she had sucked the sugar from the sweet, white base of grasses that were coming up in sunny clearings in the wood.

She'd folded the empty food sack and rolled it tightly and put it in the pocket of Pastor's coat. If she found food again, she'd have a place to conserve it. The men she watched shared a jug among themselves. They laughed and sang as they sat around their fire pit. They weren't speaking any language she had heard before. She considered waiting until they were asleep and sneaking into their camp to look for food. But her body still hurt from what Pastor had done to her. If they caught her they might hurt her as he had, or kill her for sport. She would endure her hunger before she'd go near the men.

She stayed hidden until the moon rose. When the men were asleep and snoring, she knew she had to get across the river. She didn't know how deep its water was, but she was compelled to try. The moonlight made the big flat rocks vivid, the log black by contrast. The water seemed lower around the rocks, only rushing where it went under the log. She buttoned up Pastor's coat and wrapped the carpetbag in the small tarp. When she judged it to be the middle of the night, and one of the men was snoring so loud that she might not be heard, she crept down to the river.

The moon had risen high as she'd waited and was giving less light. If she moved slowly and stepped so carefully that she didn't crack a twig or stumble over stones and pebbles. If one of the men woke and looked around, she might just seem a shadow in the night.

When she came to the bank of the river, she tucked her underskirts up and over the fabric of her dress and pinned them tightly. Then she took her boots off and tied their laces together and hung them around her neck. She looked around and listened. An owl hooted, but the men were still, lying in their blankets and she sensed that they were asleep.

She stepped into the water above the first flat rock, holding the tarp-wrapped carpetbag over it. The cold water shocked the breath out of her, and she stood shuddering for a long moment. She went on, finding her footing with care, going from one rock to the next. When there was a distance between them, the pressure of the water tried to force her down, but she held her burden up over her head, and resisted, continuing on to the next slab of granite.

It was easier when she came to the log. She pulled herself up on it, and lying on her belly while pushing the carpetbag ahead of her, moving like a lizard along the length of the fallen tree. The scraping of bark against her chest and belly abraded the coat, but its buttons held and she wasn't troubled by worry of her clothes bunching and impeding her progress. There were some minutes when she could feel the velocity of the water rushing below her, and was terrified. But she moved onward by inches, until she could clearly see the moonlight on the rocks at the other side of the river.

When she knew she had crossed the deepest part of the rushing water, she stopped and let herself lie on the log to rest. But her hands continued to grip the carpetbag, her knees gripping the log beneath her. She was crawling like a frog swam, and trying not to scrape her dress to a tear or pull the buttons from the coat, using her feet and knees to propel her forward. Her shoes, hanging down from her neck, snagged. She had crawl backwards to free them. It was an awkward and slow crossing. But she made it to the eddy and its short beach on the other side. She silently prayed as Nancy McCreary had taught her when she was a very small child. She thanked God for bringing her across the river safely.

In the dark, she found a place in a thicket of manzanita, deep past the rush on the other side of the river and back in the trees. She crossed the river and walked far from the men and their camp.

Though clouds had dimmed the moon, she took off the wet coat and hung it from a branch and stripped the tarp wrapping from the carpetbag. The bag was dry. Its heavy fabric felt good to her fingers. She opened it and felt through the clothes inside. Everything was dry. She pulled down her wet underskirt and drawers and hung them on branches as she had hung Pastor's coat.

She felt in the carpetbag until her fingers recognized buttons, and she took out under things and the other frock the minister's wife had given her. She spread the dress she had been wearing on a bush. Its lower skirt was as wet as the bottom of her underskirts, but its bodice had remained dry. She was comforted to find that the buckskin packet she'd worn tied around her chest was still dry and warm from her body. She slipped the fresh dress over her head and buttoned it up, immediately feeling less cold. She pulled another underskirt and set of drawers out of the carpetbag and put them on. The ground was soft, and she was very tired. She knew her search for the crossing had moved her far to the east, but she was on the south side of the river now. She couldn't stay awake any longer, and she slept.

When she woke, it was bright morning. She heard the chucking of a squirrel. She pushed the tarp and carpetbag away and sat up. Her eyes cleared, and she saw two brown men. They were thin and had broad faces and black hair. They were squatting just a short distance away, watching her.

One was wearing almost nothing. He had a short buckskin skirt and a band around his waist. He was as naked as the boys tied in Cobey's barn. He was old, older than she remembered Ootie looking. His hair was long. The other was a young man, wearing overalls and a much-mended brown shirt. His hair was cropped. They seemed calm, just watching. She knew she should run away, but she was still too tired. She didn't have the energy to stand up or to run.

They said something to each other in low voices. Then the older man said something to her. She couldn't understand what he was saying. He offered her a skin canteen and indicated that she should drink, and she did. Then he gave her something to eat, and she did. She didn't know or care what it was that she was eating or drinking. The old man spoke to her again, and the younger man said something. She was frustrated, trying to understand, but unable able to concentrate on their strange talk. She wanted to curl up and go back to sleep.

But she wasn't afraid of them. For some reason she seemed to have once known but then forgotten, she felt the men wouldn't hurt her. The younger man laughed, and said something that made the older man laugh. He looked at her and said something more. She put her head down and closed her eyes. She didn't think the men were going to hurt her.

She turned away from them and covered her head. She had no idea what they were saying to each other. Then the young one spoke to her in English, "You Indian. No talk Indian?"

She still didn't understand him, but she thought she should.

The old one was demanding in his manner. He asked "Hopopi?"

Food, and hearing the old man speak in a familiar way, gruff and soft at the same time and bringing up memories of a different time, made her feel alive again. The younger man who spoke to her asked slowly, "Girl. What name you got?"

She lifted her face and looked at them. She did understand him. She could answer. It was the first time she had spoken aloud in weeks. She swallowed, and though hoarse, began.

"My name is Napas. I am an Indian like you. Thank you for finding me. Can you tell me how to get to Crane Valley?" She heard her voice clearing. It seemed odd to be talking again.

He tilted his head to look questioningly at her. "You say hopopi Napas?"

"Yes."

"White people at Arnold town say *Napas* kill Henon. He was nodding his head. Picture is same you."

"I didn't! Please believe me. I didn't kill him. Anna killed him. I need to go south. Please help me. I need to cross all the rivers."

"Hu!" the old man said. His wide smile wrinkled his face.

The younger man's eyes shone. "It good kill Henon. He kill many Indian. Bad man." They looked at her as though she were a hero.

"We help." The old man said something. Both men laughed. It disturbed her that she didn't know what they found funny.

The young man noticed her discomfort. "Tunitosewe say you talk much for Indian girl. Maybe you white, but it good you kill Henon." Both men still had huge smiles on their faces. They wanted her to have killed Pastor, but she was very sure she hadn't. She wanted to, though. She just didn't get the chance and ought not be honored.

And, then, all in a rush, her memory was clear. She remembered who she was and where she was. She also remembered why she had been walking.

"Can you help me get to Crane Valley?"

"Cray Valley?" He looked puzzled. "We help you hide. Come. Is danger. Now we go."

The river had taken the last of her energy. There were many more rivers to cross between her and the home she wanted to reach. But she was so tired. She knew she had to go with them to stay alive. She couldn't go on, but she had to try.

Napas knew that if she tried to keep walking alone, she would die somewhere, in the woods, or crossing the next river. Or white people would find her. These men were her only chance.

When she began stumbling, the young one gave her things to the older man. Then he swung her over his back and carried her. He and the old one never slowed their pace.

Chapter Forty-six
~ A Tower of Stone ~

In the early afternoon, the two men gave her some dried meat from a pouch one carried on a hide strip around his neck. They stopped each time they crossed a creek to drink but they wouldn't stop to rest. She felt better and walked with them, trying to keep up.

That morning, the old man had put on Pastor's coat though it was a warm day. It looked like it was still damp from the river, but he didn't seem to mind. The young one had opened her carpetbag, pulled all her dry clothes down from the branches and bushes and stuffed them inside. When the younger one carried her, the older man carried the carpetbag.

They'd led her through more miles of uphill and downhill striding, until she fell, and then they let her rest for a while. When it was time to walk, the younger man once again hoisted her up on his back as he had at first, and they went on.

In late afternoon, the three of them broke through dense woods of huge trees and tall bracken and stopped. Napas leaned up against a tree, and wanted to sleep. But the men pointed to a gap where she could see through the trees.

A large clearing was ahead of them. She saw that they'd come to what she recognized to be an Indian village. But she saw little movement and very few people moving about. Only a couple of houses showed smoke. Most were dilapidated and coming apart. The older man caught her and put his hand across her mouth. She knew to keep quiet. She had no desire to talk.

The older man touched the younger man's shoulder. The young man nodded, and the old one reluctantly took off the black coat and handed it to the girl. He turned without saying anything and left them to go on to the village. She started to follow, but the younger man pulled her back. She pointed after the older man, looking up quizzically.

He pulled her back farther into the woods. "No. You *no* go Indian place."

She was dismayed. She wanted to go there. It looked safe there, and she wanted to rest.

"More walk. I walk. You walk. Then eat," he said. And they went back deep into the woods. It grew darker. They crashed through a small rivulet and stopped. The man filled a pouch with water. They walked again just a short way and suddenly were on a well-traveled path. The Indian seemed to know where they were going, and though she was exhausted, she followed without complaining. They left the path again and were in the trees.

They walked until it was almost dark. They passed some huge rocks and after they passed them, the Indian stopped and turned off the path. He held up his hand indicating that she should stop and wait for him. He went through some bushes. She heard a squeak and a rustle as the man emerged from the manzanita and budding elderberry with a dead rabbit in his left hand. He was smiling at her.

"Trap good. We got food." He helped her up into a cleft between two of the rocks. Then she saw that they were in a protected place, in a high position. The place was like a cup, formed by boulders that were much taller than the man was, maybe as tall as two men were. There were traces of old fires that had been built there other times. Soon the Indian had skinned and gutted the rabbit and had it skewered it over a new fire.

After they'd eaten, the Indian scooped up the debris of their meal and took it down and away. It was full night when he came back. The rocks made shadows, but the fire was still glowing. The Indian man got down on his hands and knees.

"Down. Come," he ordered her. The Indian man belly-crawled through a low opening, slithering between two slanting wedges in the rocks.

She hadn't noticed the opening before. She didn't question him. She tucked her dress up to free her knees, and then she spread the tarp out, putting the coat and carpetbag on it, folding its edges up and over the items. She got on her knees, pushing the stack ahead of her. When they'd crawled through, he said, "We rest now."

She took her boots off, lay down, and slept. When she woke up stars were shining above her, but it was still early in the night. In the darkness, she knew the man was awake and watching her.

"I, Opototo, go now," he said. "You push rock." He pulled her up, took her hand and she could feel a large barrel shaped rock. He rocked it, and she realized it wasn't attached to the rock face that surrounded them.

"You want me to stay here?"

"You stay. Push rock. Safe place. You push rock no white man see safe place. Tomorrow I come. Bring food. Bring Wokli."

She understood. When he left her, in the darkness, she pushed the rock against the opening. She heard him doing something to the ground on the other side, and then it was quiet and he was gone. She wondered what a wokli was.

The next day, with dawn, she could see that she was in a tower of stone. The place where the Indian man had left her was like a great nest. Its bottom was soft sand and it was as wide as the kitchen had been at the Henon house, not big, but a man could easily stretch out full length. She had to pee. She looked around to find a place and discovered that a narrow and twisted crevice, almost invisible against the cracks of a rock face, opened to another room of greater size.

It had reeds and a tiny pool at one rock's base and a cavern where another rock overhung. There was a small opening in that room also. It was too small for the Indian man, but she slipped into it, saw where it led, and in less than a minute, she was out in the pines on the outside of the big mass of rocks.

She took care of her body's needs, washed her face and hands in a small stream, and slipped back into the nest room. She was safe. The stone castle protected her. Napas knew if people were after her, crossing the river wasn't enough. Men with guns and horses would be hunting her. They wouldn't just kill her; they'd kill the Indians who helped her. Thinking better, once she'd had a long restful sleep, she wondered why the men thought she had killed Pastor. She hadn't. She wanted to. She would have. But she hadn't.

She had been walking a long time and was just beginning to feel healed from where he had ripped into her body. She could feel the rough tight place on her face and knew she was scarred. What seemed far worse to her was what he had done to his own little daughter. It was true that Trial wasn't like other children, but she was his and Anna's child. She was a harmless little innocent. This was the clearest thinking

Napas had done about what had happened at the Henon place. She'd lost time somehow. She didn't know how many days she'd wandered. She knew it was more than two weeks, maybe more than three weeks.

She looked down at her wrists and hands and saw how thin she had gotten. She pushed her sleeves up. The bones of her arms looked like the blades of knives. Her feet wobbled in her shoes.

Napas leaned back against a slope of granite in the morning sun. There was something good about this place in the rocks. She still felt full from the rabbit she'd eaten the night before. The sun was warming the sand where she sat. She wondered about the killing. Anna must have accused her of killing Pastor. If the woman had taken the wagon and gone to Avery with her daughter as she said she was going to do, the white people there would *want* to believe her. Napas understood how it had happened. Anna must have been afraid that she'd be jailed, and then, who would take care of Trial? What would become of a child like her? Who would ever take in a child who would never talk or be able to work for her keep. If Anna told the truth, the law would hang her. If she lied, she kept her daughter. Poor woman.

It was possible that Anna didn't know herself that she had wielded the axe.

Napas felt guilty when she'd run away from the thin, sick, odd-thinking woman and the backward little girl who needed her. But she couldn't stay. She couldn't. And, now she knew she was the accused. If she had stayed, she'd have already been shot or hanged for his murder.

"It's not wrong to save one's self," she repeated over and over, speaking aloud but in a whisper. She wanted relief from her conscience, which was wracking her with more and more torment. What would become of the woman and child she had left? What could she have done?

She heard the rock being pushed and went to help by pulling at it. It came away easily, and Opototo came in with food. Then, she found out what the wokli was. Wokli was a *woman*. She was a beautiful woman. She was perhaps a little older than the Indian man, and much taller than Napas. Her face was wise and kind. She had a large basket that she'd slid ahead of her through the opening, just as Napas had pushed her own bundle.

In the basket were smaller baskets. There was some sort of mashed nuts that tasted a little like the hominy she had eaten at Miss Lucy's and something like the rice she had eaten at the White Dove. It wasn't as good as meat and potatoes, but it was much better than the cold and often burned pancakes that Anna had given her to eat. She ate every bit. There was some kind of dried meat too. But Wokli shook her head and said something to the man when Napas reached for it.

"She say you keep. No eat. Maybe eat tomorrow."

"She wants me to save it?"

"Yes. Save. If soldiers come, Napas alone here." He looked as though he wanted to say something more, and then he did. "Much men look for Napas. Soldiers. Deputies. Bad men. Men want kill girl for money. I see on trail, on road. Have guns."

"They'll kill me."

"Yes."

"And I can't be near your village because they'd kill all of you for helping me."

"Yes."

A frightening thought came to her. "Will you sell me to them?"

"Sell to white men?"

She had been sold before, more than once. "Yes. Please don't sell me. Please don't. Let me go away, but please don't sell me." She knew fear and desperation were in her voice and that she was begging.

The man looked very offended. He whispered to Wokli, and she looked even more offended. The woman said something in strong words to him, but she was watching Napas. Wokli's eyes were slitted and her mouth was pulled back.

"Wokli says you no think good. You look Indian, but not think Indian. Indian not sell girl who kill Henon."

They were disgusted and angry with her, but seeing she was humble and ashamed, the man and woman took deep breaths and their faces relaxed. "You think good now. Save food." Opototo said.

Their faces softened. Wokli smiled at her.

"You want me to save food in case you can't come back every day."

"That good." He was pleased she understood. She was happy she'd finally expressed herself correctly.

Wokli went back out through the entrance, and returned soon with a soft blanket made of strips of rabbit fur, and a full skin that looked like it came from a big grey and black furred animal.

Wokli grinned so her perfect white teeth showed. She said something to Napas, and Opototo trans-lated. "Wolf skin good for Napas. Sleep with wolf skin and dreams make you be strong."

"Aren't wolves evil animals?"

"No, wolves are what wolves are. They have brave power. Make girl spirit strong."

Chapter Forty-seven

~ The Conspiracy ~

Dr. Grainger sent for Richard, Tom, and Edward, asking them to come to the mansion in all haste. Edward needed to drive by Tom and Lucinda's house to find Richard. The young McCreary had been gone from the office all afternoon. Edward was relieved that he had found him, and the men could answer the doctor's summons together.

Dr. Grainger had examined Frederick and found a large knob massed in the man's abdomen. His patient had not recovered consciousness and the doctor feared his diagnosis. Edward Harrington had said that McCreary had come to the office raving earlier, but the doctor didn't think that the man's disorderly behavior was related to his collapse. He had seen this coma combined with a swollen belly many times, though not usually in offices or in mansions. More often men in his profession saw this symptom when they were called to backstreet boarding houses, mining camps, or alleyways.

He did his best to prepare the man's sons. They sat quietly, listening to all that the doctor both said and implied. Then, late in the afternoon, when they were in the dining room and Ada, one nurse and the doctor were the only ones at the bedside, Mr. McCreary gasped. Blood came streaming out of his mouth in such volume that Ada and the nurse had to turn him lest he choke. The doctor had to help them, but blood kept gushing and the man died.

The body was in no condition to be viewed by his sons. Dr. Grainger did not call for them, but he washed and went down to the parlor to talk to them while the nurse did her work at the bedside.

"Did he have a cancer, Doctor?" Richard asked.

"No. I don't think that was the cause."

"Then what was the cause our father's death? You'd said in your earlier opinion that it was not caused by his deranged state."

"This was caused by alcoholic poisoning. I've seen it often and am certain. He was bleeding internally. The blood vessels soften and explode after a time, in some people who drink. I am some at fault for not paying enough attention to the widening of the veins on at the sides of his forehead and his neck. I had hoped the laudanum would have helped take away his need for drink. And, perhaps it did, but too late. Or perhaps I didn't prescribe enough. However, the blame was his own."

"Are you sure, Doctor?"

"Yes, Tom. The manner of Mr. McCreary's death confirmed my diagnosis. From the moment of his collapse, death was inevitable and ultimately of his own doing.

"I must make out a county certificate. If you would prefer, I will not enter details. Heart failure is always a concurrent cause, and that will suffice to put on paper."

The body was cleaned, and the undertaker called. Tom and Richard went out in the garden to wait until they were requested to approve the manner of their father's lying out presentation.

Ada's work taken over by the undertaker. She went to bathe and change her soiled clothing. When she again looked the proper for the McCreary housekeeper, she went out in the garden to talk to Tom and Richard. "Ye will get word to Mason quickly, I suppose. The lad needs to know of his father's passing. Yer father can lie out one day more, but not beyond that."

"Yes, Ada. Mason is on his way home. We will arrange Papa's funeral for the day after tomorrow, whether our brother is here by then or not. We'll tell Papa's friends also."

"Good, all's well. I have something more to talk to ye both about. It is a very delicate matter, and I'd not bring it up now, but that it is bothering my mind so."

"Anything, dear woman. You can bring up any-thing, and we will try to settle it for you."

Richard had taken both the woman's plump hands in his, and Tom bent toward her. They waited for her to speak.

"Ah, me. I don't know how to begin, but here 'tis. I think our little MeMe's been found. I think she is here in this country and is pursued for a crime of murder."

Richard's eyes widened. He'd not considered that their housekeeper might have seen a poster.

"Ada, how can you think this?" Tom asked, peering down at her from his height, and seeming more like a judgmental wraith of a man than the man she had known as a lively, cheerful boy.

"Why, there are posters all about the town with a face like hers. I know in me bones it is our girl, right there on the paper. Ye know I can't read but some words, but I know a murder poster when I sees one. Have no worry. This mouth is closed. I've said nothing but to you that it's our wee girl."

Richard put his arm around Ada and looked at Tom.

"We have our woman, brother. We need not bring another into this." He led the confused Ada to a garden bench. Anyone passing or looking through the mansion's iron fencing would think they were commiserating in their grief over Mr. McCreary's death.

Ada was more than willing to become party to their plot, stating emphatically what she felt. "If that dear child murdered someone, he well needed murdering!"

"You understand, dear Ada, that if you help us, you become our accomplice in breaking the law," Tom said. "It may be a capital offense, Ada."

"I owe it to the girl. I should have helped her long ago. Though they hang me like poor Mary Surratt, I'm with you boys!"

Alone with Lucinda that evening, Tom said with some bitterness, "Our Papa's heart failed, but not today." The woman, though not long a wife, knew her husband well enough to understand his meaning. Her sister had shared the story of Frederick's brutal reunion with his son on the day of Tom's arrival in Angel's Camp. She put her arms around her husband to comfort all his deeply held grief.

A telegram arrived from Ples the next morning.

I arrive in A Camp with Dickey and Ootie. Leving today. Ples

Mason sent a similar message. He arrived within two days, too late for the funeral, but Frederick McCreary's death was far overshadowed by the need to find MeMe.

The brothers were driven to do that before the sheriff and his deputies, or some bounty man claiming reward, apprehended her. Tom had managed to get newspapers and to charm information from any local people who could have had more information on what had taken place in the region of Avery.

The gruesome nature of the murder made most people curious about all its sensational details. This wasn't a knife fight that resulted in murder along the placer camps. It wasn't a brawl in a tavern, and it would whet an appetite for vengeance. This was understood to be the vicious murder of a man of religion by an Indian woman who worked on his property. It gave vigilante license to whoever looked for an excuse. Indians had become scarce. None were seen, not even around the sites where the natives had been used for labor.

"Bounty hunters are coming into Murphy's Camp," Tom told Mason and Richard. "We must begin the search. We can't wait until Ples gets here."

"Yes, but this is what will help us. MeMe has been gone for over a week. The widow didn't report her husband's murder for that long. Sheriff found him laying on his bed in a foul condition. It seems obvious that the man's wife is the murderess and should be hanged, not our sister."

"But if there is a Native around, he or she will carry the blame no matter what the crime. You know that as well as I," interjected Richard. "The Murphy's paper says dogs have been called out to track her."

"They'll find a cold trail if MeMe was gone a week before they began," said Mason. "There's been rain almost every day."

Richard voiced the possibility that it wasn't MeMe. "It might not be our sister who was on the poster."

"Did you see the drawing? I know it's she. Papa thought so. Ada, too."

"But the sheriff's office said no one but the widow gave a description. The news office had their artist draw the picture from her description. I don't know its accuracy."

"My mind and heart tell me the wanted woman is MeMe."

Two days later, three riders pulled up in front of the office of McCreary Hauling. Mr. Dickey, who had been there eight years earlier, wasted no time leading them to the right building on the right street of Angel's Camp. Ootie had never been away from his tribal region before, and was silently guessing at the reason he was called to go with the traveling party but saying little. The tattoos on his face told Tom that he'd never pass as a Mexican, even with a sombrero. The brothers were responsible for his safety now too.

Ples was proudly riding a horse, not sitting in a wagon or carriage. He'd invented a device to protect his leg and give it the strength so that he could finally mount a horse, though not in any way as he had been in his cavalry days. He had leapt into the saddle in those days, joyous now that he could ride again, if only with help.

The white men were introduced to Edward Harrington and the office staff as friends and fellow land investors with whom Mason, Richard and Tom McCreary would be spending much time in the following weeks.

Edward was puzzled, but accepted the explanation. He had never known the brothers to be foolish or brash, and he remembered Mr. Dickey's first visit to the office with Henry Stegler. He knew Ples well from the brothers' stories. An Indian serving man made a kind of sense to him, for he heard that Dickey lived apart from his wife and might need someone to care for laundry and meals.

Ples, Mr. Dickey and Ootie were taken to the mansion, where Ada would make them comfortable. All their meetings would be held there. There would be no chance of the office staff or the Harrington family members of finding out what the six of them were doing.

When Ootie refused to stay in the house, Richard told him emphatically that he couldn't stay elsewhere for the man's own safety. But, the first morning, on rising, the brothers found Ootie had taken his blankets to the wide porch at the back of the house.

"House air not good," the man said by way of explanation.

348

Chapter Forty-eight
~ Blue Tail Fly ~

For nearly a full month, Ada kept the coffeepot hot. She never knew when one of the members of the conspiracy would drop into the mansion. It served as the clearing-house for their various searches. Though Ada couldn't read or write, she had the kind of mind that liked to keep track of things. She kept track of where each of them was, where he had been, and where he would be going next.

The group had agreed to meet back in Angel's Camp at the mansion on the 12th of April, if not before, and each man was to check general delivery of the post office nearest his area of search as often as possible during the interim. Often two or more of the men worked together, particularly if there was a lead or a suspicion of where MeMe might be.

Much money passed hands. Roust-a-bouts were hired to quiz ferrymen. Miners were paid to give information on who was seen at rivers or streams. The McCreary party was careful not to give any appearance of its search. Usually they posed as men looking for property or business investment to justify the questions they asked. Ootie always stayed with Dickey. By the 12th of April, the men sat in the dining room with Ada, bemoaning their lack of success. "Five times I've been mistaken for a bounty hunter when I made the mistake of asking questions that were too obvious, or when I asked the wrong person. Twice I've been mistaken for a reporter from San Francisco seeking a good story," Tom complained.

"Everyone is interested in the violent Indian woman who murdered a preacher," Mason said. "But I've heard stories about the victim that make him *less* than a true minister of God."

The men around the table nodded their heads.

"The reward has gone higher. Have you seen the latest posters? Dead or alive, they say. They mean dead. In the Gold Dust, a deputy bragged that Indian women's bodies had been brought in, but the widow couldn't identify them so no bounty had to be paid," Tom said. "They were killed ruthlessly and shamefully ~ for sport as well as for money."

Ples sorrowed aloud. "It's been over a month and no one has found MeMe, not the sheriff or any of his deputies, not a constable from another county, not a bounty man."

"And we haven't either," Mr. Dickey grumbled.

"This isn't something I wanted to say," Tom began. "But she may be lost. It was raining even more up in the hills a month ago. Where would she have gone? What would she have found to eat? We've been to Avery. Mason and I crawled through the woods on our bellies. We didn't want to arouse suspicion, but we wanted to get into that Henon place and take a good look at it."

"We saw the lean-to where we think she was kept. It wasn't worthy of any human being. There was a pallet, some bloody covers, a few basins, a tin plate and mug. No window, only a door with a string to hold it closed" Mason said. "If it was truly her room, she has been badly hurt."

"What I keep wondering is, maybe she's dead." Richard looked down at his hands. No one wanted him to say what all were thinking.

"Heaven protect and preserve us. The child can't be dead!" Ada broke the moment's silence.

"We've worked so hard, Ada. We've found no clue," Mason said. "We've walked the woods in all directions around Avery."

Ples twisted around so he could get to his feet. "I'm not giving up. Tom, I lived a long time with nothing to eat and only polluted water to drink. I stayed alive to keep my promise to Wiley. She is still alive, I know she is."

Ootie, who never had said anything, put his head back and the corners of his mouth turned up. He nodded his head.

"Ples is right. She alive! Now I go find Napas. Pah! None you know how." He stood up, went to the door and started to open it to leave.

Tom, nearly a foot taller than the Indian, bounded out of his chair and took Ootie's hand from the doorknob, closing the door and keeping own hand on the knob lest the man persist. But Ootie wrenched the knob away and opened the door. He walked out.

"You can't go alone, Ootie. Every man out there is gunning for Indians." Tom was impressed, and somewhat shamed, by the old man's determination, and went after him. "Wait. Ootie. Wait. I'm going with you. If you have any ideas, I'm ready to follow you. Whatever you say, that's what I'll do."

Ples hobbled right behind him. Mason, Richard, and Mr. Dickey followed as Ootie led them through the house.

Ada came to watch them. "Aye, and ye all go along. Army's only as good as its captain. Maybe 'tis the right one for the job we've got ourselves at last."

Ootie led them down the back hallway and out the big doors to the back garden. He squatted down and waited for the men to join him. All but Ples and Dickey circled around and got down too.

"Dang it, Ootie. My rheumatism won't let me squat like you do. I'm stayin' standin'," Dickey said by way of excuse.

Ootie still hadn't said a word since he stated that he was going to go and find his granddaughter.

"What is your plan?" Richard prodded him.

Ootie grunted, and said something in his language that no one there understood. Then he made the biggest speech of his life. "Need Indian to find Indian. Use Indian to find Indian. I goin' up Avery place. I goin' fine some Indians."

"You won't find Chancys. You're one of a kind up around here, old man."

"Dickey's right, Ootie. All around here are Miwok. Can you speak their language?"

"No, but I fine Indians. I goin' Avery. I goin' fine Napas."

"How? Just how are you going to do that?" Tom questioned.

Ootie smirked at Tom as though Tom understood nothing. "In Avery, Indians come fine me."

"You sit yourself down in Avery and you'll be dead in about two minutes," Mason said.

But Ootie wasn't going to change his mind, and the others had no better plan. They went to their saddles to start for the town of Avery.

When they'd traveled as far as Murphy's Camp,

352

Mason, Ada and Mr. Dickey took a room at the hotel to wait. Tom, Dickey and Ootie went on to Avery. Tom was going to play the role of a gambler, then buy a berth in the livery to sleep near the horses.

Dickey went into the biggest tavern in Avery. He made sure he was heard loudly ordering that 'his Indian' sit out by the horse trough and wait for him. Ootie made a show of filling a pipe with sweet tobacco and smoking it slowly, playing a 'tame' Injun servant awaiting his master. When Dickey came out, the two men walked over to the inn. Dickey left Ootie outside again while he registered. "My man is going to sleep alongside the building. Any trouble about that?" Dickey asked at the desk.

The hotelier would have obliged a two-headed pig for the opportunity to rent the best room he had, and Dickey had just taken it for the night. "Sure. We got a watchman. I'll tell him your Injun belongs to one of the tenants."

"He's the best goddamn Indian I ever had for running errands an' getting 'em done right. Don't want to lose him."

"No worries, sir. He'll be all right. I'll make sure no one bothers him out there." Appreciate you didn't bring him inside.

Five hours later, the streets long dark, had grown quiet, Ootie lit his pipe again. About a half hour after that, a shadow moved up next to him, and a quiet, low-pitched voice asked, "*Noko hu tija?*"

Ootie didn't know Miwok, but he understood. He answered in Chukchansi, "*Dawa ku.*" He couldn't see the Miwok's face, but he pulled out his pack of sweet tobacco and broke off a big hunk. He gave it to the

Miwok.

"Enlish. I talk Enlish, Miwok," he said.

The man pointed to the eastern sky and made the sign for sun, and a sign for water, and disappeared.

The next morning, Ootie was gone when Dickey got up. Dickey checked the horses, and went back into the hotel dining room. Somewhat concerned, he ordered breakfast.

At around nine, Dickey went out to check the horses again. Ootie was there, sitting up against the wall of the livery. "We go now," Ootie said. He seemed satisfied.

"Go where?"

"Get Ples and Tom. Mus go over river. Go in more mountain. Fine Napas."

There was argument, for it was a little more complicated than Ootie's directions implied. The men had to make preparations. They brought a covered carriage, sturdy enough for the hills, and packed it with whatever they could think of that might be needed - if they should find MeMe.

Ootie was sure that they would find her, but he didn't know exactly where. He only knew that they had to cross the Stanislaus River and go east.

After that, the old man would have to find more Indians who would take him to a Miwok named Tunitoswe. And they had to carry gifts with them. Ootie was vague about the gifts. Dickey wanted specificity. "What kind of gifts, Ootie?"

"Food, med'cin, clothes, knife, iron pot. You know what."

Six of the seven conspirators went into Tuolumne County, only Richard stayed back in Angel's Camp, tended to the office. He had to hold a semblance of normalcy that protected the venture. Ada went with the others, as confident as Ootie that MeMe would be found.

Ootie drove an unmarked mule wagon from their company sheds, loaded with the gifts packed to look like peddler's goods. Tom and Ples rode their own horses alongside. They slept along the road just outside of the town of Columbia. It was easy to pass themselves off as vendors, selling supplies to the camps. Wherever they stopped, Tom wove a story of how he and his partner worked as a peddler team with a fiddle and a deck of cards. "The more we entertain, the more we sell."

His story and joviality brought a moment of humor to people wherever they stopped for food to rest the mules.

On the chance that Ootie was right, and they'd find MeMe, Tom wanted it well established that they were familiar faces, normal sorts of travelers in the gold country.

Mason, who was well known in Tuolumne and other counties through his visits to the freight liveries as one of Frederick McCreary's sons, drove the closed carriage. Mr. Dickey and Ada rode inside. "And now it's an actress I am!" exclaimed the plain-faced old woman, primping in her finest clothes and overplaying the role of great lady.

"You are Mason's auntie, Maybelle Miller, remember that and make no slips of your tongue in the hotel."

Dickey retorted. "And this week or two, however long it takes, I'm your husband."

"Ye'll not take liberties with me. It'd be the death of ye."

Ada raised both eyebrows so that they arched high. "Not only would I knock ye out of this fine carritch, but think man, me cursed husbands all take sick and die. Do ye too wish this t' befall ye?"

"I have no intention of taking liberties with you, Ada. I already have a wife. I may have a chance to pay her a visit before I go back to Crane Valley and my store."

"Ah, Mr. Dickey, sir. Bein' serious, do ye think Ootie will find our girl?"

"He may. Indians have their ways. He's been my friend since I came to Crane Valley. He was almost dead when I found him. His wife was dead and all his family but his daughters who stayed living with their mother's people up near Coarsegold Creek. He'd come down in the valley hunting. "His kill was taken and he was beaten half to death. When he recovered, he worked for me around the store. And I've paid him fair.

"I used to give him things for his family too. They'd come across the mountain every week or so bring a rabbit or squirrel and take what we gathered for them."

Ada listened seriously. "I heard stories about the English who came and murdered my own people for their land. Me, meself, survived the famine. But I never knew of worse done than what I knows was done here, to these people, in the land of gold."

In Sonora, they took a suite at the city hotel. Mason drove the closed carriage on to covered storage in McCreary Hauling station's livery garage. The three, passive players in the drama, then began the long wait.

Ootie had great faith in what he had learned from the Miwok in Avery. The McCreary brothers had only hope. Tom's hope was tinged with cynicism learned in the Shenandoah Valley. "The Indians may have sold her to bounty men, Ootie."

Ootie made no reply.

But Dickey snapped at Tom. "Indians might sell her if they have grievance against *her*, but not for killing someone who was no kin to them. Not knowing better, they'd calculate that she had her reasons.

"Ootie? You agree?"

Ootie smirked and said, "Miwok say Henon bad man. It good he killed."

"Bad, huh. What'd he do to get Indians against him any worse than any other white man?" But Ootie was done talking. He ignored the question as irrelevant.

A plan was agreed upon. Ootie, Ples and Tom would take the wagon and a couple of horses and go up into the higher forest country to the east. They'd be dressed and would mime the part of gold camp peddlers. If they found MeMe, they'd bring her down to Sonora. Tom would send a wire from Sonora to Henry Stegler to hire rooms for them in Stockton near the waterfront and watch closely for their arrival.

Mr. Dickey, Ootie and Ada would take MeMe to Stockton using the covered carriage. Ples, Tom and Mason, well armed, would ride alongside. Once there, where ships were arriving and departing, goods being distributed, foreigners arriving to start new lives, the mountain affairs of Calaveras County counted for little. What would the murder of one man up in the Sierra signify? It would signify nothing. Too many men died nightly in the cities of San Francisco,

Sacramento and Stockton.

Up in the trees, at dawn, three days later, on a track off of Italian Bar Road barely wide enough for the wagon Ootie emerged from the woods with another Indian man no taller than he was. The man was wearing Indian clothing and looked to be older than Ootie.

"This my frien'." Ootie said. "He want look at you."

Tunitoswe looked at Ples and Tom. He looked at the men's hands, told them to open their mouths, and he stretched up to smell their breath. He looked back and whistled. A fine-looking short haired and younger Indian came out of the trees wearing the garb of any miner or laborer. He wore boots instead of moccasins. Tunitoswe said something to the young man, and the young man looked at them and said, "Tunitoswe say you go up road to clear place. You wait in clear place. Wait behind rock. If Napas know you, she come wagon."

"We drive down to a clearing, and wait?" Tom repeated.

"Wait behind rock. Now go up road." The Indian spun around and sprinted off into the woods.

A half hour through a winding road they came to a clearing. It was narrow, and surrounded by pines. There was a big chunk of granite in the middle, with a scrubby lone oak trying to grow out of one side of the granite's scree. They halted the mules, and Tom turned them out to drink and graze. Ootie stayed up on the seat of the wagon, watching.

After twenty minutes, Tom got out his cards and laid out a solitaire game on a flat piece of granite a short way from the wagon. Ples looked to the northwest and thought for a minute. He snapped his fiddle case open and tuned the instrument up. Scanning the trees again in the northwest direction on a hunch, he touched bow to strings. Tom glanced about nervously. But they had seen no other people on this remote track all that morning, no one but the Indian who directed them here.

Ples played, "Blue-tail Fly," played it again, then a medley of hymns MeMe would know. Tom caught on, and sang along. They were a duet with Tom singing "Billy Boy" and "Yankee Doodle," and then Ples fiddled his way back to "Blue-tail Fly" again. Ootie didn't know the words but he sang too, though not any song that the others recognized as music.

There was movement at the edge of the trees, and two dark haired figures were coming out toward them. The smaller one was carrying a bag of some kind. The larger one had something in her arms. Ootie squinted his eyes, and jumped down from the wagon to begin running as fast as his ancient and arthritic legs would allow.

It was apparent now that the figures coming toward them were women. Tom got up and began to run toward MeMe. Ples put the fiddle down. Ples wanted to run too, but couldn't. He went hopping on his crutch, and dragging one leg. Across the thin early grass of the clearing, Ootie bent and wrapped his arms around the smaller figure. As Tom caught up, Ootie released MeMe to proudly stretch himself as tall as possible.

"I tol' you," the old Indian said.

>>>O<<<

Chapter Forty-nine
~ Safety in Stockton ~

MeMe was subdued and shy. She was eight inches taller and eight years older than the child the men remembered. She was no longer a child. Their little sister looked up at them. There was a deep, nearly healed wound puckering across the right side of her face. Scarecrow thin, she looked gaunt and older than they knew her to be.

"You're Tom. Aren't you?" Her voice was barely audible. "You are still skinny, but you grew so tall."

"Oh, MeMe, I am Tom. We've been looking for you for such a long time." His eyes were running tears. He'd kept the promise he'd made to his brother in the Shenandoah.

When he dried his face, he took a close look at her. Her hair was ragged and her dress too short. Her boots had worn thin and the heel on one was gone. She'd wear the scar of a facial wound all her life. But in her brother's eyes she was profoundly beautiful.

"I knew Ples was making the music. I knew it was Ples! That's when I was certain the white men were you. Wokli said an Indian and some white men had come for me. I wanted it to be Ootie and you and Ples, but I was afraid."

The Miwok woman stepped closer and lifted a fur skin that looked like it came from a very large grey wolf. She draped it over MeMe's shoulders. MeMe reached up and touched the woman's face. The woman's eyes showed wariness of the white men. Still, she bent her head down to the girl and said something to her. Then she looked at each of the men as though she were memorizing their faces. She bowed to each and disappeared into the trees.

"What did she say to you, MeMe?" Tom asked.

MeMe only smiled and didn't answer.

Tom didn't pursue the question in spite of his curiosity. The handing of the fur by the handsome Indian woman to MeMe had seemed ceremonial. It gave him a feeling of reverence that was contrary to his nature but not unpleasant.

The men quickly unloaded all the items from the wagon: iron skillets, bags of dried corn-meal, white flour, sides of bacon packed in salt and barreled, packs of clothing - but no items that would call attention to their wearers by seeming too new. There were boxes of varied medicines, knives, needles, threads of many kinds, and at Tom's insistence, some rifles and shells. It was illegal to give firearms to Indians, but they already were committing a capital offense. If these Miwok were driven higher into the mountains, rifles and shells could help them hunt and protect themselves.

Ootie and Tom carried the items deep inside the line of trees, while Ples stayed with MeMe. She looked at the man she had known young perfectly formed. He was now twisted and lame, but his eyes were as kind as they always had been.

"Ples, people think I killed someone, but I didn't," she said.

"It doesn't matter, MeMe. Nothing like that matters," he answered. "All that matters is that you are with us again." He helped her up into the wagon while Ootie and Tom hitched the mules.

Ples was careful and gentle as he showed her how to tuck down and keep hidden in a false box behind the driver. It had been a very long since she had felt a light, soothing touch from a white person. He moved slowly and she wondered what had happened to the man she had known as a boy. He was still handsome, but could scarcely walk without the help of a cane.

Ples took all her things out of the carpetbag and wrapped the buckskin packet and her clothing in a small tarp. He put them on the low shelf that ran the width of the wagon beneath the driver's bench near her compartment.

Tom and Ootie returned. They took the shovels from a rack on the side of the wagon and walked into the trees on the other side of the clearing walking away with the carpetbag. The bag had been her valued companion for over a year and she had clung to it during these past hard weeks.

"Must they take it?" she asked Ples.

"It could identify you, and bring trouble to those who helped and hid you. They will bury it very deeply." He looked at her, a petite and lovely young woman just emerging from girlhood, sitting on the edge of the wagon. She smiled at him, nodding her understanding and agreement.

"I'm sorry," he said, taking her hand. But it is necessary to protect you."

"What happened to your leg?" she asked.

"The war."

"I didn't know there was a war."

He laughed, and she felt everything was all right. The Ples she remembered was soft faced and young. This Ples had lines around his blue eyes and on his forehead, He was thin and a short trimmed beard as blond as his hair. He was twisted to one side and couldn't stand straight. She might not have recognized him but for his music and the soft sound of his voice.

When Ootie and Tom came back she climbed into her hiding place. It wasn't the first time she been hidden in a wagon.

As they went back down Italian Bar Road, past the camps, and through small hamlets, there was one fearful moment. A group of lawmen rode by them just outside of Columbia. Ootie wore a sombrero and kept his head down, but Ples and Tom, waved cheerily and chatted with a cluster of men working along the roadside. One man remembered them and asked, "Good sales, Peddlers?"

"Mighty fine, sir. Mighty fine," Tom answered. "Be back in a couple of months with more goods to trade." The lawmen lost interest and road on.

By midnight, they were in Sonora. Mason was waiting in the dark livery. He slid the doors opened as soon as he recognized the team and wagon. Soon the wagon was inside, and the men dismounted to get the mules unhitched and turned out into the corral behind the livery.

"Let her stretch out and walk for a while."

"Our brave sister isn't one to complain. But she needs to move about."

Mason helped Tom extract MeMe's aching, but very alive, body. She had trouble standing, but when finally upright, she looked up at the strong mass of Mason McCreary standing around her with Tom, Ootie and Ples.

"Are you Wiley?"

"No, little sister. I'm Mason."

"You can't be Mason. He was the littlest! How'd you get so big?"

He picked her up and tucked her head into his neck and chest. "MeMe, you're bigger too. You didn't weigh as much as half a tick last time I saw you. Now you just go stretch and move about," He showed her where she could relieve herself and wash. There was no light but what the moon gave, but she felt better with exercise after the long ride.

Mason and Tom and helped MeMe up into the soft luxury of the carriage. "This will be much more comfortable than the wagon. Mason and I are going for the others now. Ples and Ootie will stay here with you.

Soon we'll hitch the horse team and travel again. Sleep if you can."

Ples strained to climb up into the carriage with her. He sat across from her and took her hands in his. "We still need to keep you well hidden. We'll stop only when we can do it safely. You mustn't show yourself even when we get to Stockton.

"Ada is here, and she'll ride with you. Mr. Dickey will also. You'll have good company. Now rest. I'm armed and Ootie is keeping watch. We are here to keep you safe."

The next day, as they sped down into the great valley, crossing through puddles and dips that brought spring run-off nearly to the carriage body itself, Ada found time to make her apologies to the child she felt she had once cruelly abandoned.

The young woman, who had been that child, accepted

her words graciously. MeMe also felt guilt. She too had abandoned a child. She reached over and took Ada's hand and held it as Trial's little face kept coming into her mind and filling her memory. She saw scenes of the girl at play, or sitting happily on Anna's lap. They were good scenes, but the bad scenes came too. Were it not that a nail had bent down with the child's weight, letting the rope slip, sweet, innocent Trial would have died.

MeMe shuddered, knowing that though she was safe, it would be a very long time before she felt comfortably herself again.

Once when Opototo brought food to her in the place of rocks, he told her a horrible story. He told her that there were many men in this part of the country who took Indian's hair and head skin like hunters took the tails of raccoons or squirrels. It was no difference to them.

He said that Pastor Henon had been the worst of them. It afflicted her to think she had been purchased with a bag of her own people's scalps, for surely that was what had been in the big bag Pastor carried. She remembered that Wokli came again that same day, and Opototo left them alone in the safe place of stone. The woman asked her by signs if Henon had violated her. MeMe hadn't wanted to answer. But Henon *had* hurt her in terrible ways. She raised her head and nodded.

Wokli pulled at Napas' skirt, and acted like she was Napas' mother looking her over. But after the examination, the Indian woman grinned wide. She said the first English words Napas had heard her speak. "Bad hur'. No pox."

Then Wokli called Opototo back, and wanted him to ask MeMe a more complicated thing. "You bleed with moon now already?" Opototo asked.

"Yes." She understood and shyly answered him.

Wokli said something more to Opototo with a very serious look on her face. Opototo asked, "How many day since bleed?

It wasn't something MeMe had been thinking about, but she did remember. She was bleeding just before she crossed the river. She remembered because she worried that wolves would come through the trees to devour her, because they could smell her blood. Since two days before I crossed the river," she answered.

He translated her words into Miwok, and Wokli was very happy. She danced around in the rock castle where MeMe had been living.

"Wokli know it very good you bleed," Opototo said. He was grinning too. "Girl not want baby from Junyapoc. Get bad baby from bad man. You lucky Napas! You no get bad baby."

Someday she'd ask Ada how bleeding was connected with having babies, but not today. Ada was sound asleep, and MeMe wasn't ready to talk about all that had happened.

Until they were safely in Stockton, nestled in the apartment that Henry Stegler had hired for them near the waterfront, MeMe had assumed that Wiley was with Richard in Angel's Camp. When Richard arrived alone, it became time to tell her that Wiley had been killed in the war.

The girl left the company of the family and went alone to the room she and Ada shared in the apartment. The scene outside her window was something she had never seen before. Ships and small boats were unloading cargo, and workmen scurrying to load wagons on the docks. But her thoughts stayed with Wiley. He was the brother who told her stories of bravery and read poems to her from his schoolbooks. She would never again. He was gone, like Nancy, like Ples's mother. The window couldn't compete with the memories she had of people she'd loved and who were gone.

When she had spent enough time in a thought-filled mourning, she came back to the central room that was used as a parlor. "What else has happened to the family since I've been gone?"

Mason, grinning to cheer her, spoke up first. "Our brothers are married! They married Mr. Harrington's daughters."

"And you? Mason, are you getting married too?"

"MeMe, I'm only seventeen! I'm not going to get married for years and years. I'm going to veterinary college back east. I'm studying now, and I inspect the stock for all of our company stations. I'm very overdue in Mariposa even now."

"Doesn't your father do that?"

Tom spoke solemnly. "Richard, Mason, Edward Harrington and I run the company now."

She had seen from their faces as soon as she had spoken that Mr. McCreary was dead. Her jaw hardened. She couldn't honestly give them sympathy. She wasn't sorry.

Too many seconds went by.

Then Richard broke the silence. "MeMe, I wish I'd been there to help in your rescue. I wanted to be."

"Richard was at the heart of the whole thing. He sent the telegrams to bring us together," Tom said.

"Richard was the only one who understood that we needed Ootie with us to find you. We would never have found you without Ootie and Richard."

Ootie held his head very high.

Mason turned to her. "Richard is the brains for all of Papa's business now. We are all part of it, but he and Edward Harrington make the decisions.

"We've told you about us," Tom said. "What about you, MeMe? Mason and I saw that place near Avery where you lived. Were you there long?"

"No. I was there just over a year."

"Where were you before that?"

Ada spoke was curious. "Yes, dear child. Tell us where yer been. Mr. McCreary told us that ye were adopted by church people. Ye were such a wee girl, I'd held hope that he had found good folk for ye."

MeMe didn't want to tell her family that their father stripped her down to her shift and sold her for twenty dollars. She floundered trying to find an answer. Ples was the one who perceptively noticed her awkwardness. He kindly and quickly pulled the attention away from her and toward himself. "Come on, boys. Get your banjo, Tom. Let's have music. Mr. Dickey, you can entertain us by dancing with Ada.

When both Dickey and Ada made protest, Ples gave a reminder. "After all, Ada, you played Dickey's wife for a few days of masquerade at the Sonora Hotel."

After the laughter subsided, Tom said, "Tomorrow we all go on our separate ways. Tonight we will be merry!" He opened the fiddle's box, tuned the instrument up and began to play.

MeMe was going to The Willows. From the brothers' perspective, she wouldn't be safe in Angel's Camp or anywhere else in the gold country. From her perspective, the ranch had always been her only goal. "It's still as beautiful as ever at The Willows, MeMe." Ples said.

"Ada, I'd like you to come too. I'm forever a bachelor, and for company as well as propriety, MeMe needs a woman in the house. The ranch house is not the mansion in Angel's

Camp, but you know it is a good home. You would each have your choice of rooms. And, dear Ada, I will defer to your judgment in regard to meals and care of the house."

"I'd go with you, surely, gladly. 'Tis only that I'd promised Mr. McCreary I'd give the rest of me days to serve his family."

Richard eliminated that concern. "If you go, your service to the family continues, Ada. Merab McCreary is the perfect center of our family."

"Then I go back to The Willows with my girl tomorrow! Ye boys must go and hire a serving girl to pack up me stuff from the mansion and send it all down on a wagon. I needs me stuff."

"Ada, *ye* must promise to make the whole McCreary family welcome twice a year. We'll spend the Fourth of July and Christmas with in Crane Valley each year."

Tom grew animated, always an easy thing for him to do, and addressed Merab. "MeMe, you will meet our wives! They are dear girls. You will like them, I promise."

"The Harringtons too." Richard added. "Edward and Carrie are our best friends."

Richard moved across the room to sit on the carpet at MeMe's feet. "They helped us through some bad times after our mother died, MeMe. They will be like parents to you, as they are to us. Mama would have liked Carrie."

Ada's eyebrows arched, and she reached to take MeMe's hand. "Aye, an' that's the truth. Mrs. McCreary would have seen the good in the Harringtons.

"But, that Carrie Harrington stole all the McCreary boys right away from me. Young men, you know she did. And know ye now, as me name's Ada Cotter, I'll not let her steal Merab McCreary from me."

Chapter Fifty
~ In the Clearing ~

In Crane Valley, as spring turned to summer, Mr. Dickey made sure that everyone knew that Merab McCreary and her companion, Mrs. Cotter, were staying at The Willows as guests of its owner, Ples Landers.

Some families had moved away from the valley; others had moved in. In the Sierra, there seemed to be a glamour that came with wealth, and it shielded both the McCreary family and the Landers family from old gossip. The memories of most people grew dim for all but scandal and affairs of money. The story of Nancy McCreary's adoption of a little Indian girl was not scandalous enough to hold in memory, while Aaron Landers and Frederick McCreary's grand financial successes were well remembered and often mentioned.

The Brauns were still in the valley, but the hearty German born family had never quite understood that Indians were supposed to be eliminated in the Sierra. They hired Indians to dig wells and latrines and let the natives live in the woods behind their pastures. The Braun girls had married, but people in the valley still called them the Braun girls.

Mr. Scruggs had died and Mrs. Scruggs moved down to the Visalia to a son-in-law's ranch in the center of the great valley. Reverend Taylor no longer dealt with sometimes annoying school children. He was by this time a full-time reverend with a new church and pulpit. The schoolmaster was a popular man named John Hatfield.

The Barretts had moved down to Millerton to grow grapes. Their son, who had gone to college in the East, was back in California, a justice at the courthouse there.

The McCreary and Harrington families came, as promised, to spend the Fourth of July, 1870 at The Willows. They stayed a very pleasant week at the ranch. Tom and Richard brought two wagons with tents and cots, and two wagonloads of barreled foodstuffs. Mason helped Tom set them up down near the orchard for the young couples to ease the burden on Ada and Ples of housing such a crowd. Carrie found everything to her liking, especially the three McCreary brothers' joy in their homecoming and their pride in their sister. The brothers had already ridden separately to Crane Valley to visit their sister and Ples. Tom, Richard, and Mason constructed and spread a simple story of how their sister had been miraculously restored to them. They wanted no questions raised that would threaten her security.

The story the Harrington family and the Crane Valley community heard soon after MeMe's return to The Willows was this:

Ples Landers, with other musicians he'd known before the war, went by wagon to perform at a May Day festival in the little town of Madera. He came upon Merab who was working as a drudge for a family there. Ples persuaded the head of that family, by means of a generous monetary gift, to release her to his protection.

Ada's move away from the Angel's Camp Mansion was easily explained. After Frederick McCreary's death it was natural she would want to find other work. The brothers gave out the information that they had hired Ada Cotter to serve as a companion for their sister who preferred to stay at The Willows, her childhood home. Angel's Camp, Edward Harrington was the first to suggest that McCreary Hauling provide an ample yearly income for Merab McCreary.

During the much-anticipated Fourth of July visit, Carrie and her daughters were delighted with the lovely and quiet Indian girl who was in truth Merab McCreary. If any of the three women had noticed a wanted poster, and seen in it a resemblance to MeMe, it was never mentioned even among themselves. The girl Merab was a member of the family. They were happy to give her their loyalty as well as love.

However, Ada knew that although Carrie, Louisa and Lucinda were too discrete ever to ask, they must wonder at the scar on the girl's face. It threatened to be disfiguring and was a blemish in the girl's beauty. The housekeeper took an opportunity one morning during their visit to hint that the family where MeMe had been living in Madera had treated her badly.

"It'll take her a time to recover, ye know. Ah, but she will be better now's she's home. There never was such a good woman as Nancy McCreary. She raised the child right here in Crane Valley, and a good child she was.

"She's a lovely girl, Ada. We love her as much as we love her brothers," Carrie responded. Her daughters beamed their concurrence.

"We'll do well, Mrs. Harrington. She'll be happy here at The Willows. I'll see to her care and she will thrive!

Ye needn't worry. My job is to fatten her up some, and make her as pretty again as she was as a child."

That afternoon, when Louisa, Lucinda and MeMe had gone for a walk down to the creek to wade, Carrie and

Ada were conversing in the kitchen of the ranch house. "You must come with MeMe to visit us, Ada," Carrie urged. "Perhaps you would consider coming to Angel's Camp in the fall? Louisa and Richard are planning to move into the empty mansion for they are starting a family. It's wasteful to leave the rooms in our house so empty."

She expanded the invitation. "Maybe MeMe will want to move closer to us by then. She could live with us, or in the mansion. You might like coming back to Angel's Camp. We would love to have you both nearer."

Ada had to deflect this idea. It would be a long, long time before it would be safe for MeMe to be seen north of Crane Valley. "Ah, Mrs. Harrington, you are very kind. But me thinks our girl will need more time here in her old home before we should begin to think of doing such travel.

"You know Mr. Landers has hired a tutor for her. MeMe wants to learn to read. In't that a grand idea!

"And Mr. Landers has ordered a fine piano for the front parlor. It'll be coming soon. He's put a fancy sewing machine in his mother's old sewing room and MeMe is showing off how she knows to use it. Young Mr. Landers is very good to both of us, he is." She stopped walking to take Carrie's hand. "But, don't ye fret. Someday, oh yes, someday, bye and bye, we'll come to visit. I'd like that and I gives me word."

Later that summer, Ples convinced Ootie that it was time for him to come and live at The Willows. He could sit in a rocking chair on a porch and watch the world go by. Ootie firmly refused Ples' invitation until Mr. Dickey told him that he was thinking of retiring, selling his store and moving to Stockton. "Come with me, Ootie. We are used to each other. Mrs. Dickey wouldn't mind. Her voice is sharp, but her heart is usually good."

"I remember wife, Dickey. I stay here."

"You won't come with me?"

"Nuh. I go wit' Ples." Ootie laughed. "Indians gone. E'n all a Monos gone. I stay by Napas."

By late September, Ootie had moved into the little room Frederick McCreary had built for Ada. He was offered a room in the house but refused declaring again that house air wasn't good.

There was an inconsistency in his acceptance of the small room near the bunkhouse, since its air might not be good either.

Ples and MeMe tactfully chose not to make mention of that, and even Ada held her tongue.

The weeks passed, becoming months. Spring became summer. Ples proved to be a tender companion, never failing in his kindness. He purchased simple books and sat with MeMe and listened to her halting reading. Anything she or Ada needed, he ordered for them. MeMe's brothers and their wives sent her letters. Carrie Harrington did too. She looked forward to the day when she could read and write well enough to answer their letters with her own.

Ada and Mary Hopkins were good company. Ootie was always nearby, to be gruff or jolly as the mood suited him.

MeMe healed.

~~<O>~~

A day came during late October when MeMe and Ootie climbed the hill behind the barn and came to the clearing. MeMe had packed food for them in a hamper and an old blanket for them to sit upon. Ada had thoughtfully considered the steep path, and pursing her mouth, she declined the invitation to join them on a picnic. She claimed that her ankles were too swollen.

Ples could have ridden up the hill to picnic with them, and MeMe was persuasive, but he was busy trying to perfect embellishments on some new music he wanted to learn and play for his parents. He had learned to read music during his hospital stay and became proficient in more than a countryman's melodies. His parents were due to visit the following weekend. He'd play them an Italian concert worthy of Washington, D.C.

Ada was bustling about in preparation for that visit from Mr. and Mrs. Landers. She was goading Mary Hopkins into polishing the furniture and making sure the windows sparkled when it wasn't yet needed for it hadn't been two weeks since the last time she'd made Mary wash them. The hired men were tidying the orchard and carrying buckets of water to rinse summer dust from the veranda's planks.

In the high clearing, the cross of sticks that the boys once put on MeMe's Indian mother's and sister's grave had weathered away. Over the summer, the girl had visited the high meadow many afternoons. She'd stacked a triangle of stones to replace Wiley and Tom's cross. The visits strengthened her legs and lifting stones strengthened her arms. She was becoming healthier each day.

MeMe had never taken Ootie to the meadow with her before. She had some apprehension. Her mother was Ootie's daughter. Mr. Dickey told her that Indian people didn't like to speak of their dead. When they reached the meadow, she didn't point out her mother's and sister's grave to Ootie. To distract him from even noticing the low mound and stone pyramid, she showed him the chamois bag he had given her when she was tiny.

She shook the pebbles out of it into his hands. "I have fifteen now. When the lupine blooms in the spring, I'll have sixteen."

She counted out six of the stones. *"Ye-et, po-noy, so-pin, ha-pa-nay, yit-sil, ka-pi-li.*

The old man's eyes brightened. He remembered that day and was proud she remembered what he'd taught her.

"You'll have to teach me more numbers, Ensay." She looked earnest, and hoped that she would be able to learn her mother's language. His language.

But Ootie bristled. "No teach Indian way. You be white woman now. Se-en, eight, ni', ten. Li' dat."

"No. I am an Indian woman. Teach me," she insisted.

"Indian gone. Only white people now. You be white."

MeMe could hear the bitter and sorrowful tone in his words. She put her arm around him.

"When I was with the Miwoks, Ootie, the man named Opototo told me that there are only six houses in his town that still have people in them. He said that once there were a hundred families living there. Now there are only six families left, only twenty-eight people in all are left of Tunitotsewe's band.

"Opototo has to leave the Miwok to work for the white men he hates. That is how he earns money to bring food home to his father, Wokli, and the people that are left.

The miners have driven the game away and sawn down the oaks. There are no acorns. The Miwok near the river have no food, but what Opototo can bring them." She took the old Indian's calloused and rough hand in hers. "You did that too, didn't you? You worked for Mr. Dickey to provide food and clothing for the Chancys over the mountain, our Chancys."

Ootie gazed at her, thinking that she thought he was better than he was. What he did was only what all men did for their families. He changed the subject by pointing out the view of the valley from the clearing. "One time, this big Chukchansi valley. One time..."

She knew that in Ootie's way of speaking one time could have meant yesterday, a hundred years ago, or a thousand years ago. "One time those Monos came down this side mountain n' took valley. Grandfather die. Many men die.

"That Graveyard Meadow up mountain bad place. Many Chukchansi people die. "We no good fighters. We must move over far away. Give up valley. *Monos* take valley." He looked as though he was more ashamed that his tribe lost Crane Valley than angry that the Monos took it.

Then he grinned at MeMe. He clenched his fist and raised it to the view.

"Now I, Ootie, take valley back!"

Ples had told MeMe that there were two Indian men who lived with their wives and children in the woods behind the Braun ranch, Mono people. The men worked for Braun. She hadn't seen them, but she believed him. After a little while, she said, "There are still a few Monos left in Crane Valley, Grandfather. They live up behind the Braun ranch. You didn't take the valley back completely."

He shrugged, as though what she'd said had no bearing on his triumph. And maybe it didn't.

"What was my name when I lived with my Indian family?" MeMe asked after some time had passed.

Ootie wouldn't tell her. He frowned. All he'd say was "Napas not to look back. Look to front. Eyes put on front to look to front not to look to back." He was finished talking, so she didn't ask any more questions. But she knew he liked to listen to her. She told her grandfather more about her time with the Miwok. "Opototo's family is gone, Ensay. His sister-in-law is the only woman able to take care of the people who are sick or old. You saw her. She came out of the trees with me."

"She tall!" he said emphatically. He'd been impressed by the Miwok woman, and smiling, nodded his appreciation of her to his granddaughter.

"Her name is Wokli. She gave me the wolf skin. She told me I should go home and stay alive."

"Good! You *be* white woman. No Indian mark on you." He touched all the tattoos he had that weren't covered by his clothes as though he were counting them.

"But I'm still an Indian, Ootie. Do you want me to *pretend* to be white? I don't want to do that."

He looked intently at her. "I pretend be white. Lift boxes. Sweep floors. I not be killed." He clenched his fist for emphasis. "Indian not pretend, he killed."

She stood up and opened the picnic basket she'd carried up the hill. She took out the bottle of water and two cups, some cheese from the Braun girls, potato salad from Ada, salmon from the Waukeen and smoked by Johnny Ferguson, one of the new neighbors in the valley.

She had gone out early that morning to pick the first of the fall grapes from the vines around the garden fence, and she'd added them to the feast. They ate quietly. Mockingbirds and Jays came to light on the branches around them, waiting to harvest crumbs. MeMe looked out across the meadow at the ranch down below.

Then, with his stomach full, Ootie's mood seemed lighter. The leaves were just beginning to turn on the deciduous trees in among the conifers, but the heat of the summer was over. The old man got up, walked around. He went into the woods, came back and gave her an obsidian arrowhead, as shiny and as black as his hair was white.

Then he walked along the edge of the meadow twice, and he came back to where MeMe was sitting to throw his arms wide to the sun.

"This good Spirit Place," he said and sat beside her again.

"Yes, it is. I thought of this meadow so often when I was gone," Merab said. "I wanted to come back here, but I needed you to find me first." She looked up at him. "The county sheriffs and bounty men would have caught and killed me, or I would have died alone in the Sierra as I tried to get back home. The Miwok found me but I couldn't stay with them. I was dangerous to them. They didn't have enough food for themselves. They couldn't keep sharing with me.

"You saved me, Grandfather. Tunitotsewe told me you were the man who saved me."

He tried to divert her from this subject. "One time some some white woman save you. Good woman. My fren, tha' woman."

"Yes," she said. "I know she did. She was my second mother, the one I can remember. I will love her until I die." Tears filled her eyes and she blinked them back. "But Ootie, you saved me too."

The Indian man's granddaughter had water in her eyes and was still talking. She embarrassed him with her praise. It was time for him to scold her. "You talk much. Maybe you white woman already," he smirked.

Tunitosewe had also told her she talked like a white woman. It wouldn't be too hard to pretend she was white. She knew Bible stories, all the hymns and prayers, and how to set a table; Merab McCreary was a white woman's name. The two of them sat for an hour more. MeMe could feel that Nancy and her Indian mother were there with them. I have good ghosts, she thought. And she wondered if her tiny sister was hovering around also. She closed her eyes so that the ghosts would stay around her, making her strong.

Then, mischievously, while she was drifting into reverie, Ootie punched her arm. She thought he was tired of the picnic and wanted to go back down the hill. But that wasn't it. His dark eyes were twinkling and he had a demand to make of her.

"Stay here," he said, and pointed out and gestured out indicating the view below them of the ranch house, garden, orchard, corrals and barn.

There was a slim ribbon of glimmering water in the Waukeen far below them still, though the rains hadn't started yet. She'd decided long ago that she didn't want to be anywhere else. It was easy to feel agreement with the old man. She didn't respond, but sat feeling happy and safe.

Ootie sensed her unspoken compliance and winked at her. "I think you be Ples woman. Him broke from war, need good woman." He pointed at her and looked very serious. "You broke from scalp-take-man, need good man. Ples good man."

She hadn't yet talked about her life or Pastor, but her grandfather sounded as though he knew what had happened to her. She wondered if Tunitotsewe told him everything that the Miwok knew about her. It annoyed her to think she was talked about.

"I have a scar, Ootie, but I'm not broke," she snapped.

He didn't seem to mind that she was sharp with him.

A little more time passed. MeMe took a deep breath pulling in all the sweet spicy fragrance of fall. She thought she could hear the fiddle now and then, not playing a song, but sending bright clean separate notes riding up through the trees. The clear sweet notes were calling her back to the ranch house as surely as they had called her from the woods.

She sat up straighter and leaned over toward her grandfather and tapped his hand thinking he might have fallen asleep in the sun like old people did. When he looked up at her, she was the one who winked.

"I am going to stay here, Ootie. This is my place,"

Looking sly and self-satisfied, MeMe told the old man something she hadn't yet considered telling anyone. "Ples doesn't know I'm his woman, Ensay, but I am."

Ootie's grin was so wide, that seeing it she felt she

needed to caution him. "You don't have to tell him, Ootie. It's better that he find out for himself."

When the breeze began to chill, MeMe tossed scraps of bread left from their sandwiches out to the blue jays. She picked up the picnic leavings to pack them neatly into the basket. She carefully folded the plaid blanket and handed it to Ootie to carry. Grandfather and granddaughter walked down to the ranch house together. Ootie closed his smile down until it was so small it only showed in his eyes.

He didn't want Napas to see how proud he was of her. The old Indian was amazed that a girl so small, thin, and young could have such confidence. He thought for a while, and decided that it came from a Miwok wolf skin.

Notes, References, and Acknowledgements

As an effect of the Gold Rush, the number of Miwok Indians in eastern California diminished from approximately 6000 people in 1848 to approximately 100 people by 1880.

Levy, p.99 (ref.p.318)

It is estimated that in 1800, after centuries of Spanish and Mexican rule in the geographic area that is now the state of California, there still numbered more than 150,000 Native Americans. By 1900 the Native population in the same area had been reduced to a mere 15,000 people.

Cook, p.401 (ref. p.318

The part of the eastern Sierra where Crane Valley is situated was in 1856 within the boundaries of Mariposa County. Later that same region was assigned to Fresno County. At the present time, it falls within the boundaries of Madera County.

Between 1910 and 1912 the San Joaquin River in the area known as Crane Valley in the Sierra was dammed and became Bass Lake, now in Madera County. The town once called Fresno Flats is now called Oakhurst. The author has never found historical evidence to support the story of a dispute between the Chukchansi Yokuts and Mono Paiutes over Crane Valley. It is family legend only.

References

Part I

*The Oregon Trail

~Schissel, Lillian, *Women's Diaries of the Westward Journey*; Schoken Books, New York, 1982, p.129

*Crane Valley

~www.lib.virginia.edu/scholarslab/resources/counties

~ww.maderacounty.com/countyhistory

~www.learncalifornia.org/doc.asp?id=118

*The California Genocide of Native Americans

~Cook, Sherburne F., *The Conflict Between the California Indian and White Civilization, University of California Press*; 1976

~Josephy, Alvin M., *500 Nations*; Alfred A. Knopf, New York, 1994, p. 349

~Levy, Richard, *Eastern Miwok, in Handbook of North American Indians, vol. 8 (California)*; William C. Sturtevant, and Robert F. Heizer, eds. Washington, DC: Smithsonian Institution, 1978, p. 401

~Starr, Kevin and Richard J. Orsi, eds., *Rooted in barbarous soil: people, culture, and community in Gold Rush California.*; Berkeley and Los Angeles: University of California Press, 2000, p.25

~Starr, Kevin, *California, A History*; Modern Library, p. 99

~1850 California law for the government and protection of Indians, April 22, 1850

~www. pbs.org/indiancountry/history/calif.html

Part II

*Scarlet Fever

~Ulrich, Laurel Thatcher, _The Life of Martha Ballard, Based on Her Diary, 1785-1812;_ Vintage Books, A Division of Random House, Inc. New York, _1991, p.44-45_

~www.abc.net.au/science/slab/antibiotics/history.htm

~www.britannica.com/EBchecked/topic/526724/scarlet-fever

*Black Bunting

~www.fdfriendly.com/subcategory.asp?id=65&storeId=

~www.ehow.com/about_6389742_history-wearing-black-mourning.html

*Knights of the Golden Circle

~Bossenecker, John, _Badge and Buckshot: Lawlessness in Old California;_ University of Oklahoma Press, _1997, pp. 135-136_

~Smith, Wallace, _Garden of the Sun, A History of the San Joaquin Valley, second edition; William B. Secrest, Jr. ed., Craven Street Books, 2004_

~www.sonofthesouth.net/mexican-war/knights-golden-circle.htm

Part III

*The Foreign-born in Gold Rush California

~en.wikipedia.org/wiki/_California_Gold_Rush_

~www.history.com/topics/gold-rush-of-1849

*Religion in the Gold Country

~www.historichwy49.com/churches.html

~www.calaverascohistorical.com 209-754-1058

~www.angelscamp.gov/index.php?option=com_content
    209-736-2963

~www.cpeacock@history.pcusa.org

*The California Battalion in the Civil War

~Wells, Roy H., *California Cavalrymen in the Army of the Potomac, The California Hundred of the Massachusetts Cavalry; copyright 2006 (online pub.)*

~Faust, Drew Gilpin, *This Republic of Suffering: Death and the American Civil War; Alfred J. Knopf, 2008*

~www.historywell.com/contact/contact.htm

~www.militarymuseum.org/2ndMassCav.html

~www.acws.co.uk/archives/index.php?page=Englishme n&   dir=history

Part IV

*The Chinese Laundry (pák kòp piú gambling game)

~www.gamesmuseum.uwaterloo.ca/archives/culin/1891

*Housing the Mentally Ill

~*Insanity and Insane Asylums, Report of E.T. Wilkins, M.D., Commissioner in Lunacy for the state of California, 1871, made to His Excellency H.H. Haight, Governor, Dec. 2nd, 1871, Lane Library, Cooper Medical College, San Francisco, CA., p. 34*

Part V

*The Eastern Miwok

~Cook, Sherburne, *The Conflict Between the California Indian and White Civilization;* Berkeley and Los Angeles, CA: University of California Press, 1976.

~http://museumca.org/goldrush/silver-native.html

~http://www.yosemite.ca.us/library/central_sierra_miwok_dictionary/images/page_27.png (Miwok Language)

~(see also: page 314, reference I, The Genocide of Native Americans)

*The Seaport of Stockton

~www.hagginmuseum.org/collections_history.htm

~Smith, Wallace, *Garden of the Sun, ibid, pp. 494-497*

~~<<<O>>>~~

I give my tremendous gratitude to my two editors, Helen Ferguson Lindstrom, of Beaumont, California and Deloris Montgomery Mahnke, of Porterville, California. Their comments and corrections improved the book. I am also very grateful to Beverly Krantz Richardson, Porterville, California for her careful reading of portions of the raw manuscript. Other people I thank are Dr. Roy H. Wells, Benecia, California, who shared his expertise on the Civil War and California's military involvement; John Noel, Exeter, California, for his advice on subtle points of literary nuance; Nioma Wilson Patrick, of the Angel's Camp Museum; Charlene Peacock, of the Presbyterian Historical Society; Judith Bixby Boling and Roger Boling, Visalia, California and Marjorie Chester Rogers, Columbia, California, for contributing detailed knowledge of the Civil War and the Gold Rush eras; and of course, the Exeter Writer's Guild and its hard working members who gave my work encouragement, chapter by chapter.

This novel is a modest but sincere tribute to Sade E. Smith, born in 1876 in Fresno Flats. My great aunt told me stories of my Indian great-grandmother's life. The events of this book are fictional, but inspired by those stories. Aunt Sade died in 1973, leaving no direct descendants. Her stories were the wolf skin that strengthened my spirit.

The shadow behind this book is a sweet man named Bob Ross. Bob let me talk out ideas without interruption - but always with attention and interest. He took over many of my domestic and familial responsibilities so I could work. Long ago I entrusted him with my life. I've never been sorry.

sr / 9.22.2012

Sylvia Ross is the author-illustrator of *Lion Singer* and *Blue Jay Girl*, books for children. Her stories and poems have been published in a number of anthologies, and also featured in *"News from Native California,"* an esteemed quarterly magazine. She is of Native (Chukchansi Yokuts) descent and an Oregon Trail descendant on both sides of her family. In early adulthood, she worked as a cell painter for Walt Disney Productions in Burbank, California. Later she taught for many years at Vandalia Elementary School in Porterville, California, which was, and is, the school attended by most of the children from the Tule River Indian Reservation.

East of the Great Valley is her second novel. Her first novel, *Acts of Kindness, Acts of Contrition,* a mid-century themed novel concerning cultural issues between 1940 and 1980 was a finalist for the James D. Houston Award in 2010. Though born and raised in West Los Angeles, Mrs. Ross and her husband have made the Great Valley of California their home. They live in Eastern Tulare County.

25127776R00227

Made in the USA
Charleston, SC
21 December 2013